TO HUNT AND PROTECT

THE FIGHTING TOMCATS HUNTER/ KILLER SERIES BOOK TWO

M L MAKI

ROSE HILL PRESS, OLYMPIA, WASHINGTON

ISBN-13: 9781734909920
ISBN-13: 9781734909937

The views presented are those of the author and do not necessarily
represent the views of the Dod, or the US Navy.

Cover design by: Megan L. Maki

Printed in the United States of America

To Hunt and Protect is a work of historical fiction and speculation
using well-known historical and public figures. All incidents and
dialogue are products of the author's imagination and are not to be
construed as real. Because of the speculative nature of this work,
we have changed some present day timelines, such as the fact that
the aircraft carrier battlegroup depicted in this book has never
existed. Also, we have changed the historical timeline in the present
to suit the nature of the work. Any resemblance to persons living
or dead who are not historical figures is entirely coincidental.

To all those men, and now women, who sail and fight beneath the seas. The perfect battle is one you are so prepared for, that no enemy is willing to fight.

To those steely-eyed frogmen who go down range to protect the freedoms so many of us take for granted.

Thank you.

Of all the branches of men in the forces, there is none which shows more devotion and faces grimmer perils than the sub-mariners.

WINSTON CHURCHILL

CONTENTS

CHAPTER 1

USS SAN FRANCISCO, PACIFIC OCEAN NORTH OF THE PHILIPPINES

1000, December 21, 1941

The USS San Francisco SSN-711, a Los Angeles class nuclear powered attack submarine, silently glides through the South Pacific waters. Its executive officer, Lieutenant Commander John Morrison, knocks on his captain's door.

Commander George Cumberland opens the door, then sits back down, "What?"

"A message from Admiral Ren, sir. The Carl Vinson and it's group is about sixty miles behind us."

Cumberland grabs the message and reads it, "What faint fucking praise. We fucking sank an Akula class, one of Russia's best, and this is what he sends?"

"It's 1941, sir. We are allies with the Russians."

"Yeah, but the enemy didn't know that. Okay, is that all?"

"Commander Miller has asked if you want to cancel the scheduled propulsion plant drills in light of the situation?"

"No. I want them at their best. Run the drills. Carry on."

"Yes, sir." Morrison walks aft to control.

The Boatswain, "XO in Conn."

Morrison walks up beside the engineer, "Commander Miller,

1

the drills are still on."

"Is he a monster?"

"He's our boss."

"Roger."

MM1(SS) MALLORY'S RACK, USS SAN FRANCISCO

1032, December 21, 1941

Mallory sits on the deck holding photos of his boys, tears clouding his vision. MM3(SS) Gustaf walks by, sees him and stops, "Dude, are you okay?"

"Fuck no, I'm not. My boys are gone. They're fucking gone. Forever fucking gone."

"They didn't die."

"No, it's worse. They will never, ever, ever exist."

"Your still producing sperm, right?"

"Gustaf, you're an idiot. You don't get it."

"Look, I lost my folks. They won't be born until '46 and '48."

Mallory looks up at him, glaring, "Exactly. In six years, you will have your parents. They will be babies, but they will exist. My kids will never exist."

"They could."

"Gustaf, you're not that stupid. Do the math."

"You're what, thirty-six?"

"Thirty-five."

"Your oldest is?"

"Fourteen."

"So, when you crank him out, you'll be sixty-eight. You should still have a few good sperm. Granted, you'll be eighty-six when he graduates from high school."

Mallory shakes his head, "You still don't get it. Picture this. You have this beautiful, vain, gold-digging twenty-year-old co-ed. A sixty-eight-year-old geezer walks up and says, 'Hey, before I went back in time, we were married. Well, we got divorced because you are a bitch that fucks a guy you met at a comic-con, but we had two kids together and I really want my boys back, so let's fuck.' Yeah, good plan. That should work."

"Okay, you're fucked. I get it now."

"Most deployments some dude loses a grandma or something. Everyone here has lost their family. Some of you will get your families back. Those of us with kids, though, we're all well and truly fucked."

"Dude. I'm sorry. Um, I need some sig's on my Upper Level Watch Qual."

"Sit."

BASE LIBRARY, BRENDENMEYER NATO AIR BASE, GERMANY

0045, December 21, 1941

Sophia Newberg looks out a window. Nazi's are everywhere. The base headquarters, where her husband worked, is still smoldering. The library is hidden in a copse of trees, but that won't last. She hears a door open and snaps around, clutching a book. Her husband, Jerry, in his BDU's is carrying two gasoline cans. "Thank God, where did you get them?"

"Motor pool. This job makes me sick."

She takes a can from her husband and pours it out onto a pile of books. "I know, but we can't let this information get into Nazi hands."

He walks across the library and pours his can out on another pile. When they are done, she strikes a match and puts it to two twists of newspaper. She holds them for a moment, looking around at the stacks of books. "I never thought I would ever do something like this. God, forgive me." She drops the brands on the two piles.

Jerry asks, "Did you disable the sprinklers?"

"Yes, I did." They watch the flames catch and take hold. They look at each other and he grabs her hand. "Let's go." They run out and get into a stolen 1935 Mercedes and drive to a gate in a remote corner of the base. There, they open the fence lock and drive out into 1941.

USS SAN FRANCISCO

1300, December 21, 1941

John Morrison stands next to the OOD, LCDR Greg Backes. A phone talker reports, "Maneuvering is ready to commence propulsion plant drills."

Backes, "Very well. Announce it."

The BMOW announces, "Commence propulsion plan drills."

Morrison asks, "Greg, how are you doing?"

Backes looks his friend in the eyes, "It sucks. Our families evaporated like a precious dream you can't hold on to when your alarm sounds."

"Yeah, no Lisa. She was born in 1961. Her mom and dad are only kids."

"Yeah, Carol was born in sixty-three. She's not at all going to be interested in an old man."

"Where did your grandparents live?"

"At this time, I think they lived in Minnesota. They moved to California when he got a job with Lockheed. What about yours?"

"Captain in Conn."

Cumberland looks at them, "A word, XO." He turns and leaves.

Morrison, "Yes, sir." He looks at Backes and follows his captain forward. He knocks, then walks into the Captain's stateroom. "Yes, sir?"

"I've noticed the crew's morale seems lower than it should be. I would think they would be pleased with our kill."

"It's the time travel, sir. They have all lost their families. They are all mourning their loss."

Cumberland glowers, "They need to get over it. Their families weren't issued with their sea bags."

Morrison, stunned, "It seems to me sir, their families loaned them to us. We train them, work them, and hopefully return them in good order when their career ends. They will work through it in time. But, sir, these men loved their wives. But, I think, it's the loss of their children that are hitting them the hardest. Meanwhile, it is probably good to keep them busy and give them the space to grieve."

"Space to grieve? No. We have a war to fight. You realize we should exceed the Tang's record. Even you might get a star." Cumberland smiles and nods, "Hey, that's right. You're not a legacy anymore. How old is your admiral dad?"

"Thirteen. He's living in Norfolk while my grandfather hunts submarines in the Atlantic."

"What rank is your grandfather?"

"Right now? I think he was the XO of a destroyer. Don't recall its name."

"What rank did he retire at?"

"Vice Admiral. His last command was Fifth Fleet in the Med."

"What side was your birth grandfather fighting for?"

"My mom's father was interned in Idaho where he joined the 100th Battalion even though he was born in Sacramento."

"Your saying he was American? Not Japanese?"

"Yes, sir. My mother's grandfather was born in Japan. The family legend is that he was madly in love with a woman from an important family. She loved him too, so they eloped and fled to San Francisco where they converted to Christianity and married. My grandfather fought with the 100th Battalion while his wife and child were interned. He died in Germany. My dad's father is, I think, a cop in New England."

"So, you are descended from a line of heroes?"

"They fought for our country as so many others did."

"You know you'll be kicked out of the Navy because of your ethnicity."

"No, sir, and you don't know that either."

"They might let you stay on as a steward."

"And they may leave me right where I am."

Cumberland smiles, cocking his head, "Don't get your hopes up."

USS CARL VINSON

Captain Johnson, commanding officer of the Carl Vinson sits in the carrier group commander's office. An aid knocks and enters with a message. Admiral Ren signs for it and reads. "What the hell?" He hands the message to Johnson.

TO: COMCG-72

FRM: SSN-711

REG: TIME TRAVEL EVENT

Sir. San Francisco has a number of minority personnel in positions now forbidden to them; i.e., the XO, LCDR Morrison is a Japanese American. Please advise as to when these servicemen are to be transferred and when replacements will be made available.

CDR Cumberland

Ren watches Johnson's face as he reads. Johnson looks up, "You're kidding, right? What's he thinking?"

Ren, "We've met Cumberland. Do you know Morrison?"

"No, sir, but Captain Klindt may."

"Please call him."

"Yes, sir." Johnson goes to the phone.

Ren reads the message again, then goes back to his work. In a few minutes Captain Klindt, the reactor officer, knocks and enters. Without preamble, Ren hands Klindt the message from Cumberland.

Klindt reads the message, then carefully reads it again, then looks up, "We must not do this, sir."

"I agree. The commander is correct, though, regarding regulation and executive order. What do we do?"

Klindt is silent for a moment, "Are we required to follow the orders of a history book, sir?"

"What do you mean, Captain?"

"I seems to me that a history book is informative, but not a directive. Just because the history says it happens, does not in itself mean it will happen. I think we should continue to comply with 1990 Naval directives until updated by higher."

"So, we kick the can down the road until we get guidance? I assume you would expect that guidance to come from Nimitz?"

"I believe Admiral Nimitz would probably keep things as is and kick the decision upstairs. What we need to do is demonstrate to him, and higher, that our people, as they are, are indispensable. In truth, sir, they are. Commander Morrison is a nuclear and submarine qualified officer who has graduated from command college. Where would we get another ethnically correct officer in 1941?"

"True. Do you know Commander Morrison?"

"I do. He was a junior officer when his father took command of the destroyer Coontz. I was a lieutenant on the Bainbridge at the time and attended the ceremony. Later, we served on the sub tender Fulton together. He's a bright, squared away officer. His father retired a rear admiral."

"How is it a Japanese is named Morrison?"

"He's Japanese American, sir. I don't know the whole story, but his dad was in the Navy and married a Japanese woman. They both died in an accident. His father was best friends with the Morrisons and they adopted and raised him."

"So, you have no issues with him in a command position?"

"Absolutely not, sir."

"What do you know of Commander Cumberland."

"We have never met, sir."

"Okay, then. Gentlemen, we will adopt the Klindt, split the hair with a razor, plan. All remains status quo until specific guidance is received from higher."

WARDROOM, BATTLESHIP TIRPITZ, NAVY YARD, WILHELMSHAVEN

1143, December 21, 1941

Leutnant zur See Helmut Schmitt shovels food into his mouth. Yesterday was his duty day and he still has much to do on this afternoon. If his men get all their work done, he may even have time for some beers tonight.

Leutnant zur See Hansel Zimmerman asks, "Did you hear that the Captain is back from Berlin?"

"Ya."

Schmitt is from Bremerhaven where his father still serves as shipwright. He grew up around the Navy. "My friend, do not believe rumors. If we had won all the battles rumors say we have, the world would be ours. If we got all the promotions rumor suggest, we would both be admirals."

"You are not interested?"

Schmitt smiles, "I am very interested in what the Captain actually has to say."

Over the announcing circuit, they hear the voice of Kapitan zur See Karl Topp, the commanding officer of the Tirpitz, "Good afternoon, Tirpitz. Two days ago, a time travel event took place in the Rhineland. A Luftwaffe facility, with many advanced weapons, came back to us from the year 1990 to our time to help us defeat the British and the cursed communists. Some of this technology will be coming to our ship. We must learn to us it. That is all."

Zimmerman looks at Schmitt wide-eyed, "I had not guessed this. Ours are anti-aircraft divisions. Perhaps the technology will come to us."

Schmitt smiles, "Perhaps."

USS SAN FRANCISCO

2258, 21 December, 1941

EM1(SS) Stan Wankowski sits in the enlisted mess and tries reading a Robert Heinlein novel. His eyes are unfocused and filled with tears. He wipes his face and focuses on the words.

His chief, EMC(SS) Andrew Hines, sits down next to him, "It's okay."

"What?"

"It's okay to grieve."

"The worst fucking thing is my kids, Chief."

"You brought pictures, right?"

"Yeah, but what the fuck, Chief, they'll never exist. All I'll ever have is those pictures. It hurts."

"You're right." Hines waits, quiet, then, "Nothing I can say will fill the hole in your heart. I can't. No one can. What I need you to know right now, is that you have a right to grieve. We all do."

Stan blows his nose, "Thanks, Chief."

"When you need to talk, find me, and we'll talk. I know you need to hold it together for the guys, just like I do. We need someone to be like a grief partner. If you are okay with it, we can do that for each other."

"Thanks, Chief. My kids were just fucking awesome. They were amazing. Now they will never exist. The world has lost so much possible awesome because they are gone."

"I and Jasmine didn't have kids. I'm thankful for that. But she...I ache because she is gone. I physically hurt."

"You know, Chief, I don't think there has ever been a ship whose crew lost everyone. We're in uncharted territory."

"We are. What are you reading?"

"Heinlein. 'Stranger in a Strange Land.' It seems apropos."

"Yeah, it does. You read a lot. Have you ever come across our situation in fiction?"

Mallory, carrying a couple of candy bars and a soda, sits down across from them.

Stan says, "The Final Countdown. It was an eighty's film."

Hines, "Yeah, but the hero gets the girl and they go back home. God can't be so cruel as to keep us here. Maybe paradox will force whatever the mechanism is to send us back."

Stan asks, "What was the other sub? The one that fired the first torpedoes?"

Hines, "Probably Japanese. Maybe that's why they know we went back."

"Maybe. It was sunk, right?"

"Yeah. The Stoddert hit it with an ASROC."

Stan, "Unless that sub was destined to die, we've already changed the past."

Mallory says, "I read a book."

Stan, "I don't think 'Curious George' will help us here, Mallory."

"Funny, Stan. It was 'The Talon Sword.'"

The two electricians look at each other.

Stan, "I didn't think your reading list included science fiction. Hell, I didn't think it got much past the playmate profile."

"I mostly read westerns. Louis L'Amour is my favorite."

"Back to 'The Talon Sword. Do you have a copy?"

"No, but I might be able to scare one up."

Hines asks, "Do either of you recall the mechanism and the date?"

Mallory, "I'm pretty sure the date was 19 December, 1990 to 19 December, 1941. But the book was fiction, right?"

Stan, "That novel created a huge stir after it was released because it was based on a paper the author found in the Bodleian Library at Oxford. The Ministry of Defense tried to stop its publication, and then tried to force the recall of the published books. They never said why, as I recall. The device could have been built."

Hines, "In the novel, was there a mechanism for going back to 1990?"

Stan, "I don't remember one."

Hines, "Okay. We need a copy of that book if it is aboard. We probably ought to acquire it quietly."

USS SAN FRANCISCO

0530, 22 December, 1941

Commander Cumberland gets up, looks in his mirror, grabs his ditty bag, and walks to the head. He hears on the bitch box, "Captain, we are reaching the end of our box. No new contact."

He pushes a button, "Very well. Right turn for a westerly leg."

"Aye, sir."

"Fucking box. The goddamned admiral has us in a fucking box when there is a carrier a few hundred miles south of us that we could kill. The goddamned flyboys are getting all the action." He finishes shaving and wipes his face. Then he returns to his cabin and gets dressed. A few minutes later, he is walking into the control room.

"Captain in control."

"Carry on." He walks through into sonar, "Anything?"

ST1(SS) Brown says, "We just picked up some explosions to the south east. It sounds like they are coming from the Lingayen Gulf. The reverb seems to indicate the noise is originating in shallow water."

"Okay."

Brown suddenly pulls off his head phones, "Whoa!" To his right, Guthrie does the same. "Loud explosion to our south."

Cumberland, "How close?"

"Distant, but loud." Brown puts his headphones back on, "I'm hearing venting steam and the grinding of a ship breaking up. A secondary explosion. A third. The Japanese are getting hammered."

"I see. Our kills."

"Sir?"

"Keep me posted." Cumberland leaves sonar and walks through control to the wardroom.

Master Chief Godoy sits in the Chief's mess, his legs propped on a chair, reading. ENC(SS) Giblin comes in, warms Godoy's coffee, pours himself a cup and sits down.

"Thank you, Jim."

"How are you?"

Godoy, "I'm committing a cardinal sin. I'm thinking."

"Yeah. That sort of thing can get you into trouble. Need a sounding board?"

"If you don't mind."

Giblin takes a sip of lifer juice. "I got your back, COB. You know that."

"Yeah. This time travel thing. If it's a one-way trip, the boys have all lost everyone they love and Christmas is coming."

"We still spending it in PI? Shit, no, of course we aren't."

"Nope."

Giblin, "With assholious rex in charge, that is going to make things even worse."

"What has he done now?"

"I saw him as we killed the Russian. The fucker was giddy. First time I've seen him happy."

"It was within our orders. Why do you suppose he was happy about it?"

"That's the thing, COB. I don't know. I've been over it again and again. At first, I thought it was that everything worked. That combined with survivor high. Now, I don't know."

"We need to keep an eye on him. It's something we always need to do anyway. What do we do about Christmas?"

"I don't know, COB. Thing is, everyone is hurting. There are no crewmembers who are not impacted to pick up the slack."

"I'll talk to the skipper. That and get the wardroom and goat locker on it. We have to take care of the guys."

CHAPTER 2

USS SAN FRANCISCO

1415, 22 December, 1941

The captain storms in for the hundredth time. "Captain in control."

LCDR Miller, the OOD watch, says, "We're at 400 feet approaching the north end of the box. Sonar says the carrier group is continuing north out of its box."

Cumberland, "Take us to periscope depth."

"Periscope depth, aye, sir. Helm, ten degree up bubble come on one hundred fifty feet."

LCDR Morrison walks in. "XO in control."

Cumberland smiles, his face tight, "So, XO, are you working on any great ballads to honor the heroic pilots today, or is it just the wife who writes?"

"Just her, sir."

"A shame."

Miller pushes a button, "Sonar, Conn, we are coming to periscope depth. Do we have any close contacts?"

"Con, sonar, no close contacts."

Miller, "Right standard rudder. Let's clear our baffles."

Cumberland, "There's nothing there. Go ahead to periscope

depth."

Miller, "Aye, Captain. Helm, make our depth sixty feet."

Cumberland, "Are you going to look up her folks? Maybe Grandma is a hotty."

Morrison, "I've not thought about it, sir."

They can feel the wave motion as the sub shallows out to sixty feet.

Cumberland, "Up scope." He steps to the periscope and does a quick 360. "No surface contacts. Send our position."

Radio says, "Yes, sir."

Cumberland steps back, "Want a peek, rock star?"

"Yes, sir." The waves are running fifteen feet in long Pacific swells. It is afternoon and the sun is shining overhead.

Radio, "Message, sir. We're being directed to search for two downed airmen west of our position."

Cumberland raises his eyes to heaven, "Very well. Plot a course. Let me know when they're found." He walks forward out of control.

Morrison, "Sir, do we have permission to surface for a proper search?"

Cumberland stops and turns and lowers his head glaring, frozen. A moment passes, then, "Yes, of course. Carry on." He abruptly turns and leaves.

Miller whispers to Morrison, "What the fuck was that about?"

Morrison looks at Miller, then, "Take us up. Call for the SAR swimmer and some strong guys. Mallory and Wankowski are off watch. I'll man the bridge. Once we're up, ventilate the ship."

"Yes, sir."

The sub rolls in the swells. This is their second pass through the area. Morrison can see a helicopter searching to their south. BM3 Billy Jackson says, "Sir, I see green." He points.

Morrison calls down by sound powered phone, "Right full rudder. All stop." He gets the repeat back. Submarines perform horribly on the surface, yet the boat swings around.

Jackson, "I see him. He's there."

"Rudder amidships. Ahead 1/3. Steady as she goes. Tell the helo we've found one." He turns to the SAR swimmer, BM1 Sarvis, "Can you get him?"

"Yes, sir." Sarvis climbs down out of the sail and onto the rolling deck.

Morrison on the phone, "Send Mallory and Wankowski up." The two men come up into the sail, then work their way onto the deck. The steady themselves as another wave washes over the deck.

Mallory gets on the exterior ladder, "Sir, is this the fun or the adventure?"

"A little of both. Be careful."

"If I was careful, sir, I would be selling insurance." Mallory climbs down beside Sarvis and hooks onto the track system that ties him to the boat.

Wankowski starts down the ladder and sings, "Be all that you can be," in his deep, gravelly voice.

Morrison, "That's the Army song, Ski."

"Exactly, sir."

The three men huddle just aft of the sail as the limp body

comes along side. Sarvis times the waves and jumps into the sea. The SAR wraps the pilot in his arms and Mallory and Wankowski pull them aboard. As they maneuver the pilot aboard, the helicopter approaches from the south. Morrison hears, "The helo has spotted the other airman south east of us. They're asking if we can recover it because of the sea state."

"Affirmative. Does the helo want to pick them up off our deck?"

"If they're alive, yes."

Morrison shouts down, "How is he?"

Sarvis, "He's dead, sir. Multiple GSW."

"What's a GSW?"

"Gun Shot Wounds. Sir, he was machined gunned in his chute."

"What's his name?"

"Ensign Robert 'Bo-Bo' Bolen, sir. He's a F-14 pilot from the Black Knights. It's on his patches."

"Roger. Garry, Stan, we'll lower a rope to help. We need to haul him up." On the phones, "Tell the helo we have Ensign Robert Bolen of the Black Knights. Once we have him inside, we'll go after the other pilot."

They reverently lift the body to the sail and carefully lower him down into control.

Morrison, "Left full rudder, ahead one third. It's going to put us in the troughs, so hang on."

As the sub comes about, Morrison hears from behind him, "Yeah Hoo!" He leans out and looks back. Mallory has his feet spread, his lanyard wrapped around his hand, and is riding the sub like a bull, his left hand flying in the air.

Morrison thinks to himself, "Thank God, the periscope doesn't depress that far. Old Stick in the Ass would be pissed."

They come up on the second body and repeat the process of getting it aboard. Sarvis reports, "This one is the same. Multiple GSW."

"Understood. What's his name?"

"Ensign Chris 'Klutz' Brandt. He's also a Black Knight."

"Roger." He again lowers the rope. On the phone, "Tell the helo, and higher command, the body of Ensign Chris Brandt is on board. He was also machined gunned in his chute."

Cumberland climbs up as they are hoisting the pilot's body up into the sail. "XO, why are we bringing them aboard?"

"We were told to, sir. It's the sea state."

"Jesus Christ. Now, we're a fucking morgue." Without helping, Cumberland climbs back down, then stops part way, "Don't you fucking dare drip dead guy on me."

They wait for the captain to clear below, then carefully lower the pilot down the trunk.

JAPANESE SUBMARINE I-76

2310, 22 December, 1941

Commander Yahachi Tanabe stands like a statue beside the periscopes. They are running on the surface at night recharging their batteries. The smell of diesel permeates everything. The thrum of the diesel engine vibrates the whole boat. The bridge watch passes down a sightings report; negative contacts. It's more to show they are awake and alert.

The commander walks to the chart table. Their position is accurately marked, as is the estimated forward progress of the American carrier. Lieutenant Kadono says, "We should be ahead of schedule, Captain."

"Yes, but this assumes much. We assume they wish to travel to Hawaii, and we assume they are not zig-zagging significantly. We can hear nothing while on the surface with the diesel running."

"Shall we shut it off and listen?"

"We are only a third through our charge cycle." The captain thinks, "Yes, do it. We drift for thirty minutes just to listen."

"Yes, sir."

USS SAN FRANCISCO

ST1 Thurman Thorsen stiffens, listening, "Con, Sonar, surface contact, bearing 304. Designate Sierra 4. It sounds like a distant diesel boat on the surface."

Cumberland materializes behind him, "Where?"

Thorsen points at the waterfall display, "It stops here, sir. That is when I caught it."

"Why not before?"

"It's far away, sir. Sorry."

"Thorsen, do better. I depend on you."

"Yes, sir."

Cumberland storms back into control, "Start a track on Sierra 4."

"Yes, sir."

Cumberland paces as they lay down the datum. The OOD, LCDR Steve Miller asks, "Do we have any idea where the American submarines are?"

Cumberland looks up, "No. We just don't know."

"Yes, sir."

Time drags by.

Cumberland pushes the button, "Sonar, Conn. Any information?"

"No, sir. No diesel. No screws."

JAPANESE SUBMARINE I-76

Commander Tanabe walks to the sonar station, "Anything?"

"I think I hear something to the south and east. About 155. It is very faint, sir, but it has the thrum of multiple screws."

"Far away?"

"Yes, sir."

"I see. We will motor for an hour or two and look again. Perhaps we may triangulate."

"Yes, sir."

Tanabe returns to control, "Restart the diesel. Return to base course."

USS SAN FRANCISCO

Thurman sits in a trance, listening. He picks up whiffs of the battlegroup ninety miles behind them. The carrier's four huge screws cannot be disguised. He hears a new sound. The unmistakable sound of a diesel. "Conn, Sonar. Sierra 4 is back. Bearing is 348."

Cumberland materializes behind him, "Is it close?"

"Closer, sir. I think they were drifting. I heard bubbles, then their diesel started back up."

"Why did they shut down?"

"I don't know, sir."

Cumberland rushes back into control, straight to the tracking table, "What do you have?"

"Sir, it looks like it was drifting."

"Why?"

Miller, "They may have stopped to listen."

Cumberland, "I thought World War 2 subs had their sonars on the deck."

Miller, "Our subs had one on deck and one underneath. I don't know enough about Japanese subs."

"We need to know. Miller, get us behind it and work up a profile. At least we can learn what type of boat it is."

"Yes, sir."

USS SAN FRANCISCO

2335, 22 December, 1941

Wankowski in maneuvering, the reactor and propulsion plant control room, is turning over Engineering Watch Supervisor to ET1 Alan Washburn, "So, air in the banks, shit in the tanks, water all around, clean, crit, and the same old shit. I had it, you got it."

"I got it. Get some sleep."

They hear, "Man the tracking party. Rig for silent running."

"So much for sleep." Wankowski exits maneuvering, passes through a hatch into the tunnel which passes through the reactor compartment, and walks forward into control. "Request to enter as tracking party."

Lt. Hank Thoreau, the submarine's weapons officer, now

standing OOD, says, "Enter."

Mallory shows up a minute later and joins Wankowski, "What's going on?"

Wankowski points at the table, "Single track cruising along fat, dumb, and happy."

Thoreau joins them, "Diesel boat on the surface. We need to build a profile and figure out if they're friend or foe."

Wankowski, "You know, sir, if an American sub spotted the Vinson at night, they would think it was Japanese."

Thoreau, "I know. It keeps me up at night."

Mallory, "Would they know we are out here?"

Ski says, "Think."

Mallory, "Fuck. We have no reliable way to contact them except just showing up. Unless they were close enough to see the flag, they might take us under fire in broad daylight."

Thoreau, "Exactly. We would have to sink them to save the carrier."

Mallory, "Yes, sir. That would totally, unequivocally suck."

A new bearing comes in and they get busy. Time crawls as they work their way behind the Japanese sub at a depth of 300 feet.

The XO walk in and straight to the table. Thoreau joins him, "They are motoring along on an intercept course to the carrier group."

"Con, Sonar. Sierra 4 has secured engines. They're submerging."

Morrison, "All stop. Diving officer, hover the boat."

"Yes, sir." The submarine uses rudder, dive, and sail planes to control depth. Trim is controlled by adding or removing water from the trim tanks located fore and aft. As the sub coasts to a stop, the trim tanks have to be adjusted exactly to keep the boat trim.

Thoreau picks up a phone, "Sierra 4 has stopped again, sir."

Cumberland comes into control, "How close are we?"

Thoreau, "About a half a mile, sir. We're drifting."

"Are we drifting closer?"

"Very slowly, sir. We are both slowly drifting north east, sir."

"What is their depth?"

"About 100 feet."

"Carry on." Cumberland walks into sonar. "Are we getting a good track, Gordon?"

ST 2(SS) Gil Gordon says, "Yes, sir. We're learning a lot. These boats are really noisy."

"Can you reliably give me a nationality?"

"No, sir."

Cumberland takes a deep breath, "Okay. Keep me posted."

"Yes, sir."

Cumberland goes back into control. He can feel his boat settling a little bow down. He goes down the stairs to the crew berthing, "I need twenty people to walk aft to the engine room."

Sailors grumble, but get out of their racks and get dressed. Cumberland, "Grab TLDs and go. You're human ballast."

"Yes, sir."

Morrison stands behind Gordon, "Do we have a 60 hertz or 55 hertz engine?"

"It seems to be all DC."

"Okay, and we know it's two three-bladed screws."

"Yes, sir. A bearing on the right shaft has a noticeable defect."

"How close are we?"

"Maybe 500 feet, sir. I can hear their feet on the deck plates."

JAPANESE SUBMARINE I-76

Engineer Third Class Ushio is taking advantage of the listening period to adjust the throttle linkage on number two diesel engine. He's using a small wrench and is twisted in a difficult position so he can see what he is doing in the poor light. He moves to get a better look and takes a deep breath of the very humid, human sweaty stink. The wrench slips in his hands, then falls and rattles down to the bilge, "Kuso!" Shit.

His engineer first class yells, "Baka Yarou!" You idiot.

USS FRANCISCO

Gordon raises a hand, "Sir, I heard spoken Japanese." He plays the recording.

"Wow. Good job, Gordon."

Morrison walks into control, "Captain, she's Japanese. Gordon caught voice, sir."

Cumberland goes immediately into sonar to listen.

Morrison goes to the plot table. The two subs are slowly drifting north on the current. The carrier group is getting closer by the minute.

JAPANESE SUBMARINE I-76

Commander Yahachi Tanabe studies the plot table. The American group will likely pass several miles in front of them. "We will make our attack from below the waves. Ahead 2/3rd on battery."

"Yes, sir." The levers are pulled and DC electric motors start turning the shafts.

USS SAN FRANCISCO

Gordon says, "Con, Sonar. Sierra 4 is moving again. This time on battery."

Cumberland rushes in, "Show me."

Gordon points to the broad cavitation noise on the waterfall, "Do you want it on speaker, sir? You can hear them clearly."

"Yes."

Gordon flips a switch and they hear a hissing sound like static mixed with a fairly highspeed vibration.

"I thought it would thrum."

"The screws are too small, sir. Let me slow it down." Gordon adjusts some switches and the blade beats of the screw are evident.

"Thank you, Gordon." Cumberland walks back into control. "Load and flood tube two."

"Yes, sir."

Thoreau asks, "Ahead bell, sir?"

"No, let's get some distance between us."

"Yes, sir."

Morrison, "We want two miles space."

Cumberland, "Yes, but we're still bow heavy. XO, go below and send ten more men aft."

"Yes, sir." Morrison pops below, "Guys, I need ten of you to quietly head aft."

One of the men asks, "Sir, why are we still hovering?"

"The captain is setting up a shot."

"Yes, sir."

Morrison goes back to control. "XO in control."

Cumberland has his hands behind his back and a smile on his face. He goes to the plot table, "Two miles. Good."

On the box they hear Kichiro, "Tube 2 is loaded and flooded."

Cumberland, "Open the door."

JAPANESE SUBMARINE I-76

Sonar says, "Sir, I heard a gurgling that sounds like a flooding tube from behind us."

Tanabe, "Thank you, sonar." He's quiet for a moment, "It is possible, yes. Left full rudder. Ahead full. Prepare torpedoes 1 and 2 for launch."

"Yes, Captain."

USS SAN FRANCISCO

"Conn, Sonar. Aspect change. Sierra 4 is turning north. They are accelerating."

Cumberland to the tracking team, "Range?"

Wankowski, "About three miles."

Cumberland, "I want five."

"Conn, Sonar. Sierra 4 is circling."

Cumberland looks at Morrison and smiles. He walks to the weapons panel, "Firing tube 2." He depresses the button. There is a swooshing shudder.

Kichiro on the box, "Conn, Torpedo. Tube 2 is fired electrically."

"Conn, Sonar. Our fish is running hot, straight, and normal."

JAPANESE SUBMARINE I-76

The sonar operator shouts, "Torpedo in the water, sir!"

Commander Tanabe, "Calm. Helm, give me a twenty degree down bubble. Right full rudder." The helm repeats back and the deck slopes down.

"Sonar, was it launched by a surface ship or submarine?"

"A submarine, sir."

"Any idea of its depth?"

"No, sir, but it is close. Only a few miles away. Bearing 245."

"Back on shaft one. We need to turn. Set depth for 100 feet."

"The torpedo itself has sonar."

"100 feet set."

"Understood. Fire one and two. We do our duty."

There is a thud whoosh as each torpedo launches.

The Mark 48 torpedo from the San Francisco has no difficulty finding the Japanese submarine with its sonar. At 55 knots, it's a short path. It recognizes the target is a submarine and detonates right against the hull.

USS SAN FRANCISO

"Conn, Sonar. Two torpedoes in the water."

Cumberland, "Very well. Did our fish hit?"

Morrison catches Thoreau's eye and mouths, "GO!"

Thoreau, "Ahead flank power limiting. 20 degrees down bubble."

Cumberland to Sonar, "What bearing?"

"Conn, Sonar. Our fish hit the Jap sub. They're the ones who fired at us." They all feel the sub shake as the pressure wave from the explosion reaches them. The San Francisco picks up speed and slopes down.

Cumberland, "Where are the torpedoes?"

"Conn, Sonar. It's hard to hear, sir."

Cumberland storms into sonar, "We need to know!"

"Gordon, 'Yes, sir." The waterfall is a mess of reverberations. As the noise of the explosion dies down, it's replaced by the flow noise of the flank bell. "Sir, they're passing astern."

"Are they turning?"

"Sir, they're continuing straight."

Cumberland nods and takes a deep breath, "Thank you." He walks back into control, a huge smile on his face. "They missed. Carry on." He walks out forward.

Morrison, "Ahead standard. Ten degrees up angle. Make our depth 300 feet. Come to 045."

The helm repeats.

Morrison looks around control, "I would like to congratulate all of you for an exemplary execution. The hover was text book and the shot well executed."

Chief Giblin at the dive panel, "How many people on a Japanese submarine, sir."

"I don't know. Those old boats typically had about seventy-five."

Giblin continues, "It's enough to be considered mass murder, right?'

Morrison, "We have a job to do. It's hard, and the consequences are dire, but it's also very important. The Japanese submarine was setting up a shot on the Vinson."

Giblin, "I agree, sir. My point is just that not all of us have a hard-on about it."

"That I understand, Chief." Morrison turns to Thoreau, "He didn't say, but continue north. When we're about one hundred miles ahead of the carrier group slow to SOA"

"Yes, sir. Speed of advance. Sir, did the Japanese hunt in packs?"

"Not that I know of." Morrison walks into sonar, "Good job Gordon, Pritchel."

Gordon, "Thank you, sir. I'm sorry we couldn't track the torpedoes in. It was just too loud."

"That's okay. We're going to sprint ahead and get back on station and back to the search."

"Yes, sir."

"How are you guys doing?"

"Is this how it's going to be?

"Until we can find out where all the American subs are located, we're going to need to get close and develop a profile."

"Yes, sir."

"Are you okay?"

"It's just…I heard them talking. I can't see them as inanimate objects. We just killed people."

"We did. We're at war, Gordon. It will take some time to wrap our head around that idea. We have two airdales on board who were machine-gunned in their chutes after they punched out. People are going to die. We may die. It's war."

"Yes, sir."

"If you need to talk it through, see me, okay?"

"I will."

"Good."

Morrison passes Brown as he walks back into control. ST 1(SS) Mike Brown, the sonar division LPO, asks, "How are you two holding up?"

Gordon, "I heard them Brown. I could hear them talking. Then we killed them."

Brown, "Yeah, it's hard. It's damn hard. The other guys can pretend it's an object we kill and not people."

Gordon, "The captain doesn't seem upset."

Pritchel, "Yeah, but our XO is cool. The captain, though, is horrible."

Brown, "Normally, it's the XO who is a mercurial ass and the captain is cool. This captain is so far the other way that Morrison has to balance him out."

Gordon, "Have you ever had a captain this bad before?"

Brown, "Yeah. My second boat. He was all over the place. One moment he was trying to be your buddy, the next, he was a tyrant. The thing about Cumberland is, that so far, he is an ass, but he is a consistent ass. I can work with that

CHAPTER 3

USS SAN FRANCISCO, 90 MILES NORTH OF THE CARRIER GROUP

0919, 23 December, 1941

A helicopter comes to a hover on its approach to the submarine. The seas have finally moderated, the swells at about five feet with a slow periodicity. The crew chief drops a line and Morrison grabs it with a grounded hook. This keeps the static electricity the helicopter generates from going down the line and grounding through Morrison. With the helo electrically grounded, Wankowski grabs the litter with the first body and helps Mallory attach it to the line to be lifted up.

Ski asks Morrison, "Sir, do you know what is going to happen to them?"

"The Vinson is having a funeral ceremony. A burial at sea."

Ski, "We could do that and save the helo."

Mallory, "And fucking chop them up in the screw. No, this is better."

Mallory and Ski attach the second litter, the body securely strapped in, and send it up. The litter is pulled into the helo, then the SENSO motions them to wait. Soon, the litter returns with two bags of mail and eight five-gallon tubs of ice cream.

Morrison, on the phone, "Sir, we need a working party to

pass below eight tubs of ice cream and the mail."

Cumberland replies, "Oh, for recovering the aircrew."

In a few minutes the ice cream is passed below and the bridge cleared. The XO carefully checks to make sure all gear is passed below. Then he carefully inspects and wipes each seal as he passes through the hatches and dogs them down. With the lower hatch shut, he announces, "Chief of the Watch, last man down. Hatches shut. Bridge is rigged for dive."

Chief Giblin repeats him.

Cumberland, "Quartermaster, sounding."

The Quartermaster says, "Sounding is 19,500 feet based on chart, sir."

Cumberland, "Very well, Officer of the Deck, submerge the ship."

Backes, "Submerge the ship, aye. Diving officer, submerge the ship."

The Diving Officer says, "Submerge the ship, dive, aye. Chief of the Watch, pass the word, 'Dive. Dive.' Sound two blasts on the dive alarm. Pass the word, 'Dive. Dive.'"

Giblin, the Chief of the Watch, announces, sounds the alarm, then announces again. He then lifts up the vent control switches. All the ballast tank valves open, letting the air escape.

Backes on the periscope, "Decks awash."

Diving officer, "64 feet. 68 feet. 74 feet. 90 feet."

Backes, "Down scope."

Cumberland, "Make our depth 300 feet. Continue north at SOA."

Backes repeats and Cumberland leaves control.

One of the helm watches asks Giblin, "Chief, why did they give us ice cream?"

Giblin smiles, "It's an old tradition. I think it dates back to the birth of naval aviation. If you fish an airman out of the water, then the carrier gives you ice cream."

"Cool. When will we get it?"

"It's up to the captain."

"Shit." He pulls back on the dive planes, "Leveling at 300 feet."

Backes, "Very well." He turns to Morrison, "Where did the mail come from?"

"The carrier must have gotten a mail run before we went back and it's just getting to us now."

"So, it's the last we get?"

"Yeah."

Cumberland on the box, "XO, could you see me in my quarters?"

Morrison pushes the button, "Yes, sir." He walks forward, knocks and enters the CO's stateroom, "Yes, sir?"

"These mail bags create an issue. It seems to me our crew would be better off if we deep sixed the lot."

"We can't do that, sir. The crew knows we have it. It's the last letters from their families, sir."

"I'm aware that destroying mail was illegal in 1990, but we're in 1941. The rules have changed."

"No, sir. That law has been on the books since colonial times. Even the censors, who reviewed mail, would never destroy it. They would send it back to the originator for editing. Besides the legal implications, sir, destroying the mail would devastate crew morale. We must give them their mail."

"Okay, I'm just concerned with crew morale."

"Speaking of that, Christmas is coming and obviously we are not going to be in port. I would like to see the wardroom and goat locker plan something for the crew."

"The SUPPO has a special meal planned. What do you have in mind?"

"Carols. Some decorations. Have a lay service."

"Do we even have a lay reader on board?"

"Yes, sir. Lieutenant Cutting reads for the protestant services and Chief Hines read for the Catholics. We also have ST1 Thorsen who reads for the non-Christian services."

"Thorsen isn't Christian? What is he?"

"Buddhist, sir. Tibetan Buddhist, to be exact."

"And we trust him?

"Sir, his religion does not mean he is not an American and a patriot. He's an excellent sonarman. He holds a BA in music from Boston U and plays several musical instruments. He's trustworthy, regardless of his religion."

"Where's he from?"

"Greenwich Village, New York."

"Greenwich Village? Is he gay?"

"Not that I know of, sir."

"I don't want a big city faggot on my boat."

"How would we replace him sir?"

Cumberland takes a deep breath, "Okay, what I say in here is private. At this time, there are no civil rights laws. I do not want any pagan ceremonies or rites on my boat. I no longer have to put up with it, so I won't."

Morrison, "Yes, sir. No Santa Claus, Christmas trees, Christmas lights, Christmas candles, and we need to have the celebration in July or August."

"What the hell are you talking about. I was clear."

"Sir, most of what we do in celebration of Christmas has pagan origins. Christianity adopted them to make it easier for pagan populations to embrace Christianity. Christmas was the winter solstice celebration and wasn't even important in the early church."

"I'm not arguing ancient history with you. You know what I want. Dismissed."

"Yes, sir. Do we have permission to put together a Christmas celebration?"

"Of course. I'm not a monster, XO."

"Yes, sir." Morrison leaves and goes back to control. Backes hands him five letters, "On course at 300 feet. No new contacts."

"Thank you. You get anything from Carol?"

"Yeah. Two letters and Travis wrote one, too."

John looks at his letters. The first two are from Lisa. The next is from his mom. The fourth is from Captain Klindt. The last is from Captain Chris Van Zandt. He tilts his head, "Hmm." He turns to Greg, "I'll be in my state room. Could you arrange a meeting for me with the COB and the off-watch chiefs and officers in the wardroom? Make it for after watch change."

"Yes, sir."

Morrison goes forward into the wardroom and gets a cup of coffee to take back to his tiny stateroom. He settles in with his coffee, "Captain Van Zandt has to be first. He was one of my instructors at command college. This is odd."

Commander Morrison,

I'm hoping you remember me from command college where I taught command ethics. I knew your father professionally and you struck me, in class, as an exceptional officer. I am now the chief of staff for Admiral Ren on the Carl Vinson. Your commanding officer, CDR Cumberland, sent a message asking if it was our intent to comply with FDR's executive order regarding internment of Japanese-Americans. The Admiral determined we will not, under any circumstance, follow orders from history books. All regulations in effect as of December, 1990 are still in effect until countermanded by our current chain of command.

We're preparing to report our presence to Admiral Nimitz. Everything we know about him says he's a fair and decent man. Still, we have no idea how this will go, or what will happen. This has a potential, though small, of impacting your career. As I, and Admiral Ren, see it, each person in this command is essential to our overall war effort and effectiveness. This is what we will impress upon our leadership.

This brings forward another question. Regarding this, I need and require a frank and honest answer. Please do not allow loyalty to cloud your answer. Could you explain Commander Cumberland's command style and reflect upon what would motivate him to seemingly recommend dismissing you from naval service?

Reply by private letter.

Respectfully,

Christian Van Zandt

Morrison sets it down and drinks his coffee, thinking. He reads the letter again. "God. He sure knows how to cut right to the point and force an answer. Okay, never be the senior man with a secret." He pulls out a pad, flips over the letter he had been writing to Lisa, and begins on a clean page.

Captain Van Zandt,

I do remember the course and the lessons it contained. As you are fully aware, you put me in a vise. Cumberland is difficult, but he is a competent officer. He is cold and he does not believe in positive feedback as an effective means of motivation. His manner is brusque with the men and myself, but he is competent and a good tactician. It was his decisions that led us into a position to engage the Russian and Japanese submarines that we successfully sunk. My instincts say he has a cruel streak, but again, he has been a competent tactician and has kept us alive thus far. In peace time circumstances, I would be concerned as to his being a good fit in command, but we are at war and there are no officers who could easily relieve him. For this reason, I see his positive qualities outweighing the negative at this time. With your permission, I would prefer to continue a correspondence on this and other topics.

Very Respectfully,

John Morrison

He pulls the sheet off the pad and puts it into an envelope. He addresses the envelope and sets it aside. "Captain Klindt next."

Greetings,

I, very much, hope this letter finds you well. I am the Reactor

Officer on the Vinson and I lead a group called the Captain's Brain Trust. We have been sorting out things since we came back in time. I should discuss the Trust's evidence. After the storm event, we lost communications with higher and the Hewitt, which was aiding a disabled Japanese fishing boat and, thus, out of the area of effect, which we determined to have about a fifteen-mile radius. We continued picking up bounced radio from the US that was playing big band music. After the loss of the Stoddert, we recovered the body of a Japanese sailor. We gave the body an internal dose check and found his reading to be nine counts. That is substantially below normal. The test was run twice, with a calibration in between. The man lived before the advent of nuclear testing. Based on the evidence we had, we were authorized to make a radio transmission in the clear posing as a lost boy on a sail boat. The ruse worked and we confirmed that the date of the transference was December 19th, and the years were from 1990 to 1941. We are still working to determine the cause. It is possible we may never know. That brings you up to date on what we've done.

As the leader of the Trust, I have been finding myself aiding Admiral Ren on a number of issues. Earlier today I was called in to give my advice regarding a message Commander Cumberland sent the Admiral. It was in regard to internment of Japanese Americans. Specifically, when he was to turn you over for internment and get a white XO. My skin crawled. He also included the other non-white members of the crew, but the focus was clearly on you. I recommended, and the admiral agreed, to not follow orders from history books. The reasoning is simple. Our presence here changes history.

Internment was a blight on the moral landscape of our nation. It was racist, a waste of resources, and allowed the theft of property. As an advisor, I will do everything in my power to eliminate internment and a number of other mis-steps our nation took.

This brings me to you. I was very much impressed with you during our time serving together on USS Fulton. I do not know your captain, but his message does not do him credit. I want to be clear. I am writing as your friend and mentor. It is for this reason I am skipping the normal chain of command and protocol. I need a frank and straightforward assessment of your commander, and whether you, and the other minority crewmembers are safe under his command. I know I can trust your response.

One last item. In my position, I will do everything possible to protect you from internment and keep you, and your talents, in the service of our navy.

Your Friend,

Captain Craig Klindt

"Wow. I have friends." He takes a deep, clearing breath. "Some of the weight lifts." He pens a reply.

Captain Klindt,

Thank you so much for your letter. Captain Van Zandt wrote me inquiring of much the same issue regarding CDR Cumberland. With you, I will be frank. Cumberland is an ass. He sees no value in positive reinforcement as a motivational tool. He is cool to cold with the crew and with me. For example, he cannot see why the crew would be saddened by the loss of their families when they have an opportunity to make history. My wife and I had dinner with him in Pearl during our last night in port. He informed us that she was an inappropriate choice as a spouse for a naval officer. But it was his behavior that was inappropriate, if not out of bounds.

Having bashed the man, I must also say he is a superb tactician and knows his business. It was his decisions that lead to the sinking of our two kills. One, if you are unaware, was a Russian Akula class nuclear sub which was maneuvering aggressively toward the Vinson. Also, though he is an ass, he is a consistent ass. We all know the importance of consistency in leadership.

Were we at peace with replacements at hand. I would recommend his replacement. In the current situation, I will deal with him as we move forward. I would very much like to continue our correspondence.

On another note, Lisa Stevenson and I broke up right before I reported to the Fulton. We had been a couple for about a year. For me, she was the one. She is a singer, songwriter. Up until recently, she was a backup vocalist with Metalsmith, as well as the bands primary songwriter. Her brother, Andy Stevenson, is the keyboardist. She married Ted, the lead singer, a few years after she and I split and divorced him eight months ago. My mom match made and suggested she borrow my apartment and escape her life for a while. We married the night before we left Pearl. I very much hope there is some mechanism to bring us back home.

Your Friend,

John

John picks up Lisa's two letters and the one from his mom and sets them with the rest of Lisa's letters, "For when I need you."

USS SAN FRANCISCO

1800, 24 December, 1941

LT Craig Cutting leads the men through a Christmas eve service. "...So, the child lay in a manger, which is sort of a trough for hay to feed animals. The family is far from home and all alone. If they knew anyone in town they wouldn't be in a barn. Normal nativity scenes show there are three wise men, but we only know they gave three gifts. In all likelihood, they didn't show up that night either. Put it together. A young couple, recently married is forced by an uncaring government to travel to a strange city when the wife is approaching childbirth. It has to be a difficult time. A scary time. What held them together? Why did this special family hold together when others fail? It is, and must be, love. We, each of us, are all we have. Find room in your day for love."

ETC John Barton, on his acoustic guitar, and ST1 Thurman, on his violin, play the first notes, then sing, "What Child is This?"

FOREST EAST OF DIJON, OCCUPIED FRANCE

1814, 24 December, 1941 (local time)

US Army SFC Henry Holmes stops the box truck he and his men stole and they all get out. It's snowing and bitterly cold. Lieutenant Victor Olsen says, "Fuck, it's cold. Why aren't we trying for the Swiss border? It's only over there."

Holmes, "Shhh, sir."

Holmes has seven technicians to feed and care for, including one woman. He starts cutting branches and small trees to cover the blue sides of the truck. Once they get started, Holmes walks back down their tire tracks with a branch. In twenty minutes, he motions south and they start out.

In their packs are jerky and other high energy, low mass foods they picked up at the mini-mart on their way off Brendenmeyer. As the sun starts to set, Holmes motions them to stop and they get off their feet and eat. He looks at his lieutenant, "Look, sir, if we make it across into Switzerland, we get interned. We're of no use to our country if we can't get home. We go south to the Med where it's warmer. If we can,

43

we steal a boat and go to Gibraltar. Barring that, we make contact with the underground and escape from one coast or another."

The lieutenant nods, "Hooah, SFC."

Technical Sergeant Tiffany Van Zandt says, "We could make for Andorra, too."

Olsen, "What's Andorra?"

Van Zandt, "It's a small principality on the border of France and Spain. It was truly neutral during the war and they took in refugees. I read once that the French underground used Andorra to smuggle out downed pilots. They could smuggle us out, too."

U.S. Airforce Master Sergeant Kelly O'Brien says, "I went there once on leave. It's in the mountains. To get there we have to cross all of Vichy France."

Holmes, "First, the coast."

Van Zandt, "It's Christmas eve." She looks at each of her companions, "Merry Christmas. God, I wish I was home."

Holmes, "Yeah, I know. For now, we've got to let it go, or we won't survive. We need to cover about thirty miles in this snow tonight."

USS SAN FRANCISCO, 90 MILES NORTHEAST OF THE CARRIER GROUP

0810, 27 December, 1941

The sub slows from a sprint. To keep ahead of the carrier, they have to spring ahead, then stop and hunt. Brown is in a near meditative state, listening and watching his waterfall screen. As they slow, a line of dots appears.

Guthrie asks, "What's this?"

Brown, "Conn, Sonar. New contact. Designate Sierra 5. Bearing is 224."

Morrison walks in, "Penny for your thoughts?"

"Sir, two screws. Twin diesels. The screws are fast. Either a large fishing boat or a sub on the surface."

"Okay." Morrison returns to control, "OOD, left standard rudder. Make our course 170."

The watch repeats back.

Morrison picks up a phone, "Captain, new contact to the southwest. We are maneuvering." The sub banks in the turn. Commander Cumberland walks in straight to the table.

"Conn, Sonar. Sierra 5 is diving. Confirmed submarine."

Cumberland pushes the button, "Very well. How far are they from the fleet?"

"Best guess, fifty miles."

"Too fucking close." Cumberland storms into sonar, "What the fuck were you doing, Brown? How could you miss a fucking World War II diesel, fucking electric submarine? Can't you fucking hear?"

"Sir, we were sprinting. We ran right by it."

Cumberland stomps into control, "Call the tracking party. Load and make ready a torpedo in tube 3." He hovers over the tracking table that marks their position and the bearing lines to their target.

"Conn, Sonar. The Long Beach has accelerated to flank speed. Their course is toward Sierra 5."

Cumberland pushed the button, "You better not have cost me a kill."

The tracking party arrives, marking down the new bearings

of the target as they are announced from sonar. Soon they have a range and course for the target. Wankowski says, "Range is 42 miles. Their course is 210."

They hear, "Tube 3 loaded with a Mark-48. Fish is spun up."

Cumberland, "Ahead flank, power limiting."

"Conn, Sonar. We are cavitating."

Morrison on the box, "Understood."

Cumberland under his breath, "Ain't no one on this ocean that can hear us."

USS FIFE DD-991, 20 MILES NORTH OF CARL VINSON

Commander James Lamoure says, "XO, take us to General Quarters. If the Long Beach gets in trouble, we'll need to sort it out."

LCDR Margaret Lafferty, the XO, says, "Aye, sir."

"Combat, Sonar. The San Francisco just kicked it in the ass, sir."

Lamoure pushes the button, "Sonar, give me a bearing."

"Yes, sir. Bearing is 038. Bearing is constant."

"Understood." Lamoure turns to Lafferty, "The submarine Long Beach is playing with got by the Frisco. Cumberland will be pissed."

"Do you know him, sir?"

He nods, "We were in ROTC at the same time. I did a number of midshipman events with him. As I recall, he attended UCLA."

"What about you, sir?

"University of Oregon."

"The Beavers?"

He smiles, "The Ducks. I'm almost offended. I guess I can't expect much more from a ring knocker."

Lafferty looks down at the Annapolis ring on her right hand and smiles. "Yes, sir.

USS SAN FRANCISCO

Cumberland, "Ahead 1/3." The order is relayed to maneuvering where the throttleman slowly shuts down the throttle. As the screw stops thrashing the ocean at speed, the flow resistance in the water causes the ship to slow. At normal throttling rates, the throttleman shuts the throttle completely for a little while as they coast down. The slower screw is no longer creating and collapsing steam bubbles along its edge: what is called cavitation. The noise made by water flowing along the hull diminishes.

Brown, "Conn, Sonar. Sierra 5 and Long Beach are both at 186."

Cumberland invades sonar, "Do you hear torpedoes in the water?"

"No, sir. I hear active sonar from the Long Beach and also from dipping sonar. There is a helicopter out there. Two, no three, sono-buoys. An S-3 is up there, too."

"What a coupe if I can steal a kill from all of those. Sort them out." He turns and struts into control, "Give me a firing solution on Sierra 5."

Sonar calls bearings to the tracking party and they plot the subs position on the chart. As all the vessels move, the bearings change. They use trigonometry to calculate range based on these changes. Wankowski, "Captain, Long Beach and Sierra 5 are a single datum. They are in close proximity and maneuvering around each other."

Cumberland spits out, "How far away?"

"About ten miles."

"Conn, Sonar. "Aspect change. Long Beach is maneuvering around Sierra 5."

Cumberland pushes the button, "How far apart are they?"

"Close, sir. Less than a mile."

Cumberland, "Fuck. Fucking hell."

"Conn, Sonar. Sierra 5 is backing. Long Beach is pacing it on their port side."

Cumberland, "Understood." He releases the button, "They're in easy range. Why don't they fire?"

"Conn, Sonar. Gertrude, sir."

Cumberland rushes into sonar and hears, "Vessel authentication bravo, bravo, delta, one."

Cumberland, "What?"

They hear, "USS Dolphin, we are new in theater and haven't received the codes yet. I'm willing to offer ice cream and coffee as a bribe, though."

Cumberland, "What the fuck is he doing?"

Brown, "Bribing an American sub so it will surface." On the box Brown says, "Conn, Sonar. Sierra 5 is friendly. She's American."

Cumberland, "How do you know?"

They hear on the Gertrude, "What vessel?"

Brown, "Could a Japanese sailor speak English that well, sir?"

"We are the USS Long Beach CGN9. By the number on your

conning tower you are the Dolphin, a V class boat. Oh, another thing, if it makes you feel better, you're welcome to take a pot shot at us, if you must. Your torpedoes won't work."

Cumberland, "The Long Beach is a fucking cowboy. He has no idea how this mother fucker might react." He storms back into control."

"Conn, Sonar. Sierra 5 is flooding tubes and blowing ballast."

Cumberland studies the chart. Backes acknowledges sonar, then makes eye contact with Morrison.

Morrison shakes his head, "There is nothing we can do, but wait."

"Conn, Sonar. The Long Beach just floored it."

Morrison, "Very well."

"Conn, Sonar. Sierra 5 is surfaced. They are shutting torpedo doors."

Morrison, "Very well." He takes a massive clearing breath.

Cumberland, "Take us back on station. Carry on." He walks out of control.

Morrison, "Left standard rudder. Make our course 035. Ahead standard."

Backes, "He seems disappointed."

"Greg, we almost killed an American sub. That sub almost killed the Long Beach. We need to be better at telling friend from foe."

Quietly, Backes asks, "Does it matter to him?"

"It has to." Morrison walks into sonar, "Brown, how are you doing?"

"Okay, sir. It was a ballsy thing the Long Beach did."

"How did you read it?"

"Sir, she knew the sub, US or Japanese, could only fire in a narrow arc ahead or behind. He approached on the beam and kept the beam on the sub. The Long Beach is a big, loud, old boat, but she got it done."

"What can you tell me about the sub?"

"Diesel electric, twin screws. She has four-bladed screws. The Japanese had three. If that is common practice in the two navies, we can use it to identify nationality. I got an audio track for training."

"Thank you."

CHAPTER 4

USS SAN FRANCISCO

1104, 27 December, 1941

MM3 Karl Gustaf knocks on the XO's door. Morrison says, "Enter." The XO's room is really small. Gustaf enters and shuts the door behind him. He takes a deep breath and says, "Sir. I know how we went back in time."

"Okay." Morrison sets down his pen and turns from his desk. The MM3 is rocking from foot to foot, his shoulders hunched, and there's a twitch in his left cheek. "Is it something you did?"

"No, sir."

"Then relax. Want a soda?"

"Um, sure."

Morrison pulls out two bottles from the small fridge he brought aboard, "Not that new crap. I have the original swill." He hands one to Gustaf and opens his, "Go ahead."

"Have you heard a book called the 'Talon Sword'?"

"Yes. Oh, it was about a time machine. Gustaf, that was fiction."

The young nuke presents the book open to the relevant scene, "December 19, 1990 to December 19, 1941. That's what happened to us."

Morrison reads the passage, "That's way too close to be a guess. I've no doubt you've an explanation. Please continue."

"My roommate at prototype was nuts about this book. Nuts as only a nuke can be nuts."

"Yes. Super nerds, continue."

"The time machine is located in the Australian outback, just like in the book. See, the author was a Lit major and wouldn't know anything about machines. But in the book, his descriptions were exacting. He got the information from a paper in the Bodleian Library at Oxford. The British Ministry of Defense really built the machine there."

"On December 19, 1941, no time travel event occurred."

"No, sir, not in our time line. The thing is, that machine discharged terawatts of energy and nothing happened. No melting. No damage. Where did it go? According to my roommate, the buildings were rusted and abandoned in 1990. He knew a guy who had seen them."

"No time travel occurred?"

"No, sir. Not until time marched forward to the right point and the antenna focused the energy around it, where ever it was, and drew that place back in time. My friend built one of the antennas and he is stationed on the Carl Vinson, sir."

"Damn. Right. It's been years since I read this book. How do we get back?"

"We can't, sir. It was a one-way trip."

"Are you sure."

"It's the physics of it, sir. Doctor Heinlein used frequency and voltage to choose the time it drew from. The process cannot be reversed without using negative energy."

Morrison finishes, "And negative energy is hypothetical. What happened to everything in the future? Did they all just die?"

"No, sir. They're trucking along with their lives in their own time line. Except, by now, the Navy is desperately searching for a missing carrier group."

"Wouldn't doppelganger us keep trucking along?"

"Sir, that would violate the Conservation of Energy. Even Einstein cannot break the laws of physics."

"Don't go Scotty on me. That's Miller's position."

"Yes, sir."

"Can I borrow the book?"

"Yes, sir."

"Who knows about this?"

"You, me, and my LPO, Gary Mallory."

"Send him to me and keep your yap shut on this."

"Yes, sir."

A few minutes later, Gary Mallory knocks and enters, "Yes, sir?"

Morrison, "Mallory, Gustaf came to you about the 'Talon Sword' thing, right?"

"Oh, fuck, sir. I told him to shut his mouth about it."

"Have you told anyone?"

"No, sir. If it's true, it's the kind of information that could get you lynched."

"Okay, I agree. I want you to keep quiet about this while I figure out what to do about it."

"Um, sir. I did mention the book to Wankowski and Hines. I didn't say anything about Gustaf's friend."

"Okay. Keep quiet about it."

"Yes, sir. I heard you got married right before we left."

"I did."

"I'm sorry, sir."

"Me too. I know you lost your boys. God, this sucks."

"The kids are the worst. They will never exist."

"Yeah, I see that."

"Sir, what are you going to do about your wife?"

"There is nothing I can do."

"We could memorialize her and all the people we lost."

Morrison's eyes widen, "Yes, we could and we should."

Mallory smiles, "I'm not as stupid as they all think."

"I've never thought you were stupid, Gary. Have you thought about what you are going to do after the war?"

"No, sir."

"What were your retirement plans."

"Get a job close to my boys."

"What are you going to do now?"

"I'm going to take a lesson from Willie Nelson in the 'Electric Horseman'. 'I'm gonna get me a bottle of tequila and find me one of them Keno girls that can suck the chrome off a trailer hitch and just kinda kick back'."

Morrison laughs, "So, that is what your persona wants. What does Mallory the person want?"

"My family back."

"I'll set up the memorial."

"Will the skipper allow it?"

"He's not a monster."

"Really?"

Remember, say nothing about the book."

"Yes, sir."

Mallory leaves and Morrison slumps in his chair, "This is fucking hard."

He pulls out a note pad:

Captain Klindt…

USS CARL VINSON

0630, 4 January, 1942

Admiral Ren, Captain Johnson, CO of the Carl Vinson, Captain Van Zandt and Captain Klindt sit with Admiral Nimitz and his staff; Captain John Duncan, his chief of staff, Captain Lewis Burbank, his logistics officer, and Commander Philip Morton, his intelligence officer. Nimitz holds up a paper, "Tell me about this submarine, the San Francisco."

Ren, "She's a 688-class nuclear powered submarine. Because of the nuclear power plant, she only needs to surface for food, maintenance, and crew rest. They do, however, require very specific and demanding maintenance."

Nimitz, "I see. The same as for this ship. How long is its core life and can it be refueled?"

"The core can be refueled, but in the end, the dive cycles on the hull are the more restrictive. We should get thirty or forty more years from her."

"Who commands her."

Klindt, "His name is Commander George Cumberland."

"Your subs have commanders? Ours use lieutenants."

"Yes, sir. We want a senior and responsible officer in charge of a nuclear power plant. The XO is a lieutenant commander, as are some of the department heads."

"What are their general capabilities and missions?

"They are being used now to defend the battlegroup from other submarines. They can perform a number of other missions, including intelligence gathering, surface vessel or submarine attack, tracking Soviet boomers, and other things."

Nimitz, "What is a 'boomer'?"

Ren, "A special purpose missile submarine." He explains the design capabilities.

Nimitz, "Do any of you know this Commander?"

Ren, "I have met him, but I don't know him well."

Klindt, "Sir, I know his XO well. We served together about a decade ago. Commander Cumberland is new in command and has made some errors. He has, however, successfully engaged two submarines. One was a Russian nuke boat."

"He sank a Russian submarine?"

"Yes, sir. It came back in time with the rest of us. When he engaged it, the Russian was maneuvering aggressively against the Vinson."

"We want to keep that secret."

"Yes, sir."

"What were his mistakes."

Klindt, "It's how he treats his crew. Commander Morrison says he has a poor manner with his subordinates. To quote, 'he's an asshole, but a competent asshole."

Duncan, "What prompted this?"

Ren, "Cumberland sent a message asking when he should send his minority crewmembers, including his XO, for internment, and get them replaced by white men. We cannot function without these people, as I discussed."

Klindt, "For clarification, I worded my request in such a way as to force Morrison to speak clearly. As it was, he was reluctant to speak ill of his commander."

Nimitz, "Klindt, what nationality is the XO?"

Klindt, "He's an American, sir. His mother was Japanese, and his father was Irish-American."

Nimitz, "I want this communication in the raw."

Klindt stands, "In my stateroom, sir."

Van Zandt also stands, "I'll get mine."

Nimitz nods. "Ren, I agree with your conclusions regarding female and minority servicemen. Until we receive specific guidance from the President or Congress, they are to remain at their posts. You know I want you and the brain trust to report to the President. It will be an opportunity to convince him we are right on this."

Ren, "Yes, sir. Who will replace me?"

"I've already called for the Enterprise to sortie. Admiral Halsey will command."

Johnson, "What do you want us to do?"

Nimitz, "Raid Tokyo. The country needs a lift. American

bombs dropping on Tojo will give it to them. No general bombing. Stay focused on military targets."

USS SAN FRANCISCO

1235, 4 January, 1942

ST1(SS) Thorsen sits his panel in meditative silence. ST3(SS)William Curtis, a twenty-three-year-old, six-foot black man, stands watch with Thorsen. He's learned to be quiet. But he has to ask, "Do you think we're going to pull in?"

Thurman, "What?"

"Do you think we're going to pull in? We're near Hawaii."

"I doubt it."

They hear a thrum. Curtis, "Hear that?"

Thorsen, "Yes. I'm sorting it out." Thorsen pushes the button, "Conn, Sonar. Multiple surface vessels, 310."

Miller walks in, "Your best guess?"

"I'm hearing multiple screws. They're far enough away to be a point source. The rpms are different, so it's more than one ship."

"A battlegroup then. Thank you." Miller walks to the chart table. He pushes the button, "Captain, we have a battlegroup coming out of Pearl."

"Okay."

"Captain in control." Cumberland studies the table, then walks into Sonar, "Thorsen, can you make any sense out of it?"

"Working on it, sir. There are at least three four-screw ships. How many carriers did we have in '41, sir?"

"I don't know. It could be battleships or cruisers."

"Yes, sir. Right now, they're just unfamiliar contacts. When we sort them out, we'll designate each track."

Cumberland returns to control, "Miller, get a good sound track on each of these new contacts and keep looking for Jap subs."

"Yes, sir."

USS SAN FRANCISCO SSN-771

0725, 5 January, 1942

Commander Cumberland waits on the bridge in a survival suit as a helo approaches. "Morrison, "I'll be back later today. You know my standing orders."

"Yes, sir." Morrison reaches out with the grounding rod and catches the dangling rope. First, the helo lowers a litter with a mail bag and boxes of supplies. Outgoing mail goes up with Cumberland's bag. Next a SAR swimmer is lowered. The SAR hooks up Cumberland and the two of them are lifted into the helo. When the helo lifts them clear, Morrison lets go of the rope.

Morrison is the last one down, "Chief of the Watch, last man down. Hatches secured. Bridge rigged for dive."

The watch repeats back and they go through the exacting routine of diving the boat. As they settle at 300 feet, he tells Backes, "I'm going to check what we got for mail and supplies. Make our course 290. Sprint out at full to clear datum and slow for search in 90 minutes."

"Aye, sir."

Morrison walks aft and finds the supply office of Lt. Ed Cameron, the only non-nuclear officer on board. "Ed, what did we get in the mail?"

"It's all official, except for a couple of letters for you and one for MM3 Gustaf."

"He's on watch. I'll bring his back to him. Can I see the official mail?"

"Yes, sir. Is the captain getting relieved?"

"Not that I know of. He's attending a meeting with the other skippers and Admiral Halsey. Please don't spread that rumor."

"Yes, sir."

USS CARL VINSON, 700 MILES NORTHWEST OF HAWAII

Cumberland's helicopter overflies the fleet. He can see the Enterprise with its escort of heavy cruisers and destroyers mixed in with the Carl Vinson group. They land on spot 4 near the island. A petty officer in white flight deck jersey and float coat helps him out as the rotors spin down. Cumberland grabs his bag and is escorted to the island. Captain Van Zandt is waiting for him. Van Zandt opens the hatch and ushers him inside. "Now that we're inside and you can hear me, welcome aboard."

"Thank you, sir."

Van Zandt, "I'm with Halsey's staff. I was Ren's chief of staff. We've forty minutes before the meeting, so let's get a cup of coffee."

"Yes, sir."

Van Zandt escorts Cumberland into the Admiral's outer office, "Two coffees, please." They go into Van Zandt's office and sit down. An aid brings in their coffees and leaves. Van Zandt looks at Cumberland over his cup, "I ought to get to the point, Commander. Why were you in such a hurry to get rid of your XO?"

"He's a Japanese American. It's my understanding Japanese Americans were interned during the war. I was just trying to comply with the law."

"So, you're a racist?"

"No, sir. Not at all. I was just trying to comply with the law."

"Fair. Buy why? Is his performance unsatisfactory?"

Cumberland is silent for a moment, "Morrison is a legacy and no doubt has friends, even now. You said you were with Admiral Ren's staff?"

"I did."

"Lieutenant Commander Morrison is a legacy. His adopted father retired as a rear admiral. His adopted grandfather retired as a vice-admiral who was 5th Fleet. That grandfather is serving on a destroyer somewhere right now."

"I'm aware of Morrison's family. I served with his father. It begs the question, though. Is his performance unsatisfactory?"

"No, sir. I feel he is too friendly with the blue jackets and way to fast to offer praise, but he's a competent officer. I wouldn't recommend him for command yet."

"Why?"

"As I said, he needs to learn how to be a firmer disciplinarian. It's the only way to hold a command together."

"I see. Can I tell you a story?"

"Of course, sir."

"When the Revolutionary Army was struggling through the cold winter in Valley Forge a soldier rode out of his encampment and noticed a group of soldiers struggling to put a log on the top of the wall they were building. Each time they lifted it, they lost their grip and the log fell. The men were cold and tired and hungry. He could see they were ready to give up. The corporal in charge of the work stood apart, yelling at them, so they picked up the log one more time. The soldier, sitting his horse, asked the corporal why didn't he help his men. The corporal said, 'Don't you see I'm a corporal?' The mounted soldier quietly dismounted and helped the soldiers raise the log into place. He then told the soldiers, including the corporal, that if they needed further assistance, they should send for him. The mounted soldier was General George Washington. Now, would you say General Washington was unsuited for command?"

"No, sir."

"So, the question in front of me is not at all whether Lieutenant Commander Morrison is suited for command. I have the assurances of Rear Admiral Klindt, who served with him, that he is. He was one of my students when I instructed at Command College, and I was also impressed. The question, then, is whether you are suited for command. Vice Admiral Halsey has been advised of the command climate on the San Francisco. He's waiting for my advice. What do you suppose I should tell him?"

Cumberland swallows, "I assure you, Captain Van Zandt, I will adjust my command style to accommodate your expectations."

"Please do. Shall we?" Captain Van Zandt stands.

CHAPTER 5

USS SAN FRANCISCO

0810, 5 January, 1942

Backes watches his watch standers do their jobs. He's learned not to hover, but trust his men. The helm asks Chief Giblin, "Chief, is there a sport you like?"

Giblin, "You're asking if there is a sport that matters. Yes, one."

"Not baseball, right?"

"No, baseball is ninety-five percent waiting for something to happen and five percent of the happenings. They've fallen down the rabbit hole of statistics to the point that we know how a batter does against left-handed Jewish pitchers on damp Tuesdays in August. Then they're disappointed when their worthless statistic doesn't pan out. It's beyond stupid. The only sport that matters is politics."

"Chief, politics isn't a sport."

"Sure, it is. It has seasons, teams, and rules. It also has winners and losers."

"Conn, Sonar. New contact. Designate Sierra 6, bearing 285. Twin screws and diesels."

Backes pushes the button, "Very well." He pushes another button, "XO, we have a contact."

A minute later Morrison walks straight into sonar, "So,

Brown, what do we have?"

"I think it's a sub on the surface. Two screws. Twin diesels."

"How many blades."

"Three."

"According to Admiral Nimitz, the American subs in theater have four. We still need to confirm. Good job." Back in control he checks the table, "Greg, let's rig for silent and call for the tracking team."

"Yes, sir." The word goes out. All unnecessary noise generating equipment is secured and the off-watch crew hits their racks. Backes asks, "How good do you think their sonar is?"

"I think it's crap. But I know we do well to overestimate our adversary, rather than underestimate them and court disaster.

"Yes, sir. Then, I'll cancel the Van Halen concert in the crew's mess."

Morrison nods, "Good idea."

They wait as they close with the contact.

USS CARL VINSON

Admiral Halsey walks up to the mike and says loudly, "Carry on," blasting everyone's ears. "Sorry about that. Can everyone hear me?" They all chuckle and nod their heads. He continues, "Before we lay out the plan, I would like each command to stand, introduce themselves, their unit, and their XO. I'm sure you all know who I am. Standing to my right is my chief of staff, Commander Miles Browning. Next to him is Captain Chris Van Zandt, who served as Admiral Ren's chief of staff before I nabbed him."

Then, Captain Johnson introduces himself and Captain Patterson. Then Captain Murray introduces himself and his XO, and so on around the room. Captain Cassin Young stands, "I'm Captain Young of the heavy cruiser San Francisco. My XO is Commander Jenkins."

When his table is up Cumberland stands, "I'm Commander Cumberland of the submarine San Francisco, and my XO is Lieutenant Commander Morrison, who is still on board."

When they've all introduced themselves, Halsey continues, "Right, the Carl Vinson Task Force brings a number of new weapons to the fight. We need to update our formations and our battle plans to incorporate these new systems. First, as most of you have noticed, the new ships are rather short on guns. That's because they use guided missiles instead. It's a rocket that can be aimed in flight. They are extremely effective against aircraft, but they need clear lanes of fire. We will be putting the Long Beach and Horne outside the inner ring around the two carriers; the Long Beach to port and the Horne to starboard. In an aerial threat, the missile ships will orient toward the threat. The Fife and Jarret will be out front and Commander Lamoure of the Fife will be ASW commander. The Vinson also has a number of ASW assets and Commander Lamoure knows how to use them. The supply ships will stay on the starboard side of the carriers and the rest of our destroyers will ring around the group. Questions?"

Captain Ellis M. Zacharias of the Salt Lake City asks, "Who is the AAW commander?"

"Ellis, I know that was your job, but it now falls to Captain Tenzar of the Long Beach. His radar and control systems far outstrip what our older ships can do."

Captain Young of the cruiser San Francisco asks, "Yes, sir, but do the contraptions really work."

Captain Tenzar says, "My missiles have a range of 85 nautical miles and I can engage eight aircraft a minute with a 90% hit rate. Horne, with half the systems, can engage four more. We will not be able to completely eliminate a persistent swarm attack, but we can attrite them long before they are in your range. Should we encounter Japanese jets, we're the only platform capable of engaging them."

Captain Young, "Our gunners are good."

Tenzar, "I have no doubt they are. This isn't a question of skill. No gunner can hit an aircraft flying 1200 miles per hour at 40,000 feet. Jets operate in an envelope unlike anything you've ever seen."

Halsey, "Gentlemen, we're all on the same team." He motions to Browning, who uncovers a map of the Pacific Ocean. "We'll approach from here. During the approach, the Enterprise will do all the patrols and the cap, preserving fuel on the Vinson. The Vinson will maintain four fighters on ready 5 and continue ASW patrols. Once we are at our initial point, the Vinson strike group will attack Tokyo, focusing their attacks here and here and here. Upon completion of the strike, we're authorized additional attacks if it seems advisable. We'll retreat in this direction. Vinson will maintain enough jet fuel in reserve to fight for two days. I want all ships to keep fuel reserves at 80%. Questions?"

LCDR Sherman of the USS Dunlap DD-384, "Why eighty percent, Admiral?"

"If we kick over a hornet's nest, I want to maintain the option to make a hasty strategic advance to the rear." The men chuckle. "Let's break for supper. I want CO's and XO's to split up. I want 41's and 90's at every table. You need to get a chance to know one another."

Cumberland stands and sees Captain Young motioning for him. He walks to the table and offers a hand, "Sir."

"Good afternoon, Commander. Have a seat."

"Yes, sir."

Young introduces the table, "This is Commander Grey, XO of the Long Beach, Captain Zacharias of the Salt Lake City, and Captain Hartt of the Quincy." He turns back to Cumberland, "Now, how is it your ship is named the San Francisco?"

"It's the next in line. Your ship gets decommissioned after the war."

Young says, "It's only eight years old."

"Yes, sir."

"Do you know why?"

Cumberland is quiet for a moment, thinking, "I think it was two reasons. The technology had marched on and your ship was not updated, which made your cruiser unnecessary. That and Congress clamored for a war dividend. The war cost a great deal to fight. For America it was war bonds, which is debt."

"So, it wasn't because of battle damage?"

"No, sir. In the early eighties they authorized my boat to reuse the name. We were even offered some of the silver set that your boat carries right now."

"Did you accept?"

"The commissioning crew did. We've only a portion of the set because room is quite limited on a submarine."

Captain Zacharias asks, "What are the capabilities of your submarine?"

Cumberland, "First, like the Long Beach, it's nuclear powered, meaning she is built with about twenty-five years of fuel. The power plant is air independent, meaning it has no need to surface for air. We scrub carbon dioxide from the air and generate oxygen to breath. The World War II submarines were surface vessels that could submerge to fight. Modern submarines are true submarines. They only surface to enter or leave port for provisioning."

Zacharias, "Very good, sir. How well do you fight?"

Cumberland, "We've already sunk two submarines. Our torpedoes have internal guidance. Meaning it has integral sonar that enables it to guide itself on to its target, close, and destroy it. They are very advanced."

Captain Hartt asks, "When was your submarine commissioned?"

Cumberland, "1981, sir."

Zacharias turns to CDR Grey, "The capabilities of your ship, sir?"

"The Long Beach primarily has missile systems. We're optimized for surface to air with two Mark 10 missile launchers. My captain described our capabilities. We do have guided torpedo launchers for anti-submarine, as well as rocket propelled guided torpedoes for engaging submarines further away. We have two missiles launchers for anti-ship and two for land attack. The land attack missiles cannot function right now. A satellite system they require doesn't exist. We also have two 5-inch guns, but they were put in as an afterthought."

Hartt, "Is it our guns that make us obsolete?"

Grey, "The lack of missiles is the problem. If you find yourself in the yards for repairs, with any choice as to your new configuration, opt to receive missile systems for self-defense and area-defense. In 1990 the primary function of cruisers is battlegroup anti-air. Destroyers can function in an anti-air environment, but are optimized for anti-submarine. Our frigate is basically, a smaller, less redundant destroyer with the same mission."

Zacharias asks Cumberland, "How good are the destroyers and frigates at finding submarines?"

Cumberland, "Against World War II diesel electric boats, they should be fairly effective. No one was focusing on making them quiet. Against my boat, and boats like mine, they're no threat. In exercises, we've had to assign sailors to pound on the hull with a hammer so they have a chance of hearing us."

Young, "You're that good?"

"I am."

USS SAN FRANCISCO

Morrison, "Bring us up to 150. I want to spin a 180 to look for traffic. Come to periscope depth behind and to their starboard side."

"Yes, sir."

"Load and make ready a Mark-48 in tube 3."

"Yes, sir."

Backes, "Are we rotating tubes to make sure they all work?"

"Yes, exactly. It's what the captain started to do."

Backes issues the orders and Morrison watches, silent. In an hour, they are coming alongside the still surfaced boat on its rear starboard quarter. Morrison, "Take it, Greg."

Backes, "Up scope." Backes spins a quick 360 and settles on his target. "Sir, the sail has a symbol and the number 9. It also has the meatball flag painted on its side."

Morrison, looking at the image on the screen, says, "Take us down."

JAPANESE SUBMARINE I-9

Lieutenant Watanabe studies the sky for aircraft. He looks down and sees the feather of a periscope off the starboard rear. "Clear the sail!" He calls down to his skipper, "Captain, submarine abaft our starboard beam!" He pulls the phone jack and slides down the ladder to shut the first hatch. He continues down and closes the last hatch, "Last man down, hatch sealed, bridge rigged for dive." The boat is already angling down and turning to port.

His CO, Lieutenant Commander Sasaki says, "Descend to 250 feet. Lieutenant, did you see more then the periscope?"

"Only that. It was fast, sir. We are traveling at 10 knots. No submarine is that fast submerged."

USS SAN FRANCISCO

Backes, "Do we turn with them?"

Morrison, "Ahead 2/3rds, right standard rudder. New course 165. We need space to set up a torpedo shot."

His orders are repeated back.

Morrison, Make our depth 500 feet." To Backes, "It's unlikely they have guided torpedoes. Even if they do, they probably can't work as deep as we can."

"Conn, Sonar. I'm losing Sierra 6 in our baffles."

Morrison, "Understood, Brown. We need some space for a torpedo."

"Steady on course 165, leveling off at 500 feet."

Morrison studies the chart table, "Very well. Left standard

rudder. Make our course 348. Open the torpedo door."

The watch repeats back and the submarine leans in the turn.

JAPANESE SUBMARINE I-9

Sasaki, "Sonar, commence active pinging. Can you give me bearing, range, and depth?"

The helm, "Captain, passing 010."

USS SAN FRANCISCO

They hear the ping against the hull. "Conn, Sonar. Active pinging."

Morrison, "Very well." To Backes, "We could fire now, but I would rather our nose was pointing at him."

"Yes, sir."

JAPANESE SUBMARINE I-9

Sasaki studies a paper chart that is being updated. "Control, Sonar. Target is bearing 167, range 6 miles. Approximate depth, 150 meters."

Sasaki looks at his XO, "How?"

USS FIFE

LTJG Laura Wakefield is standing OOD. She is the only JG with her Surface Warfare Officer qualification, and the only one allowed to stand OOD. On the squawk box she hears, "Bridge, Combat, we're picking up active sonar at 285."

She pushes the button, "Understood, Combat. Do we need to maneuver?" The sound powered phone growls, and she picks it up, "Bridge, OOD."

Her engineer, LCDR Peter Gregory says, "It seems distant and I don't think it's American. I'm passing it to the Vinson and directing Easy Rider 31 to the area."

USS SAN FRANCISCO

The helm reports, "Steady on course."

Morrison, "Fire tube 3."

On the box they hear Kichiro, "Conn, Torpedo. Tube 3 fired electrically."

"Conn, Sonar. Fish is running hot, straight, and normal."

"Very well."

JAPANESE SUBMARINE I-9

"Control, Sonar. Torpedo in the water!"

"Calm please," LCDR Sasaki admonishes, "What is the bearing?"

"345, sir."

Sasaki, "Set all six torpedoes to the reciprocal course, 165. Full depth setting."

They can hear the pinging of the incoming torpedo. "Set, Captain."

"Fire one through six." The sub shudders as the torpedoes leave their tubes.

USS SAN FRANCISCO

Morrison is quiet as their torpedo closes its target. "Conn, Sonar. Sierra 6 is firing multiple torpedoes. Constant bearing."

Morrison, "Ahead flank, cavitate. Full rise on the planes. Right full rudder."

The watch standers repeat back the order and the sub starts to turn and climb. "Twenty seconds to impact. Ten, nine, eight, seven, six, five, four, three, two…" The San Francisco shudders from the nearby explosion that destroys the I-9.

"Four hundred. Passing 020."

"Rudder amidships. Steady as she goes."

"Three hundred. We're going to broach."

Morrison, "Ahead 1/3rd. Helm slowly center the bubble."

"Two hundred."

Morrison, "If we broach, we broach."

It takes time to slow the engines back down from ahead flank. The dive planes can't be quickly changed either. The inertia of the submarine is too much. A rapid control change, against the mass of the water, could damage the controls.

EASY RIDER 31, NEAR THE USS SAN FRANCISCO

LTJG Buddy 'Babe' Ruth, pilot of Easy Rider 31 has ordered the dipping sonar rigged out. They have a Mark 56 torpedo mounted on the left side of the fuselage. He and his co-pilot, ENS Sara 'Bubbles' McNeal, watch as a couple of miles away frothing bubbles come to the surface. At first it is white, but it quickly turns black. Ruth turns his bird, "Turn on the camera Bubbles."

She flips the switch and calls on the radio, "Fife, Easy Rider 31. We are seeing a black froth of oil bubbling up." She gives the map coordinates.

Ruth sees movement out of the corner of his eye and turns the helo hard around, "What's this?" They have a perfect view of the San Francisco broaching. The bow comes out of the water and splashes back down.

Bubbles, "Fife, Easy Rider. Our sub just broached in front of us."

"Roger, Easy Rider. Make contact and see if they need assistance."

Bubbles, "San Francisco, Easy Rider 31."

USS SAN FRANCISCO

The submarine settles down and sinks back into the water. The broaching maneuver looks dramatic, but inside the boat, it isn't. The deck just slowly tilts back to level. Morrison, "Take us to periscope depth. Up scope." He spins the periscope and spots the helo, "Turn on the VHF."

"...Francisco, Easy Rider 31."

He keys the mic, "Go traffic for San Francisco."

"San Francisco, we can confirm a good kill. Debris and oil in the water. Do you need assistance?"

"Negative, Easy Rider. We were dodging counter fire from our target."

"Understood. Good hunting."

"And to you."

"Commander, your boat. I need to write a report."

USS CARL VINSON

Commander Cumberland is lead into Admiral Halsey's conference room by Captain Van Zandt, who leaves and shuts the door. Only Vice Admiral Halsey is in the room and he does not stand, or offer a hand. "Sit."

Cumberland sits at attention.

"I've read Captain Van Zandt's and Admiral Klindt's reports on you. I want to be absolutely clear. Your primary job is to train every officer and bluejacket under you. I will not tolerate a tyrant. Absolutely not. Do not think for a minute you are irreplaceable. I don't need a new commander. I need a new seaman recruit. He bumps everyone else up, and then, I'll have a new commander. Am I clear?"

"Yes, Admiral."

"Okay. We have two San Francisco's. On the radio, you will be Sierra November, while both boats are in the same group. Now, get a cup of coffee and tell me about your submarine."

USS SAN FRANCISCO

Morrison comes back into control and hands his report to the radioman, "Tell me when it's sent and confirmed."

"Yes, sir."

USS CARL VINSON

There is a knock on the door and a messenger enters and hands Admiral Halsey a message in a folder. He reads it, writes a reply, and hands it to the messenger. Then, he slides the message over to Cumberland.

FRM: SSN-711

TO: COMCARGRU-2

REG: AFTER ACTION REPORT

On 2010 GMT, 6 January, 1942, San Francisco engaged a Japanese submarine 40 miles northwest of the carrier group. Markings indicated a hull number of 9. Fired one Mark-48 torpedo. Said sub sunk.

V/R

LCDR Morrison

For

CDR Cumberland

Cumberland stares at the message as his face reddens, then tightens. How dare Morrison get a kill. He struggles for control, then, calmly, "Thank you, Admiral. This is great news."

Halsey tilts his head, "You obviously have a good crew and an effective XO. Carry on, Commander."

Cumberland gets up, "Yes, sir." He walks out into the outer office where Van Zandt hands him a folder, "These are the current addresses for the grandparents of your crew. Not all the information is completely vetted for accuracy, but Admiral Nimitz wants your crew to write home."

Cumberland stares at him for a moment, uncomprehending. He takes a deep breath, "Yes, sir. I'll hand them out, but my crew is quite busy."

"Nimitz did not send it out as a request. The Navy department is contacting every person on this list. Your crew are required to write home, and so are you. Thank God, we have your crew's service records on board, because you guys don't have the room."

"Yes, thank you."

"Good day, Commander. Don't forget to recognize your XO for the great job he did protecting the fleet."

"Yes, sir."

USS SAN FRANCISCO

Morrison climbs down from the bridge, "Chief of the Watch, last man down, hatches closed, bridge is rigged to dive." They start the process of submerging the boat.

Cumberland finishes removing his exposure suit and hands it off to a petty officer. "I'll be in my stateroom. Get us back on station."

Morrison, "Any word from the meeting?"

"No changes in our mission." Cumberland abruptly walk away.

Miller, now on watch, asks Morrison, "What got up his ass? No congratulations for killing a sub. He looked, well, more angry than normal."

Morrison shakes his head, "Let it go." Louder, "Make our depth 300 feet. Come to course 287. Ahead standard."

The orders are repeated and the sub sinks deeper into its domain.

Mallory and Wankowski feel the sub tilt down. Mallory, "You know, it was damn nice fighting the boat with Morrison in charge."

Wankowski, "Yes, but we best not revel in it. Commander Cum-while-killing is back on board."

Mallory, "You think he's happy that we killed a boat?"

"No. Probably pissed off because the credit goes to Morrison."

Mallory, "It's his boat. He gets the credit."

"Yeah, but he's a ball hog. He has to make every shot."

They hear over the 1MC, "This is your Captain speaking. Uh, good job with the kill. Um. We are steaming to the approaches of Tokyo Bay, so there will be more. Um. Keep sharp. That is all."

The two men look at each other. Mallory, "A genuine compliment. Where did our captain go?"

Wankowski, "You don't suppose someone on top has figured out old Cum-while-killing?"

Mallory, "God. Maybe. Who is our Admiral?"

"I don't fucking know. Next time we're in control, we can ask."

They hear, "Secure from cleaning stations."

CHAPTER 6

USS SAN FRANCISCO

2023, 5 January, 1942

Morrison walks in from the communal shower wearing boxers, a shower robe, and flipflops. He hangs his ditty bag up and sits down to tidy up his desk. He sees new mail and picks it up. He opens a letter from Captain Van Zandt.

LCDR,

I have had a few discussions with Admiral Halsey regarding CDR Cumberland. As I am writing this Cumberland has not yet landed on the Vinson. Halsey plans to discuss his expectations with the CDR after our CO's meeting. Based primarily on your recommendations, it is not our intent to relieve CDR Cumberland at this time. If opportunity presents, I will speak to him as well.

Also, Cumberland will be delivering a list of addresses so that most of your crew can write home. Nimitz has made it mandatory that they do so. As I am certain that you agree, it is important to reconnect each of us time travelers with our families. There are a few exceptions. You have a small number of crew members, such as TM2 Kichiro, who's family live on occupied Guam. Some live on the contested Philippines. We have provided names to General MacArthur and requested he evacuate the Godoy's and the other Philippine servicemember's families out of PI. It is a tall order, so there are no guarantees.

Admiral Klindt has left the Carl Vinson, as you may know. He put on two stars and is being assigned to DC. He and I discussed your situation. He will send you a letter as soon as he is settled, so he may continue your correspondence. Meanwhile, I am and will remain here for you.

Best Regards,

C.B. Van Zandt

Morrison says to himself, "It's a wonder Cumberland didn't chew my ass as soon as he got back. That also explains the 'good job.' He opens the next letter, which is from Klindt.

Dear John,

I will be promoted to rear admiral in a few minutes, and then I am flying to Hawaii on my way to Washington, DC. I will be standing up the nuclear power program, and, likely assuming control of the Manhattan Project. I will keep you informed of my wanderings.

Know that I expect ORSE inspections and such will continue once I have my team stood up. We absolutely must retain our discipline as operators. Our units are far too important to let quality lapse.

I have informed Admiral Nimitz and Admiral Halsey of the issues your unit is facing. Captain Van Zandt will also keep me posted.

Please do all you can to keep morale and effectiveness up in your unit. The San Francisco is irreplaceable. Know also, it is the intent for the Navy to keep your subs name, even though there is a heavy cruiser for the same name. Have the crew drop the letters SSN from their correspondence and admit nothing of the details of your unit. We are calling it an anti-submarine vessel. A descriptive, non-descriptive term.

John, you are my friend. There are a group of us who, upon our trip back in time, have the opportunity to make our world a better place. All the people of my brain trust are in the group. I would like to include you. With that in mind, start thinking of ways we can improve our country's future.

Your Friend,

Craig

"Woah." He reads the letter again. "We probably have only eight months until ORSE. I'll make sure we're ready. With Klindt running it, I know it'll be a ball breaker."

There is a knock on the door. "Come in." He folds and puts away the letters as Cumberland walks in.

"XO, here is a list of addresses for our crew. They need to write home."

"Yes, sir. I and the COB will take care of it."

"Good." Cumberland hovers in the doorway, then, "Tell me about the sub."

"Brown picked it up 45 miles away on the surface, right when we completed our sprint back into position. We sprinted closer, pulled a 180 and inspected it by periscope. We have good video. It's one of the bigger subs designed to carry an aircraft. The hull number was 9. They spotted the feather from the mast and dived. In their dive, they turned north. We ran south to get range for the torpedo shot. They started pinging us. We got our nose on it and fired a '48. They counter fired all six tubes. Sonar reported no bearing change, so I put them on the beam and drove for the surface. Either, they were unguided, or our knuckle fooled them. The fish passed astern. Once we know we were clear, we slowed, but still broached. A nearby helo, Easy Rider 31, confirmed our kill. Oil and debris."

"You broached?

"Rather broach than eat a fish."

"You could have dived, rather than climbed."

"True, sir. I just believed diving at ahead flank would be a much more dangerous maneuver under the circumstances."

"Okay. Something you should know. We have someone reporting the goings on to the Admirals."

"I see. We shouldn't have anything to hide."

"Damn it. It rubs me wrong. I expect loyalty."

"Yes, sir. What did they say, sir?"

"Halsey expects his commanders to train their crews. We need to do more training."

"Yes, sir. I got a message from Admiral Klindt. He said to be ready for ORSE on schedule."

"What? There is no Naval Reactors."

"Admiral Klindt is being assigned as NAVSEA-08. He's standing up the organization."

"I see. That must be what Halsey was getting at. Okay. Do you know the man? I've never met him."

"We served together on the Fulton. He's a sharp operator. An ORSE from him will miss nothing at all."

"Have you been writing him?"

"He's been writing me. You don't ignore correspondence from an Admiral, sir."

"No, you don't. Do you have those letters?"

"I didn't keep them."

"From now on, all correspondence to or from Admiral Klindt goes through me. Understood?"

"Yes, sir."

"Are you the mole?"

"The mole, sir?"

"Never mind." Cumberland leaves, closing the door behind him.

Once he's gone, Morrison pulls out all the letters and rolls them up in a sock. He opens an access panel, reaches his arm through the hole and spins a bracket that pops loose a wall panel. The sock is carefully hidden in the wireway beyond. No one wants to touch someone's happy sock. He puts everything back and gets ready for bed.

SPECIAL WEAPONS BUNKER, BRENDENMEYER NATO AIR BASE, GERMANY

1100, 6 January, 1942

Reichsmarschall Hermann Goering strolls around the bunker complex, his baton behind his back. The stench of fire is still strong. "Why did you ask me here Oberfuhrer?"

SS-Oberfuhrer Erik Von Bergan, "Mein Reichsmarschall, interrogations of captured enemy personnel indicate this was a special place. This is where the Americans kept their atomic devices."

"There are no such devices here, Oberfuhrer."

"No, but one aircraft successfully escaped from the base. The reports are that four devices were under its wings. Those devices came from here."

"I am busy, Oberfuhrer. If they are gone you waste my time."

"The aircraft went somewhere. The men who manned this facility went somewhere. May I draw aerial resources to find them?"

Goering waves his baton, "Keep it a reasonable effort and do not bother me with it again unless you gain results."

Bergan snaps his heels together and salutes, "Heil Hitler."

Goering returns the salute and goes to his staff car.

USS SAN FRANCISCO

0823, 7 January, 1942

Kichiro and Trindle finish the weekly test on a Mark-48. Trindle, "What's with the captain?"

Kichiro, "He still hates me."

"Does he? He told me I was doing a good job yesterday. I about fell over."

"It all started after he went to the carrier. Do you suppose someone chewed his ass?"

"Kiche, all your seeing is the negative. He may have had an Epiphany."

"Dude, do you even know what that word means?"

"Yeah, it's like, you know, a good idea or something. I heard a nuke say it."

"It means a life changing discovery or realization. It's from the bible, man. When Jesus showed back up to the Apostles and stuff."

"How do you know about it?"

"Dude, I went to Catholic schools as a kid. That, and I'm not as stupid as you're acting."

"So, you were learning to be a priest, or something?"

"No, dumbass. It's where I went to middle school and high school. Religion was a required class."

"Okay. I thought Guamanians worshipped, like totem poles, or something."

"When the Spanish took us over hundreds of years ago, the islands converted to Christianity."

Trindle, "Okay. Have you written your family?"

"Have you?"

"Yeah. Just kind of a hi thing."

Kiche, "You didn't use a crayon, right?"

"No, dude. It was a good letter. What about you?"

"Where does my family live?"

"Guam, right?"

"Yeah. Who's running Guam right now?"

"A governor or something, right?"

"No. The Japanese hold the islands."

"Oh shit, man. Are you okay?"

"Yeah, I'll manage. I tell you. Someone chewed the captain's ass and he's going to unwind."

USS SAN FRANCISCO

1000, 14 January, 1942

Cumberland is in control as Backes runs his watch team and a drill set is going on in the engine room. Morrison walks in and straight to Sonar, "How are we doing, Brown?"

"It's quiet, sir. Reverb from the fleet in our baffles. Biologics. That's about it."

Morrison puts a hand on Brown's shoulder, "Good. As we get closer to Japan, we're all going to get a little more jumpy."

"Fair enough, sir."

Morrison joins Cumberland and studies the chart, "About sixty miles before they plan to launch."

Cumberland, "Morrison, I have an idea for a new fire drill. Could you run it back to Miller and go over it with him?"

"Yes, sir." Morrison takes the papers and heads aft."

Once Morrison is gone, Cumberland walks forward and into the XO's stateroom. Other than the small safe, nothing is locked. He goes straight to the safe and opens it. There are just the code books and papers that are supposed to be there. Next, he quickly opens the drawers of the desk, carefully running through the stuff in the drawers. There is a stack of letters in a desk cubby. He lays them out on the desk and sorts through them. All but two are unopened and they are all from his wife or mom. "Fuck." He looks in the coffin locker under the bed. Nothing. He puts down the locker and lifts the mattress. He is straightening the covers when he hears, "Captain to control."

Rushing out of Morrison's stateroom, he almost runs over the supply officer, Lt. Ed Cameron.

Cameron, "Sorry, sir."

"Yeah." Cumberland turns aft for control.

"What's going on, sir?"

"Don't worry about it, Lieutenant." A few more steps and Cumberland is in control, "Report."

Backes, "Sonar reports a single screw surface vessel at 354.

Designated Tango 19."

"Okay. Work up a firing solution and maneuver us astern." He walks into Sonar, "Report."

Brown, "Sir, from the change of bearing it's about thirty or so miles away. One fast screw, so it's unlikely to be a sub or warship."

"Okay. Um, good job."

When Cumberland gets back into control, he sees Morrison studying the table. "Sir, we ought to make an approach on her starboard beam. If we approach a fishing boat from the rear, we may foul in her gear."

Cumberland works his lip for a moment, "It's a point. Backes, approach the contact from the rear starboard quarter. Don't get fouled in its gear."

"Yes, sir." Backes passes the order.

Cumberland, "Let's get the tracking party team in here. Even if it's just a fishing boat, it's still good training."

"Tracking party to Control."

Morrison, "Sir, should we report it?"

"After we know what it is."

"Yes, sir."

In twenty minutes, they are coming up close to the contact at periscope depth."

"Conn, Sonar. The fleet is only 20 miles away."

Cumberland, "Up scope."

Morrison, "Understood, sonar."

Cumberland does a quick spin and settles on the contact, "Fishing boat. About 60 feet. Shit, it has a radio mast. Turn on the VHS."

"Yes, sir."

"Carrier Group 2, Sierra November. There is a fishing boat with an aerial at your 038."

"Sierra November, Group 2. Acknowledge. Why didn't you sink it?"

"Conn, Sonar. A cruiser just kicked it in the ass."

"Group 2, we need positive ID to engage."

"Understood. We are taking it under fire."

"Roger. Clearing datum." He hangs up the mic. "Crash dive. Make our depth 600 feet. Ahead flank. Right full rudder. Make our course 290."

Watch repeats and the sub's screws churn the water in a steep dive.

JAPANESE PICKET BOAT

The lookout shouts, "Captain, a submarine!"

The boat's commander sees the periscope slip beneath the waves, then a churned froth where screws near the surface. He turns to his radio operator, "They have a large powerful submarine out here. Call it in."

The first salvo from the USS San Francisco CA-38 lands close. The radioman is thrown out of his chair as the boat rocks from the near miss and water cascades down on them. He gets back to his console and starts to type as the Salt Lake City gets a direct hit with its first salvo. The shells pass right through the light-skinned vessel and explode under it, blowing the boat to pieces and killing all hands.

USS SAN FRANCISCO

Kichiro slides out from under the torpedo racks where he was cleaning the floor rails with a vacuum. He can hear the thunder against the hull. The whole ship is shaking, "What the fuck?"

TMC Kennedy, "It isn't depth charges. Nothing is close enough to drop them."

Cumberland on the 1MC, "The explosions you heard was our surface fleet engaging a Japanese picket boat that we located for them. We are clearing datum and getting back on station. That is all."

Morrison walks into his stateroom with a thousand things on his mind. As soon as the door shuts, he freezes. His letters from Lisa and his mom are scattered over his desk. "That sonofabitch."

He carefully checks each one. All the ones he hasn't opened are still sealed. He looks around. It's obvious his room has been tossed. After decades at sea, he has specified spots for everything. "Obviously, he didn't believe me. I wonder if he put a camcorder in here." He searches exhaustively for more than an hour and restows his things to their proper places. Then, he sits down and writes a letter to Van Zandt. When he's done, he checks the sock and stows the new letter with the others until it can be sent.

USS SAN FRANCISCO

1212, 14 January, 1942

Morrison studies the chart. They are arriving back on station 60 miles northwest of the fleet at 300 feet and 1/3rd.

"Conn, Sonar. Possible submarine on the surface at 281. Designate Sierra 7."

Miller pushes the button, "Very well." He pushes another button, "Captain, possible surfaced sub at 281."

"Let me know when you have range, bearing, and blade count."

"Yes, sir."

"Conn, Sonar. The Long Beach just went to ahead flank."

Miller pushes the button, "Roger, sonar."

Morrison, "Call for the tracking party."

"Conn, Sonar. The Fife just went to ahead flank. The Jarrett is also accelerating. The other ships are keeping station."

Miller, "Roger, sonar." He asks Morrison, "What do you think they are doing, sir?"

"Conn, Sonar. Long Beach has slowed. It looks like they changed their position in the battlegroup."

Morrison, "Roger, sonar. Be prepared for some loud noises."

"Yes, sir."

Morrison, "They're unmasking their batteries."

Miller, "A drill?"

The tracking party enters and takes their station. Morrison shakes his head, "Not this close to Japan."

Miller, "Jap fighters and bombers don't stand a chance."

Morrison nods, "You would think so, but we just bombed the shit out of their home."

"Conn, Sonar. Sierra 7 has just changed course toward the fleet. The screws are three-bladed."

Wankowski, "Sir, we have position, course, and speed."

Miller calls Cumberland.

Morrison, "Load and make ready a Mark-48 in tube 4."

"Load and make ready tube 4, aye."

Cumberland walks and goes directly to sonar. When he's back into control, he asks, "Status of tube 4?"

FC1 Anthony Walters, "Loading, sir."

"God damn it." Cumberland pushes a button, "Kichiro, get the lead out of your ass. I want it flooded and ready. Come on!" He turns to Miller, "Take us to periscope depth. I want to see it."

"Yes, sir." He passes the order. They wait while the range narrows. Submarine warfare is a patient game. TMC Kennedy, on the box, "Conn, Torpedo. Flooding tube 4."

Cumberland, "About time."

IMPERIAL JAPANESE SUBMARINE, I-57

Lieutenant Nakamura is on the bridge with two ratings. All three are studying the sky. Nakamura, "Be observant. They tell us the new aircraft are extremely fast and hard to see."

Petty Officer Sato asks, "Wouldn't the noise give them away?"

"I am told they fly faster than their noise."

Sato, "Then the pilot wouldn't hear himself fart."

They all chuckle.

CHAPTER 7

USS SAN FRANCISCO

1322, 14 January, 1942

Kichiro, "Chief, one of the lights are out."

"Check the bulbs."

"I did." He pushed the bulb test button and they all come on.

Kennedy, "Load tube 1." On the box, "Conn, Torpedo. Tube 4 is down. Loading tube 1."

Trindle at the rear of the torpedo, "Locking the bridging rails. Bridging rails are locked. Extending the bridging rails. Stay clear forward."

Kichiro in its front, is preparing the Amphenol. He checks the spacing, "Stay clear aft."

Trindle extends the hydraulic rails that bridge the space behind tube 1. He installs the pushing arm onto the rear of the torpedo, unlocks the torpedo from its cradle, and cranks a handle to raise it for moving forward. "Raised from the surface."

Kichiro inspects the tube. "Aye. Motion." He pushes the lever that moves the torpedo over the extended rails in front of the tube.

Cumberland materializes in Torpedo, "What the fuck is going on?"

Kennedy, "Just a sec, sir."

Kichiro uses a flashlight to make sure the torpedo does not foul on anything as it slides into place. "Guide center. Guide slot."

Kennedy, "Guide center, guide slot, aye."

When the fish is most of the way into the tube, Kichiro removes the cover over the screw and carefully installs the Amphenol, screwing it into position.

Cumberland, "Let's go!"

Kennedy, "Slow and careful."

Trindle, "Ready aft."

Kichiro, "Weapon in motion." He holds the cable with his flat palms as it slides into position.

Kennedy, "Mark."

Kichiro, "Mark, aye." He releases the lever and motions stop. "Warning, weapon must be restrained at all times." He locks the hold lever for the torpedo, then releases the push arm. "Track down one. Clear forward."

Trindle, "Clear aft."

"Motion." The arm is withdrawn. Kichiro installs the fire latch pin and reports it. "Positive control of breach door. Caution." He swings the door partly shut and installs the other end of the Amphenol on the torpedo tube door. He then carefully shuts the door, making sure nothing binds.

Cumberland, "Come on. Let's go."

Kennedy, "Slow and careful."

Kichiro, "Rolling breach ring tube 1. Stand clear." The ring is turned to the lock position. "Ready to flood."

Kennedy, "Flood tube 1."

Kichiro, "Flood tube 1, aye." He slowly opens the flood valve and allows pressure in the tube to equalize with the water pressure outside the submarine. "Tube 1 flooded. All lights are lit."

Cumberland pushes a button, "Conn, Captain. Do we still have a solution for Sierra 7?"

"Affirmative, Captain."

Cumberland pushes the button, "Opening the door."

Kichiro pushes the button for the doors, "Chief, safe tube 4."

Kennedy, "Got it." He flips the firing circuits to off on tube 4. "Tube 4 is safed."

Kichiro, "Doors open on tube 1."

Kennedy pushes the button, "Conn, Torpedo. Doors open."

"Doors open, aye."

Cumberland pushes the button, "Conn, Captain. Match bearings and fire."

Morrison repeats. They hear and feel the air discharge that pushes the torpedo out of the tube.

Cumberland, "Now. What happened?"

Kichiro, "Sir, the light was good on tube 4 when we loaded it. It went out when we flooded."

"Chief, what would have happened if we fired without the indication?"

Kichiro, "We would die."

Kennedy, "Sir, if we fired the torpedo, it would either not start, or it would circle."

Cumberland "I want to know why it failed. Carry on." He runs upstairs to control.

USS SAN FRANCISCO

When the captain enters control, Miller announces, "Fish is running straight, hot, normal. The fleet's been attacked, sir."

Cumberland, "Very well. My scope."

Morrison backs away from the periscope and Cumberland takes over.

IMPERIAL JAPANESE SUBMARINE, I-57

Lieutenant Nakamura spots an explosion in the sky far away. Looking carefully, he can see small grey dots racing across the distant sky. "We are killing them."

They do not see the torpedo as it races toward their boat. Modern torpedoes do not leave a trail of bubbles, or any indication of their existence. Nakamura is lifted up and out of the bridge in a cloud of spray. He finds himself in the water. He can see the bow and stern of his boat pointing toward the sky. Sato swims to him through the cold water. "Sir, what happened?"

The bow of the sub rolls on its axis nearly 360 degrees as it falls slowly on its starboard side and begins its last dive. "We were torpedoed. There are no aircraft around."

"So fast?"

"Yes. It must be."

USS SAN FRANCISCO

Morrison, "Sir, there might be survivors."

Cumberland, "After that? No way."

"Sir, we have to look. Law of the sea."

Cumberland, "The British didn't in the Falkland's."

"Yes, sir, and they were criticized."

Cumberland, "Look. If you find any of your family or friends, surface and bring them down for tea and crumpets." Cumberland stomps out of control.

Miller and Morrison look at each other. Morrison, "Wankowski, Mallory, get your survival suits. Call for the SAR swimmer. Oh, Wankowski, Mallory, draw small arms." He pushes a button, "Kichiro, Trindle, lay to control with rifles, flak vests, and side arms. Miller, blow ballast."

"Aye, sir. Shall I order up some Dramamine?"

"If you need." He picks up the VHS set, "Any unit, San Francisco."

"San Francisco, Sylvester 270. How might I help you?" Sylvester is the call sign for VF-6 off the Enterprise.

"We have sunk a Japanese submarine and are checking for survivors. Could you relay a request for a helicopter?"

"Can do."

The sub starts rocking as it settles on the surface. "Miller, your boat. I want to shift any bodies or prisoners directly to the helo."

"Aye, sir."

Morrison grabs the phones, lowers the ladder, opens the hatch, and climbs up into the sail. Kichiro and Trindle come up into the sail with M-16s, helmets, body armor, and side arms. Next up is the SAR, BM1(SS) Sarvis in his wet suit. "Japanese, sir?"

"Yes. I saw a couple get ejected from the sail."

"Okay." He climbs down onto the deck below.

Next up are Mallory and Wankowski, "We'll do our bit to keep them away from our guns." The two strong guys climb down and hook up to the rail.

Trindle, "I see one." He points off the port bow.

Morrison calls down, "Left standard rudder. All stop." As the sub slowly comes left, he says, "Rudder amidships. Back 1/3." As the way comes off, "All stop." He shouts down to the men on the deck, "We've stopped."

Sarvis jumps into the waves.

Morrison, "Trindle, Kichiro, aim at the Japanese."

"Yes, sir."

"Um, sir, the SAR is getting in the way."

"I know. Hold fire and just point." He calls on the phone, "What is the status of the helo?"

In the water, Sarvis approaches two men who are floating together. He notices the rank insignia of an officer and an enlisted. He points at the officer then the San Francisco. "You're going with me."

The officer holds out his hands to stop the SAR. Sarvis dives down, grabs the legs of the man and pulls him down and away from the other. Two powerful strokes and he has the officer facing away from him in a hold as he swims for the boat. When he gets there he says, "This guy is a fighter."

Mallory and Wankowski time the waves and grab the Japanese, hauling him on board. Sarvis reverses, pushes off the sub and swims for the other man.

Mallory holds the Japanese while Wankowski searches him. The lieutenant has a bill fold and pen. Once they know he is unarmed, they zip tie his hands and feet. Mallory sets the man against the sail.

When Sarvis gets to the young enlisted Japanese, he's desperately trying to remove his life jacket. Sarvis dives under, comes up behind him, get an arm around him, and swims for the sub.

The lieutenant on the sub tries to roll into the water. Mallory picks him up with one hand and cocks a fist.

Soon, both Japanese are aboard. Wankowski shouts up, "Sir, can you talk to these guys?"

Morrison removes the phone and goes down. Hanging from the ladder, he says, in rough Japanese, "We no harm."

The officer speaks a torrent of words so fast; Morrison can't understand him. "Slow down. My Japanese is bad."

"Who are you?"

"Lieutenant Commander Morrison. I'm the second in command of this boat."

"What is this boat?"

"You are prisoners of war. You will be treated fairly. Are you injured?"

"You sink us?"

"Yes."

"You're Japanese."

"I'm American."

"You are Japanese."

"No. No, I'm American." Morrison hears the helo in the distance, "Your names?"

The lieutenant spits, "You are a traitor."

Morrison wipes the spittle from his face, "And you're a prisoner." To his men, "He called me a traitor. Be careful not to get shocked by the helo."

"Aye, sir."

Mallory, "Did you get their names?"

"No, and I don't know how to read it off their uniforms."

"Roger that, sir."

Morrison climbs back up the sail as the helo approaches. Both prisoners are hoisted aboard and the helo flies off to the Enterprise. That done, they clear the bridge for dive. Morrison is the last man down. Once in control, he sees Cumberland standing silently in the corner. Morrison goes through the dive routine and they slip under the sea.

When they're at 200 feet, Cumberland hands him a message, "While you were talking to your cousins up topside, we got this."

The message reads:

Bravo Zulu on engagement with sub. The attack on Tokyo area was highly successful. Japanese have high performance jet aircraft and counter-attacked the fleet with a swarm of Harpoon missiles. Sunk: USS FANNING DD-385 AND USS DUNLAP DD384. Damaged: USS SALT LAKE CITY CA-25, USS SAN FRANCISCO CA-38, USS LONG BEACH CGN-9, USS FIFE DD-991, USS CARL VINSON CVN-70

Carrier is still fully functional. Upon completion of emergency repairs to Salt Lake City and Long Beach, we will retire to Pearl Harbor.

Continue patrolling. Note, there are a number of USN submarines operating in and outside Tokyo Bay.

Halsey.

Morrison, "Damn. The fleet got hammered and we lost a lot of our ASW."

Cumberland, "We did. While you were helping your relatives, their pals were destroying our fleet."

"Sir, I was trying to do the right thing."

Cumberland raises his voice, "Listen up. Put it in the pass down log. From now on, we practice unconditional submarine warfare. We do not recover survivors. We do not warn civilian targets. The only good Japanese is a dead Japanese. That is all." He turns and walks out of control.

Miller, "Can he do that, sir?"

Morrison, "Only the President can set national policy, but the captain sets policy for his ship. He may get into trouble for it, but he can do it."

USS SAN FRANCISCO, 50 MILES WEST OF THE FLEET

2111, 14 January, 1942

ST2 Gil Gordon, the watch 3 team lead sonarman, sits quietly watching the waterfall display and listening to the ocean. The pounding repairs on the Salt Lake City can be clearly heard over the fleet noises. Because the Long Beach is moving slowly, it is quiet for a change. Even among the new ships, the Long Beach is the loudest. He mentally mutes the known noises and listens for outliers. Their sub has been tracking south and north to the west of the fleet. He picks up another sound. He hears it before he sees it on the waterfall. He focuses the waterfall on the area where the sound is coming from. "Conn, Sonar. Two contacts bearing 145. Two submerged submarines in close proximity. Designate Sierra 8 and Sierra 9."

"Conn, aye."

Lt. Henry Thoreau, the watch team 3 OOD comes in, "What do you think?"

"Gordon, "Two subs, sir. They could be American or an American chasing a Jap. I don't have a blade count yet."

"Could they be Japanese?"

"Sir, I thought the Japanese didn't hunt in packs."

"Maybe they have changed. Good job."

Thoreau goes back into control and pushes the button, "Captain, two submerged contacts to our southeast."

"Roger. Call me when you have course, range, and speed, and if they're Japanese."

"Yes, sir."

The conning officer, LTJG Eric Forester, "Are we changing course?"

Thoreau, "No. We need more information. If we change course it complicates the sonar and the math."

"Sir, the math isn't that hard."

"For you, math-tenant. Steady as we go." Forester grins. He has a degree in math from Cincinnati University.

"Conn, Sonar. Sierra 8 and 9 are both two screw vessels with three-bladed screws."

Thoreau, "Very well."

Forester, "Should we call for the tracking party, sir."

"Fire control has it for now. Let them sleep. This is your first deployment, right?"

"Yes, sir."

"Submarine warfare is a patient art. It's less fencing and more Samurai."

"I don't understand."

"Fencers swat and stab, hoping to create an opening. Samurai patiently circled until one found an opening. With one strike it was over."

"How many patrols have you been on?"

"This is my third patrol and first war."

Fire control reports, "Sir, Sierra 8 and 9 are close together. Bearing 132. Speed 3 knots. Course 015. Submerged. They are both confirmed submarines."

Thoreau pushes the button, "Captain, Sierra 8 and 9 are working together and approaching the fleet." He repeats the bearing, speed, and course. He pushes another button, "Load and make ready tubes 1 and 2 with Mark-48s." He studies the chart table. "Come to new course 042. Ahead standard."

Morrison walks into control. "XO in control."

"Carry on." He goes to the table and studies it and nods to Thoreau, "Good job." He goes into sonar, "Gordon, how do these compare to our other Japanese tracks?"

"Sierra 9 is a close match to Sierra 3. The two are so close together they have to be working together. They can't be more than 3 miles apart."

"Thank you." Morrison goes back into control and sees Cumberland at the chart table. "Sir, Sierra 9 matches Sierra 3, a confirmed Japanese sub."

He nods, "Thoreau, you're a studied man. When was the last time a sub killed two other subs at once?"

Thoreau, "To my knowledge, it's never happened. Submarines have killed more than one surface ship at a time, but never have two subs been engaged at once."

Cumberland, "Never. We'll be the first. Let's get behind them."

Morrison, "Sir, if we shoot from behind, we may hit the fleet if a fish misses."

Cumberland sighs, "If we shoot from the side, we can only hit one at a time."

Morrison, "Front quarter, sir? We've little risk of counter-battery from their torpedoes and it's safer."

Cumberland takes a deep breath, "We won't hit the fleet, XO. Are you trying to give the enemy a fair chance?"

"No, sir. I just don't want to risk the fleet."

"Set it up. Call me before we shoot." Cumberland walks out.

Morrison, "Come to 030."

I-5, JUNSEN CLASS JAPANESE SUBMARINE

LCDR Takahashi studies his charts. "The Americans are moving very slowly. Continue on course." The nearest American warship is 28 miles. "It is the carrier we want."

USS SAN FRANCISCO

Morrison, "Ahead 1/3rd."

He walks into sonar, "Gordon, as the noise clears, we'll need separate bearings."

Gordon, "Yes, sir. These diesel electrics are surprisingly quiet submerged."

"Yeah, they're so slow there isn't as much flow noise as you would expect."

Morrison walks back into control, "Time to call the captain." He takes his place behind the scopes.

When Cumberland comes in, he goes straight to the chart table. "Sonar, give me a bearing for 8 and 9."

"Aye, sir. Sierra 8 is 041. Sierra 9 is 047."

Cumberland, "Match bearings. Tube 1 for Sierra 8. Tube 2 for Sierra 9. Doors open."

I-5, JAPANESE SUBMARINE

Sonar, "Sir, I think I heard a transient. A rumble to our northwest."

"It's a reflection from one of the damaged ships."

USS SAN FRANCISCO

Sir, doors open. Bearings matched."

Cumberland, "XO, fire the shots?"

"Sir?"

"Kill them. You call yourself American, so kill them."

Morrison goes to the fire control board and pushes the button for tube 1, "Fire 1." Thud, whoosh.

"Conn, Torpedo. Tube 1 fired electrically."

Conn, Sonar. Torpedo 1 is running hot, straight, and normal."

Morrison pushes the button on tube 2, "Fire 2." Thud, whoosh.

"Conn, Torpedo. Tube 2 fired electrically."

"Conn, Sonar. Torpedo 2 is running hot, straight, and normal."

Morrison, his face still, turns to Cumberland, "One has an 85 second run. Two has 78."

I-5, JAPANESE SUBMARINE

"Control, Sonar. Two torpedoes in the water. Bearing 221."

LCDR Takahashi, "Are they going ahead or astern?"

"Sir, the bearing is constant."

"Ahead full. Give me a bearing for the nearest ship. Flood tubes 1 through 4."

I-11, JAPANESE SUBMARINE

LCDR Moto shouts, "Flood tubes! Ahead full! Blow ballast! Prepare to start engines!"

USS SAN FRANCISCO

"Conn, Sonar. Sierra 8 and 9 are flooding tubes. 9 is blowing ballast."

Morrison, "Very well."

Thoreau, "25 and 32 seconds."

Cumberland, "They don't have time to flood, open, and fire."

Morrison, "Yes, sir."

Cumberland, "Are you worried you might have killed your relatives?"

Morrison, "No, sir."

Cumberland smiles, "Was it hard to push that button?"

Morrison, "No, sir."

Cumberland, "Did you like it?"

Thoreau, "10, 9, 8…"

Morrison, "It's our job."

Thoreau, "4, 3, 2, 1." They feel the impact of the explosion through the hull. "5, 4, 3, 2, 1." The second explosion hits and resonates.

"Conn, Sonar. Sierra 8 and 9 are breaking up. Good hits."

Cumberland, "Well, Morrison, I doubt any of your family survived that."

"Sir, none of my family could be out there."

"You know what I mean." He picks up the 1MC, "Gentlemen, we have just successfully destroyed two Japanese submarines with two torpedoes fired at the same time. Good kills. Carry on." He hangs up the mic. "Morrison, take us to periscope depth so we can report in." Cumberland walks forward out of control.

"Yes, sir." He issues the orders. As they are working through the procedure, Morrison walks into sonar, "Gordon, Pritchel, how are you doing?"

Gordon, "I'm feeling sick, sir. How many did we just kill?"

"I don't know. Likely over one hundred. Guys, this is what submarine warfare is."

Gordon, "Yes, sir. It's terrible."

"I agree, but it's necessary. If they sink the carrier, we're out of business."

"Gordon, "I'll deal, sir."

"Look, I know it's hard. It should be hard. If you need to talk, come see me."

"Thank you, sir."

"Thank you." Morrison goes back into control. They perform the required circle before coming to periscope depth.

Thoreau, "I'm placing us between the kills so we might get some debris pictures."

"Good call."

Thoreau continues the maneuver and Cumberland walks in with the message and leaves. Morrison, "Up scope." He does the quick 360 and takes the pictures. "Oil and debris in the water, Also, bodies."

They get the reply back on their message, "Good job. Continue."

CHAPTER 8

USS SAN FRANCISCO

0807, 15 January, 1942

The fleet slowly retreats, the San Francisco coursing north to south, protecting their eastern flank. Morrison wakes up naturally and rolls out of bed. He puts on his robe and flip-flops and goes to the officer's head to shave. Halfway through his morning ablutions, Miller comes in, uses the urinal, and washes his hands. Then, he looks in every stall. "John, do you know what's going on with the captain?"

"I just woke up."

"It's been coming on for a while. He keeps hassling you about your Japanese heritage. He seems happy only after we've killed a sub. As soon as the kill is confirmed, he's almost giddy. Then he leaves to rub one out."

"You don't know what he does."

"Yeah, but it's likely."

Morrison finishes shaving and washes his face. Turning to Miller, "How are you and your guys dealing with the killing?"

"It has us kind of fucked up. We've sank five subs. Killed about three hundred people. It's the job we signed up for, but shit, it's hard."

"It is."

"How are you dealing with all the discrimination from the

captain?"

"It thrills the shit out of me. No. But, listen, as long as he's focusing on me, he's leaving everyone else alone."

"A point. I hope we get some liberty soon. This boat is turning into a pressure cooker."

"We're at war. We'll pull in when we do. Keep a close eye on your guys morale. With everything else, we have to stay on top of it."

"Yes, sir. Have you written your grandparents?"

"Yeah. My grandmother is living in New Jersey and my grandfather is the XO on a destroyer in the Atlantic."

"Cool. My grandpa is building life boats and life rafts outside of Boston. What about your birth parents? Are they interned?"

"My mom, yeah. She's in Utah. They lost everything they owned in California."

"The whole thing was fucked up."

"Hopefully, we can make a difference."

On the 1MC they hear Cumberland, "San Francisco. I just got word that the USS Salt Lake City has succumbed to the damage inflicted on it by the Japs. Another loss. That is all."

They look at each other. Morrison, "Damn it."

MORRISON HOME, OFFICER HOUSING, CAPE MAY NAVAL BASE, NEW JERSEY

1320, 16 January, 1942

Elaine Morrison walks into her kitchen with the mail and the paper. Across the front page is a picture of the USS Carl Vinson and the headline, "1990 NAVY FLAT TOP HAMMERS

THE JAPS!" She glances at the headline, then goes straight to the list of lost units. The USS Livermore is not on it. "He should be back soon."

She puts the paper down and goes through the mail. A letter from the Navy makes her heart stop. She sits down, ripping the letter open:

LCDR and Mrs. Henry Morrison,

This letter is to inform you of a family member currently in Naval service. On December 19th, 1941, due to a time travel event, a battle group with the USS Carl Vinson, CVN-70, appeared in the Pacific waters north of the Philippine Islands.

You have a descendant family member in this battle group. His name is LCDR John Morrison. Currently, he is the executive officer of a 1990 ship named the USS San Francisco. According to our records he was adopted by your son, retired Rear Admiral Mitchell Morrison in 1956 after the death of his birth parents, Lt. Andrew Fallon and Kinuko Fallon. He has been given your address to write to you. Please write to him and support our new service member at the address below.

Sincerely,

Captain Donaldson

Assistant Director of Department of Naval Personnel

She reads the letter twice, then looks at the enclosed photo. It's obviously his academy picture as an ensign. His Japanese heritage is obvious.

Her thirteen-year-old son, Mitchell comes into the kitchen, letting the door bang shut behind him, "Hi Mom, can I go... Mom, what is it?"

"Your father is fine, Mitchell. Where do you want to go?"

"That letter is from the Navy, isn't it?"

"It is."

"Can I see it?"

"Your father is fine."

"Okay, Mom. Can I see it?"

"Yes. You have a son from the future."

"That's not funny." He takes the letter and reads it.

Elaine, "No, it isn't."

"I become an Admiral? Cool. Can I go to Bobby's house?"

"Be back before dark, Admiral. You're not cleared for night maneuvers."

"Yes, ma'am."

USS SAN FRANCISCO

1712, 20 January, 1942

The off-watch officers are quietly eating their dinner. The captain looks up, "This room is a mortuary. Don't any of you have something to say?"

Morrison, "Sir, do you think we'll be pulling into Australia?"

"I doubt it. They'll need us to patrol."

The supply officer, Lt. Ed Cameron, "Sir, it would be nice to re-provision."

Cumberland, "How many days do we have left?"

Cameron, "Sir, we could make it another six to eight weeks, but we're out of fresh food and who knows when we'll be near a port again."

Backes, "Sir, do we know where we're going next?"

Cumberland, "We need to get cut loose to hunt Jap subs. Instead, we'll be escorting the bird farm. I don't know what Halsey is planning. Morrison, has your vaunted connections revealed anything to you?"

"No, sir, but I may have an educated guess."

"Go on. I've no doubt our wardroom waits with bated breath for your scintillating analysis."

Morrison stares at his commander.

"No, please. What are your thoughts?"

"Sir, we may be dropping off a squadron of jets to defend Australia. Unless they had a time transference that was conveniently next to a military airfield, they will need our help."

Cumberland, "That's not it. No way Nimitz would dilute the power of the carrier. When we get to Australia, we'll not pull in. I don't want to pull in until we are out of torpedoes and we have a broom on our mast."

MM1 Mallory is eating in the enlisted mess with his watch team. He sees a radioman, "Hey Sparky, where are we going?"

The RM2 just smiles.

Mallory, "Radiomen. They know everything and say nothing."

The RM3 says, "G'day, then." He puts his tray in the scullery and leaves.

Mallory and Gustaf look at each other and smile. Mallory, "No way the captain will let us pull in. No way."

Gustaf, "Have you been there?"

"Once. It was amazing. The people were really nice."

"Any advice?"

"Don't try to drink an Aussie under the table. It can't be done. They don't tip. When an Aussie buys a round, you need to as well. That, and don't be the kind of ass that fucks it up for the next boat."

"Are the girls pretty?"

"Oh yeah, and they have this amazing accent. And they're nice girls. Be nice back, and don't fuck it up for the next boat."

MM3 Black, "Will we have to wear our uniforms?"

Mallory, "Wear it and don't bitch. It's a bit of a chick magnet. It really is. Just don't be an ass and ruin it for the next boat."

MM3 Black, "I detect a theme."

USS SAN FRANCISCO, 400 MILES SE OF WAKE, 100 MILES WEST OF THE FLEET

0130, 29 January, 1942

Brown is watching the waterfall and chatting with Guthrie, "You doing alright?"

"Yeah, I guess. When I said all that about them leaving, it was like an intellectual exercise. Now that it's real, I miss them terribly, especially Lorna. It's like an empty ache in my heart."

"That's what love feels like. It's hard dude. No making it easier."

"What do I do?"

"Live through it. You have a right to grieve. Grief takes time."

"Thank you, Mike."

"No problem, if…" His hand shoots up.

Guthrie, "Man made. Shit, that's a lot of boats."

"Yeah." Brown pushes the button, "Conn, Sonar. Multiple targets bearing 300."

Morrison in control, "Roger." He pushes another button, "Captain, multiple contacts at 300."

Backes comes back from the head and Morrison quietly briefs him. Morrison heads for sonar. "What have we got, Brown?"

Brown points at a jumbled mess on the waterfall. "It's a mess, sir. But, it's positively a bunch of ships. If we were closer, we could itemize them."

"Okay, good job."

Morrison walks back in to the chart table and is joined by Cumberland, "What do we have?"

"Sonar just picked up a large cluster of ships near Wake Island."

"That wasn't included in the fleet movements we received. It has to be the Japs."

"Report it and continue on, sir?"

"Hell, no. It's a hunting ground and we still have torpedoes."

"Yes, sir."

Cumberland announces, "Conn, come to 295. Make our speed 20 knots." He walks into sonar.

Backes repeats his order, then goes to Morrison, "We're going out of position?"

"We are."

"We're not checking in?"

"We're not."

Backes sighs, "Roger that."

MM3 Gustaf snakes out of the shaft alley he was cleaning, "Fuck this shit." The main shaft, just inches above where he was working, picks up speed. He goes to the upper level and tells Mallory, "The shaft alley is as clean as is it going to get at this speed."

"Okay. It's about time to end the field day, anyway. How are you doing on your upper level qual?"

Gustaf looks down, "It's coming along."

"Go get it. If you see any of the others working on their quals, collect them, too. I've warmed up my pen."

"Aye, aye."

TMC Kennedy is going over training with his watch crew when they feel the change in the ship's movement. Kichiro, "Captain killer has found another victim."

Trindle, "You think?"

"Yeah. That mother fucker only gets in a hurry when it's time to kill."

Kennedy, "Kichiro, Trindle, do you want to share your wisdom about the Harpoon missile?"

Kichiro, "Sorry, Chief."

USS SAN FRANCISCO, 50 MILES SW OF WAKE ISLAND

0605, 29 January, 1942

Morrison carefully studies the many sea mounts in the area; charting and adjusting their course to stay as far from the undersea mountains as possible. Cumberland walks back in, straight to the table and studies it, "What are you doing, Morrison?"

"This area is littered with sea mounts, sir."

"They're all at least 1500 feet below the surface."

"That's their charted depth in the seventies, sir. We don't know what they are now."

Cumberland, "Ahead 1/3rd." He walks back into sonar, "Thorsen, what do we have?"

"There are two groups of ships. One group close to the island, and a second group further to the east. The easterly group is a bunch of ships. As we slow, we'll categorize and sort them out."

"Are any of them carriers?"

"I think several have four screws."

Cumberland, "Carriers, or maybe battleships. Focus on those." Back in control, "Load and make ready tubes 1, 2, 3, and 4."

The order comes down and the torpedo team gets busy. Kichiro, "Evan-san, I called it."

Kennedy, "What's that, Kiche?"

"When we went to that full bell during training, I told Evan-san that the captain had found something to kill. Hatch one open."

ISOKAZE, FUBUKI CLASS JAPANESE DESTROYER

The CO, LCDR Hiro Yaman is on the bridge, reading dispatches and listening to his watch team. North of him the four aircraft carriers, the Akagi, Kaga, Hiryu, and Zuiho, are always changing course to chase the wind. The Isokaze is the southernmost destroyer in the task force, which makes place keeping a little easier. A rating approaches, salutes, and hands him a message, "They are launching the attack. Good."

USS SAN FRANCISCO

Morrison walks up behind Thorsen, "How many?"

"At least 24. The closest is probably a destroyer about ten miles out at 328. There are at least six four-screw vessels. I've been sending bearings." He sweeps his headphone off and pushes the button, "Transient. Transient. Explosions forward."

Morrison goes back into control. Cumberland, "God damn it. These are our kills! They passed them by."

"Conn, Sonar. More explosions in the group near Wake Island at 064."

Cumberland, "Stay on course."

Backes, "Yes, sir."

"Conn, Sonar. More explosions at 355."

Cumberland, "They won't sink them all. We'll get a few. Open doors on tubes 3 and 4."

Thorsen and Curtis are keeping the tracking party at the table updated with the bearings to the various targets, but there are so many targets, the table is a bit confusing.

Morrison, "Sir, we're passing ahead of that destroyer."

Cumberland, "There's no fucking way they could ever hear us. Tangos 17 and 12 are four shaft ships and they're entering range. Target tube 4 on 17. Target tube 3 on 12."

Miller relays the orders.

Cumberland, "Miller, Giblin, come here." ENC Giblin looks around, then approaches the captain, "Sir?"

"Miller, push the button for tube 3. Giblin, you push the button for tube 4."

They hear, "Bearings matched and cross-checked."

Miller pushes the button. They feel and hear the thud whoosh of the fired torpedo. "Conn, Torpedo. Three fired electrically."

"Conn, Sonar. Torpedo running hot, straight, and normal."

Cumberland, "Chief, fire 4."

Giblin, "No, sir. It's your job. I'm not doing it."

"GET THE FUCK OUT OF CONTROL!"

Giblin returns to his watch at the dive panel. Cumberland pushes the button. After torpedo and sonar have reported in, he walks to Giblin, "Get the fuck out of control!"

"Sir, I have to be relieved, sir."

"I got your watch. Go."

Giblin leaves.

"XO, find another chief."

"Yes, sir."

The captain walks away, leaving the dive panel station empty. Morrison sits down at the panel and calls torpedo.

"Conn, Sonar. Tango 7 has started pinging."

Cumberland, "We're at 300 feet. Continue on." The high-pitched ping is audible throughout the boat.

DESTROYER ISOKAZE

"Captain, Sonar. The submarine is ten degrees to starboard and one mile. Depth is 300 feet. It is moving at 12 knots to the north."

LCDR Hiro Yaman, "Very good. Set depth charges to 300. Stand by to drop on my mark. Left rudder, come to new course 010."

USS SAN FRANCISCO

TMC Kennedy takes the watch. Miller is counting down the torpedoes they fired. "Conn, Sonar. They have us. Tango 7 is changing course toward us."

Cumberland walks into Sonar. Miller, "10, 9…"

Morrison, "Shut the doors. 5 degrees down bubble. Left full rudder. Ahead flank cavitate."

The orders are repeated and Cumberland storms out of sonar. By now the screws of the destroyer are as audible as the explosions from the aircraft attacking the fleet to the north. "Morrison, what are you…?"

"Conn, Sonar. Splashes over us."

Cumberland, "Splashes?"

Morrison, "They're depth charging us, sir."

Cumberland, "Carry on."

Morrison, "Rudder amidships. Steady as she goes. Make our depth 600 feet. Ahead 1/3rd."

"Conn, Sonar. Fish 3 is a hit."

The orders are repeated back. Because of the burst of speed, the sub continues downward quickly. The sub shudders as the depth charges detonate 300 feet above them and to the rear. "Conn, Sonar. Fish 4 is a hit."

Cumberland, "Another double hitter." He smiles.

Morrison, "Give me a fix on tango 7. Sir, on their sonar, they just saw what we can do."

Cumberland, "I got it."

"Yes, sir."

"Conn, Sonar. Tango 12 is breaking up. Several other ships are sinking."

Morrison, "Thank you, sonar."

Cumberland, "Ahead 2/3rds. Right standard rudder. Two degree up bubble."

"Conn, Sonar. Something up there just blew up. I think it's tango 14."

ISOKAZE, FUBUKI CLASS JAPANESE DESTROYER

A rating rushes onto the bridge, "Sir, the Zuiho and Kaga are sinking. Admiral Kondo is switching his flag to the Akagi." They hear a rumbling explosion and turn to the sound. They see the battleship Haruna's center lift up, then collapse, the ship broken in two. Then, close by, the Maya also rises at the middle and collapses down into two sections.

LCDR Hiro Yaman, "The submarine's torpedoes hit their targets. Right full rudder. Sonar, we need to know where it went."

"I am fairly sure it went to the south."

Yaman, "We go into the teeth of the lion."

JAPANESE BATTLESHIP HARUNA

Captain Takama Tamotsu gets up off the deck and walks out onto his bridge wing. Looking aft he can see, through the water raining down from the explosion, the center of his ship settling, the bow and stern rising up. The bow turns to the port, while the stern continues straight, and smoke and steam rise from the center, which is now awash. He nods, "Tell the men to abandon ship."

A lieutenant, "Can we not save her, Captain?"

"Where once we had a single ship, there is now two. Abandon ship."

The lieutenant bows and gives the order. Tamotsu, "All of you on the bridge, go to your abandon ship stations." They bow and depart. Tamotsu stands alone watching his ship die, and waiting.

JAPANESE HEAVY CRUISER MAYA

Captain Nabeshima Shunsaki hold onto a bridge station as the bow of his beloved ship rises into the air. Looking aft he can clearly see one of the bronze screws still turning as the stern section capsizes. The bow spins 180 degrees, throwing him into the water. Around him float the dead and wounded, "What could do this?"

USS SAN FRANCISCO

Cumberland, "Open the door on tube 1."

"Conn, Sonar. Tango 3 is sinking. Tango 21 is sinking."

Cumberland, "Match bearings. Porter, come here."

The conning officer walks to the captain, "Yes, sir."

"Conn, Torpedo. Door is open on tube 1. Torpedo is ready."

Wankowski, "Captain, we have a good solution for tango 7."

Cumberland, "Very well. Porter, push the button."

Porter, "Sir?"

"Push the fucking button."

"Yes, sir." Porter pushes the button.

"Conn, Torpedo. Tube 1 is fired electrically."

"Conn, Sonar. Fish 1 is hot, straight, and normal."

Miller, "34 seconds. Porter, return to your watch, please."

The young man, his eyes wide and mouth ajar, looks at his department head and mouths the word, "Why?"

Miller gives a small shake of his head.

ISOKAZE, JAPANESE DESTROYER

A lieutenant approaches, LCDR Hiro Yaman, "Captain, the carrier's Akagi and Hiryu are lost. The battleship Haruna broke in half and sank. The heavy cruisers Maya and Ashigara are lost. The Admiral is dead. What are your orders?"

"We sink this submarine..." His legs piston upward as the bow of his ship tilts down. The explosion is so loud, it breaks his ear drums. His back hits the overhead and he is bounced through the hatch into the water. When he surfaces, his ship is broken in two.

USS SAN FRANCISCO

Cumberland, "Yes!" He goes to the chart table and studies it. Pushing the button, "Sonar, are any of the Japanese ships going to survive?"

Thorsen, "Sir, I have no idea. The fleet is getting hammered from the air and the noise is deafening."

Cumberland rushes into sonar, "What do you mean, no idea?"

Thorsen, "Sir, I cannot predict the fall of bombs that I cannot see. Just because a ship is not hit now, doesn't mean it won't be, sir."

"Okay."

Back at the chart table, "Morrison, could you conn us in?"

"I recommend we don't do that, sir. If we get hit by a sinking ship or a missed bomb, that would be it, sir. And sir, we've been away from our position for a while."

Cumberland freezes for a beat, he sighs, "Conn us back into position. Once back in position, we'll report in. That is all." He walks forward out of control.

Morrison, "Right full rudder. Make our course 195. Ahead standard."

Of the 28-ship Japanese carrier group and the twenty-ship landing group, only four destroyers manage to avoid destruction. Still, the landing force takes Wake Island.

CHAPTER 9

USS SAN FRANCISCO

1526, 29 January, 1942

Morrison announces himself and enters. Giblin sits in a chair drinking coffee. Morrison, "You okay?"

"Am I going to mast?"

"I don't know yet. That was ballsy thing to do. Do you want to explain your decision?"

"Sir, I do my duty. I serve my country and I don't shrink away from everything that means. Thing is, it is not my responsibility to initiate weapons release. I don't have to kill those sailors and I won't. Furthermore, sir, there are others on board who won't. If someone has to be the lightning rod, it might just as well be me."

"I don't know what he'll do."

"That's the thing, sir. None of us do. It's crazy."

"As soon as I can, I'll let you know."

"Yes, sir."

USS CARL VINSON

Admiral Halsey sits reading reports. Captain Van Zandt knocks and walks in, "Our sub reported in, sir." He hands Halsey the message.

TO: CARGRU 3

FRM: SIERRA NOVEMBER

REG: FLEET ENGAGEMENT

San Francisco identified and engaged Japanese carrier group west of Wake Island. Two four-shaft vessels and one destroyer sunk by torpedo. Back on station 70 miles ahead of fleet.

V/R

Cumberland

Halsey grunts and hands the message back. Van Zandt, "He left station without reporting in and engaged without reporting, sir."

"Captain, I like my captains aggressive. This explains the reports, so credit him with the destroyer, battleship, and heavy cruiser. Thank you."

USS SAN FRANCSICO

Morrison knocks on Cumberland's door and enters, "You wanted to see me, sir?"

"I want a captain's mast for Chief Giblin. He disobeyed a direct order. He will be charged with disrespect, disobeying a direct order, and cowardice before the enemy."

"Sir, why are you having people push the fire button?"

"It's a measure of their loyalty to our nation. Any crew member unwilling to kill the enemy is a pinko communist and needs to be punished and removed."

"I think I understand, sir. You recognize that busting a chief requires a message off the ship, sir."

"I do. He was out of line."

"I understand your point, sir. The write up, by necessity must contain the circumstances of the discipline. Are you comfortable with sharing your practice with higher?"

"So, what you're saying is, you will report me to your friends and get me relieved?"

"No, sir. I'm saying the details, by law, must be included in the report. Discipline of this nature on a nuclear vessel must be forwarded to NAVSEA-08. That's the law. That may put you in a difficult position, sir."

Cumberland sighs, "What do you recommend?"

"A suspended bust for failure to obey the order and we keep it on the boat. His record stays clean and so does yours."

"I want him off the COW watch."

"Yes, sir."

"Morrison, I'm growing tired of you thwarting me when it comes to discipline."

"Yes, sir. Are you going to continue doing your communist tests, sir?"

"When it suits me. I noticed you pushed the button."

"Yes, sir. I'm a submarine officer and understand the need. Most enlisted crewmembers have not grappled with pulling the trigger themselves."

"It's time they started. Let me know when you have it set up."

"Yes, sir."

Morrison goes directly to the chief's mess. Kennedy and Giblin are drinking coffee and talking. Morrison, "Kennedy could you relieve the COB and have him meet us in my office?"

"Yes, sir."

"Giblin, with me. In a few minutes, he, Giblin, and the COB are in his office. "Giblin, I understand your position. Let me explain what is going to happen."

"Yes, sir."

"You're going to be placed on report for failure to follow a direct order."

Godoy, "XO, this is fucked up. It's bullshit. Absolute bullshit."

Giblin looks Morrison in the eyes, "What did he want?"

Morrison, "It isn't relevant."

Giblin, holding eye contact, "Sir, it's the only thing that's relevant. I understand the necessity of maintaining unity of command, but under this captain, that is almost impossible."

Morrison, "I agree. Unity of command is critical under any commander. The core of this issue is simple. The captain issued you a direct order and you refused to follow it. This was not due to cowardice or disrespect, but because the order, as you saw it, was inappropriate in its intent. The problem is, as a subordinate, you do not have the liberty of determining the intent behind an order."

Giblin, "Yes, sir."

Godoy, "So, this whole thing is going to leave the boat? You know I have the right to pass my comments with it."

"I see no reason why this needs to leave the boat. That is all, gentlemen."

Godoy silently leads Giblin back to the goat locker. Once they're sitting with a cup of lifer juice, Godoy asks, "Did you read the subtext?"

"All I heard was mast. I'm fucked."

"The captain was going to charge you with cowardice and disrespect, as well. Morrison talked him down to the one obvious charge and made it a suspended bust."

"I didn't hear that."

"A bust must leave the boat with all the details. A suspended bust doesn't. Morrison protected you as much as he could. You did refuse a direct order in combat."

"I did, but it was fucked up."

"I know. It's probably going to get more fucked up. Given the circumstances, I think you are lucky."

"Aye, COB."

"I need to get back on watch."

USS SAN FRANCISCO

1802, 29 January, 1942

The Captain's Mast is being held on the mess decks, and being run over site TV. Cumberland, "I find you guilty of one count of Article 92: failure to obey and order. I order you demoted to EN1, suspended for six months, with no loss of pay or restriction. Chief, I'm going light on you, as this is your first offense. I expect my orders to be followed. Dismissed."

Cumberland leaves the mess deck and the crowd disperses. Mallory and Gustaf walk aft. Gustaf, "Shit, man. That was fucked up. Did you hear what the chief did?"

Mallory, "I was there."

"Did the captain really yell at him?"

"I would say it was more of a scream from the pits of hell itself."

"Were you scared?"

"He wasn't yelling at me."

"You weren't even a little afraid?"

"Truth? It was fucking terrifying to see the guy in charge that out of control."

"You're in control all the time. What would you do?"

"How many people have we already killed?"

"I haven't killed anyone."

"Not true. Not even a little bit true. Our ship has killed a lot of people. Hundreds. Maybe over a thousand. As a crew member you share in that the same way you get the unit citation or Battle E when the boat does."

"I never thought of that."

"Think it through. Talk to me if you need to."

"Mallory, you didn't answer my question."

"Your upper level watch board is tomorrow. Get your card."

Morrison walks into his stateroom and sits down. He closes his fists and silently screams. He gets out his letters and carefully sorts through them. He opens Lisa's next letter.

My Darling Love,

I so hope and pray that you're okay, happy, and well. In the quiet of our home, I can hear you breath. I'm a poet and a songwriter. I'm someone who is supposed to fathom the depths of the human soul and distill its essence, so I may share the truth. Right now, I feel like a giddy love bird, instead. I should say that I know we will have hard times. I recognize we will struggle and disagree. We are two very different people. Misunderstandings and disagreements are a real part of life and love. What I know more powerfully than anything else, is that you totally, unconditionally, and fully love me. A part of me fears I am unworthy of your love, but I know, to the very fiber of my being, that you are worthy of mine.

I walk a stormy desert beach

To see what drifts ashore

Cast my eyes upon the waves

For the man I adore.

All I see is the wind-swept sea

Crashing on the shore.

The only one for me.

Your life is on the sea.

I had to let you go.

It is the life you know.

It's how my life must be.

I love my sailor. My sailor loves the sea.

How can I love a man,

Who's first love is the foam?

How can I find a place,

To be our house and home?

How can I hold him,

When his heart will always roam?

The only one for me.

Your life is on the sea.

I had to let you go.

It is the life you know.

It's how my life must be.

I love a sailor. My sailor loves the sea.

I cast my gaze upon the waves,

And see a distant mast.

Endless, crashing, changing sea,

And a ship, my love, at last.

The sea that stole my love from me,

Returns my love at last.

The only one for me.

Your life is on the sea.

I had to let you go.

It is the life you know.

It's how my life must be.

I love a sailor. My sailor loves the sea.

He's everything to me.

He is what he must be.

I need to moor with him.

So, he can moor in me.

I love you, my love. I love you exactly as you are. If I need to buy a boat, so we can share our loves, then I will. God, I love you.

Your wife, Your love,

Lisa

He collapses onto his bed, "My boat will never return." He buries his face in his pillow, sobbing.

CAPE MAY NAVAL BASE, NEW JERSEY

1032, 30 January, 1942

Elaine Morrison stands on the quay with her son, Mitchell, and her eleven-year-old daughter, Margaret. Finally, they see the USS Livermore, DD-429, steaming into Cape May harbor. Its sides are streaked with rust, but it glides gracefully toward the pier.

Ida, the captain's wife, joins her, "It looks a little rough."

Elaine, "It does."

Mitchell, "Hi, Mrs. Huber."

Ida, "Hello Mitchell. How are you liking your school?"

"It's okay. I'm doing good in math."

Ida turns to Elaine, "I wish we could know more about their schedule."

"It is what it is. Did you hear about the Carl Vinson?"

"The future carrier? I did. I'm thinking it's some kind of war time propaganda."

"It seems Mitchell here has a son named John on board one of the ships. John is a lieutenant commander."

"That...that would be quite impossible."

"Impossible, or not, he exists. We have his picture on the wall."

Ida asks Mitchell, "How do you feel about this?"

"It says I retire a rear admiral. That means I have to work even harder in school."

Elaine, "Why is that, dear?"

"Admirals can't be dummies. I hope someday I get to meet him."

Ida, "What would you do?"

"I would ask him everything I need to know so I could grow up. If I adopt him and be an admiral and everything, I have to be a really good student. I need to be like dad."

Elaine, "But, darling, you have years to get ready."

"Yeah, Mom, but if I don't start now, by then, I won't know enough."

They hear, "Moored, shift colors."

They wait as the brow is installed, shore services hooked up, and the engineering plant shut down. The official party goes aboard for debrief. When the official party leaves, liberty is called. The off-watch sailors stream off the ship. They pile on base buses for the gate and the pleasures of the small sea side town.

Finally, LCDR Henry Morrison walks off the Livermore with the CO, Commander Vernon Huber. He smiles uncontrollably as he walks up to his family. He pulls them all into a hug. "God, Maggie, you've grown like a weed. You too, Mitch."

Mitch, "Dad, we got a letter from the Navy."

Elaine, "Mitch, we'll talk about it at the house. It's odd dear, but nothing bad."

Henry, "Okay."

Mitch, "I'm going to be a rear admiral. I bet you are, too, Dad."

They climb into their Chevy sedan and Henry fires it up. "What's this about?"

Elaine, "I'll show you the letter when we get home. Have you heard anything about a carrier battle group coming back in time from 1990?"

"Yeah, they hammered the Japanese in the Philippines real good. Gave McArthur a fighting chance."

Elaine, "Well, Mitch has a son on one of the ships."

Henry, "Huh. I guess it could be. Hell, we've been serving in the Navy a lot of generations. Really it shouldn't be much of a surprise."

Mitch, "Dad, it said he was adopted by retired Rear Admiral Mitchell Morrison."

Henry, "Don't let it go to your head, son. You still have to earn it."

"I won't, Dad. I promise."

Henry, "Good. What rank is he?"

Mitch, "A lieutenant commander and XO like you, Dad."

"XO of what?"

"The San Francisco."

"The San Francisco is a heavy cruiser."

"Dad, the heavy cruiser wouldn't still be around in 1990, would it?"

"You're right. Did it give the ship's class?"

"No." They pull up to their house and everyone gets out.

"Odd." They walk into the living room and Henry looks at the picture of John on the mantle. "He looks Japanese or Chinese."

Elaine, "His mom was, I think, Japanese. His dad was Irish, from the name, and a naval officer. It seems John's parents died and Mitch took him in. Here's the letter."

Henry carefully reads it, "San Francisco, 711. No way we have made over six hundred heavy cruisers from 1942 to 1990. Must be a destroyer or destroyer escort."

Mitch, "Dad, could it be some type of ship that don't even exist yet?"

"I suppose it could. Darling, have you written him?"

"I have. Mitch has, too."

"I will as well. Japanese or not, he's family."

CHAPTER 10

USS SAN FRANCISCO, 50 MILES EAST OF SYDNEY, AUSTRA-LIA

0928, 4 February, 1942

Morrison, on the periscope, does a quick 360, "No traffic."

Cumberland walks into control and hands him a radio a message.

"Conn, Sonar. The carrier is in the harbor."

Morrison, "Very well. Sir, want a look at sunlight?"

"I want Halsey to agree. While they are in port fucking around, we have work to do. There are convoys coming here all the time. Somewhere, the Japanese must have some submarines."

"We have the reply, sir."

Cumberland reads it, "God damn it. Okay, plot our course to Sydney Harbor. We're to follow the Horne in tonight, then moor inside them."

Morrison, "Sir, the Horne will screw up our anechoic panels."

Cumberland hands him the message, "We surface at the hundred fathom line. Let me know before we blow."

"Yes, sir." Morrison reads the message.

FRM: CARGRU-3

TO: SIERRA NOVEMBER

REG: PORT VISIT

711 will follow the Horne into port this evening. A place is being prepared to moor the 711 inside the Horne. Shore power, water, and sewer connections will be provided. Once moored, off duty service members shall be granted liberty. The crew is required to wear service dress white uniform the first day and liberty uniform thereafter. They shall be briefed that they are forbidden to disclose the nature of your unit. They are to describe it as the anti-submarine ship, San Francisco. It is typical for sailor to brag on their kills. That is allowed in general, as it is good for morale. No specific details will be released (locations, weapons, tactics, procedures). Any sailor violating security shall be disciplined and at minimum lose liberty privilege. CO and XO will report to my office at 0800 02/5/1942.

Halsey

Morrison stays in control as the sub waits to pull in. As the sun sets, they approach the Horne and blow ballast at the one hundred fathom line. The sub rolls in the Pacific swells. Cumberland, "Morrison, I got the bridge. In about twenty minutes muster the line handling party."

"Yes, sir."

Morrison raises the scope. The Horne is only three miles away. It starts flashing blinker code. Every submarine officer is conversant in this code. "Tell the captain the Horne wants us close."

Backes, "The captain says, no closer."

"Roger." He relays the message using the signal light in the periscope mast.

About an hour later, it is full dark as they pass between the headlands. The Horne picks up a pilot. The spotlights on the pilot boat never point astern. In another twenty minutes, a blacked-out tug approaches. The line handling detail ties it to the port side and they start the slow process of mooring between two barges. The wharf is completely dark, making it difficult. A second tug joins the first, and slowly, they push the submarine between two barges. Sailors on the pier throw their monkey's fist, and the boatswain announces, "Moored."

Miller walks into control, "Any light up there?" Morrison shakes his head, and goes back to the periscope. Miller continues, "If it's okay with the boss, I would like to keep steamers until morning. I'm worried about hooking up at a strange port in the dark."

"Sounds reasonable. Let's see what they have set up. Once the Horne is in, they may turn on the lights."

"Where is the Horne mooring?"

"They tucked us between two barges. The Horne is mooring to the barges. We'll be tucked in nicely."

"So much cloak and dagger."

"It's necessary."

"Yeah. Does it look like World War II out there?"

"It looks dark. I think the lines are secure."

Cumberland passes down, "Secure the main engine. Retract the outboard."

Morrison, "The Horne is working itself in. They may need to tie off to us." He grabs the sound-powered phone, "Captain, XO, do you know if the Horne plans to tie any lines to us?"

Cumberland, "I don't know yet, Morrison. I'll ask." He comes back on, "They plan to tie over us."

"Yes, sir. I'll retract the masts."

Cumberland grunts, "Yeah. Secure sea and anchor. Once the Horne is parked, they'll turn on enough lights to hook up services."

Morrison, "Yes, sir." He flips the handles on the periscope and announces, "Retract all masts to their stowage position." To Miller, "I have your answer. Once the Horne is moored, the lights will come on."

USS SAN FRANCISCO

2335, 04 February, 1942

Mallory gets into his dress whites with watch team 2. Watch team 3 has duty and watch team 1 has it tomorrow morning. Gustaf, "Where are we going?"

Mallory, "If you're going with me, we're going to Bondi beach."

"Why?"

"Save the questions until after we're there. You coming?"

MM2 Joe Jackson, "Mind if I join you?"

Mallory, "Sure. If I can, I'm getting a room, so bring a change of clothes. We don't have duty tomorrow."

Gustaf, "My other whites?"

"Yes. Trust me. Just trust me."

They hear, "Liberty call for watch team 2."

Gustaf, "Watch 1 is getting screwed."

Mallory, "Suckage works its way around. That's how it works."

Jackson asks Gustaf, "Haven't you learned the Law of Continuity of Suckage?"

"Yeah."

They climb out of the hatch, salute the watch and flag and go ashore. They see Horne and San Francisco sailors walking toward the gate and follow them out. Soon, they're in a taxi on their way to Bondi. Mallory, in the front seat, asks the driver, "Sir, how late are the bars open in Bondi?"

"What mate? They're open until they close. There is no mandated closing time."

"Okay, we're looking to have a beer in a decent place that isn't crawling with sailors."

"I know a good place. When you want to go back, the barkeep will call me."

"I was hoping to let a room somewhere if its reasonable."

"I know a pub that has some rooms behind it. Will that work, mate?"

"It will."

They pull up to the Slaughtered Lamb. Mallory, "How much, sir?"

"Twenty P."

"Do you take the American?"

"Not the coin."

Here's a dollar, thank you."

"No, mate. Let me make change."

"Okay."

Coin in hand, they walk into the bar. The bar is wood with shake siding. There is a line of two by two windows on each side of the door. Mallory leads them in. The room isn't large, but along the back wall is a nice wooden bar with stools. Of the five tables, three are occupied by Australian Army.

Mallory tells his companions to pick a table and walks up to the bar, "Three beers, and do you have rooms to let?"

"The room is two dollars and I don't want it wrecked."

"It won't be wrecked by us. We're just thankful to not have to sleep on the ship."

"Ten cents a beer."

Mallory pulls out his wallet, "Do you have anything to eat this late?"

"We've got some stew heating bye. It's been there a bit. That, and some bread."

Mallory hands him three dollars and gets change back. He carefully navigates to their table with the precious beer. He takes his first sip as if it was communion wine, and savors it.

One of the soldiers says, "Looks like the yanks 'er getting their first taste of real beer."

Mallory looks over at him and smiles, "I've been to Aussie before. I love your beer."

"You've been to Sydney?"

"Melbourne, about six years ago."

"Well, mate, all Melbourne has is VB and that's rubbish compared to our Tooheys."

Mallory takes another drink, "Yes, I'm inclined to agree."

The digger they've been talking to comes over, "I'm Dan Potter, a corporal of the coastal artillery."

Gary Mallory shakes his hand, "Gary Mallory, a machinist mate first class off the San Francisco. These two are Joe Jackson and Karl Gustaf."

The man introduces his mates, then orders a round just as the food comes out.

GARDEN ISLAND NAVAL STATION

2350, 4 February, 1942

LCDR Joh Morrison is walking along the road out of the station when a grey sedan pulls up beside him and the rear window opens, "Are you lost, Commander?"

John peers into the car, "No, sir. I was walking to the carrier."

"Well, get in. We can drop you off."

John climbs in and discovers the rear seat passenger is a two-star admiral, "Thank you, sir."

"Admiral Lee. You're welcome. Bill, to the Vinson, please."

"Lieutenant Commander Morrison, sir."

"You from the San Francisco?"

"Yes, sir, the anti-submarine ship."

Lee chuckles, "I was CAG on the Vinson when we came back in time. I know what the San Francisco is. It's an LA flight 1, right?"

"Yes, sir."

"You're the XO?"

"Yes, sir."

"You're on liberty, so why are you hoofing it to the Vinson?"

"I've some mail for Captain Van Zandt."

"And the mail bag won't do it?"

"Sir, are you going to drag it out of me?"

"If I have to."

"It's a trust issue, sir."

Lee sits back, "Fair enough. May I guess?"

"Sir, I'm having issues with my commanding officer. I've been keeping Van Zandt and Klindt informed. I'm worried about the security of my mail."

"I'll be seeing Craig in a couple of days and would be happy to hand deliver your letters to him. You can drop Van Zandt's in his box."

"Sir, what are you doing here?"

Lee laughs, "A fair question. I need to talk to a couple of pilots, but I let them go out for a beer first. Now, I'm hoping to intercept them on the way back."

"Can I ask what you do?"

"Sure, I'm NAVAIR Jets, and Klindt is NAVSEA-08."

"Yes, sir."

"I can tell you he's being promoted to Vice-CNO for special projects."

"Who will be '08'?"

"He'll keep that."

"Okay. Sir, do you have any insight as to what is going on in DC?"

"There is a lot I know, but little I can share. They're very happy with the success of the battle group. Off of Wake, you managed to sink four carriers. Three of them were at Pearl Harbor."

"We sank a battleship, a cruiser, and a destroyer. And sir, we're getting short on torpedoes."

"The Camden has some on board. When you leave Sydney, you'll be full. We're working on making new ones. It'll be a while."

"Thank you, sir. Here are the letters for Admiral Klindt."

Lee puts the letters in his shirt pocket. "Take care, Commander. That and be careful, your ethnicity may mark you for discrimination."

"I understand about that, sir. My father was Irish."

Lee laughs, "Are you in contact with your family?"

"My dad is about thirteen right now. His dad is the XO on a destroyer on the East coast. I've sent letters, but I've no idea if they received any yet."

"You remember which one?"

"I just found out. It's the Livermore out of Cape May."

Lee, "If it's okay with you, I'll check on them."

"Please do, and thank you, sir." Morrison gets out of the car and walks up the officer's brow. He salutes and shows his ID, "Request to come aboard for delivery to Captain Van Zandt."

The lieutenant junior grade studies his ID and face, "What ship are you on?"

"The anti-submarine ship San Francisco."

"What the hell is that?"

Morrison smiles, "We're not the heavy cruiser. We came back in time with the rest of you."

Captain Holtz steps up after John, "CAG, reporting." The officer salutes. Holtz, "What's up Commander?"

Morrison, "I'm the XO on the San Francisco, sir. I'm trying to deliver some personal mail for Captain Van Zandt."

The quarterdeck watch, "What's the San Francisco, sir?"

Holtz, "While on this watch, you should know the vessels that make up your battle group and you should recognize the face of every CO and XO. Get your shit straight, Lieutenant. Morrison, I'll show you the way."

"Thank you, sir."

"Thank you for sinking all those Japanese subs. Were it not for what you did while we were trying to recover the Salt Lake City, we could have all been sunk." They climb the stairs to the 03 level, then walk through the maze of passageways. "Aren't you seeing Halsey tomorrow morning?"

"My captain and I, yes."

"Hmm. I see." He stops at a door, "This is his stateroom. It was mine before I made CAG."

John slides three envelopes under the door.

Holtz, "Now, can I offer you a cup of joe while you share your story?"

"Yes, sir." They walk into the CAG's office and Holtz puts on the pot. As they wait, John explains his struggles with Cumberland, "The thing is, sir. He's a damn fine tactician and he's really aggressive. All these are traits that are needed in the force. But he abuses the crew."

"Do you want him relieved?"

"Actually, no, sir. I do want people outside the boat to know we're struggling. Of late, he's actually gotten better."

"I, of all people, know a person can make a change for the better. I also know, we really need you out there. I really appreciate you being frank with this."

"Sir, do you know where we are going?"

"I'll not rain on Admiral Halsey's parade. He'll tell you the plan tomorrow. Are you staying on your boat?"

"Yes, sir."

"How did you get here?"

"Admiral Lee gave me a lift."

'Papa' Holtz smiles, "Lee used to sit in this chair, and I've known him since I was an Ensign. He's a very good friend to have."

"I got that impression, sir. Can I ask you what the two of you fly?"

"The Tomcat. We flew the Brick before. When we leave here, it's liable to be a target rich environment. The Japanese will know we're here. How long do you think you'll need to sanitize our exit?"

"A day. Two to be careful."

"Thank you. Now, the President and Admiral King have decided to keep your existence secret for now. Can you and your crew deal with that?"

"I served a tour on the Parche, sir. It isn't a problem."

"Okay. It won't be forever. Where we're going, it will be really handy if they don't know you exist."

"I agree, sir."

"Okay, I'm calling for a car to take you wherever you want to go."

"Sir, it's just down the wharf and through the construction area."

"Yes, but I don't want a hyped-up security guard thinking you're an infiltrator. Speaking of which, don't go out on the town alone."

"Yes, sir."

THE SLAUGHTERED LAMB, BONDI BEACH

0122, 5 February, 1942

The six servicemen are laughing and enjoying their beers when the shore patrol walk in. They are in their tropical white uniform with the band on their arm. The laughter dies down. The second-class leading the patrol walks right up to the men, "What unit are you with?"

"I'm Corporal Potter of the coastal artillery. Who are you?"

The petty officer says, "No, him," pointing at Mallory.

Mallory stands up to his full six-foot four-inch height, "I'm MM1 Gary Mallory, at your service. We serve with distinction aboard the anti-submarine vessel San Francisco. I'm not drunk and not driving, so what is your issue, PO2?"

The five-foot four-inch second class petty officer stands his ground, "I think you're drunk and disorderly."

The bartender joins them, "Young man, they're not causing a problem, so take a piss."

"What?"

Mallory, "He's telling you to leave. We're guests in this country, so be a good lad and move along."

"Shut up." The petty officer rotates like a turret toward the bartender, "Unless, you want to be banned from serving the Navy, you will shut up and go away."

The bartender says, "Unless you want to spend a day in jail, petty officer, you will piss off. We've no time for a wanker, so bugger off."

The petty officer points a finger at Mallory, "This ain't over."

Mallory, "Have a good day, shipmate."

The shore patrol detachment hang outside the bar waiting for the sailors to leave. Gustaf, "Why are they still here?"

Mallory, "No other sailors have found Bondi Beach yet, so he only has us to fuck with." He turns to the bartender, "Sorry, Bruce. They single out assholes to be shore patrol."

Bruce, "You've been out a fighting and deserve a coldie in peace."

Potter, "Have you done any fighting?"

Jackson, "We've sunk five Japanese submarines."

Bruce, "Crickey."

Potter, "You with that carrier that attacked Tokyo?"

Gustaf, "Yeah, the same group, but we're on another ship."

Potter, "What kind?"

Mallory, "Anti-submarine."

"A destroyer."

"Like that."

Potter, "You've got quite a stack of lettuce, what are they?"

Mallory looks down at the four-high stack of ribbons under his submarine dolphins, "Well, this one is for making my rack real good."

Gustaf, "Come on, Mallory. Really?"

"Look, I've been in eighteen years. You just acquire stuff. The highest is the Navy Achievement Medal. The silver star means I have four or more. I have five."

Potter, "What are the others?"

Mallory sighs, "This row is Good conduct, Presidential, and

Meritorious unit citations; next, Battle E, National Defense, and Armed Forces Expeditionary Medal; bottom row, Sea service, Expert Rifle and Expert Pistol. It all sounds much more cool than it is. A lot are just for me being in theater or on a ship when they are issued."

Bruce, "What are the Achievement Medals for?"

Mallory, "Three were end of tour medals, just for doing well at a command. One was for a big repair I did. The other, I can't talk about it. It was a spooky thing."

Bruce, "Wow. You boys need another round?"

Mallory, "Sure. I got this one."

Bruce, "This one is on the house. Yous rattled Tojo's cage."

Gustaf, "They're still waiting outside."

Mallory grins, "Let them wait. We ain't doing anything wrong and we have a room."

CHAPTER 11

PORT AFT MISSILE LAUNCHER, TIRPITZ DEPARTING WIL-HELMSHAVEN

1832, 4 February, 1942

Oberleutnant zur See Helmut Schmitt stands with his men beside their launcher as Germany's only remaining battle-ship goes to sea. The new launchers have two of the new missiles on the rails. He smiles. The missiles they are carrying were made in America. He is looking forward to giving them back to them, one at a time.

The ship turns and he sees the cruiser, Koln. It also has four missile launchers. Four destroyers in their group each have one. "If the Royal Air Force shows up, they're going to get a surprise. We need to test it and know how to use it, but, still, it is amazing."

They secure from manning the rails and he goes back to play with his new toy.

USS CARL VINSON, GARDEN ISLAND WHARF, SYDNEY, AUSTRALIA

0725, 5 February, 1942

Cumberland and Morrison sit waiting for Halsey. Captain Van Zandt comes in with a steward, who serves coffee. After the steward leaves, Van Zandt says, "Admiral Halsey is visit-ing with Vice Admiral Royle, head of the RAN. I'll be giving you your briefing."

Cumberland looks at Morrison, puzzled, then, "Yes, sir."

Van Zandt, "I'm aware that you would very much prefer to be at sea. The reason we're in port is to prepare to fly off the Blue Diamonds to defend Australia and facilitate repairs to the Fife and Carl Vinson. This is an opportunity for your crew to get some well-deserved liberty, and for you to perform needed maintenance, and get re-supplied with more torpedoes. If you have repairs that are beyond ships force, bring them to Captain Tucker, our reactor officer. He has additional resources. We'll be in port for at least two more weeks. More likely, three."

Cumberland, "Why so long?"

"The Fife is getting a new bridge. It's the kind of extensive repair that takes time."

Cumberland, "Why didn't you just send it home?"

"We can't be without the antisubmarine capabilities of the Fife."

Cumberland, "Sir, while you're in port, we could be patrolling."

"It's been discussed. If we need to sortie you, we will. For now, Halsey wants you in port."

"Do you know why?"

"Halsey expects the Japanese will send submarines to engage us when we leave. You will leave two days before the rest of us to sanitize the area. If we had you out there, the Japanese could start learning to counter your capabilities and one may slip through. If you shock them all at once, you'll catch them unprepared and lay waste."

"But, sir, the convoys."

Van Zandt, "Put yourself in their position. Would you reveal yourself by sinking a merchant ship? Also, the Japanese did not use their submarines for unconditional warfare. They considered them to be part of the fleet, and used them to sink our warships. The convoys should be quite safe. I grant, it's a gamble, but they gave him three stars to make these kinds of decisions."

Morrison, "Where do we go from here?"

Van Zandt, "We know you've been chomping at the bit to get on the offensive. Once you escort us clear of Sydney and into the IO, you will be cut loose to transit the Atlantic to hunt U-boats. We're still sorting out the schedules, basing, and details. They'll be given to you before you sail."

Cumberland, "Yes, sir."

Morrison, "Yes, sir."

Van Zandt, "That done, Morrison, could you please give us a minute?"

"Yes, sir. If it works for you, sir, I'll find the reactor department here and meet you back on the boat?"

Cumberland, "Do that."

Morrison leaves Halsey's office and walks down the ladder until he gets to the second deck. No one is around, so he asks himself, "Forward, or aft?"

He walks forward and finds photo dosimetry and knocks. The window slides open and a female second class says, "We're closed. Um, sorry, sir."

"I just need directions. Where is the reactor office?"

"Starboard side, aft of the mess decks, inboard, sir."

"Thank you."

He finds the office, knocks, and walks in. The office is huge. It's bigger than the mess decks on the sub. A third class is sitting at a desk, "Can I help you, Commander?"

"Yes, is the reactor officer aboard?"

"No, sir. The engineering duty officer is Lieutenant Commander Petrea."

MMCM Hatzenbeuler walk out of his office. "How can I help you, Commander?"

"John Morrison, XO on the San Francisco. I was told by Halsey's chief of staff to look into working with you for maintenance."

The third class says, "The San Francisco went back to the States."

Master Chief says, "We have two." Turning to Morrison, "Doug Hatzenbeuler. Petrea is in 2 RAR right now. I'm the bull nuke. Want a cup of coffee while we talk?"

"Sure."

"Do you pollute your coffee, sir?"

"Oh, no. Just the straight swill."

They sit down in the chief's office, "Not everyone knows we still have a sub. What kind of shape are you in?"

"Not terrible, but there are always things that need doing. Do you have a nuclear certified welder?"

"We have four. We can do that."

"We have a couple of steam plant valves that really should be replaced. The seats are cut."

"No problem. They don't last forever. Do you have the new valves?"

Morrison, "We do, but if we could draw them from the Camden or you guys, so I can keep my inventory, I wouldn't say no."

"No problem. How's morale?"

"It's been hard."

"Yeah, it hits everyone differently. The parents on board have it the worst."

"They do. I think it helps to give them a meaningful mission and keep them busy. How well are you manned?"

"The department is at near one hundred percent. We lost our reactor officer to DC."

"Yeah, he's NAVSEA-08 now. Did you hear he's getting a promotion?"

"I didn't."

Morrison, "Vice-CNO for special projects and NAVSEA-08. It probably means another star."

"Do you know him?"

Morrison, "Yeah, we served together when I was a J.G. and he was a lieutenant."

A black-haired female LCDR knocks and comes in, "Who's our guest?"

The two men stand. Hatzenbeuler says, "Commander Petrea, this is John Morrison, XO of San Francisco. John, Liz Petrea, our reactor training assistant."

They shake hands and sit. She smiles, "What can we do for the sneaky underhanded half of the service?"

"I'm lobbying for maintenance assistance and contemplating a few crew transfers."

"I'm not swapping my cream for your crap, Commander. Not happening."

"Not what I was thinking about. I was considering voluntary cross decking if anyone was interested. Generally, there are always a few. Also, if you have a surplus of NUBs, I wouldn't say no"

"We have a satellite nuke school on board that is approved. We may be able to produce some students for you, eventually."

"Thank you. How are your training resources?"

Petrea, "Pretty good. We've a reactor casualty simulator if you want to run your ETs through it."

"I do. What can we do for you?"

"I would like to let our student trainees get tours of the sub so they know a bit of what that half of nuclear power is about."

"No problem. Are your phones hooked up?"

"The office phone is." She writes down the number. "Are you doing anything tomorrow?"

"Nothing pressing."

Petrea smiles, "Could you show me the town?"

Morrison smiles back, "Okay. Where and when?"

"Nine, officer's brow."

"I'll see you then."

BONDI BEACH, NSW, AUSTRALIA

0830, 5 February, 1942

Mallory and the guys are walking the sidewalk along the beach in their dress whites. Gulls call and float on the thermals against the blue sky. Gustaf, "God, I'm going to burn."

Mallory, "We might even end up with a boot line across our foreheads. It'll be worth it."

They see a group of girls walking toward the beach change direction and come toward them. Mallory, "Now, remember you guys, don't be a jerk. These are nice girls. Not whores."

A red head says, "Hey there, sailor."

Mallory, "Hi. Are any of you ladies local? We just pulled in."

The red-head smiles, "We all are. We work the night shift at Cockatoo Island."

Gustaf, "What's that? You work with birds?"

The girls laugh and the red-head says, "I'm Amy Randolph. This is Sharon Tinkler, Debby Guiles, and Mary Burns."

Mallory, "I'm Gary Mallory and these two are Karl Gustaf and Joe Jackson."

Amy takes Mallory's arm and starts walking, "What do you want to know?"

"All my corny lines are failing me now. I'm just hoping we can talk. It's been quite a while since I talked to a girl." He notices that Debby has paired off with Gustaf and the other two are with Jackson. He smiles.

"So, your plan was to troll for girls using your uniform as bait?"

"Yeah, something like that. I reminded the guys that you are all nice girls and they were to behave."

She giggles, "Well, we're mostly nice. What ship are you on?"

"The San Francisco. It's a good boat, but the skipper is an ass."

"You married?"

"I was divorced before we went back in time. I lost my two sons."

"Oh my God! How?"

"Time travel. Ours is one of the ships that came back in time."

"Oh, so, they're not born yet, and…and given the age difference, they never will be."

"Exactly. My ex was a bitch, but I love my boys. Loved."

"That's hard." They sit on a bench. "What's the future like?"

"Wow, there's a big question. As I understand it, we have changed history, so the history I remember is probably all wrong."

"Do we win?"

"Yeah. It's seriously ugly at times, but we won. I was born in 1954."

"What did your dad do during the war?"

"He went to grade school. He's about eight years old right now, and my grandpa is a logger in Minnesota. My uncle Gary is in the Army going through basic training."

"Was. Um…is he a hero?"

"He is to me. He died on the invasion beach in France. I never knew him. This time, maybe he will live."

"How did culture change?"

"Oh, wow. Another huge question. It might have been a little different in Australia. Basically, right after the war ended, a cold war with the Soviet Union began. They called it that because America and Russia never actually directly fought. Instead, they used alliances; their ally versus our ally. That kind of thing. Anyway, after the war, most of the women lost their jobs so they could be given to the men returning from the war. There was an enormous baby boom. Returning servicemen married and started making babies like crazy. In the late forties and the fifties American culture got really vanilla."

"What do you mean?"

"Well, the cultural pressure was to be white, protestant, and average. Any diversity was frowned on. Blacks, Natives, and Latino's were massively discriminated against, as was anything society considered deviant."

"What was deviant?"

"Oh, atheism and agnosticism were not tolerated. Men with long hair. Women with short hair. Women wearing pants. Homosexuality, lesbianism. It was a great time if you fit in and a terrible time, if you didn't. So, the baby boom kids grew up. In the sixties and seventies there was a backlash. Things got really herbal and really wild. They called the kids flower children, and such. The kids swore to never trust anyone over thirty. This generation swore to never trust their own children."

"What is herbal?"

"They smoked marijuana. It's a plant that is dried and smoked like a cigarette, but it makes you high. I'm the wrong guy to ask, but it's supposed to be something like getting drunk."

"So, the world goes to shit?"

"Partly. It was a different time."

"What about you? Were you a flower child?"

"No. I grew up on a farm. My dad was a logger. We were so busy just surviving, there wasn't much time for that shit."

"Why didn't you become a logger?"

"I wanted something more for my kids. My brothers were

loggers. Well, one is a bit of a dead beat, an herbalist. I couldn't afford college, so the Navy was my ticket out." He looks at the sky. "Do you suppose the sun has crossed the yard arm?"

"What?"

Gary grins at her, "Want lunch and a beer?"

"Sure." She leads him to a café.

Mallory, "You order. I don't even know what I'm looking at." She orders and the beers come fast. He asks, "What is the drinking age here?"

"Eighteen."

He smiles.

She does too, "So, were you thinking if I'm old enough to drink, then I must be old enough to shag?"

"You caught me. Yes."

"I might say no."

Gary looks her in the eyes, "It isn't important. I'm enjoying your company. I'm not expecting more. It's just nice to know I won't end up in jail if we do."

"I see your point. I'm twenty-three."

"I'm thirty-five."

"Okay. You said you have kids?"

"Had. Two boys. Billy and Johnny. Bill is fourteen and John is twelve. Now they don't exist."

She touches his arm, "I'm sorry."

USS SAN FRANCISCO

There are five letters on Morrison's desk. One from Klindt, one from Van Zandt, and three from his family. He opens Van Zandt's:

Good Morning,

I've arranged to do the briefing on the 5ᵗʰ. I read your letters early this morning. If you can prove he's tampered with the mail, that's an Article 134-32 violation. It would be grounds for his dismissal. That said, I'm glad he's settling down some. I'll say this, he's a pretty aggressive commander, and Halsey likes his leaders aggressive. Hopefully, moving forward, the two of you will balance each other.

Keep me posted.

C.B. Van Zandt

He opens Admiral Klindt's:

Dear John,

There is a lot going on in Washington right now, but I have not lost sight of your situation. Please keep me apprised. We are standing up maintenance facilities for your unit, but as you know, these things take time. Thank you for letting me know when your most recent exams were. We will schedule your next to work around your operations. That said, expect an inspection in about two months.

I will also be pulling some of your senior enlisted and junior officers into the new vessel program we are standing up. They will be replaced by less experienced men. I know that will hurt, but it can't be helped.

I hope the Navy got through to your adoptive parents. Last I heard, the other LCDR Morrison is doing well. I've included the address of your birth father's parents and your birth mother's parents. We are doing what we can to alleviate the suffering and tragedy where we can.

Something Nimitz once said: He was the only person who could lose the war in a day. If you think about it, that is true for your unit as well. We need you out there being aggressive, but losing your unit would be a disaster. Please take care of your unit and yourself.

Your Friend,

Craig

"Okay, so be aggressive, but not too aggressive." He sighs, "If it was easy the Air Force would do it." He opens the letter from his grandmother.

Dear John,

We were startled to get the letter from the Navy Department announcing your existence. They included your picture. It is obviously your Academy photo. If you have a more current picture, could you please send it? As I write this, your grandfather, Henry, is out to sea.

I should be completely clear, John. You are welcome in our home and we welcome you to our family. In fact, we are all very much looking forward to meeting you.

We are putting together a package of things you might need in hopes that it catches up to you. It will have the usual stuff and will include enough to spread around to your crew. If you are anything like my husband, I expect that is what you will do. If you have any specific needs, please let us know. We know how hard it is to serve at sea and want to be a comfort to you.

There was a front-page article in the paper about the carrier group attacking Japan. I tell you; it was a morale boost. The article mentioned a heavy cruiser, but nothing about your San Francisco. I assume they have a reason and will respect that.

Please share our highest regards for your captain and crew.

Elaine Morrison

He puts the letter down and wiped his eyes, "God bless you, Grandma." After a moment, he opens the one from his grandfather.

Hello Commander,

I hope this letter finds you well. I write this shortly after arriving home and hearing my son proudly say he is going to be a rear admiral someday. He has dedicated himself to working harder in school so he can be smart enough. We'll see how long that lasts, though that boy has surprised me in the past.

I expect there is a fair bit of family history you could share. I trust you will only share what will be beneficial to our family. If there is an illness that could be nipped in the bud, or such. Otherwise, I would as soon not know when I will die, etc. All that is way too morbid.

I know Elaine made clear that you are welcome. I heartily agree. Mi casa is su casa.

I'm pretty certain what an anti-submarine vessel would be in 1990. That's all I will say. Mitch is trying to sort it out. I can see good reasons to leave it as is. You are welcome to write me at my FPO. But, as I am sure was true for you in 1990, it takes forever to get mail. I made some suggestions for your care package, but Elaine already had it well in hand.

Take care of yourself,

Henry

He sits for a while, "They were always wonderful." Then, it's the letter from his father.

Hi John,

I hope it is okay that I don't call you son. For me that would be too weird. Mom said it was okay to write you. I really want to meet you. I have a million questions I want to ask and I don't want to ask them in a letter. For one, it would be way too long. I hope I wasn't a jerk to you as a dad. I guess you are doing okay, but maybe that doesn't mean much. I really hope you are okay. Dad, I think, knows more than he is saying, but that's pretty much normal for him, because the Navy requires it. Your mom's name sound Japanese. Are you part Japanese? Do you have one of those curved Jap swords? Uh, Japanese, sorry. The most important question I have is, what do I need to do now, so I can be a good father and good officer when I grow up?

Yours,

Mitchell Morrison

This letter makes him smile, "You already are the great man you need to be." He picks up his pen and starts writing.

CHAPTER 12

QUEEN VICTORIA BUILDING, SYDNEY, AUSTRALIA

1635, 5 February, 1942

Karl Gustaf holds hands with Debby Guiles. She's a pretty, brown-haired girl with a quick smile. They see an ice cream shop, "You want a cone?"

"Sure. Hey look." They see MM2 Jackson walking, relaxed and laughing, with the other two girls. "Are you jealous of your friend because he's with two girls?"

"No, that isn't how the math works."

"What do you mean?"

"When one guy is with two girls, he has to divide his attention between the two, so both the girls only get half a guy. Also, because the girls know each other, their attention is also divided. I'm sure he's enjoying himself, but I'm having the better time."

"So, relationships are just math?"

"Well, some of it is. Have you heard of an American mathematician named John Forbes Nash, Junior?"

"No."

"Oh, wait a minute. He came up with his theorem in 1950. How could you. He basically invented game theory. It's a school of math. Um, a type of math can describe human behavior, including dating. I learned about him in college."

"You've been to college?"

"Yeah, I dropped out after my sophomore year because I ran out of money."

She hugs him, "You sound so smart."

AMY'S COTTAGE, BALMAIN, WEST OF SYDNEY

Gary wraps Amy up close and rolls, so they're side by side in the bed, "Oh wow. Wow. Just wow. Amy, you're amazing."

She lightly caresses his face, "You are too."

"I...today, I hoped to get to talk to a pretty girl. Your beautiful. Your funny. Your amazing."

She smiles, "When do you leave?"

"I have duty tomorrow. I don't know when we're leaving, but we are supposed to be here for a couple of weeks. Maybe three. They don't tell us when."

"Okay. I need to get a little sleep before I go on shift at midnight. Can I see you again?"

"Absolutely. I would really like that. Where do you want to meet?"

"You think you can find this place?"

"If you write down your address, the taxi can."

She climbs out of bed, in the nick, and writes her address on a note card. He lounges in the bed admiring her, "You're incredible."

"Your good for my self-esteem. We need to get a shower."

"Okay."

USS CARL VINSON

0850, 06 February, 1942

LCDR Petrea walks down the brow and sees John waiting at its foot. She gets to him and smiles, "Tell me you have a car."

"Yes, I do. Now hopefully, I can drive on the wrong side of the road. Is that in your skill set?"

"No, I'm afraid not."

"Well, I'll muddle through. If I scare you, please say so."

"I'm from New York."

He laughs and opens the wrong door for her, "Oops." They settle into the Ford sedan and he pulls out. "I thought first to drive into Sydney proper, then we can explore."

"That works."

They drive through down town with its tall buildings and shops. He served in Scotland for three years and has no trouble driving. His navigation skills do result in the sounding of a few horns from other drivers. They drive by the Queen Victoria Building and John says, "This is supposed to be the best place to shop."

Petrea smiles, "Maybe later."

"Okay." He drives into the Royal Botanic Gardens and parks. "A walk?"

"Sure."

He hands her out of the car and they start down one of the many footpaths. Liz, "Were you married?"

John breathes, "I got married to Lisa the day before we sailed."

"Oh my God."

"It...It's hard to explain."

"I was married to Tim for three years. He…he's special."

John, "I don't want to fly a false flag. I can't even imagine being with anyone but Lisa. I just can't."

Liz, "Truth, I feel the same about Tim. He's the love of my life."

"So, this isn't a date?"

She quirks up the side of her mouth, "Is that okay?"

"It's wonderful. Way better. Okay, that sounds awful. Do you understand what I mean?"

"I do. Exactly. I just wanted off the ship and didn't want to hang with the guys."

"Okay, how do we keep this non-date from getting awkward?"

She smiles up at him, "We talk. I know I need to."

"You don't want to hear me whining about Lisa."

"I do. I do, if you can put up with me whining about Tim. I think we both could use the relief valve. So, you married her right before you left?"

"We dated for a year when I was a JO. Back then, I proposed twelve times, and she said no, every time."

"Do you know why?"

"Sure. She didn't want to fuck up her career. She was convinced it was incompatible with being a Navy wife."

"What did she do? Pole dancing?"

He laughs, "You're direct. No, she's a songwriter and back-up singer in a band. Well, she was."

Liz, "She probably still is, somewhere."

"No, she married the lead singer. When she divorced him, she left the band."

"Oh, okay. Have I heard of them?"

"Metalsmith."

"Yeah. I really liked one of their early songs. I can't recall the name, just the lyric."

"What's the lyric?"

"My heart screams out for you, but it doesn't make a sound."

He smiles, "She wrote that."

"So, you know it?"

"Yeah, but I can't sing."

"Who is it about?"

"This is going to sound massively self-centered."

"Okay, but is it the truth?"

"Yeah. She wrote it after we broke up, right after she said no for the twelfth time. I feel this empty hole where my heart was. God, I miss her."

"Yeah, I get it. You know, she was probably right."

"What?"

"Her career and yours were almost completely incompatible."

John, "I know, but we would have figured it out. If it hurt my career, it would have still been worth it."

Liz, "All the lost years to hurt."

"That's the worst part. We could have been happy for fifteen years."

"I can feel that pain. I was in a fucked-up marriage for four years. I finally found the strength to dump him and six months later, I really saw Tim."

"You worked with him?"

"Yeah. I'm a mustang. We met at 'A' school. He was a nuke and I was a diesel dyke. We met again when we were on the Gompers. He was a chief, and I was a lieutenant JG going through a divorce. The day he retired, he asked for a date. I said yes. God, I'm glad I said yes. When they opened nuclear power billets at sea to women, I signed up. He encouraged me through nuclear power school and prototype, because he understood what it was about. In every way, we lift each other up. In no way, do we pull each other down. He's a one in a billion guy."

"So, we both have an unfillable hole."

Liz, "We do. Right now, I'm not even looking for a shovel, but it's nice to talk about it."

"Yeah, it is. Did you have kids?"

"Thank God, no. That would be the worst."

John, "What year was Tim born?"

"1949. In 1967 he'll be legal, and I'll be a haggard fifty-five."

"You might not be haggard."

"Do you know anything about women? We do have a shelf life."

"Only to stupid, shallow people. Real beauty comes from within. So does real ugly. Yours is a beautiful soul."

Liz grins, "Some of my guys would disagree."

"Yep, and they would be wrong. They don't see what I see."

"John, I'm a demanding mercurial bitch on the job."

"Good. In your job, you have to be. I'm an XO. Normally, I have to be a pain in the ass, too. Lately, I need to be the nice guy."

"Why?"

"Because our captain is a flaming ass hole."

Liz laughs, "Captain Johnson is pretty cool. Tucker is, too. He has a sense of humor that is needed. We're all still demanding assholes to some of the guys. It's necessary."

"Yeah. As important as it is to care for our crews, we also need to keep them in fighting trim. Do you recall what Rickover said about that?"

"I'm pretty new in nuclear power. I probably need to complete a Rickover PQS."

John smiles, "Yeah. Anyway, he was asked why he trusted his enlisted men as much as he did. He said, 'If you send a ship out crewed entirely by officers, it would never come back. If you send a ship out crewed entirely by enlisted, it would always come back. It would just come back dirty.'"

Liz howls, "That is so true. So, fucking true. So, what is wrong with your captain?"

"He has zero empathy. I think he believes a strong face in front of the men is needed. He's incapable of caring. From time to time, he seems to be faking it. He generally fails. After we found out about the time transference, he couldn't understand why our crew was upset. After all, the Navy didn't issue them a family."

"You're serious."

"As a heart attack. The only time he's happy is when he's just killed another sub. I do have to admit, he is effective tactically, though he takes too many chances."

"How many have you killed?"

"We've sunk seven Japanese subs, one battleship, one

cruiser, and one destroyer."

Liz, "He always has to push the button?"

"Oh no. His latest game is to test the loyalty of the crew. Once the shot is set up, he'll call someone over and order them to push the button. If they refuse, he masts them."

"That's sick."

"Yeah, welcome to my world."

"Has he ordered you to do it?"

"Yeah, which was stupid. When he was on the Vinson for a meeting, we killed one. I pushed the button then, too."

"So, you have personally sunk two Japanese submarines?"

"Yeah."

"Are you okay?"

"I'm not sure what okay is. My work life is a pressure cooker, but my guys need my best."

She gives him a side hug, "Yeah, they do."

He returns the hug, "How are you holding up?"

Releasing the hug, she starts walking, "My watch station is main control. On a carrier, that is the overall engineering control center. I don't push that kind of red button. Still, everyone on board shares some of the responsibility. I've done a lot of soul searching about it. If I had to, I would, but I'm glad I don't."

"I'm glad you don't, too. I'm glad our women aren't in that position."

She stops and looks up at him, "You don't know?"

"Know what?"

Liz, "You don't know about the pilots. We have a bunch of female pilots."

"Do they have any kills?"

"Commander Hunt, Samantha Hunt, is CO of the Black Knights squadron. She's a F-14 pilot who has 35 kills."

John, "Wow. I didn't know. Did I just make an ass of myself?"

"You did. I don't believe it is any harder for a woman, than it is for a man."

"I didn't mean it misogynistically. Well, maybe a little. I just assumed it would be harder for a woman."

"You assumed wrong."

"I'm sorry. Can I take that one as a lookup?"

Liz smiles, "Maybe some remedial training is in order."

"I'm on board for that. How does Hunt's kills compare to the other pilots?"

"Captain Johnson called her the squadron, air group, Navy, and national ace of aces."

"Wow."

"Yeah, girls can do it, too."

"He looks at her, "I'm sold. I think I've hogged the conversation. Tell me about Tim. After he retired, what did he do?"

She grins, "He looked after me, took care of our house, two dogs, and a cat. He's a great cook."

"Right. Point taken. Guys can be domestic engineers, too."

"They can. He also has a wood and metal shop where he builds all kinds of cool stuff. He's made custom gates, door hinges, stuff like that. He makes stuff to order and makes custom knives to sell. We have an amazing house in Washington."

"I bet. I live in a one bedroom flat in Honolulu. What is the thing you miss the most?"

"His voice. He isn't a singer or anything. It's just, when he calls me 'darlin', I melt."

John, "Lisa has an amazing giggle when I make her laugh. I've even made her snort. It's so cute."

Liz, "Sometimes I would quietly walk into his shop and just watch him. He'd be stripped to the waist wearing a leather apron. His muscles would glisten with sweat. He was in his element, you know? The master in his realm."

"When we were together before, I loved to watch her at the piano working out a song. That is something I understand."

"Never again. It's all gone."

John, "We don't one hundred percent know that."

"We do one hundred percent know that. We know the mechanism."

"The Talon Sword?"

Liz, "Yeah, there is no mechanism for returning."

"It was a book. It may have the details wrong."

"I've gone over Dr. Heinlein's paper, and what we have of his notes. It's a one-way trip."

"Fuck. I knew in the book it was a one-way trip. I guess, I was just hoping…"

"Yeah."

"You hungry?"

Liz, "Time travel makes you hungry?"

"Nope, but time does."

"Yeah, I'm hungry, too."

As they walk back to the car, he asks, "Do you mind the chivalrous stuff?"

"No, I don't mind. I just don't expect it."

"Because you're in the service, or because you're from New York."

The get in the car, "A little of both. Women in the work force have to work so much harder than a man to prove themselves. Any weakness is jumped on as a reason why you're not suitable."

"I've never seen a mechanic use his penis as an extra hand, so I don't see why one is required."

Liz, laughing, "Oh, my God! That would be impressive."

He joins in, "Yeah, and probably painful."

He pulls up to a café with two police cars in front, "Does this work?"

"Yeah. What do the police cars indicate to you?"

"Police know their district and aren't generally well paid. If they are eating here, the food is probably both good and affordable."

Liz, "Solid analysis. I cannot find a flaw."

He gets the door for her and they go into the café. Their dress whites attract attention, but they're left alone. They are seated in a booth and given menus. He asks, "Have you been to Australia before?"

"Well, yes. A couple of times."

"My first time here. Should I try the fish and chips?"

Liz, "It's all good."

The waitress, an older woman, walks up.

Liz, "Chips are French fries. Ma'am, can I have the pasty with Earl Grey?"

"Of course."

John, "I've been to Scotland before. Can I have the bangers and mash with coffee?"

"Yes, sir."

Liz, "You were in Scotland?"

"Yeah, my last tour before the San Francisco was SUBRON 14."

"Then you have driven on the wrong side of the road."

"Yeah, I'm just not great at it."

"But you were going to let me drive?"

"Liz, I may be a bit of an ass, but I've no doubt you're as capable as I am."

"Thank you, but in the future, don't act stupid on my account. It has the opposite effect."

"I won't and I'm sorry."

"Do you understand why it's annoying?"

He is quiet for a moment, then, "Because it's patronizing?"

"Exactly."

"I had no idea how much cultural bullshit I need to work on."

"You haven't had a wife to sort out your bad habits."

"You know, that's patronizing, too."

Liz, "Probably, but it also rings true for most relationships. It's women who create a civilization. Men would be slobs and cads if it were not for the presence of women."

He chuckles, "Mostly true."

They hear, "Liz?"

Liz looks up, "Hi Commander. Please join us. Samantha Hunt, Gloria Houlihan this is John Morrison, XO of San Francisco."

Sam, "We don't want to break up a date."

John and Liz look at each other and grin. John, "It isn't exactly a date. Please, join us. We've just ordered."

Houlihan sits with Liz and Hunt with John. They sort out their orders and John asks, "How do you three know each other?"

Sam, "We share a p-way and a head."

"Okay. Liz was telling me about you."

Sam looks at Liz, then back to John, "Okay?"

Liz, "I used you as an example that women can fight. I just dodge zoomies."

Sam smiles, "I want the nukes and airedales to get along. I know it's like solving the middle east, but it's still an aspiration."

John, "I'm career submarines. I've heard of black and brown rivalries, but kind of assumed it had reached a détente years ago."

Gloria laughs, "Oh no, the battle continues."

John, "Are you both with the same squadron?"

Gloria, "Black Knights."

"Do you fly together?"

Sam, "We're both pilots."

"Oh. So, who's the Goose to your Mav?"

"My RIO is Eric Hawke."

Gloria, "Mine is Byron Standley. His call sign is GQ."

John raises an eyebrow, "Call signs? That's real?"

Sam, "It is."

"Okay, can I ask, or is that rude."

Gloria rolls her eyes, "No one likes their call sign. I was hung with Hot Pants. Sam is Spike."

John, "Liz, is this just an aviation thing?"

Liz, "It is. Nukes don't have official nicknames. I thing Rickover would roll over in his grave if we started that."

John chuckles, "You know he's alive and a lieutenant commander right now."

Sam asks, "Is that a good thing, or a bad thing?"

John, "Yes. He created the program, but he was also an eccentric ass."

Liz, "Was your interview with him?"

"Yeah. I thought he hated me."

Gloria, "Why?"

"My dad retired as a non-nuke admiral. My grandfather retired as a non-nuke admiral. Rickover hated the regular navy."

Sam, "What did he do?"

"He hit me with a barrage question. 'You're in the middle of the Atlantic at 600 feet with frozen air lines and a scrammed reactor. What are you going to do, Ensign?' It's kind of what happened to the Thresher."

Sam, "What did you say?"

"I looked him in the eye and said, 'If I'm in that situation with the training I have right now, what I'm going to do is die. I'm here so you can teach me how to keep the crew and myself alive.' He actually smiled, then we talked. I didn't try to bullshit him or convince him I knew anything. My major was physics, but that only meant I knew enough to be stupid."

Gloria, "I haven't heard the stories. I mean, I've heard of him. He was like Grandpa Nuke, right?"

Liz, "Yeah, he was way eccentric. But his eccentricities were vital for making the program to what it is."

Gloria, "Liz, did you get interviewed by him?"

"No, he died in 1986. My interview was with Admiral De-Mars. He was a demanding guy, but his expectations were more straight forward. I did get the vagina monologue."

John, "What's that?"

Liz, "He lectured me about being one of the guys and not letting my wiles or period get the best of me."

John, "Oh, my God!"

Gloria, "You think we don't put up with stuff like that?"

John, "Actually, I hadn't thought about it. Not really. There are only guys on a sub."

Liz, "But there were women in SUBRON-14. Don't tell me you've never had a co-ed command."

Sam smiles.

John, "I've been in a co-ed command. I just considered it to be a hazard to navigation. You treat everyone with the same respect and move along. Looking back, I think I was a little blind."

Liz, "Yes, you were."

Sam's smile gets bigger, "Guys, he isn't the enemy. He's just discovered a form of empathy he was blind to before. Let's give the poor man a chance to adjust."

Their food arrives.

John, "Thank you, Spike."

Sam, "I know, it sounds like the name of a bull dog."

"It does, but I guess it could be worse."

Gloria, "You mean like Hot Pants? You know, one of the helo pilots call sign is Cargo Britches. Then there's Revlon and Lipstick, it goes on and on."

John, "Geeze."

Gloria, "At least my call sign implies I have them on. I can live with it."

John, "Why do call signs exist?"

Sam, "So, no one shouts, 'Hey, John Morrison!' on the radio."

"Oh. On the radio we just use the ship's call sign."

Gloria, "When a missile is closing at Mach 4, you don't have time for long-winded formalities."

"Good point."

Sam, "We're going to Queen Victoria's Market. What are you up to?"

John looks at Liz. Liz is looking at the door. He follows her gaze and sees Cumberland staring at him. Cumberland rumbles his way to the table. Quietly, he says, "Commander Morrison, I thought you were madly in love with that rock star. Now, I find you slutting around with three women."

Sam, "Excuse me."

Cumberland ignores her, "Get your ass back to the boat. We'll discuss this there."

Sam stands, "Who are you to impugn the honor of a fellow officer?"

Cumberland waves her off.

Morrison, "I'll deal with it, Commander."

Sam stays put, so he can't get out of the booth. "No, I will deal with it. Who are you, Commander? I need a name and command when I report this to my captain."

Cumberland finally looks at her, "Who are you?"

"Lieutenant Commander Samantha Hunt, CO of VF-154."

Morrison, "Hunt."

Cumberland, "Oh well, you couldn't have known his behavior was inappropriate."

Sam, "You've insulted the honor of three officers. Your conduct here is completely out of line."

Cumberland, "Um. I didn't mean to impugn the honor of any of you three. It's his conduct I find inappropriate."

Sam, "Why?"

Cumberland, "Well, um…he was just married, and…"

Sam, "And what?"

Cumberland, "He should not be cavorting…"

Sam, "Cavorting with whom? Do you see, Commander? You cannot impugn his honor, without smearing ours. Now, your name, position, and command, sir."

Cumberland, "That won't be necessary. I think this was a simple, ah, misunderstanding."

"I think so as well. It seems to me a commanding officer should have better judgement. Do you think the admiral would agree with my assessment?"

Cumberland pales, "Um. Will you excuse me?" He turns on a heel and leaves.

Morrison, under his breath, "Jesus Christ." Louder, "I'm sorry guys. I'm sorry."

They all stand and Morrison hands a ten to the waitress, "I'm sorry."

The waitress, "It's a dollar seventy-five."

Gloria, "How much for all of us?"

"A dollar seventy-five. Who was that man?"

Gloria hands the waitress two dollars, "Thank you."

Morrison, "Commander George Cumberland. My captain." He sighs, "Commander Hunt, I could have handled it."

They leave the café. Sam, "Yes. But that would have diminished us in his eyes and done nothing to help you. He needs to be relieved."

"I know. But nuclear trained officers aren't thick on the ground. Are you going to report him?"

Sam looks John in the eyes, "I don't bluff. Not ever."

"Okay, I better get back."

Liz, "Spike, do you have room for a third?"

"We do."

John, "I'm sorry, Liz."

"Don't be. He was the ass hole."

John gets in the car and drives back to the boat alone. When he gets to the submarine, Cumberland isn't there. He changes clothes and gets to work taking care of the stack of paperwork on his desk.

CHAPTER 13

USS CARL VINSON

1630, 06 February, 1942

Hunt knocks on the CAG's door and walks in with her statement. Holtz meets her eyes, "You okay?"

She sighs, "Yes, I had a liberty incident." She hands him the statement.

"No one is dead, in jail, or in the hospital, right?"

She smiles, "No, nothing like that."

He reads through her statement, "What an ass hole. For clarity's sake, you didn't put him in the hospital, right?"

Sam chuckles, "No. I admit, a Swede solution crossed my mind. I said I would report it, so now I have to."

"What do you want done?"

"Could you put the fear of you in him?"

"Sure. That's easy enough. Seems like a reasonable solution. If he treats his XO this way, he must be an absolute tyrant to his crew."

"Liz assured me that Morrison said as much."

"She's with reactor, right?"

"Yeah. They both lost their spouses. It wasn't a date, just two grieving people commiserating with each other. That said, they are both single, equal rank, and in different commands. There would be nothing wrong if they were dating."

"I agree. Okay, I'll talk to him. By the way, you have CDO under instruction tomorrow."

"Yeah, I know. Thank you, Papa."

USS SAN FRANCISCO

Morrison stays on the boat for the rest of the day working on paperwork. At dinner, Miller, the CDO, asks, "Sir, why aren't you out having a beer?"

"Have you seen the captain?"

"He told the watch he was staying at a hotel tonight."

"Thank you."

COMMANDER'S STATEROOM, USS SAN FRANCISCO

0730, 07 February, 1942

Cumberland arrives back at the boat and goes to his stateroom. There's a message on his desk.

Commander Cumberland

Report to Commander Air Group no later than 1000, 02/07/1942.

Captain James Holtz

In near silence, "Mother fucking, cock sucking, whore, bitch, cunt." He checks himself and walks out. On his way off the boat, he tells the watch, "I'll be on the carrier."

The Horne's driver gives him a lift.

He goes aboard the Vinson, finds the CAG's office and knocks.

"Enter."

Holtz points at a chair and continues reading the report in his hand. Cumberland sits down. Holtz keeps reading. He picks up the phone, "Yes, this is the CAG. Did you receive the list I sent down? Good. Thank you." He hangs up and puts a notation on the report. He makes another call, "CAG, did we get our twenty mike? Good. Thank you." He hangs up and looks at Cumberland, "Explain yourself."

"Why did you wish to see me, sir?"

"Cumberland, don't start that shit. You know why you're here."

"Sir, the conversation was between my XO and myself. Your flyer had no business interfering. She was out of line."

Holtz, calm and measured, "You accused three officers, two under my command, of being sluts and you want me to ignore your behavior?"

"My comment was aimed at my XO."

"You are aware Hunt is a squadron commander?"

"She said, but really? I didn't believe it."

"You best believe it. She's the finest fighter pilot on this ship and she has the kills to prove it."

"As I said, my comments were aimed at my XO, not at her or the other women."

"You said. So, what kind of boat do you run where it's okay to publicly humiliate your XO?"

"His actions were unseemly, and Captain, as long as I'm the commanding officer of my submarine, how I run it is my business."

"Do you have a plan B?"

Cumberland, "What?"

"What are you going to do with your life when you are dismissed from the service?"

"The Navy needs me."

Holtz, "The Navy needs effective leaders. Do you know who is going to sign your FITREP, Commander?"

"Halsey?"

Holtz smiles, "Halsey is heading back to the Pacific. It's his war. You are staying in the Atlantic. Admiral King has made it clear that your sub is to be kept a secret for as long as possible."

"I don't understand."

"They will be leaving a naval captain to manage the fighter squadron, and you. That naval captain is me. Cumberland, I will write your FITREP. I expect a commander to take care of his people."

"Sir, you don't know anything about submarines, sir."

"I know a hell of a lot more than you think I do, and I expect you to take care of your crew, including your XO. Do you understand?"

"Yes, sir."

"Good. You may go."

OUTSIDE AMY'S HOUSE

0850, 07 February, 1942

Mallory gets out of the taxi and pays. Carrying his duffle and flowers, he knocks on the door. An older copy of Amy answers, "Petty Officer Mallory, please come in. Amy is getting ready. I'm her mother, Judy."

"Thank you, ma'am." He swallows, "I didn't know she lived with her folks."

"I understand. The last time you were together you no doubt had other things to talk about. Would you like tea or coffee?"

"Coffee, please."

A man, about five and a half feet tall, walks out of a back room. His face is set and his gaze burns into Mallory's eyes. Gary stands, towering over the older man. "I'm Andrew Randolph, Amy's father." He gives Gary a crushing hand shake.

Gary doesn't flinch. "It's nice to meet you, sir.

Judy brings in the tea and coffee services, "Dear, your crushing the lad's hand. He'll need it to fight the Japs."

Andrew lets go of Gary's hand. They all sit. Judy serves, watching her husband with amusement in her eyes.

Andrew asks, "What do you do for the yank navy?"

"I'm the LPO, the foreman, of the mechanics in our engine room. I serve on the San Francisco."

"What is that? The heavy cruiser?"

"No, sir. We're an anti-submarine vessel. We came back in time."

"Yes, I've heard about that. I thought it was rubbish."

Mallory pulls out his driver's license from Minnesota that shows his date of birth. The issue date is 1973 and the expiration just says 'active'.

Andrew studies it carefully, "You were born July seventh of 1954?"

"Yes, sir. My dad is a kid right now."

"How old are you then?"

"Technically speaking, I'm negative twelve."

Andrew laughs, "Okay."

"I'm thirty-five, sir."

"You know my daughter is twenty-three, right?"

"Yes, sir."

Amy walks into the living room in a pretty floral print dress and carrying a bag. "Dad, are you interrogating my date?"

Andrew looks up at his daughter, "I was. Where are you going?"

"Uncle Danny is taking us out."

"Separate beds."

"Dad."

Gary, stands up and hands her the flowers. She smiles, "They're lovely."

Judy, "I'll take care of them, dear. Go have fun."

She gives her mom a kiss on the cheek and hugs her dad. Andrew gives Gary his license back and shakes his hand again, this time leaving the hydraulic crushers off. "Take care of my girl."

"Yes, sir."

The get into a sedan waiting at the curb. They get in and Amy says, "This is my Aunt Ally."

"Pleased to meet you, ma'am. Where are we going?"

Amy smiles, "You'll see."

They cross a bridge and drive down to a marina. Ally pulls in and stops. She turns around, "Here's the keys, honey. You two have fun."

"Aunt Ally, you're the best."

They get out, grab their bags, and walk down the dock. Gary asks, "What are we doing?"

Amy smiles, a mischievous glint in her eyes, "You'll see." She unlocks the gate and they walk down the dock to a Sparkman and Stephan's 12 meter-yacht. "Welcome aboard the Sea Breese."

"Your aunt owns a boat?"

"Uncle Danny. Aunt Ally married up. He's actually a good Bruce. Really good to Aunt Ally."

"Does he know we have his boat?"

"I reckon he should. Was him I asked." She removes the sail lashings and covers.

"What do you want me to do?"

"You're a sailor. Do you know anything about sail boats?"

"No. Our propulsion is a little more advanced."

She grins, "Put our bags below and start the kettle. It uses an alcohol stove. Can you use one?"

"Yeah, we camped all the time." He goes below. The boat is stocked and, in a few minutes, he finds everything he needs and starts the water heating.

She pops her head in, "Leave that to boil. I need some muscle."

"Okay." He climbs topside and helps her hoist the sails. It's a Bermuda rigged sloop with lovely lines. "Does it have an engine?"

"Yeah. It's below the companion way ladder."

"I'll check it."

"Uncle Danny takes care of his boat."

"I've no doubt. We're going to take care of it, too." He goes below and checks the oil, belts, and sea cock. The sea cock is closed. He opens it and looks for leaks. Finding none, he puts the ladder back, and climbs back up to the cockpit. "The sea cock was closed. If we had to run the engine, we would have burned it up."

"Oh, crickey. Thank you. I know the sailing bit."

"And I know engines. We're a good team."

"We are, aren't we?"

He gives her a kiss, "Ready for me to let loose the lines, Captain?"

"I need to start the engine." She turns the key and the two-cylinder engine below turns, catches, and starts popping along. Gary looks over the side checking to see water with the exhaust, then goes forward to untie the bow line. He then removes the stern line, and they are off. She moves them out of the marina, then, "Take the wheel. I'll get the tea."

She comes up with two mugs.

"Tell me where to go."

"Go up wind."

"Okay." He starts to use a finger, then looks up the mast and sees a wing gauge.

She sets her mug in a holder and sets the sails, "Come off to starboard."

Gary does as instructed. The boat surges forward as the sails catch the wind. They're in a mild chop with the northeastern wind warm on their faces. She joins him in the cockpit and shuts off the engine, "It feels good. Don't it?"

"It does." She snuggles next to him.

"Where are we going?"

"I'm going to show you where I work. Then, we're going down bay to look at your fleet."

"We have to stay well clear, and I don't think you'll see mine."

"Why not?"

"The boat I'm on is secret. It wasn't in 1990, but it is now."

She's silent for a bit, "What can you tell me?"

"It's designed to hunt submarines, though it can hunt surface ships, too. It isn't designed, really, for anything else."

"Is it a nice ship to work on?"

"It was before we got our new captain. He came aboard shortly before cruise."

"What's a cruise?"

"A deployment; a trip to sea for six or more months."

She gives him a kiss, "What's your home port?"

"Pearl Harbor, Hawaii."

"Are there lots of girls in hula skirts?"

"There wasn't when I was there in 1990. Mostly, there was tourists."

"What was it like?"

"1990 or Hawaii?"

"Both."

"In Hawaii, the water is really warm. You can swim comfortably in just shorts. Also, it doesn't get too hot. Most days are around eighty degrees. Uh, about 24C. Because it's an island group in the middle of nowhere, everything is expensive. So expensive, I lived in barracks even though I'm a first class."

"What happened with your ex-wife?"

"Sissy was full of herself. She wanted me to be an admiral when all I am is a mechanic. She thought by marrying me, I would make her someone more important, and that isn't who I am."

"Who are you?"

"Me? I'm a sailor. I'm a mechanic. The symbol on my rank patch is a screw. I run the equipment that makes the boat go through the water. I like teaching the new guys. I also like doing a hard job well. I don't want anything like stardom. I don't want to be an officer, president, or politician. I just want to do an honest day's work that I can be proud of."

"I want that, too. Over there on that island is a ship yard. I work in the weld shop cleaning metal for welding. It's filthy work, but it's important."

"Wow. What building?"

"It's kind of in the middle of the island. You can't really see it."

"Okay."

They continue down the bay toward the Garden Island Naval Base, passing under the Sydney Harbor Bridge. Gary, "Always a cool view. You know, there's going to be a big opera house around here somewhere."

"Really?"

"Yeah, it becomes this huge landmark like the London

Bridge, or the Eiffel Tower."

"Wow. Okay, I need to let out the sails a bit." She gets up and adjusts the sails, then cuddles back against him. "It's a good thing it isn't too warm."

"It is."

BOTANICAL GARDENS, SYDNEY, AUSTRALIA

A photographer from the Sydney Morning Herald is looking out over the bay. He was told to find pictures of Yank sailors enjoying Sydney. He has pictures of sailors shopping or walking, but they do not capture what he wants. Then he sees a sail boat. At the helm is an American sailor in uniform. Snuggled next to him is a local girl. She is looking toward him. He brings his camera up and takes a series of photos.

S/V SEA BREESE, SYDNEY HARBOR

Gary sees the guy with the camera and waves.

Amy, "What?"

"A guy is taking our picture."

Amy waves too. They settle back, watching the scenery pass by. "That ship sticking out? What is it?"

"It's the front half of the Carl Vinson, our aircraft carrier."

"Wow. How big is it?"

"Actually, I don't know the numbers. I know it's over a thousand feet long and holds a bunch of aircraft."

"How many and stuff is probably classified, right?"

"Yeah." When they get a bit closer, a wood runabout, with a machinegun mounted, comes toward them. "It's time to give them some space."

They swing up wind until they are close hauled and sailing away. The patrol boat continues to approach and comes alongside. The Australian sailors ask, "What yous doing, mate?"

Gary, "She wanted to see the ships."

"No worries, mate. We'll radio it in. Keep three hundred feet or more from them."

"Thank you."

"Which one is yours?"

"The San Francisco."

"Stay clear of that one, mate."

"Yeah, I know."

"G'day then." They motor off.

Amy nods, "So, it's a fair dinkum secret. Wow."

"Yeah. I wasn't bull shitting you."

Amy, "Do you want to come about and run in there?"

"If you want. You didn't bring a camera, right?"

"No."

"Good." They swing about and run into the inlet where the ships are. They're building a dry dock between the Horne and the Vinson.

She looks up at the Vinson, "Do you know the air planes?"

"Yeah, those you see toward the front with two tails are F-18s. They're fighters and bombers. The skinny tailed ones with one vertical tail, those are A-6s. They're bombers. The ones with two tails and the wings folded back, instead of up, those are F-14 Tomcats. They're fighters, pure and simple and they're really cool. I wish I could show you the movie

'Top Gun'. It's so cool."

They sail down in a broad reach until they get to the finger pier and the wind dies. He starts the engine and they come about. Amy, "That big boat is a cruiser?"

"Yeah."

"You know, I'm curious."

"I do, but, sorry. If I talk about it, I would go to jail."

"Oh."

"Yeah."

"Okay. I keep asking questions that could get you into trouble. Let's get away from here."

"Okay. Where next?"

"I know a cove further up the harbor.

USS SAN FRANCISCO

1527, 7 February, 1942

Cumberland is going through paperwork when there is a knock on his door, "Enter."

Morrison walks in, "You wanted to talk to me, sir?"

"About?"

"The restaurant, sir."

Cumberland shakes his head, "Who's idea was it to cross-train crews with the carrier?"

"As I understand, the reactor officer, Captain Tucker."

"Don't you see the possibility of him stealing our crew?"

"Thought about that. None of their people are sub qualified. They can't have any of our guys that are. Commander Petrea said they're running an approved nuclear power school on the carrier. In time, we could get new crew. It would be nice if they at least had an idea of what we are about."

"Were you talking shop in public?"

"No. We discussed it on the Vinson when you sent me to the reactor department for parts and maintenance help. Sir, they're providing experienced nuke welders, valves, and other supplies. They've also offered the reactor training console. I thought it would be a good thing to run our ET's through. We have an ORSE coming up."

"Okay. That's a good idea. New nukes would be nice. I've no idea how we can get new non-nuke crew."

"They have a sub school in Groton."

"True, but the curriculum would be massively out of date."

"Yes, sir."

There's a knock on the door and Morrison opens it. The roving watch says, "XO, you have a guest on the brow."

"Who?"

"Commander Petrea, sir."

"Thank you." He turns back to Cumberland, "Anything else, sir?"

"No, go continue your date."

"Sir, it wasn't a date. She just lost her spouse, too."

"Call it what you will, it isn't a fraternization issue, so carry on."

"Yes, sir."

Morrison climbs out of the boat and walks up the brow and sees Petrea in her tropical whites. She grins, "Are you hiding on your boat?"

"Can you give me a moment to change?"

"Sure."

Ten minutes later, he's walking up the brow in his tropical whites. She dangles car keys from her finger, then tosses them to him. They walk to a Ford, and this time, he remembers which door to open for her. He asks, "Where too?"

"I found a bar yesterday. I'll show you."

"Okay. They have food?"

"The best 'tucker' I've found. Turn left, then right at the first stop. Are you okay?"

"He said he wanted to talk to me, then he fled the fucking boat. I couldn't leave until we talked."

"What an ass."

"Yeah. What's worse, when I finally cornered him in his office, he blew off the whole thing like it was nothing. Did Hunt report him?"

"She doesn't bluff, John."

"Well, I think he got his ass chewed, again."

She chuckles, "Is it becoming his hobby?"

He laughs, "It seems like it. By the way, he approved the cross-training."

"Good. Turn left up ahead, the right on the roundabout. It's called the Blue Rabbit." They find a place to park and walk in. An older gentleman greets them and finds them a table. About half of the customers are in uniform. They see a few in aviation green. Some are in the blue of the RAAF. They appear to be the only ones in white.

John, I see our comrades haven't found this place."

"Yeah. It's a hole in the wall, but it's nice. Gloria and Sam recommended it."

"Are they coming?"

Liz, "I'm not sure what they are up to. Are you okay?"

He nods, "Yeah." They order their food and a beer. "Unfortunately, I've grown accustomed to my boss' eccentricities. Captain Van Zandt and Admiral Klindt know all the particulars. I think they're waiting to get the training pipeline sorted out."

"I just heard they're standing up a nuclear power school in Washington state. It's at the shipyard in Bremerton, I think."

The waiter brings their beers. John asks, "Have you been there?"

"John, the Vinson is stationed there."

"I was assigned to the Parche in Bremerton."

Liz, "Oh, the spook boat."

"Yep. That's all I can say about that. I did like Washington. It's nice, but rainy."

"I liked it too. We're dancing around what we ought to be talking about."

"We are. Did you report him to Tucker?"

"I had to. Otherwise, I would undercut what Sam did. The CAG was the one who talked to him. What's he like underway?"

"The same as he is everywhere else. The exception is when we are stalking a target. Then he gets calm and happy. I think, after a kill, he has to rub one out."

Liz, "That's sick."

"It's weird."

"No, it's sick. I'm no psychologist, but your captain is clinical. He's like a serial killer, or something."

"Not my area, either. Don't serial killers have to always kill? We're the first sub to take a war shot since the Falkland's."

"Maybe he tortured cats."

"Liz, how could someone with an actual psychological condition make it all the way to command?"

"He would be the only one who could answer that. Look at his behaviors. What other explanation is there?"

The waiter delivers their food. John says, "I heard he went through an ugly divorce a bit before he reported."

"That explains the anger when he thinks you're in a relationship. It isn't fair for you to be happy, when he is not. That sounds narcissistic."

John smiles, "By the time we get to dessert, we'll have him diagnosed as a homicidal maniac."

"That's not an actual diagnosis."

"Okay. I don't know what to do. An XO is supposed to be loyal. I have to have rock solid reasons to recommend he be relieved. Relieving a skipper can be devastating to a command. Not that I think he's popular."

Liz smiles, "What are we going to do is change the subject, because your command knows and there's nothing you can do, yet."

"Okay, maestro of musings, we've talked about my work situation. Can we discuss the conversation we had before assholius interrupted us?"

"I would like that."

"While I was on the boat in purgatory, I did some thinking

about what you and Hunt and Houlihan said. I admit my ignorance on the topic. I've enough empathy to attempt understanding, but I think my bias gets in the way."

"Right. I'm glad you thought about it. What do you mean by 'bias'?"

He takes a sip of beer, "I'm a guy. I see the world through the lens of a guy. I can imagine how the world might be for a woman, but that's only a guess. I don't know nearly enough about the experiences of servicewomen, or how those women feel about their experiences to have any judgement. In that sense, I'm not stupid, but I'm definitely ignorant."

"And now that you see the problem, do you want to fix it?"

"I do."

"Often, we just need to be heard. If you fix our problem, then it makes you feel better, but it diminishes the woman. From the outside, it looks like she is a fragile little thing that needs help. That plays to the male ego, and does nothing to lift up a woman or truly help her."

John, "It's like training. If the instructor does everything for the student, the student doesn't learn, frustrating both of them."

"Yeah, exactly."

"So, listen like you did earlier for me?"

Liz smiles, "Yeah, it's a start."

"You know, this is lesson is the beginning of my remedial training. If I'm going to complete this PQS, you're going to have to instruct a lot more."

She grins, "I know."

"Does it annoy you that I'm such a poor student?"

"You're not. You're an exceptional student and I enjoy the company."

"I do, too. Dessert?"

"Another beer." She gets the attention of the waiter, lifts her glass and holds up two fingers.

"I didn't know you knew sign language."

"Just a few signs. The one finger salute, stuff like that."

John grins, "Oh, I know that one. Unlike Goose from 'Top Gun', I do have some control of my fingers."

"Good to know. It's because we're nukes. We've been potty trained and everything."

"Yep, and Goose was an aviator. Quite a wild creature. Uncivilized."

"John, you said your whole family were sailors?"

"Yeah, my adopted family. My pop, grandpop, and great grandpop. An ancestor probably sailed with Noah."

"Are you worried about discrimination in this war?"

"I try not to think about it."

"You have to. Some misguided red-neck could kill you."

"And I could meet wonderful people like you. I can't crawl into a hole."

Liz sighs, "Are you taking this seriously?"

"I am, but we also have a war to fight. I can't lead from the rear."

"Okay, I think I get it."

"Look, I don't want to die a stupid death. I don't. You know, in that one way, Cumberland was accidently trying to protect me."

"How?"

"He wanted to send me to an internment camp."

"Oh shit. Did he tell you that?"

"Yes. He also wrote Halsey asking for a relief."

"What an ass."

John, "Admiral Lee told me not to go out alone. His assumption is that you being with me serves as a degree of protection."

"I see that. I have duty tomorrow. What are you going to do?"

"I don't know. I'll figure it out. Hang with one of my guys or stay on the boat. Do you think it will be better in America?"

Liz, "No, it'll be worse. I don't think they have red-necks here."

"They have red-necks everywhere. Remember Crocodile Dundee? Shall we go?"

"Sure." He pays the bill and they leave. Liz says, "Let's walk." As they walk down the street, she takes his hand.

"Um?"

"Now, they know we're walking together."

"Thank you."

"Does it make you uncomfortable?"

"No, you just surprised me."

"Okay, just don't get any ideas."

"I'm male."

"Uh huh. I know."

"I also know I'm in no way ready for anything you deserve."

"What do I deserve?"

"You deserve a whole man. Someone who can bring their whole self into a relationship. At best, I'm half a man. I haven't processed losing Lisa."

"I know. I'm right in the same boat. I may deserve a whole man, but right now, I just want a friend."

John, "I can be that. I don't care much what he thinks, but if Cumberland sees us, he'll freak."

"Just a heads up. If I see him, I'm going to kiss you. Fuck that ass hole."

He looks at her, "Um, okay."

COVE WEST OF SYDNEY

2142, 7 February, 1942

Mallory goes forward to drop the anchor. He shouts back, "Back her up!"

Amy, "Backing." She puts the engine in reverse and guns it to start backing.

Gary, "About fifteen feet. Okay, thirty, forty, fifty, sixty, seventy, eighty," he puts on the brake slowly. "Ninety feet of scope. That should be good." He ties it in place with a snubber, and walks aft. "Ninety feet. With the tide coming in, we should be good. How low does it get?"

"We generally swing up and down about six feet."

He looks toward the shore, "Okay, we've about three feet to high and ten feet under our keel. At low tide, we'll have about seven. There might be a rock we didn't see, but I think we're okay."

"I'm hungry. Let's go below."

"Me, too."

As soon as they're below, she jumps into his arms and gives him a deep kiss. An unmeasurable time after, they separate and smile at each other. Gary asks, "Food?"

"Yeah, luv."

He pulls her into a kiss again. "I know it's too soon, but...I... You...um...I love you, too."

She grins and kisses him again, "I love you, luv."

Another kiss, then he says, "I'm hungry."

"I'll whack something together, luv."

"I'll help. I know a bit of how to cook." In a few moments they're sitting across from each other, eating and smiling like kids.

Amy, "I'm giddy."

"Me, too. I'm also terrified. We have to make this work."

"I don't want to think about tomorrow." They finish and clear the dishes. She leads him into the stateroom.

QUEEN VICTORIA BUILDING, SYDNEY, AUSTRALIA

John and Liz walk, hand in hand, along the third-floor shopping center. John's carrying their purchases. LCDR Greg Backes walks out of a hand crafts shop and stops, "What's up?"

John let's go of Liz's hand, "Liz Petrea, Greg Backes." He reaches back for her hand as she steps forward.

Liz, "Pleased to meet you."

Greg shakes her hand, "Pleased to meet you." He turns to John, "I've had something come up I need to talk to you about. Commander, could you give us a minute?" He moves John well away until they're alone, "What the fuck are you doing?"

"Nothing. Look, she's worried I'm going to get killed because I'm half Japanese."

"I was your best man less than three months ago."

"We're not dating."

"Don't you think it's fucking...what?"

"We're friends. She just lost her husband, too. I waited fifteen years for Lisa. Do you really think I'm looking for anyone else?"

"Don't hold hands."

"Yes, dad."

Liz, from down the hall, "Are you done arguing over me?"

John, "I believe we are."

Liz, "There's a bar downstairs. Let's get something to drink and talk."

After they've ordered and they're settled in, Liz asks, "Commander, are you pissed off at me?"

Greg, "The optics weren't great. That said, I want my friend to be happy."

Liz, "Do you want your friend to be alive?"

Greg flushes and he looks down. Then he lifts his head. "Oh."

John, "I'm not made of porcelain."

Liz, "I know, John, but you're not made of HY-80, either."

Greg, "What are you two? I'm confused."

John, "Friends, like I said. That is all I can handle right now."

Liz, "The same. Is he your friend, Commander?"

Greg, "My name is Greg. Yes, he's my friend. I've known John for fourteen years. I'm sorry, John, but I don't see anything Japanese when I look at you."

Liz, "Do you recognize that other people do?"

Greg nods, "Yeah."

Liz softens her voice, "Did you know Admiral Lee ordered him not to leave the ship alone?"

Greg looks at his friend, "No. John, why didn't you say?"

"I don't want to be a problem."

Greg, "Jesus Christ, John, you were never a problem. More than anything, you're the solution. Get off your fucking cross, we need the wood."

Liz grins, "Amen. Greg, you and I, we can't let him be alone out here. It isn't safe."

Greg, "When's your next duty day?"

"Tomorrow."

Greg, "Shit, me too."

John, "Guys."

Liz, "I'll explain this to Captain Tucker. He'll get it."

John, "Guys?"

Greg, "Are you in three section?"

Liz, "Yeah. I'll swap with the REA. He shouldn't have an issue with it."

John, "Can I talk, please?"

Liz turns to John, "No." She turns back to Greg, "He's going to have to do official stuff. We need to support that, too."

Greg, "No problem. On my end, I can clear the decks a bit. Anything where I have to be on board, John will want to be there anyway."

"Okay, Tucker and Johnson, very much, want our crews to work together. There are only three boats like ours in the world."

John, "Guys, you don't need to swap around duty days. I'll just stay on the boat."

Liz, "Won't work, John. You're an XO. You'll have official stuff you have to do. This way, we got you covered on any day."

Greg, "Liz, have you met our skipper?"

Liz, "Oh yes. We were eating lunch and a couple of pilot friends joined us. Poor John here had three beautiful women sitting with him. Commander asshole stormed in and started yelling at him for being 'unseemly'. Spike took him to task. It was beautiful."

Greg, "Who's Spike?"

Liz, "Lieutenant Commander Samantha Hunt, commander of the Black Knights squadron. She's an F-14 pilot with 35 kills. She doesn't suffer fools."

Greg, "What did Blunder-land do?"

John, "He said, 'excuse me,' and made a hasty retreat."

Greg, "You know, he'll never forgive you for that?"

"Yeah, I know. He hates me already. Thing is, he knows I can fire him at will. It tempers his behavior some."

Liz, "How?"

John, "USS Fulton. I served with Admiral Klindt for six eventful months and we became friends. He knows what is going on. Halsey, and his chief of staff, Captain Van Zandt, also know."

Liz, "How is he still in charge?"

John, "Where would we find a replacement?"

Liz, "You could…oh."

"Yeah, those optics aren't good. It's for that reason, I think we should just deal, for now."

Liz, "I'm pretty positive none of the guys I work with are sub qualified. I get it."

John, "Guys, I'll stay aboard tomorrow. It's too late to arrange anything tonight."

CHAPTER 15

S/V SEA BREESE, COVE WEST OF SYDNEY

0854, 08 February, 1942

Amy is tucked into Gary's left side, "I love you, luv."

Gary, "I love you, too."

"You're worried, aren't ya?"

"We need to talk about how we're going to make this work. I'm in contact with my grandparents in Minnesota. They would take you in, but during the war, we can't move you. I have no idea if the Navy will bring me back during the war, and it's going to last at least four more years. Can you wait four years for me?"

"I can wait as long as I must. Also, I can stay here while I wait. After the war, come get me."

"A lot can happen in four years." He rolls over and meets her gaze. "Mine is the best ship of its kind, but twenty percent of the men who served in the field I do died in WWII. It's a fact. I think I have a good chance, but it's warfare."

"I can't bear the thought of losing you." She hugs him.

"I understand, but we need to be realistic. Look, love. I'll give you the address of my grandparents, and I'll write them about you. If anything happens to me, they'll know and let you know."

"This scares me."

"I know. If you choose to be with me, it's what you're signing up for. Right now, I couldn't get out of it if I wanted to. After the war, I'm going to retire. After that, we have the rest of our lives together."

"Is that what you want, Gary?"

He smiles, "I do. I love you and I believe you're strong enough to do this. But, do you believe you're strong enough?"

She gives him a pensive look, starts to talk, then stops. Then, "It's going to be hard?"

"We'll only be able to stay in touch by letter, and those will take two to three months to go either way. You'll get nothing for months, then a pile all at once. I won't be able to tell you much, because what I do is classified. You'll hear about battles and be starved for information and fearing I will be lost. Nobody around you will understand. Maybe your mom will. It will take even longer to send a package either way. The whole thing will be an ongoing heart ache.

"Even when you do get a letter, you'll know it's from well in the past. This will be the hardest thing you'll ever do.

Amy is silent, her imagination working the images he's conjured, "I need to know what we will be."

"I love you, Amy. I want you for my wife."

"You have to say it."

"Amy, will you marry me? Will you wait four long engagement years during an awful war to be my wife?"

She smiles, gazing into his eyes, "No. luv. I will not do that. But, if you marry me now, here, while you are in port, I will wait as long as I must and follow you anywhere I must and do anything I must to be with you forever."

Shocked, he shakes his head, "Are you sure, honey? It's going to be a long time, and what if you…"

"Shut up. I'm not like that. Got it?"

Gary smiles, and blows out a breath, "Okay, then. We better tell your folks and I'll need to tell…"

It's all he gets out as she wraps him up and smothers him in kisses.

USS SAN FRANCISCO

0832, 8 February, 1942

ST1 Mike Brown walks off the brow in his tropical whites and heads toward the gate. He sees Kichiro sitting on a bollard and looking into the distance. "Hey, Kiche!"

"Yeah."

"Kiche, what's up?" TM2 Kichiro looks up at Mike, his eyes puffy and black. One eye is nearly swollen shut. "Shit, Kiche, what happened?"

"I fucked up, Mike."

"What did you do?"

"I tried to drink in a white bar."

"What?"

"They got white bars and Aboriginal bars. I went into the wrong bar and they kicked the shit out of me."

"Let's go below and have Doc fix you up."

"He's not on board. Now, I'm for sure getting busted."

Mike takes Kichiro's hand and helps him stand. Kichiro gingerly lifts himself upright, wincing. "Let's go aboard the Horne. I saw the whole thing. No fucking way you're getting busted."

"Mike, you saw nothing."

"Come on, Kiche. Practice the story. I was down the street and couldn't stop it, but I hauled you out. We waited for Doc, but he didn't show."

"Okay." They go aboard the Horne and get directions to medical. Then Mike knocks, the HM2 on duty answers, "What's up?"

Mike, "We're on the San Francisco, but our doc is on liberty and my friend got beat up last night."

"You know, I have to report a liberty incident."

Kichiro, "I was stupid to walk into a white only bar."

The HM2, "The local's beat you up?"

Kichiro, "Yeah."

"You're the fourth I know of. No shame on you to report it and the command needs to know."

"Okay."

The corpsman gets him on the exam table and starts by checking his eyes, "You have a concussion."

"But everyone says I'm thick-headed."

"Thick-headed with thin skull. You have a concussion." The corpsman gently pushes on the swollen skin, "Sorry. No broken bones that I can feel." He turns to Brown, "ST1, can you wait outside? I need to strip him down to his skivvies."

"Why?"

"Did they only hit you in the face?"

"No."

"You could have internal injuries."

"Okay. My hand hurts, too."

Brown steps out and Kichiro strips down with the help of the corpsman. Though his skin tone is fairly dark, the bruising on his body is obvious. The corpsman helps him back on the exam table, "Now, I'm going to check your internal organs. You have to tell me if it hurts and how it hurts, okay?"

"It all already hurts, man."

"Where?

Kichiro points at the bruising on his left side, where it is the worst.

"I see. I need you to exhale when I tell you and try to relax, okay?" The corpsman begins his examination.

"Oh, mother fucker, that hurts."

"Right. That's your left kidney. I need to make a phone call."

Mike, outside medical hears, "Lay stretcher bearers to medical." He opens the door. He sees the corpsman putting Kichiro into a gown. "ST1, get his stuff. You're going to the hospital with him."

"Roger that, Doc. What's wrong?"

"Not sure. The hospital should confirm that it's a lacerated or bruised kidney. He may have some broken ribs, too. He definitely has a concussion. Go with him. I'll take care of your command."

USS SAN FRANCISCO

Morrison is writing letters at his desk when there's a knock on his door. "Enter."

The HM2 from the Horne comes in, "Sir, you have a sailor, TM2 Kichiro, who was assaulted last night. He was brought to me. I just sent him to the Royal Prince Alfred Hospital. I can't issue a diagnosis. Only a doctor can do that, sir. But he has a concussion and I'm very concerned about his left kidney."

Morrison writes down the name of the hospital, "Thank you, corpsman. Do you know what happened?"

"He said that without realizing it, he went into a 'whites only' bar."

"Is he alone?"

"A ST1 is with him. I didn't catch the name."

"No problem. Thank you." Morrison is wearing his khakis, so he grabs the correct cover and strides into control and picks up the 1MC, "Navigator, lay to control." Then he picks up a phone.

"Horne quarterdeck. How can I help you, sir or ma'am?"

"This is Commander Morrison from the San Francisco. Do you have a driver available?"

"Yes, sir. He's standing by to take you to the hospital."

"Thank you. I'll be up in a sec." He sees Backes walk into control, "Greg, Kichiro got assaulted. They're taking him to this hospital." He hands him the address, "I need you to inform the captain."

"Are you going alone?"

"What else can I do?" Greg nods and Morrison shoots up the ladder and across the brow. He gets in the back of the sedan, "Royal Prince Alfred Hospital."

"Yes, sir."

A few minutes later the car pulls up to the hospital. Morrison, "I have the number to call for you. Go ahead and get back to your duties."

"Yes, sir. Sir, I hope he's alright."

"Me, too." He walks into admitting and looks around. People are staring at him. He says loudly, "One of my sailors was just admitted. Where do I need to go?"

A woman at a desk raises her hand and he walks over, "I'm Lieutenant Commander Morrison, USN. Do you know what room he's in?"

The woman looks him over, "Who are you?"

A man in a summer suit walks up beside him. "I'm Lieutenant Commander Morrison, the XO of the San Francisco. I'm looking for Scott Kichiro. He's a TM2 on my vessel."

"Oh, let me check."

The man says, "Commander, I'm Special Agent Donald Matthew, NIS." He shows his badge and offers his hand.

Morrison takes his hand, "I didn't know we had the Naval Investigative Service in 1942."

"We didn't. Like you, I came back with the carrier. I'm attached to the Secretaries office while they stand one up. What do you know about your sailor?"

The woman says, "Mister Kichiro is in room 407. The lifts are down the corridor to your right."

Morrison, "Thank you." The two men go to the elevators. "I know he's from Guam. He's a torpedoman and a very good one. He's never had a liberty incident that I'm aware of. Word I received; he was assaulted for entering a 'whites only' bar."

"Well, I suppose we'll see."

When they get to Kichiro's room and knock, Mike Brown comes out. "Sir, he got beat up, bad. The doctor is with him right now."

Matthews, "Did you see it?"

Brown, "Who are you?"

Matthews shows his badge, "Matthew, NIS."

Brown, "No, sir. I saw him after. Sir, he was with TM3 Trindle. Trindle was chatting up a girl, so they split up. He decided to try a different bar."

Matthews is writing it all down. Then, the doctor comes out.

"And who do we have here?"

Brown, "Dr. Davison, this is my executive officer, Commander Morrison, and this is Special Agent Matthew. He's a Navy investigator."

"I see. My patient needs to rest. He has cracked or broken ribs, a bruised left kidney, a bruised heart, possible liver damage, and serious concussion. He also has three broken fingers in his left hand. Officer, I would like him left alone for a bit."

Matthews, "Is he sedated?"

Davison, "Of course not, he has a concussion."

Matthews, "Then, I need to talk to him."

Davison, "No. You will wait. You have no jurisdiction here. Let him recover a bit. There's a waiting room down the hall. Thank you, gentleman." He leaves.

Once Davison is gone, Matthews moves toward the door and Morrison puts a hand on his arm, "Special Agent, it will wait."

"The kid is awake. I need to interview him."

"The doctor was clear. The waiting room is over there."

"Why?"

"I'll not have his recovery endangered by you. Not going to happen. We follow the doctor's orders."

Brown, "Special Agent, my XO knows who-flung-dug and origami. I wouldn't mess with him."

"Who-flung-dung?" Matthews smiles, "Okay?" He turns and walks toward the waiting room, Morrison and Brown following. "You know, Commander, if I chose to, I could prosecute you."

Morrison, "And explain to Admiral Halsey how I temporarily delayed you in your duties based on the orders of an attending physician, and by doing so, slightly slowed a criminal case you have no authority to prosecute? Do what you have to do."

Brown, "Sir? I need to tell you something."

"Yes."

"I told Kiche to say I saw the assault, because of the captain."

"Were you anywhere near the bar where this happened?"

"No, sir. I ate out and came back to the boat. I just don't want to mess up a criminal case."

Matthews, "What's wrong with your captain, petty officer?"

Brown, "Special Agent, he's a fuck head that has it out for Kichiro. Kiche is a good guy and an excellent torpedoman. He prevented a hot run during combat where we had an active torp in a tube. Did the captain ever thank him? No. He tried to mast him as we were leaving Pearl on a trumped up, bull-shit charge. He bad mouths Kiche in front of the crew. Other than having the bedside manner of a tyrannosaurus rex and the leadership ability of Jack the Ripper, the skipper is great."

Matthews looks at Morrison, a question in his eyes. Morrison, "ST1 Brown is accurate and succinct, as usual. Halsey knows about the issues with Commander Cumberland. It's Halsey's decision."

Matthews, "What do you think, Commander?"

"I think I'm his XO and all of this begs the point. What are you going to do about Australians beating up my sailor?"

"I'll work with the local law enforcement."

An orderly comes in, "Commander, Mr. Kichiro has asked for you."

"Thank you." Morrison and Matthews stand. Morrison looks at him, "I'll let you know."

"I go in first."

"No, you don't. He's not a suspect in any crime."

"You don't know that."

"Neither do you. I have a generally positive view of NIS. Don't give me a reason to adjust that opinion down."

"What would you do?"

That's the thing, Special Agent. You don't know what I can do, so, let's work together on this."

Morrison leaves and Matthews sits down. He looks over at Brown, "Is he bluffing?"

"Commander Morrison, sir?"

"Yes."

"Sir, have you ever heard of the western writer, Louis L'Amour?'

"Yes."

"One of my favorite Louis L'Amour quotes is, 'Lie to a liar, for lies are his coin; steal from a thief, for that is easy; lay a trap for the trickster and catch him at the first attempt; but beware of an honest man who knows he is right and just keeps coming.'" Brown pulls out a paperback and starts reading.

Matthews, "Okay, but what does that mean?"

Brown looks at the agent for a long while, stretching the stare out, "It means, a guy like you best not fuck with Commander Morrison. I've known him for years and I've never known him to lie."

Morrison walks into Kichiro's room. Kichiro is laying on his back, his face turned to the wall.

"Kiche?"

He starts, "Um, sir?"

"How are you?"

"I hurt like hell, sir. Do you need a statement?"

"We will, eventually. Right now, I want to know how you feel?"

"I pissed blood, sir. Like a fucking vampire, or something. It hurt like a mother-fucker."

"I bet."

"I'm sorry, sir."

"For what?"

"They had a sign. I thought it was stupid. Also, I figured it was only meant for their native people. I thought it was okay."

"I would have thought the same thing."

"Yeah, wow. Like, I kinda forgot you're Japanese."

"It's okay. I don't sound like Jerry Lewis in his stupid movies."

Kiche chuckles, then winces, "No, you don't. Every once in a while, I would like to hear you say, Godzilla."

Morrison smiles, "I just haven't seen him yet. I need to know if you're up to an interview. I'll try to pile everyone who needs to hear it in at once, so you only have to go through it once. If you need to stop the interview, just let me know."

"Okay."

"Now, something you should know. Brown told us he told you to lie about him seeing the incident. Please, don't lie. Okay?"

"I won't sir."

"I, or Brown, will be back in a bit." When he gets out of the room, he sees Cumberland navigating toward the room with two uniformed law enforcement officers. He changes direction, "Officers, I'm John Morrison, TM2 Kichiro's XO. I take it you've met Commander Cumberland?"

"We got acquainted in the lift."

"Sir, gentlemen, if you would come with me. I have one other person I need you to meet before we see Kichiro." At the desk, "Could you see if the doctor is available to meet with law enforcement?"

"Yes, Commander."

Morrison takes them to the waiting room. "Officers, Commander Cumberland, this is Special Agent Matthew of the Naval Investigation Service and ST1 Mike Brown. We didn't catch your names."

"I'm Sergeant Louis and my colleague is Sergeant Cass."

Morrison says to Brown, "Stand outside his door. No one but medical until we sort this out."

"Yes, sir."

Smiling, Cumberland asks Morrison, "So, what has our troublemaker done to get himself here?"

Morrison, "Gentlemen, could you give me a moment with

my commanding officer?" They step out, "Sir, you're looking at this wrong."

Cumberland continues smiling, "What do you mean? He got into a bar fight and had his ass handed to him."

"Sir, please, that is not what happened. He walked into a 'whites only' bar and was assaulted. It's aggravated assault, not a bar fight. Please, don't fuck up a criminal investigation. It will just spill all over your command and make us both look bad. Besides, if we don't fuck this up, you're getting what you want: Kichiro off the ship."

"You're certain?"

"Fairly certain, sir. That's for law enforcement to determine. Understand, sir, we're lucky he's not dead, and you being all smiles when it's your guy in the hospital makes you look... sir, the optics aren't good."

Cumberland looks at Morrison. The smile disappears and he assumes a concerned manner. Just then, the doctor walks up. Morrison introduces everyone. Morrison, "Doctor Davison, could you describe the injuries to Petty Officer Kichiro and share your conclusions as to how they happened."

"Of course. Gentlemen, Petty Officer Kichiro has several cracked or broken ribs on his left side and left upper back. His left kidney has suffered significant blunt trauma. It will be some time before we can determine whether any function remains. His heart is bruised, also from blunt trauma. We are assessing possible liver damage and will not know for certain how bad it is for two or three days. He has a significant concussion caused by blunt trauma to the rear of the head. We're waiting for x-ray results to determine if there is any skull damage or other broken bones. He also has three broken fingers in his left hand. I think we should take pictures of his bruises, as several of the pictures indicate the tread pattern of the shoes worn by his assailants.

"Based on the localized nature of the injuries to his left side and back, it appears that the petty officer was hit first from behind on the head. He went to the ground and curled into the fetal position in an attempt to protect his vital organs. At this point, his assailants started kicking and stomping on him for some time. I'm speculating, but it looks like the broken fingers were caused by his placing his hands over his face, and then his assailants stomped down onto his hands and head."

Cumberland, "So, it wasn't a bar fight?"

Doctor Davison, "Not as I see it. In a bar fight, the injuries are to the head, face, and frontal torso. Also, in a bar fight, the injuries are not localized. In my experience, the injuries to your petty officer are indicative of aggravated assault; perhaps, attempted murder. That is for the officer's and the Crown prosecutor to determine."

Detective Sergeant Louis, "What was his blood alcohol content?"

Davison, "Point zed two."

Louis, "Can we have a signed statement, Doctor Davison?"

"Of course."

Louis, "May we speak with him?"

"Keep it brief. He's weak and will tire quickly. Also, please keep it very calm while in here. An increase in blood pressure with a lacerated kidney could be fatal."

The doctor leads them into Kichiro's room. Kichiro's eyes widen when he sees Cumberland. Louis introduces himself and Sergeant Cass. He calmly questions Kichiro. "Could you just run through the events as they happened?"

Kichiro, "Yes, sir. My liberty buddy was TM3 Trindle. He was talking to this girl in the Barrel House. I was bored, so

I walked across the street to another bar. It was something coup. It was an Australian word. Anyway, I like the sound of the music, so I walked in. This big guy stepped in front of me and said, "Whites only." I started to back up 'cause I didn't want trouble. Something hit me a fucking whack on the head. I fell down, so I just curled up and they started kicking me. Then somebody shouted, "Enough," and they ran off. I got myself up and headed back to the boat. The doc wasn't in. I didn't want to get in trouble, so I just waited on the pier. ST1 Brown found me."

Louis, "Did you tell the doctor what happened to you?"

"No. I just said I got beat up. He tisk, tisked, and said I was sorely used."

Cass, "Do you think you could identify your attackers?"

"The big guy in front of me, yeah. He had a block head and really long hair for around here. It wasn't that well cared for, either. I mean, it was stringy, like he hadn't had a bath. Oh, and he was a white dude."

Louis, "What is a dude?"

Kichiro, "What? Dude? A dude is a guy. A man. It doesn't mean anything special."

Louis, "Thank you. Can you think of any other relevant detail?'

Kichiro, "The corpsman said I was the fourth non-white sailor to be assaulted."

Louis, "We'll figure this out and put an end to it. Thank you for your help, Petty Officer." The officers leave.

Kichiro looks at Morrison, "When can I go back to the boat?"

"They're waiting for test results, Kiche. It'll be at least a couple of days. You don't want to rush it."

"But, sir, I'll be able to get back, right?"

Cumberland, "No. You're done."

Morrison, "Sir, could you give us a minute?"

"Tell him the truth. I'm going to talk to Halsey's staff about getting us another torpedoman." Cumberland walks out.

"Sir?"

"Truth, Kiche, it's going to take a while for you to recover. We'll be transferring you off the ship for now, but that doesn't mean you're done."

"What does it mean?"

"How many people on earth know what you do about torpedoes?"

"Not many."

"Could you help us build new torpedoes?"

"Yeah, sure, except for the electronics. I know fuck all about electronics."

"We got blueprints for that. We have the specifications for everything. With you, we also have someone who knows how to put it all together and test it."

Kichiro tears up, "I'm a Guamanian second class. No one is going to give a fuck about what I know. No one cares about a second class, third class citizen."

"I care, Kiche. Let me work it for you. Trust me."

"Yes, sir."

"Focus on the job in front of you. Focus on getting yourself better, okay?"

"Yes, sir."

"I'll see what Mike needs and talk to your chief. Take care,

Kiche."

"Thank you, sir."

When Morrison gets into the corridor, he finds Chief Kennedy and several torpedomen waiting and talking to Brown. "Guys, he's tired, but seeing visitors. I just had to tell him he'll be transferred off the boat. We're going to take care of him."

Trindle, "So, captain asshole finally gets what he wants."

Morrison, "Trindle, let's focus on taking care of Kiche, okay?"

"Yes, sir."

Morrison phones for a car.

CHAPTER 16

AMY RANDOLPH'S HOME

1615, 08 February, 1942

Gary and Amy walk into the house. "Hi Mom, Dad." She hugs them. Gary stands back. Grinning, joyous, shows her parents a small diamond ring on her left ring finger, "We're engaged."

He mom's mouth opens as wide as her eyes, immediately followed by a smile and a hug. Her dad's head swivels toward Gary, lips tight and eyes narrowed. Gary makes eye contact and holds it.

Judy, "Oh my God, Amy. Oh my God. You have to tell me all about it."

Andrew, "Excuse me, dear." He let's go of Amy and Judy, and walks toward Gary.

Judy, "Dear."

Amy, "Dad."

Andrew, "Judy, the young man and I are going to the pub."

Judy, "Dear, your daughter loves him."

"Our daughter doesn't know what love is. Come." Gary follows him out the door. Andrew is silent as they get into his Holden badged Chevy sedan. He puts the car in gear, backs up, and starts down the street. Gary holds the silence as they drive to a local pub. In the parking lot, Andrew says, "What kinda fucking game are you playing at?"

Gary holds Andrews gaze, "I love her."

Andrew, "I don't give a fuck. You're just another fucking, randy bugger who wants to shag my daughter. I forbid it."

"Sir, I very much hope I can change your mind. It would rip her to pieces if I have to break it off."

"Why didn't you ask me first?"

"Fuck. You're right, sir. I'm from 1990. It isn't a thing that is done much anymore. I should have, sir, and I'm sorry."

"Do you understand why a marriage is impossible between you two?"

"No, sir."

"I'll not have you haul our only child off to America, where we'll never see her again. That would break her mother's heart."

"Sir, after the war, travel becomes easy and cheap. If we live in America, I'll promise to bring her, and our children to see you, or bring you and her mother to see us. That said, I effectively have no family in the states. My dad is a kid. My grandparents have never met me. It seems to me it would make more sense for us to live here."

"What would you do here?"

"Sir, I can't go into details, of course, but mine is a new type of ship. My expertise as a mechanic is rare. There are only thirty or forty people on earth who would be my equal or better. Maybe not that many. After the war, my skills will be in demand. I would very much prefer to make a home here, raise my children here, and visit my family in the states from time to time."

"How many Australians know what you know?"

"As far as I know, not one."

"And Australia will need your expertise?"

"They will."

"And you're willing to live here?"

"I'd actually prefer it."

"Why?"

"One: She knows her family and I don't really know mine. Two: You guys are important to her and I want her to be happy. Three: Here, I'm part of an established community of relationships. Back home, I'm inserting myself in a place where I don't really belong."

Andrew, "Well, son, let's go have a beer so I can introduce you to my mates."

They get out of the car, and Gary look at him over its top, "Do I have your blessing, sir?"

Andrew comes around and gives him a hug, "You do."

USS SAN FRANCISCO

Morrison is on the phone, on hold. A paper on his desk has seven phone numbers, with four scratched out. He finally hears, "Klindt."

"Sir, this is Commander Morrison in Australia. I've a situation that letters are too slow to solve."

"Go."

"Torpedoman second class, Scott Kichiro, from Guam, was assaulted in a local pub and injured too badly to continue on the ship. I don't think he would be safe on the carrier, either. I would like to send him to you."

"How good is he?"

"He's one of my very best."

"So, he knows our torpedoes?"

"He's not a chemical or electronic engineer, but his knowledge of components, manufacture, assembly, and testing is encyclopedic."

"I can use him. In fact, I desperately need him. However, a second class is of no use to me. We'll get to that. What's happening with Cumberland?"

"He's still a pain in the ass. In normal circumstances, I would recommend his relief, but we've been working together okay. He absolutely hates Kichiro. When he came to the hospital, he was actually smiling. When I pulled him aside and pointed out that his conduct was inappropriate, he moderated it."

"Why does he hate Kichiro?"

"Because Kichiro is outspoken, expert, and brown-skinned."

"I see. I'm starting to run out of patience with that man."

"The problem, sir, is we have no one to relieve him."

"We have you."

"Sir, the optics are terrible and my race goes against me."

He hears Klindt take a deep breath, "We need to fix that. We're also standing up a new school to train officers and enlisted people in our specialty. They'll be needed. Keep me posted on Cumberland. Now, for Kichiro. Before you get underway, the young man needs a new sea bag and a promotion. I want you to take care of it. It'll have to come out of your pocket, so tell me what it costs, and I'll pay you back. You're to commission him as a lieutenant before he walks out of that hospital. If you get underway before he can safely leave the hospital, attach him TAD in transit to the US consulate's Naval attache until he can leave. Update his service record and ship it to me as soon as you can. Do you have all that?"

"Yes, sir." He gives a verbatim readback as nukes are trained to do.

"Do you know how the Fife is coming along?"

"No, sir. I don't."

"I would like you to make the acquaintance of its captain. Her name is Commander Laura Wakefield."

"Okay, sir. I and Commander Petrea have made our acquaintance. We're cross training our enlisted and sharing training resources."

"Good. She's sharp. John, she lost her husband. They were a match, like you and Lisa."

"She said. We...we've been sharing ears. She seems a safe person to confide in."

"She is. Good. I'm delighted when a couple of my mentees help each other."

"Thank you, sir."

"I want your feedback on Commander Wakefield. She's a nuke mustang, but I've never met her. A few months ago, she was a JG. I would like you to take her under your wing, if possible."

"Yes, sir."

"Do you think Kichiro could pass the board to earn his gold pin?"

"Not as a nuke, sir, but he knows the systems. Backes, Miller, and I can conduct the board with your permission."

"Please do."

"Yes, sir. By the way, congratulations on your promotion."

"Thank you."

"Sir, is there any news from Washington I should know?"

"None I can share over this medium. We're working as fast as we can."

"I understand."

"Give me a call at this number when you have everything set up. Good day, John, and good luck."

RANDOLPH HOUSE

Gary and Andrew pull into the driveway and get out of the car. Gary passes a serious belch and Andrew laughs, "Good beer, mate?"

"The best beer. Reason number four."

They walk into the house and Andrew stumbles toward his daughter. He puts a hand on each side of her face, "You have my blessing, daughter. Your man is a fair dinkum, right fine, cunt."

Amy starts crying, "I love you, Dad." Judy walks into the hug and they hold each other, all three crying.

Andrew, "I love you, too. Momma, do you have some tucker on? We need to feed our boy before we ship him off to duty. He has to be aboard tonight."

"I have it on, my darling man."

USS SAN FRANCISCO

0830, 9 February, 1942

Morrison dresses in his tropical whites. There's a knock on

the door, "Enter."

The messenger, ST3 Guthrie, says, "Sir, that girl commander is waiting for you on the brow."

"That girl commander has a name."

"Yes, sir. Why are you hanging out with her?"

"She's the reactor training assistant on the Vinson."

"Oh, it's a nuke thing."

"Tell her to come down."

"Sir, she's wearing a skirt."

"Okay. Thank you, Guthrie. I need Kichiro's sea bag put in my car."

"Yes, sir."

"Are you okay, Guthrie?"

"Just missing my girls, sir."

"I thought you would already have a harem here."

He turns red, "No, sir."

"If you need to talk, I'll be back tonight."

"Thank you, sir." Guthrie goes.

Morrison gives himself a quick look in the mirror, grabs a folder, and leaves the boat. When he gets to the brow, he sees Petrea waiting for him in her tropical whites. "I heard about your torpedoman."

"Yeah. I need to sort out some things for him today." They get in the car, "I need to update his wardrobe."

"Why?"

"Admiral Klindt. I talked to him last night."

"On the phone?"

"Yeah. It was a challenge to find him."

"Fill in the pieces, please."

"Kiche is too injured to deploy with us. When he's capable of traveling, we're to ship him off to Klindt's office in D.C. He's going to build new torpedoes for us."

"That doesn't explain the wardrobe change. Wait, it does. Klindt wants to commission him."

"To Lieutenant. The base CDO recommended a tailor shop. That's where we'll go. No way we can get what he'll need off a shelf. Klindt also wants him to stand his sub board. He'll never qual nuke without power school, but we're the only nuke boat. I need to give him the good news at the hospital."

Liz, "Do you think he'll pass?"

"All, except maybe, the tactical stuff. He's sharp."

"Okay. At thirteen hundred we have a high tea with Sam and Gloria. They're bringing a couple of other people."

"Okay. This afternoon, I also need to visit the Fife."

"It's in dry dock getting a new bridge. Why do we need to go there?"

"Have you met her captain?"

"No. I know the ship got decapitated by a missile and a female lieutenant saved the ship and got promoted to command. Oh, Klindt, again."

"Yep. He asked me to offer my services as a mentor. Might I suggest you do the same?"

"Sure. Do you know what Klindt is up too?"

Morrison, "If you think about it, it's kind of obvious. He's the right person, in the right position to do it, too."

"I get it. Do you think he might succeed?"

"He's the only person who could. Frankly, I'm delighted to play my part, however it plays out."

Petrea, "Yeah, me too. So, we take care of your guy. Is that where we're going?"

"Yes, to arrange the tailor first, then give him his sea bag and the good news."

"Let's go back to the Vinson. I can get him a set of bars and some other officer uniform items, like shoulder boards and a combination cover."

"Any chance you could scrounge up bridge coat buttons?"

"I'll try, but that's a tall order."

They drive to the Vinson and he helps her in their scavenger hunt. Two hours later, they leave with everything. The next stop is the tailor. They agree to a price for a full sea bag, including summer and winter dinner dress, and Morrison pays the bill. Then they go to the hospital.

Morrison carries the two bags of gear up to Kichiro's room. He knocks and enters. Kichiro is lying in bed reading a newspaper, "Hi, boss."

"How are you doing?"

"Fantastic. Ready to report for duty."

"What did the doc say?"

"He's still waiting. I can muscle through this."

"I've got another plan for you."

"Shit."

"I talked to Admiral Klindt. He needs you."

"Me? Why me?"

"His organization is thin on qualified submariners. The problem is your rank. A second class can't get done what he needs to get done."

"Then I can go back on the boat?"

"Kichiro, do you trust me?"

"Yes, sir."

"Raise your right hand." Bewildered, Kichiro complies. Morrison opens the folder he brought and reads the oath. Kichiro, in dawning surprise, repeats it. When they finish, Petrea shows Kichiro the lieutenant's bars and pins it onto his pillow.

"Lieutenant, sir?"

"It's what Admiral Klindt told me to do, and I agree with him."

Kichiro starts crying, "Me, sir?"

"You."

"If only my wife could have seen this."

"I agree."

"I'll do my best, sir."

"I know you will. We brought your sea bag. I pulled out your enlisted stuff for the lucky bag. The tailor should be up shortly to measure you for your uniforms."

"Tailored uniforms? Sir, that will cost a fortune."

"Admiral Klindt is taking care of it. I'm getting you everything, except a sword. When you get a chance, you should get one when you get stateside."

"Why, sir."

"Because you'll be working for an Admiral. We have to assume you will be attending formal events. Now, I also bear some bad news. In a week, or two, you'll be standing your submarine officer board. Backes, Miller, and I will help you prepare. We'll also be sitting your board."

"But, sir, for a pin, I have to qualify all the watches and be a nuke."

"Not if you're going to serve in a diesel boat. That might be what he has in mind. He may also be thinking you'll have an easier time directing construction with a pin on your chest. Remember, the dolphins were approved in 1924, so folks now know what they mean."

"But, sir, can I really earn them? If I don't earn them, I don't want them."

"We'll have to cut some corners to get you qualified. Most of the stuff you already know. Keep in mind, when you return to sea, it will be to a new submarine class, or as a nuke officer on the San Francisco. Either way, you'll have to qualify the boat."

"Do we have a nuclear power school?"

"We do. I don't know if that is what you want, or what the Admiral wants. We'll have to play that by ear."

"Yes, sir."

The tailor comes in and Petrea steps out. Morrison helps him get the measurements. When the tailor is done and has gone, Morrison says, "One more thing. Cumberland will have a cow if he finds out about his. Let's keep him in the dark."

"Yes, sir." Kichiro smiles, "I think he would explode."

"Probably. I need you to rest now."

"Yes, sir."

Morrison puts Kichiro's rank bars in his bag and leaves.

Once out of the hospital, Petrea says, "That was a really good thing. It felt good."

"Yeah. Kiche is a good duck."

Morrison drives them to Olivia's Tea Garden south of downtown. Waiting outside are Gloria, Sam, and two men. One has the bone structure of a Native American, and the other is a guy of average height in a perfectly tailored and sharp uniform. All four are in aviation green uniforms.

Sam says, "Commander Morrison, Commander Petrea, our RIO's Eric Hawke and Byron Standley. Guys, John Morrison and Liz Petrea." They shake hands, then go into the tea room. A young woman seats them, "Do you need a minute to look over the menu?"

Sam asks, "Guys, to do you trust me?" They all nod. "Good. We'll have the high tea with the salmon, cucumber, and cheese. For tea's; Earl Grey, Darjeeling, and the China black. Thank you."

"Of course. It will be just a moment."

Sam grins at them, "Gentlemen, is this your first high tea?"

Eric and Byron nod, and John says, "No. Scotland."

She grins, "Okay, don't stick your pinky out. It's pretentious and silly. The sandwiches and scones are finger food. The cakes need a fork. These are fun, so relax."

Eric, "You're asking the impossible of Byron."

The pilots chuckle.

John, "Guys, can I ask your call signs?"

Erick, "I'm Puck."

Byron, "I'm GQ."

Liz, "Are you a Shakespeare fan?"

Eric, "Flight training roll call, 'Hawke, E.' Puck."

They laugh. Young ladies come out with the three tea pots, cups with saucers, cream, and milk. Sam, "I'll be the mother," and she serves the tea.

Gloria, "It's a shame other communities do not adopt call signs. Your captain would be officially known as 'Shit Head'."

John nearly spits out his tea.

GQ, "We heard about your rating who was assaulted. How's he doing?"

John, "He's rather upset that he's being transferred to D.C. We're still waiting to see how bad his kidney and liver were damaged. Oh, and he isn't a rating anymore. I swore him in as a lieutenant this morning."

GQ, "Why?"

Sam, "Klindt."

John looks at her surprised, then smiles, "Yeah. He's reporting to Admiral Klindt's staff."

Sam, "Oh, good."

John, "You know him?"

Sam, "I was part of Captain Johnson's brain trust. Admiral Klindt ran it."

Liz, "When Klindt got his stars, he had Sam pin them on."

Sam, "John, do you know him?"

"Yeah, we served together on the sub tender Fulton. He was a lieutenant and I was a JG. We became good friends."

Sam, "And Liz, you served under him?"

Liz, "Yeah. "We've figured it out. Have you?"

"He outright told me. Yeah, I get it."

Puck, "Get what?"

John, "Admiral Klindt is choosing officers to mentor and asking those officers to choose more."

Puck, "Does this club have a secret hand shake?"

Sam, "No, but it does have plenty of meetings."

GQ, "You four are in? Are we being invited?"

Sam, "You are. Both of you."

GQ, "I doubt he wants me."

Sam, "I want you in the club, Byron, so you're in the club, unless you want out. If that is what you want, that's fine."

GQ makes eye contact with her, "I want in."

Puck, "Me, too, if Indians are invited."

John, "Native Americans are needed, Eric. You're probably the highest ranking Native American in military service. I'm sure I'm the highest-ranking person with Asian blood. It's central to what he's doing."

GQ, "So, he's trying to integrate the Navy. I'm for that. Where do I fit in?"

The food is brought in on three-tiered silver services.

Sam, "As the Navy ramps up the war, it has less than three thousand pilots of all types. By the end of the war, we'll have twenty times that number. When we came back, we had about eighty pilots and flight officers, and we've had losses. Who's going to lead all the new jet squadrons? Some will be led by very competent 1940's naval aviators. Most will be led by successful 1990's aviators. We understand how to use the technology. I hate counting kills, but we four are leading the pack. Our squadron is leading the pack. That will matter. If we don't screw up, all three of you will have your own squadron within a year or two. John, you'll have your own boat. Liz, if you don't end up in a design bureau, you'll have your own command."

Liz, "A woman?"

Sam grins, "I have my command. Nimitz made that decision, by the way, not Klindt."

John, "Liz, what kind of command would you want?"

Liz, "I can't command a carrier, and I couldn't serve on a submarine. I don't know if it could be done."

Sam, "That's what you don't want."

Liz, "I would have to think about it. I have trouble imagining me running a battleship."

John, "Sam is right. Wakefield has her command. If you want it, one is coming for you."

"Okay, John, but I don't feel ready."

Sam laughs, "Oh, I know that one." She's quiet, looking out the window, "You know, Admiral Lee and I had that conversation. You're never ready. No one is. He said that when you look up to those leaders above you, you think you see wise, and maybe even, noble people. What you are really seeing are old people trying really, really hard not to screw up. What matters is character. You see, those people who take command as their right, instead of their duty, are unsuited for command. Those people who worry primarily about their subordinates, and how to take care of them, have the right character and attitude for command. Guys, with the right leaders, that have the right attitudes, and serve in the right positions, we can change the Navy for the better, and give our country, and the world a better future. That's what Admiral Klindt is working for; nothing less than a better world."

CHAPTER 17

USS SAN FRANCISCO

1530, 9 February, 1942

Mallory is checking the alignment on one of the pumps when Gustaf sits down beside him, "Dude, where have you been?"

"I've been busy, why?"

"You fucking disappeared with that red-head and I ain't hardly seen you since. Does she put out, or something?"

"What happened to you and the blonde?

"We talked a while. We walked the Victoria market and I bought her lunch at a little place. After that, she took me to her house. It's way west of here. Anyway, her dad came home when we were making out on the couch. He had a fucking cow and threw me out. I wasn't feeling her up or anything. We were just kissing."

"I told you they were nice girls. So, you haven't seen her again?"

"Oh no. We met yesterday. I took her shopping and now I'm broke. What happened to your red-head? Did she part her legs for you?"

Mallory, "Will you stop with the fuck language."

"Why? You're not fucking marrying her, are you?"

"Drop it."

"You are. The president of the he-man woman hater's club is getting hitched. My God. She must have been an incredible fuck."

In a flash, Mallory has Gustaf by his shirt front, and is picking him up, one-handed, until Gustaf's feet are off the deck. He holds him there for a moment, "Don't fucking talk about my wife that way. Clear?"

"Clear man. Sorry."

"Yeah, you are."

"Dude, I was just fucking around. I didn't know."

"Well, now you do."

"You said wife. Are you already married?"

"No, it's in four days. Wankowski is standing up for me. Her best friend is standing up for her. That gives us time to go to the consulate after."

"Are you going to send her home?"

"No, not during the war. When it's over, I'll come get her."

"The last time it didn't end until 1945."

"I know. I make it to twenty next December. I know they'll keep me to the end. By then, I should be a chief, or senior chief, with over twenty-two. That retirement is pretty good."

"Did her dad approve?"

"Yeah, I got his blessing. He's really cool and he really loves Amy. He loves Amy like I love my boys. She's so different from Sissy."

"Where did you propose to her?"

"On a sail boat. I asked her to marry me after the war. That way, if she gave up on me, there's no paper involved. She said no. She'd only marry me if we did it now. She's something."

"Cool. I'm happy for you. Can you teach me how to align motors?"

"Sure."

WOOLWICH DOCK, WEST OF SYDNEY

1710, 09 February, 1942

It takes Morrison a couple of hours to drive to the dock yard. The Royal Australian Navy gate guard checks their ID and lets them through. As they drive up, they can see the work being done on the destroyer. The new bridge hasn't been installed yet and there is an erector set of metal pieces on the dock side. A crane is lifting components into place where the bridge used to be.

Morrison, "Damn. Do you know what happened?"

Petrea, "Just that it took a missile in the Japanese attack."

A yard worker runs up as they leave their car and hands them each a hard hat. The watch at the foot of the brow lets them pass, and they go aboard. As they step onto the Fife, they salute the flag, then the quarterdeck watch, and present their ID. Petrea, "Request to come aboard and speak with Commander Wakefield."

The quarterdeck watch studies their ID, "Come aboard."

Morrison, "Is Commander Wakefield aboard?"

"Yes, sir. She's in a meeting in the chief's mess." He gives directions.

Morrison, "Not the wardroom?"

"The wardroom was under the bridge."

"Understood." They meet three civilians leaving shortly before they get to the hatch for the chief's mess. Petrea knocks, and they enter.

Wakefield looks up, a confused look on her face. She stands and offers a hand, "Commander Wakefield. Can I help you?"

Petrea shakes her hand, "Liz Petrea, RTA on the Vinson."

Morrison shakes Wakefield's hand, "John Morrison, XO of the San Francisco."

Wakefield smiles, "Coffee is over there. How can I help you?"

Morrison, "Can we reverse that? How can we help you?"

"Unless you have a miracle or two, I'm not sure."

John sips his coffee, "Good coffee."

"You can't have my yeoman," Wakefield smiles.

John, "I wouldn't think of it. Do you know Admiral Klindt?"

"He was the RO on the Vinson. I know he left in Hawaii, but that's about it."

Liz, "He has a third star and an interesting gig. His title is Vice CNO for Special Projects, and NAVSEA-08."

"Wow. But, where do I fit in?"

John, "I served with him when he was a lieutenant and I was a JG. He's been mentoring me, Liz, and about a dozen other officers, especially minority and female officers."

"Again, where do I fit in?"

Liz, "I've no doubt that what you are doing is hard as hell. Important, rewarding, but hard. Might it give you a little peace of mind to know you have a friend who sits next to the CNO and advices the President directly?"

Wakefield's eyes widen and her mouth falls open, then shuts with a snap. "What goal is he working toward. Nothing is ever free."

Liz, "As a start, he wants to integrate the Navy and create protective legislation for women and minorities in the work place."

John, "There are times when knowing the struggles of people on the ground, as well as their successes is useful to a guy who's trying to get Congress to move forward with legislation. Also, by helping the next generation of leaders succeed and grow, he's building a better Navy."

Wakefield, "So, he's looking for spy's in the ranks?"

Liz, "No, Commander, he isn't some J. Edgar Hoover building a blackmail ring. He's in charge of all the new technology. He can fast track what we need."

"Like?"

John, "Like what is your highest priority, torpedoes or AS-ROCs?"

"ASROCs."

John, "Do you assume the Navy knows that?"

"Oh, probably not."

"They will tomorrow, because I'll pass that along. They're building new ships like crazy. What systems on your ship would be critical to the success of the new destroyers?"

"Number one is bow and towed sonar. If you can't find them, you can't kill them. After that, it's the torpedo systems, ASROC and ship launched. Guns and missiles are secondary, but should be fitted."

John's taking notes.

"You're going to share all this?"

"Yes. You're determining our national ship policy."

"What if I'm fucking it up?"

Liz, "You're a nuke. Who's the person most likely to understand a problem, and the best solution?"

"The person closest. Okay, I see your point. Did you two just decide to come out here and recruit me?"

John, 'Oh, hell no. Admiral Klindt sent me. Not that I wouldn't have, eventually. I was just too myopically focused on my own issues. That, and I'm a sub guy. You folks are targets."

Wakefield laughs, "A target with teeth."

John, "True. Do you want to talk with him? I have his office number?"

Liz, "It's about 0330 in Washington."

John, "I meant later."

Wakefield, "I'm sure he doesn't want to hear from me."

John, "He made a point of sending us out here to talk to you."

Liz, "So, another thing to think about. Like John and I, you are training the next generation of Navy leaders."

"Why would my people be special?"

John, "Your boat, with the Jarrett, are the only modern surface ships with an anti-submarine suite. They're already building destroyers with the modern equipment. Your XO should get his own command soon. Choose your next XO from your crew. If no one is ready, start looking around. Start shopping for sharp officers. Klindt can help you there. Given that every single competent officer in your wardroom, along with your sharpest enlisted, will likely achieve command, this ship is really the Fife school of warfare. As captain, you get to decide what that will look like."

"John, is your captain doing the same?"

"My captain is a tyrant with anger management issues, so no. I'm having to carry that load while dealing with him."

"Why haven't you relieved him?"

"Halsey and his staff know about the issues. The issue is my race. The 1942 Navy isn't sure yet that they can trust me."

Liz, "Halsey cares more about competence then he does skin tone. You're responsible for your command."

John, "Laura, as you know, the captain is always in charge. I've been directed to share every incident with higher. In the end, it's Halsey's decision and he likes Cumberland's aggressiveness. When Cumberland is gone, the ship is going to need a great deal of healing, and in truth, I've been so close to the problem, I don't know if I can be the solution."

Laura, "Liz, you're the RTA?"

"I am."

Wakefield, "Talk to the RO and Captain Johnson. See if you can swap two or three officers and a few, newly commissioned, senior enlisted onto the sub for cross training. Give the reason as cross training to build a cadre of sub qualified officers. We may need Halsey's blessing, but I'm sure he'll see the merit. John, you get to sell it to your captain.

John says, "Will do."

Laura continues, "I've a handful of officers and crew I can swap, but none of them are nukes. When we do this, we commission the enlisted first. I have two I want to send to nuclear power school. Liz and I want stars in return. I've already done some swaps with the Jarrett. One other thing, I would like a refresher board when possible."

Liz, "You're a nuke officer?"

Laura, "Yeah, I'm a mustang. I got accepted and went back through the program as an officer. They gave me this as my first assignment, rather than a nuke boat because they wanted me to have a combatant craft tour."

Liz, "Does Klindt know you're a nuke?"

John, "He does."

Laura, "Liz, the officers I send your way, I want them trained on what your helicopters and S-3s do, as well. They're qualified SWO here. I want them qualified SWO on the carrier and I want them to get their flight officer pin on a helo or a S-3."

Liz, "I'll talk to Johnson and Holtz."

Laura, "Okay guys, have you had dinner?"

"No."

"Let's go eat."

KINGS CROSS, SOUTH OF GARDEN ISLAND NAVAL BASE

Commander Cumberland walks past bars filled with sailors. The shore patrol salutes as they pass him. A teenage boy comes up, "Admiral, are you looking for a girl? I know where the best girls are. Clean, Admiral. The best in Sydney."

"I ain't an admiral."

"That's okay, sir. Still, you're a man. You gotta want a shag."

"I don't cavort with prostitutes. Get lost, kid."

He continues on and sees a hotel with a pub on a corner. He likes the song, 'Tumbling Tumbleweeds,' he hears coming from the pub, so he walks in. It's a smallish room with a jukebox in the corner. The long wood bar is ornate with mirrors behind it. It's half full with more workmen then sailors. There are several women sitting together at a table.

He walks up to the bar, "A beer, please."

The bartender draws a pint and sets it in front of him, "Ten P."

Cumberland gives him a dime. He puts his back to the bar and looks the place over. To himself, "In here, I could be in Virginia City. Out there, it's 'War and Remembrance'."

One of the women gets up and walks over, "A beer, Joe."

"Sure."

Cumberland puts a dime down. She looks up and smiles, offering her hand, "I'm a sheila named Sheila."

He smiles and takes her hand, "George."

"Are you a Yank, then?"

"An American, yeah."

"I heard some Yanks don't like being called Yanks."

"Some don't. Ever heard of the American civil war?"

"No."

"It was between the north and the south over slavery. It ended in 1865. The south called the northern soldiers Yankees. Southerners, to this day, don't like being called Yanks."

"If they lost, why do they join the Yank navy?"

"Now that is a good question. I don't know."

"Are you from the south?"

"No, I'm from California."

"Do you know any movie stars?"

"No. I've never met even one. I grew up on a ranch."

"We call them stations here. Have you ever been in one of those rodeos?"

"I have. I earned a buckle in calf roping when I was in high school." The jukebox stops. Cumberland goes over and puts in some coins and selects all country music. As 'Cool Water' starts, one of the workmen says, "Hey Yank, how about something else?"

Cumberland looks at him, holding his gaze, "I want to listen to it."

"Yes, sir."

Cumberland escorts Sheila to a table, "That was Cassy Jones. I wouldn't cross him."

Cumberland smiles, "I'll keep that in mind.

ANTONIO'S CAFÉ, WOOLWICH, NSW

After Petrea, Wakefield, and Morrison, and Flanagan are seated, Antonio comes out, "Captain, you honor my table. I'm so pleased to see you."

Laura, "Thank you, Antonio. You've met my XO, Commander Flanagan. This is Commander Petrea of the Carl Vinson and Commander Morrison of the San Francisco."

"I'm so delighted to meet you. Would you wish wine?"

Laura says, Please, your house red is wonderful."

"You are too kind. We have an excellent lasagna verdi al forno and a superb Fettucine Carbonara."

Liz, "Your lasagna, does it have spinach?"

"Ah, of course."

Laura, "I recommend anything on the menu."

"You are too kind."

They order, and as he goes back into the kitchen, an older woman serves their wine. "It's good to see you, Commander."

Laura, "Thank you, Elena. Everyone, Elana, Antonio's wife, and better half."

THE PORTER PUB, KINGS CROSS

Cumberland is laughing at a comment by Sheila when a tall man in workman's gear walks in and makes eye contact with her. She stiffens as he approaches. "Hey Sheila, you need to be making money."

Cumberland, "Is there a problem?"

"No problem for you, codger."

The man grabs Sheila's arm and Cumberland grabs his wrist, "We're talking."

"Old man, let go if you want to keep breathing."

Cumberland smiles, his eyes lighting up, "Are you actually threatening me?"

The man pulls his hand back and shifts his focus to Cumberland. "Who the fuck are you?"

Still smiling, Cumberland stands, "Are you threatening me?"

"Old man, I could split you in two before you take another breath."

"Bluster. I've never seen your graveyards." His smile grows.

"Do you want to die, old man?"

"Go ahead. I won't die."

The man goes completely still, looking into Cumberland's

eyes, "Get back to work, Sheila." He abruptly turns and leaves.

Cumberland shakes his head. Sheila immediately leaves the bar, not looking back.

ANTONIO'S CAFÉ, WOOLWICH, NSW

The four officers walk out together. John and Liz shake Laura's and Brewster's hands. John, "I'm so glad to have met the two of you."

Liz, "I'll be talking to Captains Tucker and Johnson on Monday."

They get into their Ford and drive away. Liz, "That went very well."

"It did. She's really sharp."

"Yeah. You noticed that, once she figured out what we were about, she took over the meeting?"

John, "Well, yeah. She is a full commander, and she wears the mantle of command well. Way better than I thought she would."

"A woman can be an effective leader."

John, "I know. Look, can you get past my unfortunate birth with a penis and not assume my every statement has something to do with genitals? I was referring to her elevation from JG to commander. That's one hell of a leap. Most people, regardless of crotch equipment, would struggle in that position."

"I'm sorry, John. Yes, I will try to look past the genitals. Now, that was a weird sentence."

He laughs, "Yep, and it implies a mammoth size problem."

She starts giggling, and affects a high-pitched voice, "John dear, could you please be a darling and move your penis over so I may see out the windshield?"

He pulls the car over, curling up laughing, "I'm sorry, love. It quite has a mind of its own."

Liz, "Why yes, darling, but the poor thing needs house training."

"All handled love, I've tucked it into my sock."

It's ten minutes before John can pull back onto the road.

CHAPTER 18

USS HORNE, CG-30

0630, 11 February, 1942

Cumberland and Morrison are eating breakfast in the Horne's wardroom. Morrison, "Sir, we have no shortage of volunteers for commissioning. We need to pick two senior nukes."

"I don't want to lose senior crew during a war cruise."

"Yes, sir, but we're getting two officers and a couple of junior nukes in exchange. Their officers will be cream. I suggest Wankowski and Mallory. They're our EWS qualified first classes."

"No. Absolutely not. They're also our tracking party."

"One of them?"

Cumberland sighs, "Wankowski would be the better officer. Wankowski and Forrester. We don't need two new officers, so let's give them Lieutenant JG Forrester. I don't much like Forrester's attitude."

"Yes, sir. I think they both would do well on the Vinson."

Captain Arron Grey, CO of the Horne, joins them and a steward takes his order. "Commander Cumberland, have you received the royal summons?"

"We cannot support it. Too much to do."

Grey smiles, "You do understand what a royal request means? Our host is a cousin to the King. Unless you're dead, or in the hospital, you must come."

Cumberland, "But, they're not supposed to know we exist."

Grey, "They're not supposed to know your type of vessel. You've sailors all over this city with USS San Francisco emblazoned on their shoulder rockers."

"I'll take my navigator. I'm sure they don't want to see Morrison."

Grey stares at him.

Cumberland, "Yes, sir."

USS SAN FRANCISCO

0940, 11 February, 1942

Wankowski is in the officer's seat reviewing logs when Morrison enters. "What's up, XO?"

"Have the valve replacements passed QA?"

"Yes, sir. We're squeezing them now."

"Thank you. The boys paint the bilge last night?"

"Yes, sir. Are we getting ORSE ready?"

"We've a mobile training team inspection coming up."

"I get it, sir. We can't paint underway."

"Yeah. Can I drag you out of maneuvering for a minute?"

The shut-down reactor operator, ET1 Brown, says, "I can keep my mouth shut, sir."

"I know, Brown. That isn't it." The two exit maneuvering and stand among the RC cabinets. "The CO and I would like to commission you."

"Really? I thought I was in trouble and I couldn't think of anything recent."

"I wanted to talk in private. That way, if you said no, there wouldn't be a crew reaction. Also, this comes with a transfer to the Carl Vinson reactor department."

"Don't I have to go back through power school?"

"No. The carrier will train you. It means learning a brand-new plant, while also learning your SWO."

"I'm to be a line officer?"

"Absolutely. Let me give you my best guess as to your career path. After you complete all your nuke quals and SWO quals, you'll probably report to a new sub as CHENG. Eventually, if you do well, you'll earn your own command."

"Wow. If only Ruth could know." He lowers his head. "It fucking sucks, sir. The worst is the kids. I had amazing kids. They left a hole in my heart nothing will ever fill."

"I understand. No words, nothing at will fill it. Do you want the commission, Stan?"

"Sir, I'm standing up with Gary for his marriage. Can we hold off on the commissioning so I don't outrank him?"

"Sure. I need you to get measured for your new uniforms."

"Roger that, sir."

USS CARL VINSON

0900, 12 February, 1942

Morrison stands next to his car. With Petrea when she walks down the brow are Captain Tucker and two ensigns. The ensigns have silver enlisted surface warfare specialist pins and enlisted air warfare specialist pins. Petrea, "Commander Morrison, these are our two swap candidates, Ensign William Harvey and Ensign Joseph Vaught. They had their nuclear qualification board yesterday. We'd put them on the SWO path, but they volunteered for your sub."

Morrison, "I talked to the CO and the wardroom. I have two guys to swap. One was commissioned before we went back. He's an exceptional officer who should thrive at your command. The other is our E-div LPO who Commander Cumberland agreed to commission."

Tucker, "What's wrong with the officer?"

Morrison looks Tucker in the eyes, "He's a smart, squared away, diligent nuke who loves to learn. My opinion, sir, the skipper doesn't like him because he has a permanent tan."

Tucker, "The service has no room for prejudice."

"Sir, at this time, the Navy has regulations codifying prejudice. Black people are only allowed menial jobs and cannot be officers."

"You're aware we do not run our commands that way."

"I am and I totally agree."

"Are you attending the Governor's Ball?"

"Of course, sir."

Petrea, "Can he have a plus one?"

Tucker, "He is the plus one. It's CO's and XO's."

Petrea, "Are all the squadrons invited, sir?"

Tucker, "Yes, our friend will be there. Morrison, have you met Commander Hunt?"

"I have."

"Look out for her there, okay?"

Morrison, "Sir, she'll probably end up looking after me. I'll do what I can." He turns to his two new ensigns, "The CHENG is on duty today. I take it you know where we're berthed?"

"Yes, sir."

"I'll talk to you tomorrow morning. Eight, my office."

"Yes, sir." The two men salute and leave.

Morrison, "We're going to have tea, sir, if you would like to join us?"

"Thank you, no. I'm meeting with some Australian counterparts. I'm arranging to see the work of Dr. Heinlein."

Morrison, "Wow. If it could be finagled, I would love to see it as well."

"I'll see what may be done. Good day."

John and Liz get into the Ford and head off base. Liz, "Dr. Heinlein and his incredible time machine."

"You know, one of our nukes was the room mate of one of your nukes."

"Do you know the name?"

John, "I do, but I haven't shared it. The young man could be harmed."

"I agree. Besides you, are there any other minority officers or men?"

"No other officers. Many among the enlisted."

Liz, "And, you're doing what you can to protect them. I don't envy you your job."

USS SAN FRANCISCO

1210, 12 February, 1942

Mallory is walking back down to the sub after eating lunch on the Horne. Cumberland is walking off the boat, so Mallory stands aside and waits. The bell rings, "San Francisco, departing." Cumberland reaches the end of the brow and Mallory salutes. Cumberland returns the salute, "Mallory, I want to talk to you."

"Yes, sir."

"I heard you're planning to get married tomorrow."

"Yes, sir."

"Well, cancel it. I'll not have it."

"Sir?"

"There's no way you could know a woman long enough to make that kind of decision this fast."

"Sir, I respect your opinion, sir, but I'm not cancelling my wedding."

Cumberland looks Mallory in the eyes, "All women are whores. The only variable is how they get paid and who they choose to fuck. Break it off. If you don't, I'll mast you for disobeying a direct order and restrict you to the ship until we're back at sea."

Mallory breaks eye contact, "I understand your order, sir."

"Look at me."

Mallory looks up as ordered. His jaw is twitching and his shoulders are tight, but his eyes are blank. "You'll thank me for this when you have some time away from her. You'll come to understand I'm right. Carry on." Cumberland walks away, smiling.

Mallory goes below. When he gets to the tunnel, he screams, face turned upward and fists clenched, "You mother fucking, fuck head, fuck wad, fuck tard, fuck face, fuck funnel, fuck monkey…" He hears the door shut behind him, but keeps going, "…cock sucking, God damned jack ass, little dick, Nazi, cock whore! You were a waste of sperm. If you'd been a blow job, the world would be a better place." He leans against the wall and covers his face with his hands.

LCDR Miller, "Mallory, give me a second, I'm taking notes. If you'd been a blow job…damn, that's good."

"Sir?"

"What did Cumberland do?"

"He ordered me to not get married, CHENG."

"I know you're not on watch, come with me."

"Yes, sir." Miller walks him to the stateroom he shares with Backes. The room is now decorated with Gumby's."

Miller pulls out a note book and pen, "Write a statement."

"Why?"

"Because it's an unlawful order. He cannot order you not to marry. I'll wait. Write the whole thing down."

Mallory writes for fifteen minutes, signs it, and slides it over. A detective has nothing on the completeness of a nuke's statement. Miller, "Okay, Mallory. This is what you're going to do." Miller signs and dates the statement. "Unless you, for your own reasons, want to pull out, I want you to enjoy your wedding tomorrow and say nothing about it. I'll forward your marriage certificate to the Vinson for entry into your record. We'll see about getting her a dependent ID card. We need to figure out how to split your check, so you can keep her in money."

"Sir, I was thinking about that. I don't even have a bank account. I was going to leave her with all I have now, and hope to wire more money by Western Union when I can."

"I'm delving into your personal life, but how much do you have?"

"I've nearly three hundred, sir."

"I'm not sure of the cost of living here, but that would get her through three to six months."

"She lives with her folks, and is responsible with money. We talked about it yesterday."

"How much does she think she needs?"

"None. She has a couple of hundred in the bank and a steady job in a ship yard."

"She told you that?"

"Sir, we were kind of arguing over it. I was trying to explain that I need to give, to take care of her. We went to the bank and she showed me her account."

"That's it. If you can get her account information, you should be able to wire money directly into her account. Tell her she can save it for you, because you don't have an account. Remember to keep half of what you earn here. Time may come that you have need of it."

"Good idea, sir. I was going to conspire with her dad to make sure she gets it."

"You get along with her folks?"

"Yes, sir. They're frankly awesome, sir. Sir, do you want to come?"

"I'd be honored. Are you going to invite the XO?"

"I was thinking about that. Would it mess up his liberty plans?"

"I doubt it. Give me the information and I'll see he gets it."

"Thank you, sir."

GOVERNOR'S MANSION, SYDNEY

1822, 13 February, 1942

Morrison parks the car and he and Cumberland get out, both in full dress whites with medals clanking. They walk to the front door and a footman checks them in. When they get into the ballroom, they see Admirals Nimitz, Halsey, and Lee talking to some Australian flag officers and a man in a tuxedo with a red sash.

Cumberland, "The civilian with the red sash, you suppose he's our host?"

Morrison, "Probably, sir. The sash is for the Order of the Bath. He's a knight."

Cumberland, "I find all that to be formal nonsense. Blue blood only matters when red blood runs thin."

They pick champagne flutes off a tray and walk among the guests. An Australian captain offers his hand, "Harry Howden, commander of Hobart."

"George Cumberland, commander of San Francisco."

Howden, "Amusing, we both command cities."

Cumberland, "We do?"

Howden looks at Morrison, "And you are, Commander?"

Morrison, "I'm his XO, John Morrison."

"Morrison? Any relation to Marion Morrison?"

Cumberland chuckles, "John Wayne? More like John Wang." He realizes the other two aren't laughing.

Morrison, "I was adopted by the Morrisons after my folks died in a traffic accident. I assume the families must be related to the Morrison clan in Scotland, but I don't know of any connection."

There's a stir in the crowd and it parts to reveal the U.S. Navy pilots. LCDR Samantha Hunt stands out in her dress whites.

Howden, "My Lord. Who is that?"

Morrison, "That is Lieutenant Commander Samantha Hunt, the CO of the Black Knights squadron, VF-154."

"A female fighter pilot?"

Cumberland, "I quite agree, sir. A woman's place is in the home."

Morrison, "She has 35 kills, sir." They watch Hunt talking with Wakefield.

Howden, "How does that compare with the other pilots?"

"She's the American ace of aces."

"Remarkable. Would you excuse me?" Howden walks toward a group of Australian Navy officers.

Cumberland, "You shouldn't talk up that woman, Morrison."

"I understand why you would dislike her, sir, but regardless of what you and I think, her competence speaks for itself."

"You lift up a woman like that, then they'll have expectations that are unreasonable. Better that her success is ignored. Regardless, she'll be kicked out of the Navy on a medical."

"A medical, sir?"

Cumberland, "Yes. On examination, they'll find she lacks a penis. Then she'll be discharged." He chuckles.

They watch the Governor walk up to Hunt. He's loud enough that the rest of the guests quiet, "I must meet this supposed female aviator. Hello, I'm Governor John Loder, Lord Wakehurst. Welcome to my home. You, madam, would you be this female aviator?"

Hunt, "I am, sir. It's a pleasure."

"This is rubbish." Turning to Nimitz, "Is this your idea of a joke, Admiral?"

Nimitz, "No, milord. This is Lieutenant Commander Samantha Hunt, commanding officer of the Black Knights squadron. She has 35 Japanese kills."

Governor Loder, "Preposterous. No woman could outfly a man. I hope you're not thinking of sending this female to defend Australia. I won't have it. Not for a minute."

Nimitz, "Milord, if I had a thought of sending you my most successful squadron, it would be Commander Hunt's. As it is, I'll be releasing the Blue Diamonds, commanded by Earl Carpenter. Their fighters are also optimized for air to ground."

Loder sputters, "Are you telling me this woman commands the best squadron on your vessel?"

Holtz, "Milord, Commander Hunt is, right now, likely the best fighter pilot in the world. I admit to having my doubts in the past, but she has proven herself to me."

Halsey, "Governor, please allow me to introduce you to Commander Carpenter. He commands the squadron assigned to Australia, the Blue Diamonds." He and Nimitz walk the Governor away. The conversations resume and Hunt is surrounded by pilots.

Cumberland watches this with a smile, "Morrison, do you know the Captain with Hunt?"

"No, sir."

"I thought you knew everyone?"

"No, sir."

Cumberland, "What's the Hobart?"

"It's a cruiser. A light cruiser, I think. It's the one behind the carrier nested with the Jarrett."

"Okay, go mingle."

"Yes, sir."

Cumberland walks up to CDR Wakefield, "Hello, Commander."

Wakefield, "Commander. You're Cumberland, right?"

"I am, and you are?"

She offers a hand, "Laura Wakefield of Fife."

"I heard you lost your entire chain. How are you doing?"

"We're managing. This is my XO, Commander Brewster Flanagan."

Cumberland notices that the cut of Flanagan's uniform marks him as a '41. He turns back to Wakefield after shaking Flanagan's hand, "Still, with so little time in service, you have to be struggling. What can I do to help?"

"I'm a mustang, Commander. I've eleven years of service, and I completed nuke school in 1988 as an officer."

"Oh, I see. So, you've everything sorted out. Have you ever even detected us?"

"You're good, and subs always have the advantage, but yes, we've tracked you. I've a really solid crew."

"There's no way you could ever find me."

Wakefield, "I bet we can track you for one hour. Your course, speed, and depth. Are you willing to put a case of whiskey on it? My preference is single malt scotch. The good stuff."

Cumberland, "Jack Daniels. You're on." They shake hands.

Morrison joins Hunt and three other pilots, "You okay, Commander?"

Hunt, "Hi John. Let me introduce you to John 'Marshall' Dillon, Norman 'Oyster' Osterman, and Stephan 'Swede' Swedenborg. Swede is my XO, Oyster is XO for the Tomcatters, and Marshall is the XO of the Redcocks. John Morrison is XO of the San Francisco."

They all shake hands. Oyster, "What is the San Francisco?"

Morrison, "It's being called an anti-submarine vessel."

Marshall, "Come on, Oyster. He has dolphins on his chest."

Oyster, "Oh, duh. Sorry. What is the pin under it of the sideways boat?"

"We just got them. It's a combat patrol pin. They haven't been issued since, well, World War II."

Oyster, "Cool. I couldn't do what you do. I need to see some sun."

"It does tend to pale the complexion."

"Do your nukes hug the reactor to keep a tan?"

Morrison laughs, "Nope. That just causes two-headed babies. I don't recommend it."

The announcement for dinner is made.

CHAPTER 19

ST. JOHN'S ANGLICAN CHURCH, CROYDON, NSW

1358, 16 February, 1942

MM1 Mallory paces in the little room where he and Wankowski are waiting. Wankowski is kicked back with a cup of coffee, "Chill, man."

"I don't want to screw up my vows. This is important."

"It get it, my friend, but it's one day. If she's as awesome as you think she is, then this is just one day."

"I don't want to screw it up."

"Dude, something goes wrong at every wedding. Just relax, okay?"

Morrison and Miller enter wearing full dress whites with their swords. Morrison, "How are you doing, Gary?"

"Nervous, sir. I don't want to mess up."

Miller, "You won't, Gary. All you have to do is repeat the preacher."

"Oh, yeah. Okay."

Morrison, "Tell us about her."

"Well, she has red hair, and the strength of character that implies. She has an infectious giggle and amazing green eyes. She's sweet and kind, but tough, too. She's the kind of woman you take home to Mom and they fall in love with each other." Gary smiles, "Thank you, sir."

Morrison, "You were stuck on the what. I just reminded you of the why. I'm looking forward to meeting her, Gary. I'm happy for you."

When they leave the room, they see about twenty of Amy's family and friends in the pews, and about forty sailors. Most of the crew that's on liberty are here, including several of the officers. All the officers have their swords. Morrison goes up to the priest and whispers something, and the priest nods. Then he sits down with Miller and the other officers near the back.

Gary takes his place. Stan walks Amy's mom down the aisle and seats her, then takes his place next to Gary. The organist starts the music. A pretty blonde, Mary Burns, in a mid-calf peach dress, walks to her place opposite the two men. The wedding march begins.

Amy slowly walks down the aisle on her father's arm. He's in a black suit, and she's wearing a simply cut white dress that fits her perfectly. As they proceed down the aisle, several girls hang ribbon decorated horse shoes on her arm.

They reach the altar and Andrew Randolph gives away his daughter and sits down. Gary's nerves drop away as he looks into Amy's eyes. The familiar ceremony speeds by and the priest turns them toward the guests, "Gentlemen, take your positions."

Morrison, Miller, Petrea, and the other officers form up facing each other at the foot of the aisle. Morrison, "Present..." They grasp their swords and partly pull them out, "Arms." They draw their swords and create the arch. Morrison is on the far end on the bride's side.

The priest smiles, "I present Petty Officer and Mrs. Gary Mallory. You may kiss your bride."

Gary leans over and pulls Amy into a light embrace and kiss. It's delicate, but full of passion. The recessional begins and they walk down the aisle under the swords. As they pass, each pair of swords come down. Morrison and Miller are the last to lower their swords and Morrison gives Amy the customary swat on the behind. She chirps, "Oh!"

The entire party goes to the attached hall of the church for the reception. The tables are covered in food for a buffet. A large cake sits at the end of one of the tables.

Amy goes up to Morrison, "Sir, why did you swat my bum?"

"It's a very old tradition among military officers. On the way out of the church, the bride gets a 'welcome to the family' swat."

"But Gary isn't an officer?"

"He isn't an officer, yet. We in the wardroom decided to honor you anyway."

"Thank you, then. Do you fair dinkum think he'll be an officer?"

"I put him in for promotion a few days ago. It didn't happen this time, but it will."

"Crickey. I'll need to be an officer's wife, then."

"You'll have time to sort it out. We've arranged for your ID card tomorrow on the carrier."

"Gary said."

"You know, the two of you have a long row to hoe. We still have years of war in front of us."

She looks him square in the eyes, "I know it. Life wasn't ever meant to be lollys and fairy floss. I said for better or worse, and I meant it."

"I see that."

BONDI BEACH

1634, 17 February, 1942

Gloria Houlihan, LTJG John 'Gunner' Harden, ENS Jose 'Speedy' Gonzalez, Lieutenant Mike 'Too Tall' Mohr, and ENS Truman 'Johnny' Walker set up their band equipment on a cobble stone area next to the beach. The carrier has three barbeques going, with no shortage of beer. Their host is the Navy base and the HMAS Hobart. There are sailors playing cricket and volleyball. The uniform is relaxed for this party. Some are in uniform, but most are in civilian attire. The band members are all in civvies. A little way from them, the Hobart band is playing big band music. Mohr fires up the generator. When the Hobart band takes a break, they do their sound check. Sailors meander toward the bands.

John is sitting on the grass with Liz eating barbeque off paper plates. Both are in civvies. John "Are they any good."

Liz, "They're fantastic. You'll see."

Gloria does the down count and they begin Patsy Cline's 'Walking After Midnight.' More and more people gather. Soon, most are standing to see, and as the song ends, they applaud. Then, Gunner sings Kenny Loggins' 'Danger Zone.' The '90's go nuts, but the '41s seem a little stunned. Next, Gloria sings Berlin's 'Take My Breath Away.' On this one, Too Tall rocks the base riffs.

John, "Wow. They're damn near professional."

"Yeah, John. I know."

Gloria and Gunner sing the duet, 'Golden Ring' by George Jones and Tammy Wynette. Her crystal-clear mezzo soprano and his rumbly baritone harmonize sweetly in the classic love song.

Then, Gloria goes into 'Watching Baby Walk Away,' by Lisa Stevenson.

"I didn't try to keep you,

Though I wanted you around.

I won't admit I need you,

Pride keeps my feelings down.

My heart screams out for you,

Though it doesn't make a sound.

I watched you walk away,

On a cloudy rain-soaked day.

There was nothing I could say.

I did it to myself.

Watching baby walk away.

I know I should feel bitter.

I should put it all on you.

I cast aside your offer,

I wouldn't say I do.

My heart screams out for you,

Though it doesn't make a sound.

I watched you walk away,

On a cloudy rain-soaked day.

There was nothing I could say.

I did it to myself.

Watching baby walk away.

Watching baby walk away.

Watching baby walk away

I watched my baby walk away.

The crowd applauds and cheers. Liz looks at John, his face twisted, tears in his eyes. She takes his hand and leads him away as the band begins their next song. Once they're between two buildings and out of sight, Liz asks, "What is it, John?"

John looks at her, lips trembling, and closes his eyes, "That was her song."

"Who's song?" Liz hands him some tissues out of her bag.

"Lisa's. She wrote it the night we broke up."

"Your wife? Oh shit. You said."

He nods and she takes him in her arms.

The band continues playing, Gloria and Gunner taking turns singing the lead. More and more civilians show up outside the fence, listening.

Liz, "Why don't we go?"

John, "Your friends are playing."

"John, I think you need to be away from people right now." She walks him to the car and she drives them away. They head south until they find a quiet, empty beach, and she pulls over. They get out and she takes his hand as they walk down to the small crescent of sand between rocky headlands. They find a place to sit, still holding hands, "John, do you need to talk or for us to just be silent."

"I was listening, and it hit me hard that I'll never see her again. Lisa. I built my internal life around loving her. After we broke up, I would listen to her music and know what she was feeling. At least, I thought I knew. I just knew we would be together eventually. We would be happy, and we were. Now, there's no chance. Zero. Gone. The worst fucking magic trick ever."

She puts her arm on his shoulder and they sit and talk as the sun sets behind them. John looks up at the darkening sky, "Do you know where we are?"

"A beach south of the base somewhere. I was focused on you."

"Thank you. It looks like we'll have to crawl back using black out lights and hope we don't get lost."

"Let's find a hotel."

"You sure?"

"I don't want to get lost and have some cop with an itchy trigger finger put a round in you."

In the gloom they see an inn and pull in. There are no outside lights, but they see a sliver of light under the main door, so they knock and open the door. A man behind a counter looks up, "How can I help you?"

John, "Can we get a room?"

"You two married?"

Liz nods, "Of course."

John fills out the registration and hands over the three dollars for the room.

"Keep it quiet. We run a nice place here." He hands them the key and gives them the room number. A few minutes later, they're in a second-floor room with a low ceiling and a single metal full-sized four poster bed. But there's an en suite bathroom and the room is clean.

John, "One bed?"

"Yeah." She sits on the bed and looks at him.

"Um, you know where I am. How are we going to do this?"

Liz grins, "Give me your t-shirt."

"Okay," and he skins it off.

Liz, "You get seconds on the bath." She goes into the bathroom.

He sits in the one chair, waiting. Quietly, too himself, "What the fuck am I doing? Am I sending the wrong signals? She's beautiful. She's smart as hell. But she isn't Lisa. This is wrong." He takes several deep breaths, "Be honest, man. I care about her. She's been a better friend than I deserve. I guess I need to just walk this trail and see where it goes."

Thirty minutes later, Liz walks out with wet hair and wearing his t-shirt. "You're next. While you're in there, take care of your needs, so we can sleep without your balls exploding."

His jaw drops, "Wh...what?"

"John, I've been married for a long time. Even if I'm not your one and only, when we get into bed your happy place is going to get hard, and then it's going to hurt. Just take care of it, okay? If you can sleep in your skivvies, that works for me."

"Okay." John shakes his head and smiles and goes into the bathroom. When he comes out, she's lying in the bed, still in his shirt. He climbs in next to her and she rolls to face him,

"Are we good?" She grins.

"We're good. God, this is awkward." He smiles.

"I guess I should give you some boundaries, John. If you couldn't tell by now, I'm not shy. If we wake up spooning, that's fine. If we wake up touching, even intimate touching, that's fine. Neither of us has any control of what we do in our sleep."

"I agree. You're an amazing woman, Liz."

"You're pretty awesome, too. Absolute truth, John, I think I need to touch, and be touched. It's a different kind of intimate. I'm not ready for the other."

He cups her face with his hand, "What are we?"

"I think we are two lonely friends trying to survive in a difficult time." She puts her hand to his face.

OFFICER'S CLUB, GARDEN ISLAND, RAN BASE

2345, 17 February, 1942

Sam, Swede, Gloria, and Gandhi sit around a table nursing beers. Gloria, "I tell you, Sam, he was upset. It was like his best friend totaled his Vette, ran off with his girl, and his dog died. John and Liz just left."

Swede, "What song were you singing?"

Gloria, "What does that matter?"

Sam, "Do you remember?"

"Yeah, it was an old Metalsmith song, 'Watching Baby Walk Away.'"

Sam, "That's when it happened? Do you know who wrote the song?"

"Yeah, Lisa Stevenson. She wrote most of Metalsmith's lyrics until she broke up with the lead singer, Ted."

Sam, "Do you remember his CO being pissed at him because he'd just married?"

"Like I could forget. What an ass."

Sam, "I talked to Liz. I was just curious, because I knew her husband, Tim, was the love of her life. I was wondering why they were hanging out together so soon."

"And?"

"John had just married the love of his life, too. They'd courted and broken up years before. Liz said her name was Lisa."

Gloria, "There has to be a million Lisa's out there. Rock stars do not marry sailors."

Gandhi, "I know the music. When I was in college, I listened to it a lot. I even went to their concerts. That song was about Lisa breaking up with someone way more important to her than Ted. It was written before the two of them were even an item."

Cumberland enters the dimly lit bar and walks by them.

Sam calls out, "Commander Cumberland?"

He recoils at her voice, "You again."

Sam, "Who did Commander Morrison marry?"

"He married a fucking rock star named Lisa Stevenson, why?"

"I was just wondering. Thank you, sir."

The four exchange looks and Gloria says, "Fuck. I didn't know."

Gandhi, "How could you?"

Sam, "I think you may have done him a huge favor."

They look at her, confused.

Sam continues, "Look, whether they are an item, or not, he and Liz are obviously close, so he isn't alone. All of us are going to have that moment when it hits us hard that we've lost someone, or something irreplaceable. It's already happened to some of us, and it will probably happen again. It's far, far better that he is walking that dark path with someone he trusts and who trusts him. Can you imagine what that would look like on his boat?"

Gloria, "You're right, Sam. I hadn't thought it through."

Swede, "Also, we all have something he probably lacks. We have a group of close friends. Being the XO of a ship is different. There has to be a bigger space between him and the guys. Lord knows he can't confide in his captain."

Gloria, "Sam, are you bringing Swede and Gandhi into the Admirals club?"

Swede, "We're already there, though I'm still working on the secret handshake."

COOGEE BAY HOTEL, COOGEE BEACH, NSW

0745, 18 February, 1942

The sounds of bird chirping wakes John up. It's such a foreign sound for someone who lives underwater. His arm is tucked around Liz, her back to him. Her rhythmic breathing is lovely. The smell of her hair is even better. He lays without moving and tries to analyze his feelings.

Where Lisa's concerned, nothing has changed. He knows he does not, cannot, feel about Liz what he feels about Lisa. He's equally certain the same is true for her and Tim. That said, what is he doing? What has he done? They didn't have sex.

What they did do, was incredibly intimate. People freak out about cheaters who have sex. They forget that emotional intimacy is the bigger thing. If there was even a chance at all of reuniting with Lisa, he'd feel a total ass. As it is, he still feels guilty, but irrationally so. Liz was right, they needed this... thing. Whatever it was.

She moves, then takes his hand in hers, "Good morning, John."

"Good morning."

She spins around to face him, "No regrets, okay?"

He smiles, "No regrets."

"It's two friends helping each other through an extraordinarily painful time."

"It is. So, are you okay?"

"I'm conflicted as hell. I'm sure you are, too. I think we both needed to help pull some of the poison from the other."

He looks into her eyes and holds the gaze. She doesn't flinch or look away. He moves his hand to the small of her back and slides closer to her. They smile.

USS SAN FRANCISCO

1000, 22 February, 1942

Cumberland and Morrison wait as the boatswain pipes, "Carrier Group 2, arriving." Halsey walks down the brow with his chief of staff, Captain Miles Browning. He salutes the flag and then the quarterdeck. Morrison and Cumberland salute.

Halsey, "How's the San Francisco?"

Cumberland, "We've completed the maintenance package. We'll be loading provisions and ordinance this afternoon.

We'll be ready to sortie tonight."

Halsey, "Good." They go aboard and they give him the complete tour, including the engine room. The ship is clean and squared away. The engine room is immaculate. The last stop is the wardroom where a steward serves lunch. After the steward leaves, Halsey says, "Your boat is impressive, Commander, and it's squared away. How would you assess morale?"

Cumberland, "The crew has enjoyed Australia. Some have enjoyed it too much. I think they're looking forward to going to sea."

"Leaving Australia for the sea and combat? No, I'd bet most of your men are quite happy here. How many of your crew are married, or planning to be?"

Cumberland looks at Morrison. Morrison, "One married and five engaged, sir."

Halsey, "It's the way of things. The one thing no officer can stop is true love. How old and what rank is the married crew member?"

Morrison, 'He's thirty-five and a first class. He's approaching eighteen years of service, sir, and will likely leave after the war."

Halsey, "Is he squared away?"

"I've recommended him for commissioning, sir."

Halsey, "Well, I wish him the best. Are the new officers and ratings fitting in?"

Cumberland, "Yes, sir, though it'll be a while before they can support the watch bill."

"Of course. That's the way of it. Now, this isn't the first sub I've been aboard, but it's the first that didn't stink of diesel and sweaty men. Do you understand what we need from you?"

"Yes, sir."

"Yes, sir."

Halsey, "Cumberland, I like your aggressiveness, but I'm growing weary of your antics. Why did you tell a senior rating he could not marry?"

Cumberland looks at Morrison. Morrison's eyes open in surprise, "What?"

Halsey, "The odds that someone will see you are directly proportional to the stupidity of your act. Captain Grey watched the whole thing from the Horne."

Cumberland, "Well, sir, I was concerned for his morale. I know most of these marriages never work out."

Halsey, "Do you have a problem with women, Commander?"

"Um, no, sir."

Halsey, "I understand you locked horns with a couple of our female pilots. If you can't respect the person, you God damned well better respect their uniform. Am I clear?"

"Yes, sir."

"Can you two work together going forward?"

Cumberland looks at his XO, then back to Halsey, "We, uh, we can work together, sir."

Halsey, "Morrison?"

"Yes, sir. Current issues aside, we're working fairly well together at sea."

Halsey, "Good, tomorrow, you go to sea. There are no friendly subs within five hundred miles of Sydney. We're giving you two days to clear the harbor of Jap subs. When you give us the all clear, this group puts to sea. It will be the same order of battle, until you are cut loose in the Indian Ocean. That done, we want you to race ahead, clear out any subs around the Cape of Good Hope, and report in when that is completed. Then, hunt your way north. Pass through the Atlantic gap, then report to Groton on or about 26 March. You'll get further orders in Groton. As I understand it, your job will be to clear out the wolf pack menace. Questions?"

"No, sir."

"No, sir."

Halsey, "Now, gentlemen, I happen to have a case of whiskey on Wakefield, but I do wish you both the best."

Morrison, "Who's the bet with, sir."

"Captain Johnson seems to think highly of modern submarines."

They walk Halsey off the boat. When Halsey is gone, Morrison asks, "Sir, why did you tell Mallory he couldn't marry?"

"I wanted to keep him from making a huge mistake."

"You've never even met her."

"It doesn't matter. I know you have a thing for the ladies, Commander. As far as I'm concerned, every split tail is a whore after your bank account and your future. They are sirens designed to lead men astray. Men are better off focusing on their work."

"Sir, you're entitled to your opinion, but we both know officers cannot interfere with personal lives of the men. It's unlawful."

"Yeah, well, he got married and I dodged a bullet. I want E-6 and below aboard by midnight. Everyone aboard by two. We set sail by four."

"Yes, sir."

CHAPTER 20

ROYAL PRINCE ALFRED HOSPITAL, SYDNEY, NSW

1610, 22 February, 1942

Morrison and Backes help Lt. Kichiro get dressed in his uniform. Kichiro, "So, I passed my board?"

Backes, "You did. You'll have a lot to learn, but you know enough not to kill anyone."

"Shit, man. This is awesome."

Morrison pins on Kichiro's gold dolphins, then his combat patrol pin. Petrea, from the door, asks, "The nurse is here. May we come in?"

Kichiro, "Yeah, sure."

Petrea, "Congratulations, Lieutenant."

"Thank you, ma'am."

The nurse walks in behind Petrea with a wheel chair, "Please sit down, Lieutenant."

"I've been sitting and laying down enough."

"You must be wheeled out of the hospital. It's policy."

Kichiro looks at the three lieutenant commanders, then back to the nurse, and sighs, "Yes, ma'am." He's wheeled out of the hospital. They put him into the Ford, and they make their way west. An hour later, they pull into RAAF Richmond. Morrison asks the gate guard for directions and they drive to the 'O' club.

Inside, they find a table and a Philippine waiter takes their orders. The bar is fairly full with RAAF and RAF officers. Liz attracts more attention than Morrison or Kichiro.

Kichiro, "Sir, when do I start getting paid as a lieutenant?"

Morrison grins, "You already are."

"Cool."

A USAAF captain approaches their table, "Are all of you flying out?"

Morrison, "Just Lieutenant Kichiro. Are you flying 2773?"

"Yes, I'm Captain Archer. You look like a Jap."

"I'm American."

"Okay, just saying."

Petrea, "He's Apache, Captain. Don't become one of his scalps."

Archer swallows, "No disrespect intended."

Their food arrives and Archer returns to his table. Morrison, "Apache?"

"It's an easier fabrication than having to explain yourself and your patriotism every ten minutes."

"It's a lie."

Petrea, "Who the fuck cares, John. Everyone knows who the Apaches are, and no one ever wants to fuck with one. They also know Apache are Americans. There's no further need to question your patriotism."

Kichiro, "She's right, sir."

Backes, "I agree, John. It's safer for you."

"I don't look Apache."

Petrea, "Really? What do Apache look like?"

"I'm not sure, but I'm sure I'm too pale."

"You live in a submerged tube."

"My eyes aren't shaped right."

"Really? And what do Apache eyes look like? Practically no one from 1942 knows."

Backes, "She's right. Your last name doesn't give anything away. In fact, it makes sense if you were part white. That would explain your pale skin, as well."

"Just how far are you two co-conspirators wanting to take this?"

"I'll talk to Johnson and have your service record changed."

"Jesus Chris, Liz. I would be a fraud. I won't do it." He looks over at the table where the USAAF crew are eating. He gets up and walks over. "Gentlemen, are you drinking beer before you fly?"

Archer, "Only one, sir. We don't fly for three more hours."

He makes eye contact with each man using the senior officer stink eye, "In the 1990 military, there is no alcohol twenty-four hours before a flight. If I see a second round, your careers are over. Clear?"

The men look at each other and back to Morrison, "Yes, sir."

"Carry on." He comes back to the table and sits.

Petrea, "Did you just set the record straight?"

"No, but they aren't buying a second round of beers before a flight."

Backes and Petrea look at the USAAF crew. Petrea, "Did you

ground them?"

"The flight isn't for another three hours. I just chewed them out."

Kichiro, "I have to wait three hours?"

"I'm afraid so. It's actually typical of government flights. They're never on time."

The USAAF crew come by their table on their way out. The captain says, "We're headed to the flight line for the pre-flight. We can take you, lieutenant."

Kichiro, "My bags are in the car. If you've room, that's cool with me."

"Cool?"

Kichiro smiles, "I forget. Okay with me."

Archer, "Are you guys those time travelers?"

Backes, "We are."

Archer, "Hot damn. Do we win?"

Morrison, "We do, but with our presence, everything is changed. What do you fly?"

"C-47, sir. From here we hop across Australia, jump to Egypt, hop to Gibraltar, then up to Portsmouth, Iceland, Newfoundland, and finally, Washington. It'll take three days, if we don't' have bad weather."

Kichiro, "In twenty years, or so, we'll be able to fly directly in air-conditioned comfort."

Backes, "Yeah, but then there's always the crying baby, stinky seat mate, or kid kicking the back of your chair."

Kichiro, "Come on, Commander. Be an optimist." He pushes his plate away, "I guess, I'll be seeing you."

They all get up and shake Kichiro's hand. Morrison goes out with Kichiro to retrieve his bags. "Take care, Kiche. I know you'll do well."

"Yes, sir." Kichiro salutes and Morrison returns it. He picks up his bags and follows the aircrew to their vehicle. Morrison watches the truck head for the flight line, then turns and walks back inside. A few minutes later, they're on their way back to Garden Island. They drop Backes off at the 'O' club and head out of town.

Morrison finds a quiet spot and pulls over, "Apache, Liz? What's that about?"

"John, you leave tomorrow."

"And you leave two days later."

"Are we going to the same place?"

He smiles, "No."

"Then you know."

"Yeah, Halsey told us this morning."

"I know you can't say, and that's fine. What I want to know is if you'll be okay. If…"

John shakes his head, "If? If I'll still need Liz the protector when we go our separate ways?"

"You need someone to help you out there, Cochise."

"Is that where we are? I'm vulnerable and you're afraid for me? Is that it?"

She looks away and takes a jagged breath. Finally, she turns and looks at him, "No. No. I'm making excuses for missing you."

"I'll still care about you, Liz. No matter where we go, no matter what we do, you'll hold a piece of my heart."

She chews her lip, "But is it a piece you can live without?" She slides closer to him.

He takes her in his arms and kisses her hair, "No, dear. I have no expendable pieces of my heart."

"When do you have to be back?"

"Two. I should be back earlier than that."

"I want you alone with me until one, okay?"

"Yes, dear."

I-68, JAPANESE SUBMARINE, NORTH OF SYDNEY HARBOR

0440, 23 February, 1942

Lieutenant Commander Yahachi Tanabe hears the merchant vessel over their head, its screws slowly churning the sea. The water is shallow here, so it moves slowly. The sonar operator, listening intently, says, "Commander, I think I hear a vessel departing the harbor."

USS SAN FRANCISCO, MOUTH OF SYDNEY HARBOR

0442, 23 February, 1942

Morrison shakes the pilot's hand and helps him step across to the pilot boat. The sub is rolling a bit in the incoming swells. He uses a pen light to confirm that all the disappearing cleats are in the dive position. Then, he climbs up the sail, "What's our depth?" Waiting for the answer, Morrison observes the dozen, or so, cargo ships circling outside the harbor waiting for daylight.

The phone talker, "85 feet, sir."

"Good.' He puts on his sound powered phones. He spots a flashing light from the darkness, "Captain, signal lamp at 085 relative. It's a patrol boat requesting the code."

Cumberland, "Ignore it. I'll raise them on radio."

"Roger." In the dim light, he sees foam at the stern as the patrol boat accelerates. "Sir, he's getting antsy."

"Stand by."

The bridge watch, "Sir, is the Captain signaling back?"

Morrison, "We don't want a light to expose our position. He's trying to raise him on the radio. What's our depth?"

"Twenty fathoms, sir."

There's a bright light from the patrol boat and a splash of water about one hundred yards in front of the sub. Morrison turns on his pen light and uses his hand to flash the recognition code. Another round fires and lands long and behind. "They've got our range." He keeps flashing the recognition signal.

Finally, he sees a response. "Interrogative. Unit?"

He responds, "SN. SN. SN."

"Interrogative. No answer?"

Morrison responds, "Interrogative. Radio off?"

The patrol boat replies, "Sorry, SN."

He sends, "Directive. Report Admiral H. for new assignment. Out." He turns off his pen light and stows it in a pocket.

I-62, JAPANESE SUBMARINE, SOUTH OF SYDNEY HARBOR

Lieutenant Commander Riku Kobayashi waits. He has torpedoes already loaded in his four forward tubes.

Sonar, "Commander, I confirm vessel leaving Sydney Harbor is single screw. The patrol boat fired on her."

Kobayashi, "Why? Why fire on your own vessel? Thank you. Do you have a blade count?"

"Many blades, sir. It sounds odd."

"But, one screw?"

"Yes, sir."

"Make turns for three knots. Let's continue using the cargo ship as a hat while we see what this is."

USS SAN FRANCISCO

The phone talker says, "Captain says we have fifty fathoms and to clear the bridge." They pull their cords and install the caps. Morrison inspects the bridge, then climbs down, inspecting and closing hatches.

"Chief, last man down. Bridge rigged to dive." They go through the dive procedure, open the ballast valves, and the San Francisco slips beneath the waves.

I-62, JAPANESE SUBMARINE, SOUTH OF SYDNEY HARBOR

Sonar, "It is sinking."

Kobayashi, "Was it hit?"

"I do not think so. It is a submarine, Commander."

"One screw? Odd."

I-68, JAPANESE SUBMARINE NORTH OF SYDNEY HARBOR

Lt. Commander Tanabe leans over his sonarman, "A submarine? You are certain?"

"I can hear the air leaving and the sound of the screw changing as the water gets denser."

"Load tubes one through four. The carrier groups first vessel to exit is a submarine. We must consider this."

I-62, JAPANESE SUBMARINE SOUTH OF SYDNEY HARBOR

Lt. Commander Kobayashi sips his tea and observes his watch team. Sonar, "Sir the target is a submarine. I hear the air escaping."

"Could it have been holed by the cannon fire?"

"No, Commander. I would have heard the explosion. The shells fell harmlessly into the sea. Also, Commander, the speed of the screw is changing."

"Understood. Could it be one of our friends?"

"The screw is wrong."

"Flood tubes one through four."

USS SAN FRANCISCO

Once they've settled at 200 feet with 100 feet under them, Cumberland asks, "What did you tell them? I caught their end of the conversation."

Morrison, "I told them to report to Admiral Halsey for re-assignment."

Cumberland chuckles, "An inauspicious beginning. We need more water under our keel."

It's a slow process using sonar alone to avoid all the cargo ships as the work their way out to sea. As the sun rises, the cargo ships shift their headings as they jockey for position to enter the harbor.

ST1 Brown, "Conn, Sonar. Submerged contact bearing 167. Designate Sierra 1. Same bearing as Tango 9."

Mallory and ET1 Andrew Brown are working the tracks. Tango 9 is sixteen miles to their south. Morrison, "Chart depth shows 300 feet."

Cumberland, "The ship is going to pull in. No way the sub can sneak in submerged. The harbor isn't that deep."

"Conn, Sonar. Tango 9 has increased blade count."

Backes, on watch, "Very well."

Cumberland studies the chart and smiles, "Make our course 150. Load and make ready tube 1 and tube 2 with Mark '48s."

The torpedo crew below race into action.

Ensign Harvey and Ensign Vaught are observing from the rear of control. Harvey whispers to Vaught, "Wonder why two torpedoes?"

Cumberland's head comes up, and they shut up, "If there's one, there are probably others. I don't want to lose time later."

The cargo ship turns toward the harbor, and the Japanese submarine stays on its course, creeping along the bottom.

"Conn, Sonar. Submerged target at 130. Designate Sierra 2."

Cumberland, "Range on Sierra 1?"

"Eight miles at 182. Its course is approximately 320. Speed is 2 knots."

Cumberland, "Very well."

"Conn, Torpedo. Tube 1 and 2 are loaded with Mark '48s. Tubes dry."

Cumberland, "Flood and equalize tubes 1 and 2."

Mallory, "Sir, Sierra 2 is ten miles at 136. Course is 300. Speed is 3 knots."

Cumberland studies the table. A cargo ship is steaming across them heading for the harbor. "The tramp above us will mask the noise. Open doors on 1 and 2. Match bearings. Tube 1 for Sierra 1. Tube 2 fore Sierra 2."

A moment, "Bearings matched and cross checked."

"Conn, Torpedo. Doors are open."

Cumberland, "Very well. Ensigns, come here."

They look at each other and walk over, "Vaught, when I tell you, push this button for tube 1."

"Yes, sir."

"Harvey, when I say, push this button for tube 2."

"Yes, sir."

Cumberland, "Fire tube 1." There's a thud, whoosh. "Fire tube 2." Thud, whoosh.

"Conn, Torpedo. Tube 1 and 2 fired electrically."

"Very well."

"Conn, Sonar. Both torpedoes running hot, straight, and normal."

"Very well."

I-62, JAPANES SUBMARINE SOUTH OF SYDNEY

Sonar, "Torpedoes in the water. Two torpedoes."

Kobayashi, "Calm. He could not hit us from where he is positioned."

Sonar, "One is turning, sir. Bearing is constant."

Kobayashi, "Emergency blow. Standby the diesels."

They flip the chicken switches and air is expelled into the

ballast tanks, forcing the boat to surface. They break the surface in broad daylight within sight of the coast.

A sailor on the M/V Devine, a crossing merchant ship, grabs his camera and takes pictures of the Japanese submarine. The torpedo does not care that its target is now on the surface. It just switches from submarine target mode to surface target mode. It drives under the keel at the center of the submarine, and detonates.

The sailor clicks off photo after photo as water shoots up both sides of the Japanese sub. The center of the sub raises up on the bubble of the explosion, then it drops, breaking the sub in two.

He sees the patrol boat turn toward the sinking sub.

I-65, JAPANESE SUBMARINE SOUTHEAST OF SYDNEY

Hearing the torpedoes pings against the hull, LCDR Harada Hakue orders his boat down to near the bottom. The torpedo acquires its target. The ground clutter doesn't confuse it. It explodes right against the hull. A bubble of super-hot, high pressure gas crushes the hull, rapidly increasing the pressure throughout the sub. The sailors die in an instant.

CHAPTER 21

USS SAN FRANCISCO

0551, 23, February, 1942

Morrison watches the two new ensigns as the torpedoes make their run. Sonar reports the progress of the torpedoes and the OOD counts down the time to impact. At the first hit, they flinch. At the second, they pale. Morrison, "Harvey, Vaught, could you come forward with me?"

Cumberland, "Congratulations, men, you're blooded."

Vaught, "Thank you, sir."

Harvey, "Th...thank you, sir."

Morrison leads them forward to his stateroom. "Do you need the bathroom before we talk?"

Harvey, "Yes, sir."

"Go ahead. Remember how to use the toilets."

"Yes, sir." Harvey disappears.

Morrison sits, but Vaught stays standing. "Sit."

"Yes, sir."

"Speak freely, Vaught. Share your thoughts."

"Sir, why did he do that?"

"He was taking your measure. We're a warship. We engage the enemy and destroy them."

"But, sir, we didn't even understand what was going on."

"You knew you were firing the weapons, right?"

"Yes, sir."

"Have you ever killed before? Hunted an animal? Shot a squirrel?"

"I'm from Long Island, sir."

"Okay. Killing is a hard business. There are men who simply cannot not do it. In all likelihood, they're better souls than we who can. Do you understand what I mean?"

"No, sir."

There's a knock and Harvey, face still damp, enters and sits down.

Morrison, "Are you okay?"

Harvey, "How many people did I just kill?"

"We just killed about one hundred, maybe one fifty. It's part of the job."

Vaught, "I get it, sir. On the carrier, we probably killed thousands between PI and Tokyo. It sucks, but war should suck."

Harvey, "I've never, myself, with the push of a button killed someone. They all died, right?"

HMAS BALLARAT, J-184

LCDR James Roberts, on the bridge wing, studies the sea with his glass as they approach the first destroyed submarine. There are over a dozen Japanese sailors clinging to each other and debris. Roberts sees a fin slice through the water, "Johnson, fire on the shark." As the sailor machine guns the shark, several Japanese dive below the water. Roberts launches a boat to recover the sailors, but many have already committed suicide.

I-68, JAPANESE SUBMARINE NORTH OF SYDNEY

Sonarman Hiro Sato, "Commander, two torpedoes. Two hits. I am certain of this. One hit the I-62. It blew ballast to confuse the torpedo, yet the torpedo hit it. The other, I believe, hit the I-65. It was very deep."

Tanabe is silent, thinking.

Sato, "We detected an enemy submarine. The sound of flooding ballast was distinct. Less than two hours and we lose two submarines to torpedoes. Sir, what does it mean?"

Tanabe, "We know an American aircraft carrier came from the future. We are here to kill it. Lieutenant Okamoto, what capabilities would you expect from a future submarine? One built thirty or forty years from now?"

Okamoto, his XO, says, "Their sonar would be far superior. What we use is very new."

"I agree. That means it would be very good at listening. We must be quiet. They must also be faster to deploy with a carrier group."

Sate, "Captain, the submarine I heard had one screw. I am not certain, but I think the screw was large and it turned slowly. It has more than four blades. I think an odd number. Perhaps five."

Tanabe, "Very good. We operate with the assumption that it is superior to our vessel in every way except our minds and our heart. The current is southward. We will move north and make our vessel as quiet as possible."

Okamoto, "But sir, that moves us further from the harbor."

"Yes, and further from the American."

USS SAN FRANCISCO

Morrison walks back in and straight to the chart table. Backes joins him, "The captain is in his stateroom for his after-kill jerk."

Morrison, "Greg, you don't know that's what he's doing.

"He's not sewing a quilt."

"We've sunk three surface ships and nine subs. We've killed, who knows how many people. You don't know what he's doing. We need to focus on finding any other subs out here. Why are we still heading south?"

"Because, wank-o-matic hasn't given us a new course."

Morrison, "Come to new course, 075. When we reach the hundred fathom curve, deploy the tail. At one fifty, turn north. Steer 020 for that leg."

"Yes, sir."

"When we get about twenty miles north of the harbor mouth, we'll turn a westward leg, then another southerly leg. We should box the mouth again and again."

"Do we think they could be further afield?"

"Diesel-electric subs like we are facing had very limited underwater range and endurance. They can't know where the fleet is going. They'll want to be fairly close."

"Yes, sir."

"Let's load tubes 1 through 4. Leave them dry for now."

"What if we need missiles?"

"We're looking for submarines. If the Japanese are this close with surface ships, we let the air force deal with it."

"Roger that, sir."

Morrison goes forward to the captain's cabin and knocks.

"Just a second." After a moment, "Enter."

Cumberland is washing his hands in his sink.

Morrison lays out the search plan.

Cumberland, "How good are our charts?"

"Pretty good, sir. They're based on Royal Navy surveys in the late 1970's."

"Okay. I suspect there are at least one more, maybe two, and there may be more inbound. The Japs have to know how important the carrier is. If they're out there, we need to find them."

I-68, JAPANES SUBMARINE, 65 MILES NORTH EAST OF SYDNEY HARBOR

2310, 23 February, 1942

They surface and start the diesel generators. Tanabe studies the chart, "Lieutenant, one screw only. We want to sound like a fishing vessel."

"Yes, captain."

"Do ten-mile legs, turn east a mile, then another, until we are charged up. I'll be in my cabin."

"Yes, Captain."

CONTROL, USS SAN FRANCISCO, 30 MILES EAST OF SYDNEY HARBOR

0315, 24 February, 1942

Master Chief Godoy and the helmsman are quietly talking. BM3 Bill Jackson asks, "Master Chief, did you find an in-port girlfriend?"

"Godoy, "No. In my heart I'm still married with kids."

Jackson, "Do you have any great port visit stories?"

Godoy, "Not really. I enjoyed the garden and went fishing with a family from Clontarf. It was nice."

"Catch anything?"

"I caught a couple of salmon. We ate some of it, and they smoked and canned the rest for me."

"Did they have a daughter?"

"Two. One was twelve and the other ten."

Lt. Henry Thoreau goes into sonar, "Gordon, what do we have?"

"Nothing new, sir. Way out to the east I'm still hearing the cacophony that's supposed to be convoy 2-18. There are some fishing boats around, but nothing else."

I-68, 30 MILES NORTH OF SYDNEY HARBOR

0400, 24 February, 1942

Tanabe watches from the sail as his sailors man the windlass forward, "I want five fathoms out."

"Yes, sir." They roll out the anchor, then stop it, and lock it in place.

"Now, men, tie that chaff gear very carefully. Our future rides on it."

He watches as they follow his orders, making sure the anchor chain is secure and chaffing gear is locked down. "Good, it is time." In fifteen minutes, they sink beneath the surface using the current to work their way toward Sydney.

USS SAN FRANCISCO

"Conn, Sonar. One of the fishing boats dropped anchor and shut off its engines."

Thoreau, "Very well. Mark its location. Anything else?"

"No, sir."

I-68, 2 MILES EAST AND 1 MILES SOUTH OF THE MOUTH OF SYDNEY HARBOR

1422, 24 February, 1942

Tanabe, "Right ten degrees rudder. Ahead slow." The submarine slowly makes the turn. "Now, we need to let water into our trim tanks very slowly."

"Yes, Captain."

"The bottom is likely rocky. Be careful with the water."

A few minutes later, "Rudder amidships. All stop." They hear a crunch, then the thud of the anchor hitting bottom. The submarine weather vanes in the current and stays put.

SAN FRANCISCO

Thorsen straightens up, "Conn, Sonar. Transient at 285."

Miller, "What do you make of it?"

"Sir, it sounded like something heavy hitting the bottom."

"Is it coming from inside the harbor?"

"I don't think so, sir. This came direct, before any reverberations."

Miller walks into sonar, "Do we have anything at that bearing?"

"Sir, I've been going over the trace. I think this might be something, but it's faint."

"What is it?"

"Sir, with the sound, there was the rattle of an anchor chain. But we don't have anything on the surface."

"Okay, good job. Focus on that area and figure it out. Thank you, Thorsen." He walks back into control and pushes a button, "Captain, possible contact near the harbor mouth."

The fire control tech, "Sir, I've cross bearings from the dome and tail for the transient."

Miller studies the tracks on the chart. They intersect south east of the harbor. Morrison, then Cumberland, come in and straight to the chart table. Miller, "Sonar picked up a transient that sounded like a dropped anchor. We triangulated using the tail and dome. It's about three miles south east of the harbor."

Cumberland, "Could it be an echo from our previous kills?"

Morrison, "Wrong placement, sir. What do we have on the surface?"

Miller, "Nothing."

Cumberland, "It could be a sail boat. Wind up the tail and get us closer. Bring us up to periscope depth slowly and call me before we raise the scope." Cumberland leaves.

Miller issues the new orders, then, "Wouldn't we hear a sail boat?"

Morrison, "Subs have been fooled by sailboats before. It would have to be one hell of a sail boat. The chart has the depth at 180 feet. There are no charted wrecks in the area, either."

Miller, "This is a 1970's chart. Could there be an uncharted wreck?"

Morrison, "Wrecks accumulate. They don't disappear. 180 feet down that wreck would not be hazard to navigation. It isn't a wreck."

Miller, "Debris?"

"With a chain?" Morrison walks into sonar, "I need to listen to it." Thorsen plays it for him. "That isn't a lot of chain, but I agree that it sounds like an anchor."

Thorsen, "Sir, I've been trying to clean up the sounds from before. Listen to this."

Morrison listens. There is a rhythmic creak with a very faint slow thrum. "What do you think?"

"Listen to it speeded up." The creak becomes obviously repetitive and the faint thrum becomes screw noises.

Morrison, "Wow. Good job, Thurman. It's definitely a vessel."

"Yes, sir. A twin-screw vessel with three-bladed screws."

"Right, a sub. Try to find out where it is now."

"Yes, sir."

"Damn good job, Thurman."

I-68

1610, 24 February, 1942

Two knots of current wash by the boat, keeping the bow pointed north. Everyone, except watch standers, are in their racks."

A messenger quietly knocks on the captain's door, "Sir, a group of vessels approach from the east."

Tanabe, "Understood. It's likely a convoy. If any of the vessels have more than two screws, let me know."

"Yes, sir."

USS SAN FRANCISCO

1755, 24 February, 1942

The off-watch officers are eating dinner. Morrison, "The transient we heard is worrying me."

Cumberland, "We need to check it to be certain, but it's probably some uncharted junk on the bottom."

Morrison, "Miller, has Thorsen heard anything new?"

"No, I agree with him, it's likely a sub, but it's become a hole in the ocean."

Cumberland, "It might have drifted south on the current."

They hear, "Captain, we're at periscope depth within ten miles of the excursion."

Morrison and Cumberland put their trays on the scullery board and go into control. Cumberland, "Traffic?"

"Several freighters from a convoy to the north."

Cumberland, "Up scope." Morrison goes to the starboard panel and watches the periscope view from the camera. Cumberland spins it and orders, "Mark."

"348."

"Mark."

"011."

"Down scope. The two sightings are cargo ships."

Morrison, "Tango 27 and Tango 28."

"Agreed."

Morrison, "Sir, can we rig for silent?"

Cumberland tilts his head, a question in his eyes, "Thoreau, rig for silent."

"Yes, sir." The word passes.

Cumberland walks to his XO, "What do you see?"

"Sir, about a year ago, we went out to play with the Nevada. It was a hole in the water. The thing is, we realized a lack of information is information."

"Can you get to your point?"

"We've heard nothing. If it was moving, we would have heard it. Therefore, it isn't moving."

"You think they bottomed the boat? That shit only happens in the movies."

"I know, sir."

"Your boat. Let me know what you figure out." Cumberland leaves.

I-68

"Sir, I hear something odd. It is a whooshing sound like a muffled pump."

"Where?"

"To the east, close aboard."

"How close?"

"Less than a mile."

"Any ideas?"

"No, sir, except, well, sir, if it was on the surface it would sound different, I think. We would surely hear screws."

USS SAN FRANCISCO

Morrison whispers, "We're almost on top of it. Left standard. Make our course 165."

"Yes, sir." The orders are quietly passed and slowly the big submarine turns south

Morrison, "Henry, what's this contact?"

Thoreau walks to the table, "That one? A fishing boat that dropped anchor."

"Henry, the water is 300 feet deep there. It couldn't anchor there...Oh." He picks up a phone, "Captain, could you come to control?"

Cumberland walks in and straight to the table.

Morrison, "Sir, this is what we've figured out from our sonar information. They exited the area yesterday to charge batteries. Before they submerged, they let out a few fathoms of chain from one of their anchors. That was this transient up here. Then they drifted down with the current and settled on the bottom using the anchor to hold them in place."

Cumberland nods his head, "Do we have enough information for a firing solution?"

Morrison, "No, sir."

Cumberland, "I want to kill this clever son of a bitch. How do we do it?"

Morrison, "Those old boats had their anchor forward. By dropping one, they'll weathervane with their tubes facing the fleet as they exit."

Godoy, "Sir, flush the game."

Morrison, "You're right."

Cumberland, "Good. Get us some distance and set up the

305

shot."

CHAPTER 22

JAPANESE SUBMARINE I-68

1843, 24 February, 1942

"Sir, the sound is gone. I think it turned south. I couldn't hear people. I couldn't hear a screw. It was really quiet."

Tanabe, "Thank you." He raises his eyebrow and looks at Okamoto.

"Should we have engaged it, sir."

"Okamoto, our target is the carrier. Also, the carrier is on the surface, thus it will be a far easier target. We wait."

"You think they leave soon?"

"They sent out this submarine to eliminate the threat we pose. This would not be done unless it is in preparation to leave."

"Yes, sir."

USS SAN FRANCISCO

ST2 Gil Gordon, "Conn, Sonar. Before we lost it in the baffles, I could hear people talking in Japanese."

Morrison walks in and listens, "I can't catch it all. They knew we were near, and were discussing whether to attempt to engage us or the carrier." He nods, "Right, that's positive confirmation of the sub's location."

"Yes, sir."

Morrison, "Left standard rudder. New course 050."

Thoreau, "Sir, sorry about thinking it was a fishing boat."

"Henry, it's an easy mistake to make. Unload tube 4."

"Why, sir?"

"So, we can fire a water slug to flush the game."

"Yes, sir."

Cumberland comes back in and walks to the chart table.

Morrison, "Helm, left standard rudder. Come to new course 010." The helm repeats and the boat tilts in the turn. "Sir, as we were departing the area, Gordon picked up some spoken Japanese. They know we are out here somewhere."

"How?"

Morrison, "I let us get too close. It could be they heard the coolant pumps."

"Yet, they made no attempt to engage?"

"Sir, their target is the carrier."

"Tube 4 is unloaded."

Morrison, "Very well. Stand by to flood tubes 1 and 4."

USS SAN FRANCISCO

TM3 Evan Trindle, "Chief, what the fuck? Why would we fire a water slug?"

Kennedy, "Because they told us to." The sub heels to port.

Over the box, "Torpedo, Conn. At the same time, flood tubes 1 and 4."

Kennedy, "Evan, Guiles, at the same time, open the flood

308

valves. Okay, crack open the vent valves."

JAPANESE SUBMARINE I-68

"Captain, they flood tubes."

Tanabe, "Let us turn our rudder full right. Stand by on engines. Stand by to blow ballast. Flood tubes 1 through 4. Sonar, can you give a bearing?"

"053, sir."

"Set depth to sixty feet with a one degree spread."

USS SAN FRANCISCO

"Conn, Sonar. They're flooding tubes."

Cumberland pushes the button for torpedo, "Get those doors open."

JAPANESE SUBMARINE I-68

"Conn, Torpedo. Tubes are flooded, opening doors."

Tanabe, "Blow ballast. Ahead full. New course 053."

USS SAN FRANCISCO

"Conn, Sonar. They are blowing ballast and opening doors."

"Conn, Torpedo. Doors are open."

"Conn, Fire Control. Bearings matched and cross-checked."

Cumberland, "Fire 1." Thud, whoosh.

"Conn, Torpedo. Tube 1 fired electrically."

"Conn, Sonar. Torpedo running hot, straight, and normal."

Morrison, "Cut the wire and the shut the doors. Ahead flank. Power limiting. Left full rudder."

Cumberland looks at Morrison, "Morrison, we'll broach. Why?" The sub shakes.

"Conn, Sonar. Sierra 3 has fired torpedoes. Two, three, no four torpedoes. Bearing is 307 constant."

Backes, "Captain, we've broached."

Cumberland, "Very well."

JAPANESE SUBMARINE I-68

They feel the sub shudder as it discharges the four torpedoes. The torpedoes have gyros to keep them on their set course regardless of where the nose of the submarine is pointing. The men can hear the high-pitched pings of the incoming torpedo.

Sonar, "Captain, all four torpedoes are traveling straight and on course. The enemy submarine is making noise. They are speeding up. They are turning south."

The pings get closer and louder.

Tanabe, "If we take them with us, it is an honorable death."

The torpedo explodes under the center of the surfacing submarine, breaking it in half.

USS SAN FRANCISCO

"Conn, Sonar. Our torpedo detonated. Sir, it's a hit."

Cumberland pushes the button, "Their torpedoes, where are they?"

"Conn, Sonar. They're close, sir. I think they'll pass astern."

"How close?"

"Less than a hundred feet."

Cumberland takes in a deep breath and lets it out, "Thank you, XO. I'll be in my stateroom."

Morrison finally exhales, and only then realizes he's been holding his breath. He rubs his face, "Ahead 1/3. New course," he looks at the chart. "New course 080. When those torpedoes run out, Greg, take us south east into deeper water. We continue boxing, looking for more."

"Yes, sir. Are you alright?"

"He said, thank you."

"I know. High praise."

"I need to wash my face. As I said, we keep boxing."

HMS BALLARAT

The Ballarat is still in position at the site where the first two Japanese submarines were sunk. Roberts sees a third Japanese sub surface, then explode. "Bloody hell."

The San Francisco broaches, its screw thrashing the water when the bow comes down, then it slips back under the sea.

Roberts, "Put the boat out. The Yank shark has killed another sub."

His XO asks, "Sir, is that the boat we fired on?"

"Yeah, I think so. No pictures. It's top secret."

"I can see why."

Roberts, "Yeah, me too."

"Sir, did you report to Halsey?"

Roberts, "The squadron commander did. They didn't respond with a light as was required."

"Maybe they don't have signal light. I mean, where would you put it?"

"True." They see the shadow of the submarine pass down their port side a few miles away.

USS SAN FRANCISCO, 20 MILES EAST OF SYDNEY

0830, 25 February, 1942

Cumberland walks in. Backes, "The Fife and Jarrett are outside the harbor. The Hobart and three Aussie destroyers are on their way out."

"Very well. Any submerged contacts?"

"No, sir."

"Good. Make our course 170."

BATTLESHIP TIRPITZ, 150 MILES NORTH OF THE FAROE ISLANDS

2345, 24 February, 1942

Kapitan zur See Karl Topp paces his bridge. Out there somewhere is a British convoy that was spotted by a reconnaissance aircraft the day before. They don't dare turn on their radar. It may help them see, but it is a beacon for an aerial attack. "Lieutenant, what does our mast head watch see?"

"He has only gotten there, sir."

Topp continues to pace. "Bridge, mast head. Masts of three vessels to our north. One looks like an aircraft carrier."

Topp picks up the phone, "Petty Officer, what is their course?"

"Sir, they are three, five, and nine points off the port bow. Bearing is constant, drifting west. Range no more than ten miles."

"Battle stations. Gunnerey action to port. Right standard rudder. New course 070. Turn on our gunnery and navigation radar."

HMS VICTORIOUS, 11 MILES NORTH OF TIRPITZ

Captain L. D. Mackintosh sits in his chair listening to his watch team. To their starboard steams the heavy cruiser Berwick. To their port is the battleship King George V. Station keeping in the fog is a real challenge. He hears, "Captain, radar warning."

"Battle stations, gentlemen." He rises and heads for combat. From the corner of his eye, he sees orange-yellow flashes to the south. He looks to starboard. The King George V is still there. He picks up a radio microphone, thinking the fire must be from the convoy escorts. "We're a British unit. Cease fire. Cease fire."

Three of the four 14-inch shells in the first salvo miss. One hits the Berwick in the bow, exploding with a tremendous report.

"My word." He goes below to combat.

PORT AFT MISSILE LAUNCHER, TIRPITZ

Through the view port, Schmitt watches the battle. The rumbling roar of salvo after salvo being fired hit him like hammer blows. All four turrets fire in the second salvo. He watches as the shells hit and a ship explodes. The shock wave moves the fog, and for a moment, he can see clearly. The ship is a heavy cruiser. Beyond the cruiser is an aircraft carrier and a battleship.

"What is happening, sir?"

"Three ships. We just sank a heavy cruiser."

The men cheer. Kapitan Topp maneuvers the Tirpitz to the side of the sinking cruiser as his ship fires another salvo. Three shells hit the carrier.

HMS VICTORIOUS

Aircraft Handler, Petty Officer Malcolm scrambles back to his feet on the flight deck and runs to man a hose. The debris of shattered aircraft block his way. He climbs around and gets to the cat walk and grabs a hose. Two more rounds hit the stern. This time, he keeps his feet. He hears the King George V open fire ahead of them. He can barely hear the sound of the guns. He fakes out the hose and charges it. Back up on the deck, he advances against the fire.

TIRPITZ

Kapitan zur See Karl Topp is on the phone, "I understand, Admiral." He hangs up, "Right full rudder. Ahead flank. It is time to withdraw." The Tirpitz disappears into the mist from where it came.

HMS VICTORIOUS

Petty Officer Malcolm stands at the edge of a gaping hole in the flight deck spraying water on the fires below. The sprinkler system helps put out the flames. The spilled aviation fuel, the primary fuel for the fire, has been mostly sprayed down scuppers and over the side. He hears a voice at his side, "How are you doing, Petty Officer?"

He looks over and sees Captain Mackintosh standing beside him, "I think we got it, sir."

"I think you do. I'm told you were the first to man a hose. I do believe your timely action contributed significantly to saving the ship."

"Sir, we all do our bit."

"We do, indeed."

USS FIFE, 8 MILES NORTH OF DEAL ISLAND IN BASS STRAIGHT

0625, 25, February, 1942

CDR Wakefield, "Ahead 1/3."

"Ahead 1/3rd, ordered and answered." The ship slows down from their two-hour high-speed run.

"Very well. Mark depth."

"Ninety fathoms by chart."

"Set maneuvering."

"Set maneuvering, aye."

She walks into combat, "Lieutenant Calvert, let's win some whiskey. Yankee search."

USS SAN FRANCISCO, 200 FEET AND 8 MILES WEST IN THE BASS STRAIGHT

Miller and his watch team or relaxed, but attentive. Then they hear the boo waa sound of active sonar. "Shit! Sonar, where is it?"

"It's the Fife, sir. They're about ten miles at 082."

Cumberland bulls his way into control in his underwear, "Fucking, lose them!"

Miller, "Yes, sir. Left full rudder."

Morrison walk in straight to the table. Cumberland joins him. Morrison points at the chart, "We've only 300 feet under our keel and it's getting shallower. No thermocline."

Cumberland, "Fuck! Ahead flank. Right rudder. Get us back on course."

Morrison, "Sir, it gets shallow. Can we come to 100 feet?"

Cumberland, "Two degrees up bubble. Come to 100 feet. Shit, this gets shallow."

"Yes, sir. It's what she counted on."

Cumberland, "Ahead 2/3rds. I ain't going to lose the boat on a bet."

Cumberland and Morrison study the channel and the water depth. They're fairly trapped.

USS FIFE

Calvert transferred from the Long Beach when he was commissioned. "Captain, they're slowing and staying in the channel."

"So, he won't risk his boat to beat us. Good."

Flanagan, "Twenty more minutes."

Calvert, "Captain, we have another submerged contact at 265 and 40 miles."

Wakefield, "Switch to targeting sonar for three pings. Directed in on the new contact."

After three pings, she says, "Stop search and targeting sonar. Bridge, left full rudder, take us about and return to station."

Flanagan, "You're not going to prosecute it?"

"We've humiliated them enough."

USS SAN FRANCISCO

Cumberland, "It's less than an hour. What's she doing?"

Morrison, "The last few were targeting sonar. There's something out there."

"Conn, Sonar. New contact, bearing 260. Designate Sierra 4. Twin three bladed screws."

Morrison, "Sonar, what is the Fife doing?"

ST1 Brown, "Sir, they're coming about. I think they're leaving."

Cumberland, "They found it?"

Morrison, "And they're leaving it to us."

"Hmm. Backes, work up a track. Load tube 2." Cumberland leaves.

Backes, "They probably figure we've been humiliated enough."

Morrison, "There are a lot of rocks and outcroppings out here. An ASROC has a good chance of missing, and no captain wants to dance close enough to engage with ship-mounted torpedoes."

Backes, "They have their helo's, too."

"True." He pushes the button, "Sonar, what is Sierra 4 doing?"

I-74, IMPERIAL JAPANESE KAIDAI-TYPE SUBMARINE

LCDR Reo Wakasugi studies the chart, "Make our course 235. Bring us to periscope depth."

His XO, Lt. Yuuto Sahashi, "Sir, the sonar stopped."

"Do you presume they did not find us?"

Sahashi, "Why would they stop?"

"Would you go into a hole after a dragon? They will coordinate an attack. It is why we must move."

The Conning Officer, "We are at periscope depth."

Wakasugi raises the scope and does a quick 360. "Nothing. We surface and start the diesels."

USS SAN FRANCISCO

"Conn, Sonar. Sierra 4 is surfacing."

"Conn, Torpedo. Tube 2 is loaded."

Morrison, "They're clearing datum as fast as they can."

Cumberland, "It's unlike the Japanese to run away. Flood tube 2."

"Yes, sir, but in this shallow water they must know they're vulnerable. They're probably hoping to ambush the fleet on the other side."

"Conn, Sonar. Sierra 4 has started diesels."

Cumberland, "Range?"

"Eleven miles, sir."

Morrison, "Sir, if we hit them in this deeper area, they won't become a hazard to navigation."

Cumberland nods, studying the chart.

"Five miles, sir."

Cumberland, "Open tube 2. Chief Barton, would you like the honor?"

Barton gets up from his station, "If you like, sir."

"Tube 2 doors are open."

Cumberland, "Go ahead, Chief."

Barton looks the captain in the eyes and pushes the button, "Eighty people dead, sir." He returns to his panel.

"Conn, Torpedo. Tube 2 fired electrically."

"Conn, Sonar. Fish is hot, straight, and normal."

Backes, "Very well."

The Japanese submarine does not react.

JAPANESE SUBMARINE I-74

Over the noise of their diesels, sonar on the Japanese submarine cannot hear the incoming torpedo. On the sail, Lt. Sahashi is searching a slow 360 around his sub. He sees nothing out of the ordinary. Modern torpedoes do not make a tale-tell line of white bubbles that WWII torpedoes did. Sahashi cannot even hear the high-pitched pings of the torpedo's sonar.

He feels the deck sharply lift and sees massive columns of water rise up on each side of the submarine. A rush of air comes out of the open hatch, then the deck drops, hard. Holding onto the bridge coaming, he looks aft and sees the stern moving separately from the bow. "Fuck! Fuck! Fuck! What weapon does this?"

The crew scramble up and out of the hatch of the doomed vessel.

USS SAN FRANCISCO

Cumberland watches the sinking sub on the monitor. Under his breath, "Damn, that was easy. No fun at all."

Morrison, on the attack periscope, says, "Sir, there are survivors. Can I call Fife to pick them up?"

"Do so. If need be, surface the boat." Cumberland leaves control.

"Yes, sir." Morrison picks up the VHF, "Fife. Fife. Fife. This is San Francisco."

"San Francisco, Ghost Rider 333. We're in contact with Fife. Go ahead."

"Ghost Rider, San Francisco. We just sank another Japanese submarine. There are survivors. Can Fife send it's helo's?"

"San Francisco, Carrier Group 2. Do not stop. Fife will take care of the survivors."

Morrison, "Carrier Group 2, San Francisco. Roger." He sends the coordinates. "Left rudder."

"Left rudder. No new course given."

Backes on the search scope, "Holy shit." He watches the stern sink. The bow is at ninety degrees vertical as it slips beneath the waves.

Morrison, "Right rudder. Resume course."

The helm repeats.

JAPANESE SUBMARINE I-74

Sahashi watches his boat slip away, leaving barely a ripple on the water. Then he sees two periscopes looking at him as the enemy submarine slides by. He, and the six other men who survived, won't last long in the cold water.

Minutes later, he hears the rhythmic beat of a helicopter. He watches the strange aircraft hover over them. A man in a sling comes down. He is hoisted into the machine and a sailor zip ties his hands. Forty minutes later, he and his men are let out in a field. They are greeted by two police officers and a posse of farmers with rifles and shotguns.

CHAPTER 23

WASHINGTON NATIONAL AIRPORT

1418, 27 February, 1942

The C-47 bounces once on the landing and taxies to the terminal. Lt. Kichiro looks out the window. His mood matches the rainy weather. The engines finally stop and he gets up and walks forward. "Guys, thanks for the ride."

Captain Archer, "No problem. We wish you the best."

The cargo master has the door open and is unloading the mail and packages. Kichiro grabs his bags and climbs out of the plane. He trudges through the rain into the terminal. On one side there's an empty desk. He looks around and sees a few people waiting in the lounge area.

He hears a gravelly voice, "You Kichiro?"

He looks over and immediately recognizes Rickover. He freezes. Rickover founded the naval nuclear program and died in 1986, a retired four-star admiral. Kichiro sees the three stripes of a full commander and relaxes, a little bit. "Yes, sir."

"Come on." Rickover turns and walks away. Once they're in a Navy Ford, he says, "I was told you would probably recognize me. Tell me about your submarine."

"No, sir. I recognize you, sir, but until I'm told by Admiral Klindt what you are authorized to know, I ain't telling you shit."

"Good. You shouldn't. I was told you were sharp. We're on the way to see the admiral now."

About a half hour later, they arrive at Admiral Klindt's building. Rickover parks and they go in. They show ID to a sentry, then walk into an office full of manned desks. Vice Admiral Klindt is on the phone, his back to them and looking out a window. "Yes, Senator, but we need approval this week. Good day." He hangs up, "Kichiro, good to see you." He offers a hand, and Kichiro takes it. "What have you shared with Commander Rickover?"

"Nothing, sir. I don't know what he's cleared for."

"Good. He's cleared all the way, for everything you know, including operations. You two will be working together off and on. He sits my chair for propulsion. You'll sit my chair for weapons. I'll give you about a week to get up to speed, then you're going to be bouncing between Keyport, Washington, and Newport, Rhode Island, sorting out our fucked-up torpedoes. Rickover, set him up with a room." He turns away, "David, could I talk you into a cup of joe? Commander Holloway, has Groton gotten back to you? Warren, what the hell is going on at PSNS?"

Rickover and Kichiro leave.

USS SAN FRANCISCO, 200 MILES NORTH OF THE DESOLATION ISLANDS

1400, 1 March, 1942

Morrison looks at the message, "Miller, we've been cut loose to search the Cape of Good Hope."

"Yes, sir. Speed change?"

"I'll talk to the boss." He walks forward to the CO's cabin and knocks, "Sir, we've been cut loose to search the Cape."

Cumberland opens the door, "Ahead full. Sprint and listen. Once you've sorted out the watch team, come back."

"Yes, sir." A few minutes later, he knocks and enters, "Sir?"

"Okay, I've been looking at the chart. Where do you think the German or Japanese subs are likely to be?"

"Sir, it's hard to say. Most of the continental shelf is deep enough for a diesel boat."

Cumberland, "I would put a picket line across the sea lanes. They're so slow, they pretty much have to be where the fleet is steaming."

Morrison, "Does the Royal Navy have a presence in Cape Town?"

"I don't know. They have no subs, that's for certain. We'll get in the shallows east of Cape Town and head south. Well short of the ice, we'll head west a hundred miles and repeat. If there is anything there, we should find it."

"Yes, sir."

TIRPITZ, TRONDHEIM, NORWAY

2010, 1 March, 1942

Oberleutnant zur See Gunter Schmitt is standing conning officer. Binoculars to his eyes, he is studying the water around them. Kapitan zur See Karl Topp, "Oberleutnant, we want to moor against that cliff. Do you see the concrete dolphin?"

"Yes, Herre Kapitan. Right standard rudder."

"Right standard rudder. Rudder is right. No new course given."

Schmitt, "Sir, why did we withdraw?"

"Oberleutnant, our mission is to sink convoys and threaten to sink convoys. We cannot afford to be damaged. The King George V is a fine vessel. They would damage us, if we persisted. We cannot threaten anyone from the shipyard. We bled them, and they will remember. It is enough for now."

SHIPYARD, COCKATOO ISLAND, SYDNEY HARBOR

1628, 02 March, 1942

Amy clocks out of work with her friends. Her face is filthy, except where she was wearing her respirator. Sharon Tinkler says, "Hey Amy, the girls are going out tonight. Wanna come?"

"No, hun. Have fun."

"Come with us, Amy. It ain't like we're planning a pub crawl. We're not trolling for blokes. Come have a beer."

"No, Sharon, I'm married. Married women don't hang out in pubs."

Mary Burns says, "Shar, let her be."

Debby, "Your sailor is half a world away, and he might not survive."

Amy turns on Debby, "Don't you dare talk like that!"

Debby, "It's true. In your heart, you know it. You're turning yourself into a nun for nothing."

Amy, "Debby, what about Gary's friend, Karl? I thought you two were engaged."

Debby, "Yeah, but who knows if he'll come back. Come out with us. He'll never know."

Amy, "I'll know. No. Period. I won't betray my vows. If you don't care about Karl, write and tell him."

Sharon, "Wow. You've become a stick in the mud."

Debby, "No. He was fun, and who knows."

Amy sighs, "I hope you have fun. I will never, ever go to a pub without my husband."

Sharon, "Okay. Sorry."

USS SAN FRANCISCO, 80 MILES OFF THE COAST, NW OF CAPE TOWN

1613, 2 March, 1942

Cumberland, "I thought for certain the Germans would guard the Cape."

Morrison, "I did as well."

"Conn, Sonar. Multiple vessels to the north west. Range is distant."

They look at each other and Cumberland smiles, "A convoy. That's where they are."

"It'll have escorts, sir."

Cumberland shrugs, "World War II destroyers, child's play."

"Yes, sir."

"You don't think so?"

"I brought it up for consideration. The German subs will know there are escorts as well. It will impact their tactics."

"Did the Kriegsmarine fear Allied destroyers?"

Thoreau, "I've read about that, sir. They respected them, but did not fear them."

Cumberland, "Right. Take us to 600 feet. We get ahead of the convoy and give it a free escort north. No contact with the escort, unless it's unavoidable."

"Yes, sir."

"Carry on." Cumberland leaves.

PIRBRIGHT ARMY TRAINING CENTER, SURREY, ENGLAND

0800, 3 March, 1942

Captain Louis Mossberg, USMC, sits at a table. He is not manacled and he has a glass of water. Colonel Albright sits across from him, "Let's go over this again."

Mossberg, "Enough man. Have you contacted my embassy?"

"In due time."

Mossberg leans forward, "Colonel, that time passed weeks ago. Both of us know you and your organization are in violation of a cubic shit ton of laws. We're supposed to be allies."

"What was so important about your aircraft?"

"Don't go back there. We've already plowed that ground."

"What kind of aircraft were you flying?"

"It was a Lamborghini Countach, model F. U. Does the Corps even know I'm here?"

"Come, come, Captain, you're an African officer. Your precious Marine Corps does not give one wit about you. Your best choice is to cooperate with us."

Mossberg laughs, "For an intelligence operative, you're a horrible liar. You know nothing about the corps."

"Then educate me."

"You all have Gurkhas in your army, right?"

"Of course."

"And, they are famous for being kick ass warriors. Disciplined, professional, little bundles of fucking whoop ass, right?"

"Colorfully put, but accurate."

"In Belleau Wood the Germans were more afraid of the U.S. Marines than they were your Gurkhas. Marines get the corps lore with every fucking push up, and every Marine is a rifleman first. You best understand, Colonel, the only reason I'm still here is because I want to be, and the only reason you're alive right now, is because I want you to be. When I rejoin with my beloved corps, they'll welcome me with open arms, because I'm a United States Marine and I bleed red like any other Marine. Now, can we fucking talk about something I might, I say, I just might be willing to help you with?"

The colonel looks Mossberg in the eyes. The black man's face is still and calm, but his eyes...his eyes are on fire. "Please, we can discuss this thing."

"Okay, it's obvious that you guys have no answer to the German jet I saw yesterday. If you had an answer, I would have heard it. Do you want to know something about the jet you're facing?"

"I would."

"It is the MiG-29. It's a Russian jet that was sold to the East Germans before the wall fell. It's a solid gen four jet that's as agile as hell, but it does have some issues. First, it has really short legs. It has a combat radius of about 400 miles. Less, if they expect to dog fight. It can only fit heat-seeking and medium range guided missiles. Also, it runs like an Italian sports car."

"I'll need some clarification. First, how do you know so much about them?"

"I was at Brendenmeyer to fly against them. A couple of months ago, I was sitting in the cockpit of one. Oh, that's something else. It's instruments suck. They're not at all intuitive to use."

"What type of aircraft do you fly?"

"Don't make me kick your ass. I call it an Italian sports car because it is beautiful and drives like a mother fucker, but it requires a great deal of care to keep it in the air."

"It must have been a fighter if you meant to fly against the German jet."

"Okay, we're done, Colonel. Get ahold of my embassy before I walk in myself and say hi."

"I'll see what may be done."

"I know pretty close right where it is. You know, I wonder what the American press will make of my treatment."

"Your own people treat Africans much worse."

"Yeah, I know. It's like two brothers picking on each other. They can be absolutely terrible to each other, but if someone else picks on one of them, the other will defend his brother with his life."

"Perhaps, I'll see what I can do. It would be easier if you were more cooperative."

"I might be more cooperative once I communicated with higher and received guidance as to what we are sharing, and what we are not. Until then, you are demanding that I break my oath, and that ain't gonna happen."

USS SAN FRANCISCO, 500 MILES WEST OF LIBERIA

0914, 3 March, 1942

Cumberland paces, head down, mumbling. Morrison walk in to control. Lt. Thoreau is on watch as they steam north of the convoy. Morrison first studies the chart. The convoy has four columns of six ships, with a destroyer at the van, and one on each flank. The San Francisco is forty miles ahead of the lead destroyer. Cumberland joins him, asking, "Where the fuck are the U-boats?"

"Hard to say, sir. I know at this time; some were off the American coast. Some are sitting on the convoy lines mid-Atlantic. Some are pursuing convoys like this one. We know Germany had a time travel event. That's where the jets came from. What we don't know is how that changed their strategy."

"This sucks." Cumberland takes a deep breath, "Carry on." He leaves.

Thoreau walks back to the table, "Why is the captain so moody, sir?"

"Don't worry about it, Lieutenant."

"Sir, that's terrible advice. When the guy in charge is floating way below his plimsoll mark, the only sane thing to do is worry."

"Point taken. He's worried that we haven't found any U-boats. Keep in mind, Thoreau, negative talk about the captain can way too easily take on the air of mutiny or sedition. He's the boss. You don't have to like him to work for him."

"Yes, sir."

"Conn, Sonar. New contact. Bearing 310. Designate Sierra 5. It has twin screws. Three-bladed. It sounds like a surfaced submarine."

Morrison calls the captain back in. He's bouncing as he walks in and heads straight to the table. Morrison, "We're heading straight toward it. Should we turn to get a range?"

"No, we'll catch up to it soon enough. Load and make ready tube 4."

The order is repeated.

"Sir, the range is 45 miles. Its course is 135. Speed ten knots."

Cumberland, "It's on a reciprocal course. These Germans are in a hurry to die."

Morrison, "Sir, their strategy is generally to shadow a convoy and call in a wolf pack. If we're patient, we might take out the whole pack."

Cumberland, "True. But, if we kill this one, the wolf pack won't gather. Safer for the convoy. I don't want to wait."

"Yes, sir."

"Conn, Torpedo. Tube 4 is loaded."

Cumberland, "Flood it."

They wait as the target continues straight on, getting closer.

Cumberland, "Take us to periscope depth."

The sub climbs up to 150 feet. Miller, "Left standard rudder."

Cumberland, "We're alone. Bring us up."

Miller pauses, then, "Yes, sir." He gives the order.

Morrison studies the chart table. The target is passing down their starboard side, and at the closest point, is only two miles away. Cumberland, "Open the door." He goes to the attack scope.

"The door is open."

"Up scope." He spins the scope, settles on the target, "Mark."

"024."

"It's a German sub. Fire tube 4." He lowers the periscope.

Morrison, looking at the screen, "I agree." He pushes the button. Thud, whoosh. "Tube 4 is fired."

"Conn, Torpedo. Tube 4 is fired electrically."

"Very well."

"Conn, Sonar. Torpedo is hot, straight, and normal."

"Very well."

Miller starts counting down. "Conn, Sonar. Sierra 5 is turning left."

Cumberland raises the scope again.

GERMAN SUBMARINE U-105

Kapitanleutnant Heinrich Schuch shouts, "Full left. Dive! Quickly!"

The bridge crew slides down from the bridge and shuts the hatch, "Captain, last man down, bridge rigged to dive."

"Engines secured."

"White board."

"Open valves. Engage the electric motors. Load tubes 1 through 4."

They can hear the pinging of the torpedo. One of his lieutenants, "Sir, what is this?"

"They have guided torpedoes? They must."

"Will it miss?"

"I doubt it."

The torpedo explodes against the hull of the boat, crushing and burning the sailors. The sub breaks apart as it sinks. For a time, the screws keep turning.

USS SAN FRANCISCO

Cumberland slaps up the periscope handles, "Yes." He pumps his fist. "Direct hit. No survivors." He stops, seeing his men all staring at him. "Morrison, get us back on course. Carry on." He heads for his stateroom.

WASHINGTON NATIONAL AIRPORT

1334, 3 March, 1942

Kichiro is drinking a cup of coffee and waiting for a transport from Washington state. Looking out the terminal window, he finally sees it land. A few minutes later a squared away Navy lieutenant walks in. He grins, "Lieutenant Simmons? I'm Lieutenant Kichiro. Welcome to Washington, and may God have mercy on your soul."

"Who are you?"

"I work for Admiral Klindt. Let's go, I have a car." Once they're in the car, Kichiro says, "Admiral Klindt is on the hill today. He wants to see you tomorrow morning at eight. Do you want to see your room or your office first?"

Simmons, "When were you born?"

"Oh, yeah. 1966."

"Okay, then. Were you on the carrier?"

"Nope. I'm not sure what you are cleared for."

"Oh. Are you a nuke?"

Kichiro, "Nope, a weapons specialist. Your room or office?"

"It's a work day. The office. Do you know where the room is?"

"Yeah, your rooming with me."

"Oh. Do you know I'm a mustang?"

"So am I. Most of us are. There's one officer you ought to know about. Oh, fuck it, you'll know who he is."

"Hughes. He's NRRO. I've met him."

"Nope. Here we are." They go into the building and up the stairs, showing their ID to get into Klindt's office. As they walk in, Rickover is walking out. He stops, "You Simmons?"

"Yes, sir."

"You have a board tomorrow night."

"Um, yes, sir."

"We've a great deal to accomplish, so don't sit on your rear wasting oxygen. Kichiro, when do you leave?"

"Tomorrow at 0615, sir. I have everything in order for the trip."

Rickover, "Who are you meeting with?"

"Captain Jerkin and his staff. I'll also be sharing the good news at the shop level."

Rickover, "Remember, we demand absolute compliance with standards. No deviations. No excuses."

Kichiro, "Yes, sir. I'll be focusing on testing and QA. Once I have the command on board, I'll be there until it's squared away."

Rickover, "Good." He walks out.

Simmons, "That...that was Hyman Rickover."

"Commander Rickover to you. You're a nuke, so you probably already know what he's about."

"I've heard stories, but never met him."

Kichiro turns to Simmons, "Rickover is simple. Never bull shit him. Never guess. Never promise. Have facts, not assumptions. Oh, and never chit chat. He has zero patience for idle talk. If you have nothing to report, just say so, and move on."

"How did you learn all that?"

"By fucking up and seeing others fuck up. Here's our desk. My stuff is in this drawer and this cabinet. We have an extra chair."

"We have to share a desk?"

"I'm sorry, I thought you were a lieutenant. Now, if you're a captain, or something, I'm sure we might accommodate you. Hell, neither of us is likely to be here much. Let me show you around."

"What ship were you on?"

"Lieutenant Simmons, do you need that information to do your job?"

"I don't even know what my job is."

"Me, neither. You'll find out tomorrow. Okay, here is where we keep our office supplies. Over there is the secure storage. This set is weapons systems. This is propulsion, and this half is nuke. If they need you to have access, they'll issue you a pass. Ronald is the day custodian." He turns to Ronald, "Hey, Ronald, how's it going?"

Ronald just looks at him, "Hey, back. New guy?"

"Yeah, anyway, check out stuff from Ronald, and for God's sake, do not ever leave anything laying around. Clear?"

"Hello, Ronald. Sorry." He turns back to Kichiro, "I'm a nuke. I know how to handle classified stuff."

"Okay. This section is the Manhattan files, and this is electronics."

"We have the Manhattan project?"

"We are the Manhattan project, and all other projects. You need to wrap your head around what we are doing here. The war will be won, or lost, in this room."

"What do you mean?"

"Klindt said it, and it's smart. In warfare, the side who evolves fastest almost always wins. We are creating the tools our warfighters will need. Our purview is all new technology from soup to nuts."

"I see."

"If we're fucking off, we're killing servicemen. We don't have the time."

"Got it. Sorry, I was a little slow."

"Truth, you're figuring it out faster than I did."

Captain Warren walks up and sticks out his hand, "Hi, I'm Captain Warren."

Kichiro, "Captain, this is Lieutenant Michael Simmons."

Warren looks Simmons over, "Okay. Squared away, I see. You're going to be standing up a nuclear maintenance facility on the sub tender Beaver. It's currently in Boston. You'll have a month to prepare all the shops a nuclear submarine needs to be maintained."

"We have a nuclear sub?"

Warren smiles, "Kichiro, he's cleared in on anything you know. Kichiro came to us from the San Francisco. It's currently transiting the Atlantic and will need your help."

Simmons, "In a month, I'll be lucky if I'm able to convince the crew on cleanliness and basic sub safe. Oh, do we have copies of the sub safe program?"

Warren, "We do. Kiche, I got him from here. And Kiche, we all have time to breath. You're right about fighting the war from our desks, but if we have no time to relax, our effectiveness goes down. Why don't you pack and prepare to leave?"

CHAPTER 24

USS SAN FRANCISCO, 100 NM EAST OF DAYTONA BEACH, FLORIDA

1140, 5 March, 1942

It's broad daylight and they are in sight of the beach. A German sub is stalking an oil tanker. Cumberland orders tube 1 fired. Backes counts down the shot, as Cumberland watches through the periscope. They hear the rumbling concussion from the hit. Cumberland pirouettes and claps his hands, "Got you, mother fucker. Morrison, we continue up the coast." He heads forward.

BUILDING 35, NAVAL TORPEDO STATION, KEYPORT, WASINGTON

1000, 5 March, 1942

Kichiro takes in the beautiful brick building, then walks in. A receptionist asks, "Can I help you, Lieutenant?"

"Yes, I have an appointment to see Captain Jerkin. I'm with Vice Admiral Klindt's office."

"Of course, just a moment." She makes the call.

Jerkin comes in from a hallway, "Good afternoon, Lieutenant. How can I help you?" He offers a hand.

Kichiro takes his hand, noticing the academy ring. "I need access to all your shops and personnel. I need to correct the problems with your torpedoes and start the manufacturing lines for better torpedoes."

"Lieutenant, there's nothing wrong with our torpedoes." He walks Kichiro back to his office.

"Sir, I understand your position. Please understand, I'm a torpedo expert who came back from 1990. When I say there are problems with the Mark 14, it isn't conjecture or suggestion. I know the torpedo is faulty and I know what is wrong with it."

"So, you're one of those time travelers. Tell me, in 1990 did they teach lieutenants to respect captains?"

"Sir, it is not my intent to disrespect you. My sole intent is to give the warfighters at the pointy end the exact tools they need to be successful."

"Well, I'm sorry you came all this way to waste your time. We do not desire or need your help here. Good day."

"I don't think you quite understand, sir. I work directly for Vice Admiral Klindt. He's not asking or suggesting. I've been ordered to correct the problems and set up new lines. I'm hoping we can work together to that end."

"Well hope your ass out the door and get the fuck off my base. There is nothing wrong with our torpedoes."

"Sir, I fucking know your torpedoes are fucked the fuck up, now quite fucking blustering and help me fix it."

"Fucking leave. NOW!"

"You are killing our men with your fucked up fucking attitude. We have no time for this shit."

"I'm a captain."

Kichiro picks up the phone, dials, and says, "Please connect me with Vice Admiral Klindt's..."

Jerkin rips the phone out of Kichiro's hand and slams it back into its cradle, "LEAVE!"

Kichiro nods, then smiles, "Roger that, dumb ass. The light in the corner of your eye that is flashing. It's your termination alarm." He steps out of the office and asks the receptionist to use her phone. Like gophers, people are poking their heads out of their offices or finding a reason to be in the area. Kichiro completes his call and asks, "Ma'am, is there a place where I could get a cup of coffee?"

"You're not going to leave?" She takes him to a room with a kitchenette.

"I have a job to do. It's a very important job." He pours a cup of coffee, "Thank you." He walks out to the reception area and calmly sips his coffee.

A few minutes later, Captain Jerkin storms out of his office and sees him, "You little son of a bitch. I will fucking kill you!"

Kichiro, "Sir, I wish you luck with your new assignment. Now, I have work to do. Good day."

USS SAN FRANCISCO, 40 MILES OFF CAPE HATTERAS

1822, 7 March, 1942

Cumberland, "Up scope." He spins it, "Mark."

"048."

"Down scope." He steps to the console and pushes the button, "Fire tube 3." The torpedo has a forty second run.

"Conn, Torpedo. Tube 3 fired electrically."

"Conn, Sonar. Fish is running hot, straight, and normal."

"Very well. Morrison, take the search scope."

Morrison raises the scope. It's night, but he can see the German boat on the surface. The flash of the torpedo is attenuated by the water, but in the moonlight, he sees the towers of water and the submarine break in half. "Sir, there may be survivors."

"Radio in their position." Cumberland dances out of control toward his stateroom.

"Yes, sir."

USS BEAVER, AS-5, BOSTON HARBOR

0900, 8 March, 1942

Lt. Simmons stands in the front of a makeshift classroom, "So, this is the first steps we need to take to prepare for our next mission. Questions?"

CDR Marion Netherly Little, "Can you explain why you spent half of the brief discussing cleanliness and quality work?"

"Everything we do must comply with SUBSAFE standards. It's a safety program you are all unfamiliar with. SUBSAFE details exacting standard for the cleanliness, storage, and use of materials to prevent catastrophic loss of a submarine, sir."

"We know how to work on submarines. Our crew is widely respected."

"I know, sir. It's the main reason you were selected. Your crew doesn't have as far to go as some of the others may. No one, other than me, has ever worked on a nuclear-powered vessel. Nuclear power plants require exacting repair standards. In the '60s we lost two submarines because standards had grown lax. The submarine we will be maintaining is a one of a kind. In the Pacific it sank ten Japanese submarines in about two months. It never, not ever once, missed with a torpedo."

Little, "Wow! Never missed? Back to your earlier statement, what is a nuclear-powered vessel?"

Simmons, "That will be part of the training, sir. In a nut shell, the sub uses a steam plant somewhat similar to the propulsion plant on this ship. What is different is where the heat comes from. Sir, are you familiar with Madame Curie's work with the decay of radioactive materials?"

"Somewhat, yes."

"Excellent. There are four ways in which a radioactive material may decay. One is alpha decay, where the material kicks out a helium particle. The second is beta decay, Where the material kicks out an electron. The third is gamma decay, where the material kicks out a gamma. Gamma is our term for a burst of light energy. The fourth, and most relevant, is fission. Fission is where an atom's nucleus splits into two or more fission product daughters. The atom breaks and becomes two or more smaller atoms. This reaction releases an enormous amount of heat and requires no connection to the surface for it to work. The vessel is a true submarine. The subs you are familiar with are surface ships that occasionally submerge for brief periods of time. Our unit spends nearly all of its time submerged. The limits to its time submerged are food, crew endurance, and maintenance."

"And your background?"

"I'm a nuclear power plant officer off a similar vessel, the cruiser Long Beach."

"A cruiser that sinks?"

"No, sir. A cruiser that is powered by the atom."

USS SAN FRANCISCO, 150 MILES SE OF NEW YORK

1613, 8 March, 1942

"Conn, Sonar. This one sounds different. Still two screws and two diesels."

Cumberland rushes sonar, "But, you're certain it's a submarine?"

Brown, "I'm certain it has two, three-bladed screws, and it's on the surface. Sir, that's all I know."

Cumberland goes back into control, "Load tube 2."

Morrison, "Are we going to periscope depth to confirm the target?"

Cumberland swivels his eyes to Morrison and locks on, "It's a submarine."

"Sir, if we commit friendly fire, they'll send us to Adak to count trees."

"Fine. We'll go to periscope depth to look at the pretty German submarine."

As they approach the surface, Cumberland says, "Skip the circle, just bring us up."

Morrison, "Sir, we're not in the middle of the ocean. New York is busy."

"Fine."

Backes orders the turn.

"Conn, Sonar. We've a fishing boat, near aboard, off our port side. It's drifting with engines off."

Cumberland, "How do you know it's there?"

"Sir, the slap of water against the hull, and the fish struggling in the net."

Cumberland, "Okay. Continue north of them, then come to

periscope depth." He looks at Morrison, "Just shooting the fucking torpedo would be easier."

"Yes, sir. But it also would be wrong."

"Well, I hope our German colleagues don't machine gun some poor fisherman as we fuck around down here."

Backes, "Periscope depth, sir."

Cumberland motions for Morrison to take the scope. Morrison, "Up on the attack scope." He spins a quick 360, "Mark."

"198."

That's the fishing boat. Mark."

"112."

"That's a patrol boat or a destroyer escort. Our fishermen are safe."

"This is New York. Find me a fucking submarine." Cumberland stampedes out of control.

Morrison, "Down scope. Make our depth 150 feet. Right standard rudder. New course 090. Ahead 1/3rd."

OLAF'S CAFÉ, POULSBO, WASHINGTON

1734, 9 March, 1942

Kichiro walks in wearing his winter khaki uniform. People stare, but leave him alone. A young, pretty waitress brings him a menu, "I'm sorry, sir. Most of these people have never seen a negro."

"I'm not black. I'm a Chamorro from Guam."

"Isn't Guam in Africa?"

He laughs, "No. Guam is way out in the Pacific Ocean north of Australia and south of Hawaii."

"You speak good English."

"Guam belongs to America. It's a U. S. territory, and has been since the Spanish lost the Spanish American war. May I have the steak and potatoes?"

"Have the Japanese attacked your island?"

"Yes. My family is living under occupation right now."

A MM2 at a nearby table says, "And they say education was bad in the eighties." The MM2 is in his working blue uniform, which is really black. He has the ESWS pin above a handful of ribbons on his left chest. The highest is a Navy Achievement Medal. That pin and that medal did not exist in 1942.

Kichiro, "What's your name, MM2?"

"James Maki, engineering on the Long Beach."

"You, um, the zoomy kind of engineer?"

"I am. I'm also native to southwest Washington."

"Good. You can answer some questions for me."

Maki joins him, "I would be glad to, sir."

USS SAN FRANCISCO, LONG ISLAND SOUND NEAR NEW LONDON, CONNETICUT

0400, 10 March, 1942

Despite the war, the waterfront is lit up as they approach. There's a great deal of boat traffic, as well. A guide boat comes out and leads them up the Thames River.

New London is on the left, and Groton is on the right. Soon, they are steaming past the Electric Boat Yard, where so many submarines are built. The tug boats come along side and nudge them in until they are moored on the south side of pier N. Morrison is focused on mooring the boat and ignores the people on the pier. Finally, he orders the lines heaved and the crew ties her against the pier.

There is the barest hint of sunrise as the port crew tie up to the barges with the concealing curtains. Cumberland comes up to the bridge, "Do they have the plywood to set the brow on?"

Morrison, "I'll make sure of it before it lands, sir."

A crane lowers the brow. Tied to the end of it is a four by four piece of plywood. The men pull it and tie it to the slide rail before placing the brow. Cumberland scrambles down the sail, "Morrison, we have an official party."

"Of course, sir." He looks up and the first person he sees is Rickover. He can't help but smile. He joins Cumberland. The party on the pier come aboard, saluting the flag, then Cumberland.

Rickover asks, "Commander, do your men have this evolution in order?"

"Yes, sir. They do."

Captain Warren, "I'm John Warren. I suppose you recognize Commander Rickover. The third gentleman with us is Mr. Hughes. He's NRRO."

Cumberland, "I see. Welcome aboard, gentlemen. You'll find everything in order."

Rickover, "We'll find things as they are. Don't assume."

Cumberland, "Yes, sir. My wardroom is down here." They wait while three electricians scramble up, salute, and start setting up shore power. They meet Miller in the wardroom. The steward serves coffee and cookies.

Cumberland, "So, this is a Mobile Training Team inspection?"

Warren, "It is. We'll start the admin part here, then shift to drill sets and performance testing at sea. That done, you'll resupply and receive your orders."

Cumberland, "Of course. You have our full cooperation."

Warren, "Good. Now, if you would be so good to inform your crew and let them know liberty call will go down at 1600."

Morrison, "We won't be working late?"

Warren, "We recognize your crew needs some R&R. Shall we begin? We need all the logs for the last month, and Mr. Hughes will start doing walk arounds and interviews. We'll be interviewing every crew member."

Cumberland, "Um, yes, sir."

NUCLEAR VALVE REPAIR SPACE, USS BEAVER

0814, 10 March, 1942

Lt. Simmons silently walks around touching every surface with a white glove. He looks at the contents of every Vidmar drawer, opening it and pulling out every item not on the label. He carefully does this for every single drawer in the large shop area. He finds a drawer of random bolts and nuts. He scoops every one of them out and throws them in the trash.

He looks at his glove, dirty from the drawer, and shakes his head. He puts on another pair and continues. He uses a flashlight to see behind the tool lockers. He climbs a ladder to inspect the wireways for more contraband. He tosses three magazines in the trash. He finds contraband parts. Every item he finds gets thrown away.

The hydro test bench gets special attention. He finds dirt in the hoses. He finds the test gauges are not calibrated. The chief with him writes it all down.

Finally, he turns to the assembled men, "Every time I come in here, this place best be spotless. You're not allowed any tool or part not listed. If you need a tool or part, submit it for addition. If an unauthorized part exists here, it will find its way onto a submarine and kill it. You'll have murdered 120 men.

"I frankly don't care of you are slobs in your rack. I don't care if you cuss a blue streak. What I care about is the work you do, and you will do superb, to standard, to code, to specification work. I require it, and the safety of every man on the submarine requires it. Questions?"

"Sir, why did you throw away our lucky drawer?"

"I just explained. Do you not understand?"

"Sir, all those nuts and bolts are to code. They're designed for use on submarines."

Mike reaches into the trash and pulls out a single nut and hands it to the sailor. "What component does this nut go to? What is it's torque specification?"

"I don't know."

"What is the approved thread lubricant?"

"I don't know."

Mike takes the nut back and throws it away, "Neither do I. It goes in the trash. Every nut. Every washer. Every valve you have will be designed and rated for the specific component it is used on. Those fasteners are coming. They'll be stored in supply as kits. When you do a repair, all new fasteners will be used and the old ones will be pitched."

"Why, if they're still good?"

Simmons, "Every single part you pitch should be good. All these parts are designed with a life cycle. If the life cycle is a thousand heat up and cool down cycles, we'll be replacing it at nine hundred. If a part is bad, there will be a failure on the submarine. Failures on submarines are often catastrophic."

He waits. There are no more questions. "Gentlemen, you're entering an exclusive club. The rules here are exacting, but once you have mastered those rules, you'll be one of the top mechanics in the world. This training will set you up for life, if you take it on board. If you understand, and make your own, the concepts I am teaching you. Carry on."

He changes gloves and leaves for the next shop.

AL'S WATER HOLE, GROTON, CONNETICUT

1710, 10 March, 1942

Mallory walks into the bar with Gustaf and Jackson. All three are in their working blue uniform, known by sailors as Johnny Cashes. It's a dingy place with trestle tables. Mallory holds up three fingers and the bartender pours out three beers. Mallory, "Do you have food?"

"We got spaghetti Bolognese."

Mallory, "That'll work."

Gustaf, "Was this here before?"

Mallory, "Nope. Americans have no love of history. We put up a plaque, save some little piece for a museum, then demolish the whole place to put up soulless minimarts.

Jackson, "Why are you in a funk, Gary?"

"Amy is in Australia."

Gustaf, "So. There are no doubt plenty of hotties here."

Mallory, "Dude, I'm married. There is only one woman who exists for me. I don't cheat and I don't respect people who do."

The only woman in the bar is wiping tables. There's no shortage of sailors, but there's more male yard workers from Electric Boat. A third class in dungarees asks, "What's the special occasion?"

Mallory looks at him, "What boat are you on?"

"Albacore, how about you."

"San Francisco."

"What the hell is the San Francisco? It isn't a submarine."

A second class says, "It's a heavy cruiser. My cousin serves on her."

Mallory, "Ours isn't the cruiser. Ours is an anti-submarine vessel."

"Why does it share the name of the cruiser?"

Mallory, "Because the heavy cruiser didn't exist when our boat was commissioned in 1981."

"Oh, you all are time travelers."

One of the yard workers jerks his head up and looks at Mallory.

Mallory, "We are. We're part of the carrier group."

Jackson watches the yard bird get up and come over. He's a stout red-haired man with a scruff of beard and wearing bib overalls. "I'm Ian Houlihan. I got a letter from the Navy that says I got a grand-daughter who flies jets. Do you know her?"

"What's her name, sir?"

"Lieutenant Gloria Houlihan. Her unit is the Black Knights and she's shot down a passel of Japs."

Mallory, "VF-154. They fly off the Carl Vinson, sir. That's our aircraft carrier. I've seen her at a distance, sir. But I've never met her. She was singing for the crew at a party."

"Is she a pilot or some singing floozy?"

"Sir, she is not a floozy. She's an officer."

"What kind of woman would take a billet meant for a man?"

Mallory, "Sir, I haven't met her. From what little I know, she kicks ass. Also, sir, the leading American ace is a woman."

"So, you think a woman can fight better than a man?"

Mallory, "What are we doing here, sir? Are you trying to goad me into a fight?"

"What can you tell me about her?"

"She's beautiful, with an amazing singing voice. If she's in VF-154, she flies F-14 Tomcats. They're a kick ass fighter. I think, in 1990, the Tomcat was the best fighter in the world. She must be an athlete just to fly. I think our XO has met her. He met some of the pilots in Australia. That's all I know."

"She sings and is a sailor. Fuck. Why has one of my seed gone so wrong?"

Mallory stands up to his full six foot four, "Sir, please do not disrespect an officer you do not know. We are here for a meal and a quiet beer. It would be best if you left us alone."

Ian look up at him and walks back to his table.

Gustaf, "Wow. What an asshole."

Mallory signals the bartender with three raised fingers. "Yeah, it's 1942. That guy remembers when women got the vote. He probably celebrates the occasion each year with a week of mourning."

Gustaf, "I though women could always vote?"

Mallory, "Women got the right to vote in 1920. That's only

twenty-two years ago."

The other sailors have all moved closer to Mallory's table. One asks, "Do you have women on your boat?"

Mallory, "No, we're too small to support coed showers and berthing."

"Is yours a submarine?"

"It's an anti-submarine vessel. That's all we're allowed to say."

"Think we could get a tour?"

Mallory, "No, guys. No way."

"Have you been out?"

Gustaf, "Yeah, we just went around the Cape of Good Hope."

"Have you any kills?"

The three friends go silent. After a moment, Mallory says, "Only a sick mother fucker brags about kills. You don't just kill boats. You kill men. It's something that must be done, but it isn't something to brag about."

Ian Houlihan leaves a paper with his address on the table in front of Mallory, "I'd like to meet your XO."

CHAPTER 25

1823, 10 March, 1942

Morrison and Backes sit at a table with beer and steaks. Backes, "Why do they want to speak with all my guys?"

"The inspector works for Admiral Klindt. I'm assuming he wants to measure our morale."

"Okay, John, but what is he going to do with the information?"

"I don't know. We all serve at his pleasure. That's just how it is."

Backes, "You think he might replace all of us?"

"I doubt it. Some of us may go, though."

"John, I thought he was your friend?"

"He is a friend, and a mentor. That said, we're at war. If I'm part of the problem, then I need to go."

"John, Cumberland is the problem."

"Is he? We've both had bad bosses. He's a competent tactician. He knows how to run the ship. I, though, have been undercutting him with the command. I've been tolerating the crew making fun of him. The problem, from a certain point of view, is me, not him."

Backes, "From that point of view, we're all the problem and

only Cumberland is good. Is that what you believe?"

"No. No, but have I handled it right?"

"John, you're my friend. We've been friends for years. You know I've got your back."

"I'm sorry. I'm just worried. I thought Admiral Klindt would be here."

Greg, "Yeah, I get it. I guess we're not going to be rescued."

"Nope. We'll have to rescue ourselves." They exchange an understanding look.

Greg, "How are we going to do that?"

"Have you noticed that he has calmed down about how we treat the crew?"

"Yeah, as long as he gets his regular fix."

John breaths in and nods slightly, then looks down, "That talk makes me nervous. It's disrespectful. It could be seen as sedition."

Greg, "You're right. We need to lock it down."

"Until relieved, he's the boss. I've already done what I can to inform the upper command about the issue. Also, of late, he's been listening to me."

"How long do you suppose he'll be in charge?"

"No idea, Greg."

"I have had guys asking about re-enlisting for orders."

"Miller has too. We can't replace anyone yet, especially back aft."

A lieutenant commander in winter khakis comes up to their table, "Any chance I could join you?"

Morrison, "Sure. John Morrison, and this is Greg Backes."

"Rick Lake, PCO of Albacore."

Morrison, "XO and Nav on the San Francisco."

Lake, "You're not PCO's?" He signals the staff for another round.

Backes, "Nope. Our boat has a silver leaf for a skipper."

"Oh, you're on the mystery boat. What can you say?"

Morrison, "It was built at New Port in 1981."

Lake stares at him, "You are time travelers. How did that work?"

Morrison shakes his head, "Can't go into it. I can say, it was an accident."

Their beers arrive, "Okay. What can you tell me that will help me kill Japanese subs?"

Morrison, "In this place, nothing. I'll talk to the skipper about holding a seminar or two in a secure location."

Lake, "Thanks. You know, you kind of look Japanese."

"From my mom. My dad was a good Irishman and a Navy officer."

"Do we win?"

John, "We do, but this war is playing out differently than our history did."

Lake, "Should I ask how I do?"

Greg, "Hell, no. Just do it. Trust your instincts and kick ass."

Lake, "Any chance of a tour?"

John shakes his head, "No, sorry."

"Why did they name your sub after a heavy cruiser?"

Greg, "We never said it was a sub."

"Yeah, but you're both wearing dolphins."

Morrison, "Subs become much more important after the war, and heavy cruisers did not. In our time, there are no heavy cruisers in commission, and over a hundred subs."

BUILDING 49, NSB, NEW LONDON

0915, 11 March, 1942

MM2 Jackson walks out of a room, "You're next, Gary."

Mallory knocks on the door and walks in. He stops in front of a chair and comes to attention. Captain Warren says, "Have a seat. I trust you've been through one of these before?"

"I have, sir."

"Okay. Describe all the interlocks associated with the reactor control system." This begins forty-five minutes of detailed and specific questions regarding the engineering systems and other systems on the sub. Warren, "What do you think of Commander Cumberland?"

"Excuse me, sir"

"Please, MM1, it's a straightforward question."

"Sir, it's not at all straightforward. He's the captain. My thoughts or opinions are irrelevant."

Warren, "We've heard about a number of concerning traits with your commander. I know you are on the tracking party and thus in control during engagements. Please share a candid response."

"Sir, as I recall, criticizing a superior officer is disrespect and insubordination. Something like that. You're asking me to violate the UCMJ."

Warren sets down his pen, "You are generally correct. How-

ever, there is a difference between disrespect and performance assessment. I'm asking for your assessment. To your
knowledge, has Commander Cumberland ever violated the
UCMJ, or any other law or regulation?"

"Yeah, sure. He ordered me not to get married when we were
in port in Sydney. I wrote a statement and submitted it to
Commander Miller. Cumberland has publicly mocked the
XO and other crew members. Isn't that cruelty? That's an article, right?"

"It is, article 93."

"Yes, sir. There have been a couple of times he's walked out of
control in the middle of an evolution or attack when precise
movements are required. That isn't against the UCMJ, but it
is weird. One other thing that probably isn't a crime, but
is weird; he seems to get off on killing the enemy. I've seen
him dance after a torpedo hit. That said, we've made a clean
sweep, thus far. We've sunk around twelve submarines and
a couple of surface ships, with no misses. Are you thinking
about relieving him, sir?"

"It's being considered."

"Being as you're asking my opinion; Commander Morrison
is ready for command. He's calm, where Cumberland is difficult. He's moved mountains keeping everything on an even
keel. The two seem to work together, most of the time."

"Do you think Cumberland's behavior is getting worse?"

"I don't think so. In fact, it seems to be getting a little better."

"Thank you. One thing. I have a copy of your statement,
MM1. Did you marry?"

Mallory hold up his ring finger, "Yes, sir."

"Good. I've one more question. Commander Morrison has
recommended you for commissioning. Are you willing to

become a nuclear officer?"

"Will I be assigned to the Frisco?"

"No, you'll be assigned here. We need a systems expert."

"I would be honored, sir."

"Good. Thank you, MM1."

"Can I write my wife and tell her about the promotion?"

"Of course. Could you please tell me about your wife?"

"Sure. Some of us went to Bondi Beach. It's a public beach near the base where a lot of girls hang out. I kept reminding my guys that these were good girls and not prostitutes, because so often, that is what sailors find. Anyway, Amy and her friends work at a ship yard as welding assistants. They had the day off, so they headed for the beach. Truth, she singled me out because I was the tallest. We spent the day together.

"The next day we could meet, I met her mom and dad. Dad was not at all amused. I was respectful. Anyway, we spent the entire day and night together. Somewhere in there, I proposed. I wanted to marry after the war. She flat out said, no. She would marry me, if we did it before the ship left. We were together a week and a half before the wedding."

He looks Captain Warren in the eyes, "She's tough. Damn tough. In that, she takes after her dad. He and I worked it out: the issue was me taking their only child away. I promised him, after I retire, we'd spend most of our time in Aussie. Anyway, Amy is my wife." He hands Warren a photo.

"How many years do you have in?"

"Eighteen, sir."

"You understand, that you cannot retire until after the war is over?"

"Yeah, of course. VJ and VE means free me."

Warren grins, "Okay, better than half of the war time servicemen will leave the service after the war. That isn't an issue for me. Another issue. Are you wanting to pursue a career at sea?"

"If I need to, I will. If I never submerged again, that would be fine with me. Sir, have you ever pushed a button and killed someone?"

"I haven't."

"He stopped doing it, but he would call people up and have them push the fire button. I killed a Japanese submarine. I don't know, maybe fifty, maybe seventy-five, people died because I pushed a button. I know it needs to be done, and I'm okay with that, but I have no desire to personally kill. If I serve out the war at a desk, that is fine."

Warren, "I don't know how it will play out. I do know we desperately need you here. I also know that Admiral Klindt will want you to be a nuclear officer."

"I'm already a watch supervisor. EOOW is easy. When we go out to train, can I stand the control watches?"

"Of course. Who else do you recommend for commissioning?"

"I would say Wankowski, but he already is. ET1 Brown, he's ready. He's the RC division LPO. Chief Giblin. He's the A gang chief. The captain masted him for refusing to push the button. He did it on principle. He knew there were men on board that would protest, and he wanted to be the lightning rod. You need a sonarman. ST1 Brown is our best and he's the LPO. ST1 Thorsen probably knows the systems as well, if not better. That, and he already has a bachelor's degree."

"Do you know his major?"

"Yeah, music theory, with a minor in math. He's from New York and attended one of those high schools for the arts. He knows like a hundred musical instruments, or something. He's brilliant. You know, his best friend, EMC Hines would be a good choice, too, except they already lost Wankowski."

"I don't want to cut the submarine too thin."

"Yes, sir."

WARNER STREET, GROTON, CT

1800, 11 March, 1942

LCDR Morrison, wearing his dress blues, parks his Navy Ford sedan at the curb and walks up to the Houlihan residence. The door is answered by a pregnant blonde woman, "Can I help you?"

"Are you Mrs. Houlihan?"

"I am. Molly Houlihan. What's this about?"

"Did you and your husband receive a letter regarding a granddaughter serving in the Navy?"

"Yes, her name is Gloria. Sorry, please come in. Could I get you a cup of coffee?"

"If it isn't too much trouble, please. My name is John Morrison. I've met your granddaughter. We're friendly, if not friends."

"You know her?"

"Well, to be fair, we met with a group of friends on a couple of occasions when we were in Sydney, Australia. It wouldn't be fair to say she and I are close."

"The letter said she had twelve kills. What is she like? What are your impressions?"

"She's an F-14 pilot with the Black Knights. The plane she flies has a crew of two, a pilot and a radar operator. She's the one who flies the plane."

"What is she like?"

"She's nice. Her manners were excellent when we went to a formal tea. She's really, really smart and very assertive."

"What does assertive mean?"

"Um, she stands up for herself in a positive way. Have you written her?"

Molly, "Ian thinks poorly of her, but I sent a letter to the address they gave us."

"It's very important to support your family who are at war. She needs it."

"Okay, I will, but Ian. I don't know."

John, "I'll speak with your husband."

"Are you Japanese?"

"My mom. My dad was a good Irishman."

Molly, "Oh."

They hear Ian walk into the house. Molly stands, goes to the fridge, and gets a beer, meeting her husband at the door. "Dear, we have a naval officer here about Gloria."

John stands, "Sir."

"Dear, this is Commander Morrison."

Ian gives Morrison a measuring look, "So, you know her?"

Molly, "Why don't I fetch a beer, Commander, and the two of you can chat in the parlor."

Morrison, "Thank you. I've met her. I wouldn't say I know her."

"Well, tell me, why should we support some trollop galivanting around doing a man's work. Is she too ugly to marry?"

"She's not ugly at all. The Navy should have sent a photo."

"Photos can lie."

"Sir, from where I sit, she's a star. She's a member of an elite squadron performing vital work in defense of the free world. I'm having difficulty understanding your objections."

"Are you daft, Commander? A. Woman. Should. Never. Fight. It's a man's job."

"I see. Well, I can see you've made up your mind on this matter. Being that is the case, sir, you don't deserve her. Mrs. Houlihan, thank you very much for your hospitality." He hands her his beer bottle and walks out of the house.

Ian stands to watch him leave. He sees Morrison shake each of his shoes before getting into his car.

BRITISH WELLINGTON, 10000 FEET, 15 MILES SW OF TRONDHEIM, NORWAY

0700, 13 March, 1942

Flying Officer Anthony Haversham sits in the copilot's seat of a Wellington bomber, part of the 156th Bomber Squadron. He, and his pilot, are fighting upper atmosphere turbulence. The plane is shaking so hard, they can hardly hold her in formation. The captain, Flight Lieutenant Peter Shanks looks over to Haversham, "So, Sham, did you score on that girl last night?"

"No, her nickers were too tightly bunched to get them down."

Shanks, "So, she didn't want to see your cockpit?"

"I guess not."

"Well, better luck next time. It's good to be married. You don't have to wonder where your next gash will come from."

Haversham, "And, you don't need to worry about spending your money. You've a wife for that."

Shanks, "Okay, here we go. My bird. Open the bomb bay."

"Your bird."

PORT AFT MISSILE LAUNCHER, TIRPITZ, NEAR TROND-HEIM

Schmitt looks away from his mount to his guys, "This is what we do. It's our job to protect our beloved ship. Please stay focused."

"Launchers, Missile Control, the link is down. Switch to local."

Schmitt flips the switch as his phone talker acknowledges. With the cliff off their starboard side, his launcher has the best view. Schmitt is now controlling the radar on the superstructure. He sees the British bombers in their stepped formation. "All launchers, Missile Control, weapons free."

Schmitt, "Wagner, fire one."

Schmitt keeps the pipper right on target. The missile flies true and hits a bomber. It belches smoke and tumbles. "New target. Fire two." As his missile leaves the rails, another missile hits the bomber he was targeting. He quickly shifts his aim point and his missile shifts and hits another plane. "Reload! Snell!"

He sees bomber after bomber blotted out of the sky as he waits what seems like forever. "Missiles up."

He settles on a target, "Fire one." The missile roars off the rails and hits another bomber. "Good." He looks for more targets. There are none.

WELLINGTON BOMBER, SOUTH OF TRONDHEIM

Haversham, "What the hell was that, sir?"

Flight Lieutenant Peter Shanks, "I don't know. Close the bomb bay doors. Get on the radio. Try to raise any other survivors. We need to get back into formation."

A few minutes later they understand. They are it. Their entire squadron was on this raid. The 156th Bomber Squadron has ceased to exist.

U-160, 150 MILES SE OF NANTUCKET

1215, 13 March, 1942

Oberleutnant zur See Lutz Wechsler, the XO, says, "My Captain, are we not close to one of their Navy bases?"

Kapitanleutnant Georg Lassen, the CO, says, "Watch and learn. We do not just face machines of war. We face men. The Americans are new to war. I believe they would not expect us in their back garden. So, we come here to pluck their plums, while they are powerless to stop us. We charge batteries in the night and park ourselves on the shipping lanes during the day. As we wait patiently the targets will come."

"You are not worried about their submarines?"

"I am not. Their torpedoes go straight like ours. Should they fire on us, we crash dive and the torpedoes will pass over our head."

"Yes, sir."

CHAPTER 26

THEATER, NSB, NEW LONDON

1650, 13 March, 1942

Morrison stands at the front of the room with over a hundred CO's and XO's listening to him. "So, now you understand a bit of the capabilities of the Japanese and German submarines you will be facing, as well as those of a modern, nuclear submarine. Questions?"

Lake raises his hand, "Is that why they pulled the guns off my boat and redesigned my sail and bow?"

"It is. You must surface to use a gun. Surfacing surrenders your biggest tactical advantage. As we start producing guided torpedoes, it will become unnecessary to fire a barrage of torpedoes in the hopes that one makes a critical hit. One will be all that is needed, because it is designed and programmed to make a critical hit."

"How many diesel subs were around in 1990?"

"Other countries had them and some were pretty good. That said, the US was exclusively nuclear, and we had quite a few."

"Did anyone else have nuclear subs?"

"Yes, our allies, England and France. Also, our adversaries, the Soviet Union and China. All other nations used diesel electric, if they had subs at all."

"Who made the Chinese and Soviet subs. Lord knows, they

couldn't."

"After this war, the world changes a great deal. The Soviets and Chinese dedicate themselves to industrialization. By 1955, the Soviet Union is a serious threat. In 1989 they collapse and China fills the power vacuum. Any more questions pertaining to the fight in front of us?"

"Are you Japanese?"

"My mother was Japanese American. My father was an Irish American naval officer. Questions about the fight."

"Who was better? The Japs or Krauts?"

"As I said earlier, they use somewhat different tactics. As for skill, that depends more on the officer in command. Some were quite skilled. Others were less so. I hope all of you are of the former category, and not the latter. In combat, stupid people typically die. Unlucky smart people may also die, but I believe we each create our own luck. Any further questions?"

Admiral Turner steps forward, "Thank you, Commander Morrison. I remind all of you that this briefing is top secret. Take it back to your commands and adapt the lessons. The existence of nuclear submarines is top secret. Carry on." He leaves the room, starting the exodus. A few come forward with questions. One he recognizes immediately, "Hello, Grandpa Henry."

"Hello, John. These folks have questions, and then we can talk."

"Yes, sir."

"Hi, I'm John Bole, PCO of Amberjack. You said you are very familiar with the history of submarine warfare. How well we do I do in the war?"

"Everything is changed now. What happened before won't

happen now. What is relevant is how you manage yourself, and lead your crew going forward. Most of all, do not underestimate the skill of our enemies."

"I'm George Porter, PCO of Bluefish. I take it from the lesson plan, crew training is critical. Do you use academic instruction, walk throughs, or operational training?"

Morrison, "A combination of all three. The emphasis is on demonstrating knowledge and competence through examinations, oral boards, and under instruction watches. Many things, like fires must be simulated. During that kind of training, safety observers are critical."

Porter, "What about those crew who are unteachable?"

Morrison, "Ah. In my experience there is no such thing. You're talking about the old line about how you can lead a horse to water, but you can't make him drink. As I learned from my grandfather, it's true about the horse, but what you can do is put salt in its oats and make him thirsty. If you cannot motivate your crew to learn, it's a failing of your leadership, not a failure of your crew."

Porter, "We need a complete update in how we train our crews."

Morrison, "I'm pretty certain it's coming. Thank you."

Porter, "Thank you, Commander."

Lt. Commander Henry Morrison, "I'm glad the lesson plan got passed down."

John, "It did, Grandpa."

Henry, "Does this base have an O-club?"

"It does."

"I took the train up. Do you have a vehicle?"

"I do. Is it okay that I call you Grandpa?"

"To my thinking it's a term of respect. It sounds odd to my ears, but please do." They get in John's car.

"Where is the Livermore?"

"It's in New Jersey. How are you, Grandson?"

"Pretty good." They pull up to the 'O' Club. "The lessons are coming hard and fast."

"Your submarine, what's its hull number?"

"It's the San Francisco, SSN-711. We can't talk about it in the club."

"Obviously, you're a nuclear trained officer. Did you get your training in the Academy?

"I did. My major was physics. After I graduated, I went through an additional year of training before my first submarine."

"What year did you graduate?"

"1973. You and Grandma were there. In fact, you were a guest of honor."

"Let's go in and save the classified stuff for later." They get out of the car. "The letter said Mitch will be a rear admiral. I'm not sure I want to know what becomes of me."

"I spent a lot of time at yours and Grandma's house growing up, and we were close. Dad had to deploy a lot. That's just how it goes, as we all know."

"Okay, I have to ask. Do I get a star?"

"Three."

"Wow. Okay. It's a lot to live up to."

"Remember, everything has changed now. There are no guaranties."

They sit down at a table and order a meal. "So, Mitch turns out okay. How about Gretta?"

"She marries a young ensign named Jack Gentry. They do not work out, and they divorce about a year later. When she's twenty-four and in graduate school, she meets Steven Lowell. Lowell was studying law. He's now a state senator in his home state of Wyoming. They have a passel of kids and live on a ranch. She became quite a, um, cow-woman. My cousin, Michael, used to ride competitively at rodeo. One too many broken bones, and he retired. Gretta and Steven's youngest was in Harvard, when I went back in time."

"What was Gretta's degree?"

"A doctorate in history. She teaches at a high school out there and writes books. Grandpa, our family was truly blessed."

"There has to have been dark days."

"Yeah, probably. As a kid, I never knew them."

"Did you have any siblings?"

"I was an only child when my birth parents died. Mom and Dad couldn't have kids. They talked about adopting another, but they never did."

"What is the most amazing technology to come out of the war?"

"That, I can't say. We've been forbidden to share it."

"Okay, what's the most amazing thing that you can share?"

"The jeep. It's a little four-wheel utility vehicle that created a whole industry of off-road vehicles, along with clubs and competitions. Aircraft technology really took off. Shortly after the war, high speed transport aircraft became the norm. For a fairly reasonable price, you can fly almost any-where on earth in no more than two days. In the sixties, we land a man on the moon. By 1990, there are tons of satel-lites orbiting the earth, all with different purposes. Radio is mostly replaced by television, which is like watching a movie from your couch."

"When I think of my son, Mitch, I have difficulty wrapping my mind around him being a father. How was he?"

"He was an amazing father. I learned most of what I know about leadership from you and dad."

Henry's eyes tear up, "Thank you."

U-160, 100 MILES EAST OF NANTUCKET

0912, 15 March, 1942

Sonar, "Captain, multiple vessels approaching from the north."

Lassen, "Very good. A convoy."

Wechsler charts the bearing reports, "They will be traveling very near us, I hope. Shall we load the tubes now?"

"We should."

SAN FRANCISCO, 60 NM SE OF NANTUCKET ISLAND

Cumberland and Morrison stand at the rear of control with Captain Warren and Commander Rickover. Backes is on watch, with Mallory standing the watch under instruction. Cumberland, "Captain, why do you want Mallory?"

"Because he's a systems expert and it's easier for you to re-place an MM1 than a lieutenant, Commander."

"You want Morrison?"

"No. Not right now. I want Miller, but I also understand how vital he is to your boat."

"Yes, sir. Do you have to take Giblin? His knowledge and Mallory's overlap quite a lot."

"You masted him."

"I had to. He disobeyed an order, but he's competent at his job."

"Conn, Sonar. New contact, designate Sierra 1. Bearing 075. It's a submerged submarine."

Backes pushes the button, "How many screws? How many blades?"

"Standby."

Cumberland lumbers into sonar, "What do you have, Brown?" Rickover follows him.

Brown points at the waterfall, "It looks like two, four-bladed screws, sir. Are there any other American subs out here?"

"I think so. Get a good track, regardless. It'll help later."

"Yes, sir."

Cumberland leaves, but Rickover stays, "Explain how you can tell the number of blades and screws."

"See these dots, sir? This one is slightly larger and that one is slightly smaller. The frequency for each is every four beats. Also, see that the dots muddle, then become clear again? That is the two screws harmonizing, then going out of sync. The harmony is a pair, so it has to be two screws."

"Thank you. How do you like the Navy, Petty Officer Brown?"

"Just a sec," he passes information to the tracking team. "It isn't a bad gig, sir. What we do is important and I get a paid trip around the world. I'm a confirmed bachelor with no kids, so I'm not leaving much behind."

"Is ET1 Brown related to you?"

"No, sir. Brown is a pretty common name."

"Thank you. Carry on." Rickover joins the other officers.

Morrison, "We've identified Sierra 1 as the Growler on shake down."

"Thank you."

Propulsion plant drills are announced and the inspection team heads aft with Cumberland. Six hours, two American subs, and fifteen drills later, "Conn, Sonar. New contact, designate Sierra 4. Bearing 088. Twin, four-bladed screws. Sierra 4 is submerged."

Backes, "Very well."

Morrison walks to the tracking table. Sierra 4 is in deeper water almost due east of them. On the surface there's a scattering of individual ships and a large convoy out of Nova Scotia. He draws a line to estimate the future location of the convoy. FC2 Edwards marks the range to Sierra 4. It's just east of the convoy's path. The two men look at each other and Morrison pushes the button, "Brown, what do you make of Sierra 4?"

"It's tooling around at minimum steerage and is very quiet."

"Does it sound like a Gato class?"

"No, sir. There are significant differences. It's closer to the last German we sank off of Cape Hatteras."

"Thank you." The sub is shaking with a backing bell for drills. He picks up the 1MC, "Secure propulsion plant drills. Possible hostile submarine. Captain, please lay to control."

GERMAN SUBMARINE U-160

1428, 15 March, 1942

Sonar, "Captain, I am hearing screw noises to our west. Bearing 270. Sir, there was nothing, and then it was there."

Lassen walks up behind the sonar operator, "Any idea what it is?"

"It's gone now. It was a single screw, or two screws meshed together precisely. It seemed to have a lot of blades."

"Listen carefully in that direction. See if you can hear anything else. You do well."

USS SAN FRANCISCO

Cumberland invades control, "What do we have?" Warren and Rickover follow him a moment later.

Morrison, "We have a submerged contact. Bearing 088. Range, 14 nautical miles. Two four-bladed screws. Propulsion noises similar to our target off Hatteras. It's sitting on a convoy lane."

Cumberland, "Right standard rudder. Make our course 060. Come to 2/3rds." The orders are repeated and the sub leans to starboard in the turn. Cumberland, "Morrison, do you think our drills revealed our location?"

Morrison, "The back full emergency probably did."

Rickover, "What is your plan, Commander?"

"If he's a German, he's laying lying low in wait for the convoy. I'm going to place us in between him and the convoy. If he makes a hostile act, we'll take him out. Our shot will be away from the convoy. Load and make ready tube 2 with a Mark 48."

Rickover, "Only one?"

"Fair point. Load tube 3. Normally it only takes one shot."

GERMAN SUBMARINE U-160

Sonar, "Sir, I hear a very faint thrum. It comes and goes, but it is very quiet."

Lassen, "Can you give me a bearing?"

"I think it is moving north. I am not sure."

"You are doing quite well. Anything new with the convoy?"

"Bearing is unchanged. It continues toward us."

"Very good. Thank you."

USS SAN FRANCISCO

Cumberland, "Ahead 1/3rd. Right standard rudder. New course 120. What's the speed of the convoy?"

"Speed, 10 knots. Range to first ship is fifteen miles, sir."

"Right. Sonar, do you have Sierra 4?"

"Yes, sir. They're at 170 and ticking over at minimum steerage."

"Very well."

Cumberland looks at the table, Sierra 4 is about six miles south. The convoy will pass west of both them and Sierra 4.

GERMAN SUBMARINE U-160

Lassen, "Do you have the anomalous vessel?"

Sonar, "No, sir. It has one many bladed screw and is extremely quiet. If it wasn't for that one noise transient, I would never know it was there."

Wechsler, "Sir, we know an advanced aircraft carrier came back in time when the airfield did, could there have been a submarine present?"

"A submarine cannot keep up with a carrier, Lieutenant."

"Yes, sir. Today's submarines cannot. Yesterday's submarines cannot. Do we know tomorrow's submarines cannot?"

Lassen, "If there is a highly advanced submarine out there, why hasn't it attacked us? Wait, we are very near an American submarine base. Perhaps, they cannot tell us from their own submarines. Perhaps, we have been quiet enough. Pass to the crew that they must remain silent. All persons not on watch need to go to bed. Suspend all maintenance and cooking."

"Yes, sir."

After a time, as the convoy nears, Lassen, "Flood tubes 1 through 4."

USS SAN FRANCISCO

"Conn, Sonar. Sierra 4 is flooding tubes."

Cumberland, "Flood tube 3." He begins pacing, "Come on. Come on."

GERMAN SUBMARINE U-160

Sonar, "Sir, submarine flooding tubes at 017."

Lassen, "Right full rudder. Ahead full. Torpedo, get those doors open. Match bearings. I want a five-degree spread. Set depth to fifteen meters."

"What about the convoy, sir?"

"They will have to wait."

USS SAN FRANCISCO

"Conn, Torpedo. Tube 3 flooded."

Cumberland, "Open doors. Match bearings. Captain Warren, would you like to fire the weapon?"

Warren, "Proceed, Commander. It's your command."

Cumberland looks at Rickover. Rickover motions for him to proceed.

GERMAN SUBMARINE U-160

Lassen, "Fire tubes 1 through 4. Reload immediately."

"Captain, tubes 1 through 4 fired."

USS SAN FRANCISCO

Cumberland pushes the fire button. "Conn, Sonar. Sierra 4 has fired four torpedoes. Bearing is constant."

Cumberland, "Shit. Cut the wire and shut the door. Ahead flank. Five degrees down on the dive planes. Right full rudder."

"Conn, Torpedo. Tube 3 fired electrically."

"Conn, Sonar. Torpedo is hot, straight, and normal."

"Conn, Torpedo. Door 3 is shut."

The submarine tilts to the right and angles down. Rickover, "How deep can we go?"

Morrison tells him, then, "Sir, that number is top secret."

Rickover, "As it must be."

"Conn, Sonar. The torpedoes are spreading apart. They're going to pass above and astern, sir."

Cumberland, "Ahead 1/3rd. Make our depth 400 feet. Left rudder. Come to new course 140."

GERMAN SUBMARINE U-160

Kapitanleutnant Georg Lassen hears the torpedo pinging. "Emergency blow. The Americans have guided torpedoes."

Oberleutnant zur See Lutz Wechsler, "Yes, sir. It seems they do." The sub splashes to the surface.

"Stand by to abandon ship."

The torpedo detonates under the center of the sub, breaking it in two. The destroyer in the van of the convoy, USS Rhind, DD-404, turns toward the stricken sub.

CHAPTER 27

USS SAN FRANCISCO

1620, 15 March, 1942

Cumberland stands tall, his arms moving. He looks toward Captain Warren. "Morrison, bring us back into the training area and recommence drills." He leaves, heading for his stateroom.

Warren, "We've seen enough. It's nearly dark, so please take us back in."

Morrison, "Yes, sir."

Warren, "Commander Rickover, shall we retire to the wardroom to discuss their grade?"

PIER N, NSB, NEW LONDON

1710, 15 March, 1942

The brow is lowered in the dark. No services are hooked up, because the submarine is heading right back out to sea. Lt. Brown and Lt. Mallory climb out of the sub with their sea bags. Gustaf helps them. "I'm going to miss you, Mallory."

"Yeah, I know. You're in good hands with Younger. He's a solid choice as LPO."

"It blows my mind that they made you a lieutenant."

"Captain Warren said that no one listens to an ensign. He's

right."

"Okay, dude. Have you heard from Amy?"

"Yeah, have you heard from Debby?"

"No, man, I'm getting worried. I thought maybe it was too soon...but...How many letters have you got from Amy?"

"A few."

"Has she said anything about Debby?"

Gary takes a deep breath, "It isn't right for us to get involved."

"Dude, I need the truth. Please?"

"She's out bar hoping and looking for husband two or three. Break up and count your blessings."

Gustaf starts crying, "Fuck. Fuck, man. What a bitch."

"I'm sorry, dude. I'm doubly sorry you had to hear it from me."

"It's okay. Thanks for being truthful, it helps. Take care."

"I will." They shake hands."

USS BEAVER, BOSTON HARBOR

The large submarine tender has been pushed away from the docks and her two screws bite into the cold water. Simmons is on the bridge, standing OOD under instruction. As they line up for the sea buoy, Commander Little motions Simmons over, "Are we ready to care for the submarine?"

"Nearly, sir. We will be before we arrive at Holy Loch."

"Very good. We'll be joining a convoy for the crossing. Maintaining station, even on a tender, is a challenge. As a naval vessel, it's important that we do better than the civilians. Anything less would be considered a failure."

"Yes, sir."

They see a blinker flashing. Simmons opens the blinker manual. Commander Little, "It's the destroyer Livermore. They're leading convoy HX-2. That's our ticket across the Atlantic."

USS SAN FRANCISCO

1842, 15 March, 1942

Warren, "So, your sub's material condition is overall, fairly good. We've given you a hit list of sixteen items."

Cumberland, "We've already corrected most of them."

"Good. Operations: You need to refresh the crew's training for radiation containment work. You need to correct the log taking errors we identified."

"We'll correct them immediately."

"Good. Positive remarks: Your medical records are impeccable. The best we've seen. Watch stander knowledge is solid. Your training program, overall, is good. That brings us to morale." Warren stops and looks at Cumberland, "Commander, the morale on your vessel is awful. It is the most clinically depressed crew I have ever seen. What are you going to do to fix your morale problem?"

Cumberland rocks back in his chair and looks at Morrison, who looks elsewhere. Finally, "Captain, I don't know what you are talking about."

"Your crew morale is exceptionally low compared to that of the Long Beach or the Carl Vinson. I recognize your crew has been through a great deal. What are you going to do to address your crew's morale?"

Cumberland, "I and Commander Morrison will discuss it."

Warren, "Good. I'll need a report on your plan of action, once formulated. Overall, we are giving you a grade of below average."

Cumberland swallows, "Yes, sir."

Warren, "Fix your morale problem before it impacts your mission capability."

"Yes, sir."

Warren and Rickover stand, shake their hands, and leave.

SS MARY BELL, CONVOY SC-3, 400 MILES SW OF ICELAND

0110, 17 March, 1942

AB Jimmy Calhoun stands out in the bitter cold and salt spray, binoculars to his eyes. They're at the end of the southernmost line of the convoy. The Mary Bell is a bulk carrier loaded with wood and paper. He pulls his jacket closer against the bitter wind.

His eyes are pulled to the center of the convoy where he sees a flash of yellow orange light, followed by a column of water. The second blast bounces him off the bulkhead. That torpedo hit an aviation gas tanker.

U-575, INSIDE CONVOY SC-3

Kapitanleutnant Gunther Heydemann, "Fire tubes 3 and 4."

They feel the thud, whoosh. "Captain, fish running hot, straight, and normal."

"Very well. Reload. Shnell."

"8,7,6,5,4,3,2,1, impact." The shock wave from their torpedoes hits rumbles through the boat.

Heydemann on the periscope, "Crash dive. Take us down to

80 meters. Some foolish American is trying to run us over."

They can hear the sound of the other torpedoes from their wolf pack hitting their targets. "80 meters, sir."

"Good. If we reload quickly, we may get to bite the tail, as well as the head."

U-128, WEST OF U-575, INSIDE THE CONVOY

Kapitanleutnant Hermann Steinert, "Two kills. Very good. Stand by for a stern shot." He spins the scope, "Mark."

"192."

"Doors are open, Captain."

"Good. Make our bearing 184. 5 degree spread. Match bearings."

"Bearings matched, sir."

"Fire stern tubes." They feel the shudder as the torpedoes are ejected. Steinert starts the count. He spins looking for other targets and collision dangers. "2 and 1 hit." He watches the torpedoes hit the bow and the stern of the target. "Very good. Let us dive as we reload. 100 meters."

SS MARY BELL, CONVOY SC-3

AB Jimmy Calhoun struggles back to his feet. Sea water cascades down like heavy rain. The ship feels sluggish. The captain shouts, "Double the lashings on the cargo holds!"

He immediately heads down the deck. His right leg isn't working right. He and the crew add lashings. Twenty minutes into the task, he can feel the wood pushing against the chains forward. The bow starts digging into the sea. He can feel the vibration of the engines restarting. If they can keep the wood in the holds, it might keep them afloat long enough to limp into port.

TRONDHEIM, NORWAY

1710, 18 March, 1942

Helmut Schmitt walks down a street with shops. Most of the shops are closed. The Norwegians on the street look at him suspiciously. He walks beside a home with a yard. Two young children are playing with a ball. It bounces off their hands toward him. He smiles, catches the ball easily, and throws it back.

The boy smiles at him and throws the ball to him. Laughing, he returns the throw. Then, a woman exits the back door, says something to the children and rushes them inside. She turns and looks at him, frowning.

Schmitt sighs and walks on. Zimmerman catches up to him, "What were you doing?"

"The kids were throwing the ball like my brothers."

"They are not to be trusted, Helmut."

"It seems that goes both ways, Hansel. If we strike terror everywhere, we go how will we manage the world once it is ours?"

"You think too much. I know where there is beer."

USS SAN FRANCISCO, 800 FEET SOUTH OF ICELAND, IN THE ATLANTIC GAP AHEAD OF CONVOY HX-2

2010, 19 March, 1942

Morrison is slammed awake out of deep sleep by the 1MC, "Captain to the Conn."

He gets out of bed and dresses quickly.

"Tracking party to control."

He walks aft. Cumberland is already in control checking the table, a big smile on his face. He looks at Morrison, "We've a new contact. Sierra 7."

"Conn, Sonar. Sierra 7's bearing is 094 distant. Twin, three-bladed screws. They just submerged."

Morrison looks at the updated charts. He sees that Sierra 7 is 35 miles ahead. Cumberland, "Ahead flank."

U-656, NE OF CONVOY HX-2

Sonar, "Captain, I'm hearing something odd. It sounds like a screw, but different."

Kapitanleutnant Ernst Kroning picks up a spare headset, "I do not hear anything. Perhaps it's the ice to our north."

"Sir, it sounds like it is passing to our south."

"I see. Could it be an aircraft near the water?"

"It could be, sir. It is too fast to be a submerged submarine."

"Where is the convoy?"

"The nearest is to our west and south, sir, at about fifteen miles. It will pass to our south."

"Then we need to move. We must not miss our dance."

U-352, SE OF CONVOY HX-2, SW OF SAN FRANCISCO

Kapitanleutnant Helmut Rathke stands up, "You think it a submarine, Koch. It must be very advanced. I must think on this. Where is the convoy?"

"About twelve miles, sir, to our west and north."

"I see. We need to maneuver."

U-573, 9 MILES EAST AND 2 MILES NORTH OF HX-2

Kapitanleutnant Heinrich Heinsohn listens to his sonarman. Krause is his very best. "Sir, I think it is a submarine traveling very fast. It however has left the door open for us to access the convoy. It is a mistake, sir."

"He heard Haydemann submerge and rushed forward to kill him. Sad for Haydemann, but an opportunity for us."

U-128, 8 MILES EAST, 3 MILES SOUTH OF HX-2

"Sir, there is a destroyer in the van and another to the south of the southernmost line."

Kapitanleutnant Steinert, "The convoy will pass to our north?"

"Yes, sir, about two miles."

"Very well." To the helm, "Ahead 2/3rds. Make our course 000. Keep our depth 20 meters."

USS SAN FRANCISCO, 40 MILES EAST OF THE CONVOY

Once they slow from their sprint, "Conn, Sonar. New contact, designate Sierra 8. Bearing 245."

Cumberland, "Sonar, is this the same as Sierra 7?"

"No, sir. Sierra 7 is at 082. Both are submerged submarines. Sir, new contact, designate Sierra 9. Bearing is 282. Damn, another submerged submarine. I picked up 8 and 9 on the tail."

Morrison comes into sonar, "Guys, look for more. Some wolf packs have as many as eight subs."

Brown points at two lines, "Conn, Sonar. Two new contacts

designate 10 and 11. They're near, but separate from 8 and 9. 10 is flooding tubes."

Cumberland storms into sonar, "Brown, how the hell did you miss them?"

"Sir, they were just sitting there. Now, they're maneuvering to get inside the convoy."

Cumberland looks at Morrison, his eyes wide and his face drained of color. He sprints into control, "Right full rudder. Take us about. Ahead standard. Get me a lock on 8 through 11. Load tubes 1 through 4 with Mark 48s. Once loaded, flood each tube."

Morrison, "Brown, Guthrie, don't worry about it. It's okay. Just work the problem in front of you."

Guthrie, "Yes, sir."

Brown, "Conn, Sonar. Sierra 11 is flooding tubes. Sierra 9 is flooding tubes."

Morrison, "Thank you, Brown, Guthrie."

USS LIVERMORE, 1 MILE EAST OF HX-2

The Livermore is clearing a gale to their west. The seas are rough with large period rollers. The destroyer finds itself pushing through deep troughs. Henry Morrison is on the port bridge wing, binoculars to his eyes. This is the gap where aircraft cannot patrol. From several crossings, they have learned that this is the most dangerous time.

Huber joins him, "How are you doing?"

Morrison does not put his binoculars down, "I'm cold, but death is cold, too. I'll manage."

Huber, "You think your grandson is out there?"

"If he is, sir, we'll never find him. If we find a sub, we fire on it. He knows to stay clear of us."

USS SAN FRANCISCO

Morrison looks over the chart table. The closest ship in the convoy is twenty-five miles away. They have tracks on four submarines, all fairly close together and right in front of the convoy.

U-575, EASTERN MOST OF WOLF PACK

Heydemann leans against a bulkhead, waiting. The crew is doing its duty. All is calm efficiency.

A radioman enters with the latest decoded dispatch. He reads, "Ten U-boats are missing already in March, presumed lost. High command believes the Americans have introduced a new weapon. The weapon is likely air-based, and we do not understand its nature. Any encounters with this weapon system must be reported to high command, immediately, so an effective response may be devised." He smiles, and thinks, "So, once we have destroyed it, we should inform high command regarding what we killed. Yes."

USS SAN FRANCISCO

Tube 1 and 2 are loaded and flooded. Evan is preparing the Amphenol for tube 3. "Chief, do you think they really need four fish?"

Kennedy, "The Germans hunt in wolf packs. They may need even more. We cycle through as fast as we safely can."

"Amphenol is installed. The torpedo is talking. Moving forward."

"Moving aft." The torpedo slides into place.

They hear, "Open door on tubes 1 and 2."

Evan looks at his chief, then pushes the button. They hear and feel the side slot in the sub move inward, exposing the torpedoes.

U-656, 200 FEET, EAST OF HX-2

Sonar, "Captain, new contact. Submarine at 094 is flooding tubes."

Kroning, "It is Heydemann getting antsy. We are nearly there. Open doors for tubes 1 through 4. When we have the shot, I want to be ready."

Oberleutnant zur See Ziegler, the XO, "Sir, several cargo ships are in range."

Kroning, "We want in the middle, as before."

"Yes, sir."

U-352, 300 FEET SE OF HX-2

Rathke leans over his sonarman. "Is it Heydemann at 275?"

"I do not think so, sir. I hear none of the normal noises."

"Then what? You are certain of the location of the other three?"

"Yes, Herr Captain."

"Open doors for tubes 1 through 4. Take us to periscope depth. Something is out there. I want to get shots off while we can."

USS SAN FRANCISCO

Cumberland, "Match bearings. I want tube 1 set for Sierra 8

and tube 2 for Sierra 9. As soon as they fire, we cycle through to fire tubes 3 and 4. Tube 3 will be set for Sierra 10, and tube 4 is to be set for Sierra 11. Repeat back."

The fire control team repeats back.

Cumberland, "XO, no submarine has ever fired four fish at four different targets and hit them all."

Morrison, "Hopefully, we will. We'll have to leave the doors open, so we can control them. We are firing toward the convoy."

Cumberland, "I plan to. This is a great many weapons in the water at once."

Morrison, "An idea, sir. If we dog leg the first two torpedoes fired, we can make all four hits at about the same time. So, the detonation of one doesn't mess up one of the others."

Cumberland nods his head, "Yeah, okay. It has merit." He turns to the fire control team and orders them to changes the course of each fish. This requires some math, to get the timing correct.

U-128, WEST OF U-352

Steinert, "Flood tubes 1 through 4. Left rudder. New course 286."

His XO, "Sir, aren't we supposed to fire from inside?"

"There is something out there. Aircraft? An American sub? I don't know yet. We will fire as soon as the angle is favorable. I want to hit the lead destroyer. It is likely the one coordinating with the other unit."

GERMAN SUBMARINE U-575

Sonar, "Sir, I think I hear a gurgling noise to the west, like a flooding tube."

Heydemann, "Can you hear anything else on that bearing?"

"The convoy, sir. I can also hear our other four subs. U-128 has a bearing going."

"Understood. Keep listening. We need to find that phantom sub killer." The crew chuckles. Unlike the other four subs in this wolfpack, this boat has been stripped of its guns and had its conning tower smoothed.

USS SAN FRANCISCO

Cumberland, "Thoreau, you're doing well." Everyone looks at Cumberland, eyes wide. "Yes, you're doing well, but this time, I think I will fire."

Thoreau, "Yes, sir."

Cumberland pushes the buttons, "Fire 1. Fire 2."

"Conn, Torpedo. Tubes 1 and 2 fired electrically."

"Conn, Sonar. Fish 1 and 2, running hot, straight, and normal."

Cumberland, "Come on. Refill the slug tank."

GERMAN SUBMARINE U-656

Kroning studies the chart table. "We are well placed. The convoy comes on not knowing we are about to rape them, like the plump English women they are."

His XO, Fischer, "Sir, what do you make of this super weapon?"

"Gunther, we are the superweapon. I know war is distasteful, but we fight for the Fatherland. We are the superior of any allied..."

"Captain, two torpedoes fired. Bearing is 268."

Kroning, "Too soon. What are they doing?"

Fischer, "Sir, we do not have a submarine at 268."

"Ahead flank. Two degrees down on the planes. Take us down. We must get below the torpedo."

USS LIVERMORE

"Bridge, Sonar. Activity everywhere. Torpedoes in the water. Submarines north and south."

Morrison, "Bring us to general quarters." He pushes a button, "Calm down, sonar. Give us a bearing."

"320, bridge."

Morrison, "Come to 320."

Commander Huber walks in and grabs a helmet. "What do you have XO?"

"Torpedoes in the water. Multiple contacts. We're sorting it out."

GERMAN SUBMARINE U-128

Steinert, "What are they doing? Those torpedoes are fired too far away to hit anyone. Steady on."

Sonar, "Captain, the torpedoes seem to be missing to the port and starboard."

"Very well. Patience is the key to success. We must be patient."

USS SAN FRANCISCO

"Conn, Torpedo. Tubes 3 and 4 are ready, doors open."

Cumberland, "Thank you, torpedo. Are bearings matched?"

"Yes, sir."

"Fire tubes 3 and 4."

"Conn, Torpedo. Tubes 3 and 4 fired electrically."

"Conn, Sonar. Fish 3 and 4 are hot, straight, and normal."

Cumberland, "Oh yeah! Um, very well."

Thoreau counts down.

GERMAN SUBMARINE U-352

Rathke shouts, "Hard right rudder. Ahead flank. Up five degrees. Blow ballast."

GERMAN SUBMARINE U-573

Heinsohn, "We go deep. 2/3rds bell. Full down on the planes."

Sonar, "Captain, one of the torpedoes has changed course. Bearing is constant."

The helmsman, "F...F...Full d...down."

"Relax, Wenzel. Torpedoes do not dive. They do not chase their prey like hounds."

They can hear the high-pitched pings of the closing torpedo. Wenzel, "Sir, what is that?"

Sonar, "The torpedo is close aboard."

At 235 feet, the torpedo detonates on contact with the hull, creating a bubble of heat and pressure that collapses the sub's hull inward. There are no survivors.

USS LIVERMORE

They hear the thunder like multiple depth charges exploding. When they look east, they see a German sub surface. Huber, "Get Mount 1 on the sub." Then, a towering column of water rises from the center of the sub. The sub lifts up, then drops, breaking in two. "My God!"

GERMAN SUBMARINE U-352

Rathke struggles to his feet. A wave pounds the sub, pushing him against the periscope. He grabs the hatch and spins it open, pushing a rating up. When he can see no more living crew, he too climbs up the ladder that is slowly rolling horizontal. In the sail, men are clinging to the rails. Several are hanging above the churning sea as the bow turns up to the sky. He sees the stern of his vessel slip below the water. The bow trembles. Air escapes through the hatch and Rathke shuts it, still clinging to a rail.

USS SAN FRANCISCO

Cumberland dances around control, pumping his fists, "Yes! Yes!"

Morrison, "Sir?"

Cumberland, "XO, you got it. I'll be in my stateroom." He dances out of control.

U-575, 15 MILES EAST OF USS SAN FRANCISCO

Sonar, "Captain, all four are gone. All are hit at the same time."

"I understand. It falls to us. It seems we were wrong to mock

393

the American superweapon." Haydemann sits, heavily.

CHAPTER 28

USS SAN FRANCISCO

2221, 19 March, 1942

Morrison walks into sonar, "Gordon, how are you doing?"

"Well, Commander, I just listened to a couple hundred people die. About how you would think, sir."

"I know it's difficult. It's damn difficult, but we have it to do."

"Oh, I know, sir."

"Can you stay on the bubble?"

"Oh, Commander, I never lose the bubble."

Morrison turns to the junior sonarman on watch, "How are you, Pritchel?"

"I try not to think about it."

"Guys, the time comes when you have to deal with death. The killing we do, each of will have our own way of dealing with it."

In his stateroom, Cumberland gets up from his rack and tosses a sock into the laundry hamper. He goes to the sink to wash up and looks into the mirror. His happy smile reflects back to him, "Four at once. Does it ever get this good?"

GERMAN SUBMARINE U-575

Kapitanleutnant Gunther Heydemann walks into the radio room and hands the radioman a message:

TO: 7UBFLOT

FRM: 575

REG: US Superweapon

Kptlt. Sohler, the American weapon is a U-boat with guided torpedoes. It is very quiet. 575 only survivor of WP-14.

Heydemann

"Once you type it up on the code machine, let me know, so we can go to periscope depth to send it." He exits radio and shuts the door. He leans against the bulkhead trying to catch his breath. He feels as if he's been running.

USS SAN FRANCISCO

Trindle sits on the floor, knees drawn up tightly against his body, fists balled and head down. TMC Mel Kennedy, "You okay, Evan?"

"No. Fuck, this is hard." He makes eye contact with his chief, "How many people have we killed?"

"Do you really want to know?"

"I guess...I guess, I don't. It's a fucked-up world we live in. The skipper's probably rubbing one out because he killed four boats at once."

TM1 Haataja, "Nah, he's done already. Think about this, Trindle, at least you don't have to clean his stateroom."

Trindle, "God, yes. After four boats, it's probably a fire hose."

Haataja, "Yep, his room is now painted a milky white."

Kennedy, "Guys, enough."

Trindle stands, "Roger that, Chief."

The phone talker, "Chief, they want us to reload all four tubes."

USS LIVERMORE

LCDR Henry Morrison, "Ahead 1/3rd. Right standard rudder. New course 012." He dials a phone, "Captain, could you please come to the bridge?"

CDR Vernon Huber walks in. "Captain on the bridge."

Huber looks out the windscreen, "My God." The bow of a submarine sticks straight up out of the water. Survivors still clinging to it. "Call the boat detail to muster on the port boat deck. Muster the security detail on the fan tail." He looks over at Morrison, "You think this is your grandson's handiwork?"

"Could it be anyone else?"

The BMOW, "Captain, starboard lookout reports an oil slick and debris off the starboard bow."

"Very well. You know, Henry, that oil slick could be your boy."

"Yes, sir, or it could be their next kill. Sonar heard multiple explosions at nearly the same time."

GERMAN SUBMARINE U-575

"Sir, we are ready to transmit."

Haydemann, "Very well. Bring us up to periscope depth."

USS SAN FRANCISCO

"Conn, Sonar. Hull popping noises. It's Sierra 7. Bearing 026 and moving aft."

Morrison pushes the button, "What is it doing?"

"They just accelerated to the surface, or to periscope depth. Two screws with three blades."

"Understood. Flood tube 1 and open doors. Ahead 1/3rd, half bell." He pushes the button, "Captain, we still need to deal with Sierra 7."

GERMAN SUBMARINE U-575

The submarine settles at periscope depth. Haydemann, "Raise the antenna."

USS LIVERMORE

"Bridge, Combat. Contact on radar. Bearing 052. Range 18 miles." Morrison puts his binoculars to his eyes.

USS SAN FRANCISCO

Cumberland goes straight to the table, "5 degrees up angle. Left standard rudder."

"Conn, Torpedo. Tube 1 is flooded. Opening door."

Thoreau, "Very well."

Cumberland, "Let's wait until we can see it."

Morrison, "Sir, they may be transmitting a message. It's almost certain they are."

Cumberland pushes the button, "Firing tube 1. Thoreau,

count us down." He looks at Morrison like the XO took his favorite lollipop.

"Conn, Torpedo. Tube 1 fired electrically."

Conn, Sonar. Fish is running hot, straight, and normal."

"Very well."

USS LIVERMORE

Morrison finally spots it. The feather from the periscope is difficult to pick out in the wind-swept sea. "Radar contact is a periscope. Any idea whose?"

GERMAN SUBMARINE U-575

The radioman is typing out the encoded message.

"Captain, torpedo in the water. Bearing 195. Range, close." They hear the pings.

Haydemann, "Blow ballast and continue to blow. Maybe the bubbles will confuse it."

They flip the chicken switches and air rushes into the ballast tanks, raising the sub out of the water. The maneuver does not confuse the Mark 48 torpedo. It detonates under the auxiliary machinery space, lifting the middle of the sub and breaking it in two.

USS LIVERMORE

Henry Morrison sees the German sub surface. "Another one!" A tower of water rises up from the exploding torpedo. The sub breaks like a twig. "My God, sir, look!"

A few miles from the sinking German sub, they see the sleek shape of the San Francisco surface, only visible as a shadow against the windswept waves. It settles for a moment, then sinks back out of sight. CDR Huber, "Morrison, is that your grandson's submarine?"

"It must be, sir."

"Well, I'm delighted they are looking out for us."

"As I am, sir."

USS SAN FRANCISCO

Cumberland, "Why the hell did we just broach?"

Thoreau, "Sir, you ordered 5 degrees and never changed it."

"I did? Well, get us back down to 400 feet and get us back on course." He walks out and forward.

Thoreau, "XO, did I just screw up?"

"We all did, Thoreau. He was hyper-focused on the kill and I allowed myself to become distracted."

"I'm sorry, sir."

"Me too. Chalk it up as a lesson and move along."

PORT ORCHARD STRAIGHT, EAST OF NAVAL UNDERSEA WARFARE CENTER, KEYPORT, WASHINGTON

0915, 20 March, 1942

Kichiro, with headphones on, is on the bridge of a submarine tied to the pier.

"Bridge, Torpedo. Tube 1 is loaded."

Kichiro, "Very well. Stand by." He shouts to the captain on the pier, "Final confirmation, sir. Is the range clear?"

Captain Guiles, the new command CO, says, "It is. Proceed."

"Yes, sir. The first is a Mark-14 as it was pulled off the shelf." On the phone, "Fire tube 1." They see the burst of bubbles at the bow, then the train of bubbles the torpedo leaves in its wake. It heads straight to the target, a barge with a steel plate hanging over the side and down twenty feet. It gets to the target, then goes under it, and onward, with no detonation. The engineers look at each other, and one says, "Oh shit."

Kichiro repeats the test three more times with off the shelf torpedoes. Everyone misses or fails to detonate.

"Now, sir, this next shot is a Mark-14B. This torpedo has a new level control system and a new contact pistol. Is it clear?"

Guiles, "Proceed."

The torpedo is fired. The bubbles lead straight to the barge. They hear the bang of the torpedo hitting the steel plate, then the green dye marker rises up, staining the water.

Divers recover the inert torpedo. They let the green dye disperse before they do another test. Kichiro, "Next is the same torpedo with a new sonar-based proximity detonator."

"Proceed."

The torpedo is fired. This time, the torpedo passes under the barge, but the green dye rises again, indicating the proximity trigger fired. Kichiro, "Sir, we still have a few reliability issues to sort out, but we're nearing a production model."

Guile, "You did nothing to tamper with the first four?"

"Sir, you chose them and had them loaded. I never saw them."

"Right. Your point is made."

"Thank you, sir."

ADMIRL DONITZ'S HEADQUARTERS

2015, 20 March, 1942

A lieutenant runs down the hall to the admiral's office. He runs past the startled secretary, and into the admiral's private office. He puts a message on the desk, and bends over, fighting for breath, "Sir."

Admiral Karl Donitz, commander of the U-boats, reads:

TO: 7UBLFOT

FRM: 575

REG: US Superweapon

Kptlt. Sohler, the American weapon is a...

Donitz looks up, "Have you been able to raise them?"

"No, sir. The entire wolfpack is not responding."

"Thank you. Send this out." He writes a brief message and hands it to the aid.

TO: ALL U-BOATS

FRM: BdU

REG: RECALL

All vessels currently on patrol, return to port expeditiously. Cease all deployments. All flotillas contact headquarters.

DONITZ

USS LIVERMORE, IRISH SEA

1010, 26 March, 1942

CDR Vernon Huber leans toward his XO, "So, this tender, the Beaver, is obviously important. After dropping the convoy at Plymouth, our escort has increased." Three of the new tribal class British destroyers, are in front of the tender, and the two American destroyers who made the crossing with them, are behind. Beyond them is the cruiser, HMS Ajax, and to their west is the cruiser, HMS Exeter.

LCDR Henry Morrison, "Perhaps my grandson might meet a good Scottish girl. The Morrison's are Scot."

Huber, "I, for one, wish him the very best. We made it across without a loss. Thank God. Now, we're to pull in at Glasgow and get orders. He might not be the only sailor to find a Scottish girl. We'll need to remind our ratings to be gentlemen here."

"Yes, sir."

USS SAN FRANCISCO

1016, 26 March, 1942

Cumberland paces the control room. Miller, "We're at 150, sir." Cumberland waves his hand. Miller continues, "Right standard rudder. Let's see what's out there."

"Conn, Sonar. New contact, bearing 163. Designate Tango 32. Sounds like a drifting fishing boat."

Miller pushes the button, "Very well."

"Conn, Sonar. New contact, bearing 181. Designate Tango 33. Another drifting fishing boat."

"Cumberland, "That's over a dozen fishing boats. Make our course 236. I want out of this fucking mess."

Morrison, "They're approaching the Firth of Clyde and we've

sniffed out the deep water around here. What are we going to do, sir?"

Cumberland, "We escorted them to the Firth, which is what our orders said. Now, we're free to hunt submarines. That is what we are going to do. We don't have to pull in until the 30th."

Morrison, "Yes, sir."

"Where the fuck did they all go? We haven't found one since the wolf pack."

USS LIVERMORE

Tugs carefully push the Livermore to a quay near one of the dock yards. CDR Huber and LCDR Morrison work together in practiced harmony, each doing their own tasks. Once the lines are drawn tight, Huber points out a strange looking contraption on the quay near their ship. It's larger than a gyrocopter, but that is what it looks like.

They see a door slide open, and a man in khakis and a watch coat, walks up parallel to the bridge as a crane lowers the brow. There are four stripes on the man's shoulder boards. Huber and Morrison quickly go down to the quarterdeck. Once the brow is secured, the captain walks up. The watch rings the bell, "Captain, United States Navy, arriving."

Holtz salutes the flag, then the quarterdeck. He puts out his hand, "Commander, I'm James Holtz."

"Honored to meet you, sir. I'm Vernon Huber. This is my XO, Henry Morrison."

"A pleasure to meet you both. Is there a place where we can talk?"

"Of course, sir." Huber leads them to the small captain's office in the in-port cabin. His steward serves coffee and cookies.

Holtz, "Okay, first, I should give you your orders. A 1990 submarine is going to be using the tender Beaver in Holy Lock as its home port. A submarine on the surface is very vulnerable. For that reason, I asked for a destroyer to escort the sub in and out of port. The Navy chose you. It isn't a glory job, but it's important."

Morrison, "I've met the sub's XO, sir."

Holtz leans back, "Really?"

"He put on a training class on submarine tactics and the San Francisco's capabilities when it was in port at New London."

Holtz sighs, "Good. Very good. Okay then, you know what the show is and when to dance. Interesting that you and the XO share your last name."

"He's my grandson."

"Wow. Okay, I had no idea. So, you understand a bit about just how special this submarine is."

Huber, "We saw it sink five U-boats before we even knew they were there."

"Wow. That makes it a bit easier. One concern that's crossed my mind is your crew being temporarily assigned to an overseas port. These folks have been at war for a long time. They've been dealing with shortages and rationing. I want our sailor on their best behavior. I recognize that sometimes shit happens, but we need to stave off as much trouble as possible."

"Sir, are you going to serve on our ship?"

"No, I'm a pilot. I fly out of Alconbury near Cambridge."

Morrison, "Can we ask for your title, sir?"

"I'm sorry. I'm dual hatted: Commander of Task Force Yankee and Commander Naval Forces Great Britain."

Huber, "Do you fly that gyrocopter, sir?"

"No. I fly an F-14 fighter. We'll be protecting Britain's skies, and I need you to support the San Francisco as it protects the convoys. The sub is supposed to stay out until 0800, 30 March. We'll need you out on the Firth of Clyde to meet them. Until then, you can manage your crew's liberty as you see appropriate. You'll be assigned here for some time, so I assume you'll want to get underway for training. That's fine with me, though, I need to be kept informed of your movements. If you need any repairs, coordinate with the Beaver for times when the sub is gone. If you have expenses beyond your resources, let me know, and my people will take care of you. If there is a liberty incident, injury, equipment malfunction, combat action, or other problem, I want to be informed soonest."

"Yes, sir."

"Okay, let's go over how you can do that."

BRUNO SUB PEN, BERGAN, OCCUPIED NORWAY

1230, 28 March, 1942

Fregattenkapitan Hans Cohausz studies the U-255 in dry dock. The guns have been removed. The sound of the grinders rings throughout the concrete dry dock bunker. He looks at the engineer, "What is this thing?" He points at a thirty-five-foot-long, eighteen-inch wide tube with a large bulb on one end and a sleeved tube on the other end.

"That, sir, is the new snorkel. It allows the diesel to run while the submarine is submerged."

"I thought it would be bigger?"

"Sir, it is all that is needed to provide for the diesel."

Cohausz, "Yes, but what provides for the crew? They need fresh air as well."

"I hadn't considered that. The outlet will be in the forward end of the engine room."

"Can you duct it forward and aft?"

"I suppose, sir. Why?"

"Doing that would mean the diesel uses the stale air in the submarine and the crew gets the benefit of the fresh air as it's drawn in, I wish that modification for all the submarines in the Flotilla."

"Yes, sir."

"Have the modifications to the shape of the sail been tested?"

"Yes, Captain. They'll reduce the turbulence, making the boat faster, quieter, and able to operate longer without charging the batteries."

"Good. We have another dozen submarines waiting, so, I will not delay you further."

CHAPTER 29

USS SAN FRANCISCO, ON THE FIRTH OF CLYDE

0840, 30 March, 1942

Cumberland spins the search scope. The grassy, rocky hills of Scotland close around them. Ahead is a small guide boat. Behind them, the destroyer Livermore, its guns ready. Morrison looks through the attack scope, "Fishing boat, 030. Looks like its setting sail from Wemyss."

Cumberland, "Got it." A navy motor launch is already heading in that direction. He looks away from the scope at Morrison, "Where the fuck did all the U-boats go?"

"I don't know, sir. There's no way they've given up on submarine warfare. They're committed to it."

"It's pissing me off."

"Yes, sir."

Cumberland falls silent. They follow the guide boat in. They round the corner into Holy Loch and see two tenders tied together and anchored at the center of the loch. One has a WWII style submarine and two small craft moored to its port side. The other has two long skinny barges tied to it. As they get closer, they see the one with the sub is British, and the other tender is the Beaver.

Tug boats help them spin around, then gently push them against the long skinny barges. Wood rub plates and rubber fenders protect the sub from the barge. The crane already has a brow ready to lower.

The tenders line handlers toss the lines over, and they are tied into place. They see three officers walking down to the barges. Cumberland, "Shit. That CAG wasn't kidding."

"What, sir?"

"The Captain, he's a flyboy named Holtz. He's in charge of our squadron."

"Yes, sir."

Holtz waits until the quarterdeck is set up and the CO and XO are present. Then, he walks aboard to the boatswain's pipe, "Naval Forces Great Britain, arriving."

Holtz salutes the flag, then the quarterdeck. Cumberland and Morrison salute, and Holtz returns it and offers his hand, "Commander Cumberland, Commander Morrison, it's good to see you. With me is Marion Little, CO of Beaver, and Mike Simmons, Nuclear Maintenance Officer." Two F-14s scream across the sky on afterburner. Holtz looks up, "Swede and Hot Pants. They got it. Gentlemen, is there a place where we can talk?"

Cumberland leads the group down to the wardroom, after waiting for the engineers to come up to hook up shore services. In the wardroom, Holtz, "Could you give us a succinct report on your operations?"

Cumberland goes through it, "...We haven't found a U-boat for ten days."

Holtz, "According to radio traffic, most, if not all the U-boats are in port. How are you handling IFF out there?"

Cumberland, "Sound, location, and behavior. We're building a library to help identify the different subs by sound profile. Sometimes we'll get reports regarding the location of friendly subs. Other times, we can figure it out based on their actions."

Holtz, "Right. Commander Cumberland, Western Approaches, the British convoy command, wants to talk to you. That means a trip to Liverpool. It's a hell of a drive, so we'll arrange a helicopter ride. One other thing, unless you have pressing maintenance, I want your crew to enjoy Scotland. Eventually, this will be a working port. For now, make it a liberty port. Understood?"

Cumberland narrows his eyes, then looks down, "Yes, sir."

"Okay, after four days in port, I want you back out there. By then, the torpedoes we received from the Camden should be here. With that, you can replenish. So, you get back underway 4 April. Before that, I'll need a complete plan for your next movements. Clear?"

Cumberland, "Sir, why do you need our movements?"

"So, in the weird circumstance that you need help, or have a surface ship sniff you out, we'll know where you are."

Cumberland, "But, if there's a leak, the enemy will know, too."

Holtz, "Have the itinerary hand delivered. My staff has been vetted and only they know where you are. With that, we'll still only have an approximate location."

"Yes, sir."

Holtz, "Now, I may send my chief of staff up here in my stead. I believe you both have met Commander Hunt?"

Morrison smiles, "Yes, sir."

Cumberland pales, "Yes, sir."

FLEET LANDING, SANDBANK, SCOTLAND

1110, 30 March, 1942

ST 1 Brown and ST 3 Guthrie, along with a some of the crew, climb out of the boat and walk into the small village. To the north they can see the wooden buildings of a boat yard. High Road is the main drag through town and all the commercial buildings are on it. They are all wearing their dress blues, with the peacoat, in an attempt to protect themselves from the rain.

About a block down, they find the Mac and Mc pub and walk in. In the center of the pub is a stove, fired up and warming the space. The bar is on the left of the deep and narrow space. An older woman is filling a cup for an old man. She asks, "What can I get for you?"

Brown, "Do you have food?"

"We do. We got stovies, roast mutton, salmon, or if you like, we have bangers with neeps and tatties."

Brown, "The salmon and a beer, please."

Guthrie, "What are stovies?"

"It's comfort on a plate; sausage, pork, and beef with tatties. Um, tatties are potatoes."

Guthrie, "I'll try that with a beer, please. Is American money okay?"

"It's fine. You're not the first Yank to show up. Our loch is filling up with them."

Brown, "Yes, ma'am." They find a table and she brings their beers.

Guthrie, "You know, Mike. Scotland couldn't be more different from Australia."

"Yeah, here we're kind of in the back of beyond. It's the whole point. Out here, folks won't find us."

The hear the rumble of jets overhead. Guthrie, "Are those

ours?"

The old timer says, "Unless ye brought us some jets, them is Germans."

Brown, "I don't know any of the details, but I understand, we did bring jets."

"Well, good. That should help some. What boat are ye offa?"

Brown, "The USS San Francisco. It's an anti-submarine vessel."

The old timer spins his chair around on one leg, "My name is Sheamus Stewart. Welcome to Scotland, lads."

They both stand and shake his hand, "A pleasure to meet you, sir."

"I dinna know about that. Tell me lads. If your boat's made to kill the subs, have ye killed any?"

Brown nods, "Yes, sir. Since we came back, we've sunk a bunch. In the Atlantic, we sank nine U-boats."

"Nine. Bloody hell. Nine. We've heard of none of ye."

Brown, "Nor will you. Our ship is supposed to be kept quiet."

Their food comes out and Stewart says, "Mary, darlin, I got their meal and get them another beer."

Mary, "Okay, Sheamus."

Brown gets up and asks for the restroom. Mary points to the door. He quietly asks, "Ma'am, can Mr. Stewart afford to pay our tab?"

She smiles, "He can. Sheamus is a retired landscaper. He sold his business ten years ago and is doing fine."

"Thank you, ma'am."

"Mary, please. If you keep callin' me ma'am, I'll start putting on airs and walking like the Queen."

Brown grins, "Got it, Mary. Thank you."

When he returns, Sheamus asks, "Do you lads have supper plans?"

Guthrie, "We have no plans. But we have duty tomorrow."

"Well, Mary can give you directions. Come by around five, and I'll have Laureen put on a bit for us."

Brown, "We understand that you've been on rations for a long time, sir. We wouldn't want to impose."

"We've enough, young man. Please come."

Sheamus leaves and Mary hands them directions, "Tis a bit of a walk, lads. Perhaps you should hire a car."

Brown, "Are you sure we aren't putting them out? I know food and stuff are tight."

"I told you, he sold his company and retired. They live on a farm up on the hill and grow much of what they need. Mind, I've never seen him take a liking to a sailor type before, and a Yank to boot."

Brown, "Thank you, Mary."

After their lunch, Mike says, "I need a newspaper."

Guthrie, "Why?"

"Because, I'm going to buy a car." Brown gets the paper off the end of the bar.

"All they have are old ones."

Brown looks at his friend, "Dude, you see that car? He points at a 1935 Morris.

"Yeah?"

"It's only five to eight years old. Hell, they made the Model

T until '27. That's only fifteen years ago. Buying a Model T is like buying a '75 Ford in 1990. None of these are that old."

"Do you really want a hand crank car?"

"By '42, most already have starters."

"How did you learn so much about cars?"

"My dad and grandpa collected them. The first car I ever drove was a 1924 Model T. I want a mid to late thirties Ford, if I can find one. They came with a flat head V-8."

They find themselves walking to the towns service station. Brown asks the attendant, "Excuse me, sir. Do you know where I can find cars for sale?"

"Yessir. I know a few brief fer sale. Watcha eenen?"

"I'm sorry, sir. I don't understand."

"What sorta car ye be looken for?"

"A mid to late 1930's Ford coupe or sedan."

"I know one, and a fair deal, too." He makes a call. In a few minutes, a man pulls up in a Ford coupe. It is a beautiful sapphire blue and in very good condition.

The man gets out, "You the sailor looking for a car?"

Brown, "Yes, sir, if the price is reasonable. That's a 1936, right?"

"It is. My son bought it new."

"He's willing to part with it?"

"Lad, he was lost to the war. He was on the Repulse in the far east."

"Oh, I'm sorry, sir."

"Well, yes, and I as well. It seems fitting to sell the car to another sailor, as we have no need of it."

"Mind if I look it over?"

"Please do."

Mike pours over the car, checking wires, tires, suspension, title, everything. In the end, he asks, "How much do you want for it?"

"It was nearly six hundred six when he bought it, and it's in pretty good shape. Would three hundred be fair?"

"It might be, but I have two hundred in cash, right now."

The man offers his hand, "I'll take it."

They shake hands, "Now, can you explain to me how to register it here?"

An hour later, Guthrie and Brown are bouncing up a country lane to Sheamus Stewart's farm. They see a white-washed two-story brick house, with white outbuildings. The fields are well tended and divided with stone fences. They drive by a herd of cows poking their heads over the stone fence bordering the lane. As they get closer, they see a huge garden plot. The barn is solid and clean. There are no farm implements out in the weather and the yard is clean and mowed.

Mike turns the car to back it up where it won't get in the way, when suddenly a little boy darts out into the drive way behind him, and he slams on the brakes.

Guthrie, "What?"

Mike turns off the engine and sets the hand brake. He gets out and goes to the boy, "Hey there."

The little boy stops, still, "I'm sorry, sir."

"What's your name?"

"Jean Luc Stewart. My dad was in the navy."

A woman in a cotton dress and apron dashes out of the

house, "Jean Luc, what were you thinking?"

Mike, "I saw him, ma'am."

She looks at him with beautiful brown eyes. In accented English, "I'm sorry, sir. He's normally more sensible." She pushes a strand of black hair off her face and smiles.

Mike, "How old is he?"

"Jean Luc is four. Please, come in."

She takes Jean Luc's hand and leads them into the house. It is solid and tidy. Everything is functional and clean. "I take it your Jean Luc's mother?"

"I'm so sorry." She curtsies, "I'm Laureen Stewart."

"I'm Mike Brown, and this is Leroy Guthrie. Mr. Stewart did say we were coming, right?"

"I did. Welcome to our home." Sheamus comes out of another room, "So, you've met Laureen and our wee one?"

The little boy runs to Sheamus, "Papa! Papa!" He lifts his arms to be picked up, and Sheamus complies.

Laureen, "Jean Luc nearly ran under his tires."

Sheamus, "Dinna dae that, wee one. Na git washed fer supper." He sets the boy down. Jean Luc runs out of the room. "I thank ye fer comin."

Mike, "We're very thankful for the invitation."

Laureen, "Excuse me, I must see to the supper," and she walks into the kitchen.

Guthrie, "Thank you, sir."

Sheamus waves his hand, "Tis nuttin. Yous say ye sank the Krauts, aye?"

Mike, "Yeah, we did."

"Wa is ya doin onda boot?"

Mike smiles, "We operate the sensors that detect the other ships around us."

Laureen comes out with a beer for each of them. She smiles when they all say, 'thank you' at the same time.

Mike, "Jean Luc said his father was in the navy?"

"Aye. That he was. Gun officer on da Hood."

Guthrie leans forward, "What's the Hood?"

Mike, "I'm so sorry. So, very sorry. Guthrie, the Hood was a battle cruiser sunk by the Bismark."

Guthrie, "But it hasn't happened yet, right?"

"It sank in 1941, before we came back, Leroy. He lost his son."

Guthrie, "I'm sorry, sir."

Jean Luc, with clean hands and face, comes running in and climbs into his grandfather's lap. Sheamus, "The wee one donna unnerstand. Just knew we was blue."

Mike, "Even if Laureen wanted to return to France, she couldn't now."

Laureen comes in, "I'll never take Jean Luc away from his Papa. Supper is ready."

They've been smelling the tantalizing odors coming from the kitchen. When they walk in its to a large table in a huge kitchen. The food is in pots on the table. Laureen, "Papa, the prayer, please."

Sheamus says the grace, praying for peace, and the food is handed around the table so everyone, but Jean Luc, can serve themselves. Guthrie, "Ma'am, it smells divine. What is it?"

"My father's recipe for fish stew." She ladles Jean Luc's portion into his bowl.

Guthrie, "Managing a place like this must be quite a lot of hard work."

Sheamus, "We get by. A good day's work keeps a man's belly where it should be."

Mike, "Especially, when there's food like this. It's absolutely amazing. Thank you, so much."

Laureen, "You're welcome. I learned to cook in Marseille from my father. We owned a restaurant. It's where I met William."

They grow quiet. Mike, "It's difficult. It creates a hole that nothing can fill."

"I have my Jean Luc."

Sheamus, "Did Ian McPherson sell you his car?"

"Yes, sir. He said his son owned it."

"Aye, a nother un not coming back. You've a thought to what you'll be doing with it when you're to sea?"

"I was hoping to park it near the pier."

"Aye, but some bloomin' truck is liable to run it down, and she's a fine car. Ye should leave it here. We'll fetch it for you as you need."

Laureen looks at her father-in-law in surprise. She looks back to Mike and smiles.

USS BEAVER

Morrison and Backes are enjoying meat loaf and talking. John, "I toured the maintenance shops. We'll have to keep an eye on quality, but Simmons has brought them on pretty well."

"Good. He's no doubt the right man for the job, but I wonder some what would happen if the ram rod up his ass ever broke."

John chuckles, "Some of that is going from first class to lieutenant in one difficult step."

"Your admiral friend, again?"

"Yeah. Think about it. It makes sense because our senior enlisted are systems experts and commissioning one of them doesn't deplete the officer corps we need out here fighting. It's a smart way to build a cadre of manufacturing and maintenance experts while still expanding the service."

Backes, "True, but don't those thoughts cause your academy ring to spin around in panic?"

"It doesn't, though by rights, it ought to."

"So, Simmons is a nuke?"

"Yeah, he was an ET1. They pulled him from the Long Beach."

STEWART FARM

Sheamus, Laureen, and Jean Luc walk their guests out of the house. Mike shakes Sheamus' hand, "Thank you very much, sir."

"Yer welcome, any time."

Mike, "The day after tomorrow, I'll bring some civvies and lend a hand."

"Thank you for that."

Mike offers his hand to Laureen, "It was very nice to meet you, Laureen. Supper was wonderful."

She accepts his hand, "Thank you. It was nice to meet you,

too."

Jean Luc puts up his arms, "Uppy." Mike reaches down, picks him up, and tosses him into the air, catching him in a hug.

Mike, "Jean Luc, I need you to take care of your mom and grandpa, okay?" He smiles at Laureen.

"Okay." Mike puts him down and he and Guthrie get into the Ford and drive down the lane.

Laureen, "Da, why are you match-making?"

"That one. He's a good man, Laureen, and they ain't popping up like weeds."

"Yes, Da, but he would take us from you."

Sheamus shakes his head, "He's a sailor, yes, but he has the love of good land in him. Did ya see howen he looked over the place when he got here? He knew of what he looked. Let us just see about Michael Brown. That, and you ain't no nun. I saw ye making eyes at him." He smiles at her. "I ain't getting any younger. This place will need caring for if it's to last until the wee one is ready. It's his future I'm thinking of."

"He is what you say, strapping."

"He is that."

USS SAN FRANCISCO

0900, 31 March, 1942

The weapons hatch is open and the crew is on-loading the new torpedoes. Kennedy walks down the brow from the Beaver, "Commander, the crane has a current certification and our fish are well within its limits." Outboard of the San Francisco is a barge with thirteen Mark-48 torpedoes.

Morrison, "Good. Okay, everyone. Gather around for a pre-evolution brief."

Cumberland climbs up from below, "Morrison, everything is in order. I'm going to inspect the weapons storage site ashore."

Morrison tilts his head, looking at his commander, "Yes, sir."

Simmons, with the rigging crew, join Morrison, "Where is he going, sir?"

Morrison, "Not your concern. Who is the rigger in charge?" One of the men raises his hand. "Good, let's begin."

BUILDING 38, KEYPORT TORPEDO STATION

0135, 31 March, 1942

Kichiro carefully watches a technician assemble a swash plate drive motor. It's brand new and still needs many parts to be finished before it can be tested. "Joe, pre-lube each part."

"Yes, sir. Won't the oil gum up if it gets cold?"

"It will thicken a bit in storage, but it will prevent corrosion which could lock up the whole thing."

"How will this motor control its speed?"

"There's a governor being built to prevent the motor from flying apart if it runs dry. The water resistance slows the motor when its fired."

"Won't it get hot?"

"It does, but not so much as to be a problem."

"Sir, how long have you been working on these?"

"Seven years."

CHAPTER 30

FLEET PIER, SANDBANK, SCOTLAND

1020, 31 March, 1942

Backes and Morrison step off the launch and walk up the pier. Sitting on the pier is a grey Chevy sedan with US Navy painted on the door. Leaning against the Chevy is Henry Morrison.

John, "Greg, allow me to introduce you to my grandfather, Henry Morrison. Grandpa, this is my navigator, Greg Backus."

The two men shake hands. Henry, "I would think a lieutenant commander on a sub would be at least a department head."

Greg, "I am. We have three departments; supply, engineering, and navigation. Weapons fall under navigation."

Henry, "I had no idea. I had a thought to showing you around some, John. Backes, you're welcome to join us."

Greg, "I can smell beer from here. You guys have a good time. One thing, Commander, because of his appearance, I've been trying to make sure he isn't alone in town. He bleeds red, white, and blue, but too many people can only see a rising sun."

Henry, "I'll keep that in mind. Thank you, Commander."

Henry and John get into the car and leave. John, "Where are

we going?"

"The ferry. I'm going to show you the Livermore and introduce you to my captain. I'm afraid it's part business."

"Are you being assigned here?"

"Yep. We're to escort you in and out of port. Have you met Captain Holtz?"

"I have. We met in Australia. He's an F-14 pilot."

"Are those the triangular planes I've seen?"

"They are. We have 'Top Gun' on board the Frisco. I ought to show you the movie some time. It would be eye opening. We also have 'The Hunt for Red October.' That would be eye opening, too."

"What are they?"

"Movies. 'Top Gun' is about F-14 fighter pilots, and 'Hunt for Red October' is a submarine movie about a defecting Russian submarine captain. They're good movies, but they would also give you a look at how modern military equipment works. Of course, both movies get a lot wrong."

USS BEAVER

1210, 31 March, 1942

Guthrie takes his tray of food and sits down next to Brown. Brown, "You okay?"

"Yeah, I'm missing my girls."

"I know it sucks, Leroy. I can promise you, it will fade, but it may never go away."

"Were you ever, you know, in a relationship?"

"I was married for two years. Her name was Lori and I was an idiot to marry her."

"What was wrong with her?"

"Leroy, it isn't that simple. Um, okay, is there anything wrong with sleeping pills?"

"I guess they serve a purpose."

"Yeah. What about a laxative."

Guthrie chuckles, "Well, it serves a purpose, even if it's a shitty one."

"Yeah, but you should never take a sleeping pill and a laxative at the same time."

"Oh God. Okay, that makes sense. It wasn't that either of you were wrong, just that you were wrong for each other."

"Exactly."

"Do you like Laureen?"

"I don't know her yet."

"Mike, we had dinner at her house. You know her."

"Really. Is she a laxative or a sleeping pill?"

"Okay, that's fair. What does your gut say?"

"My gut says Sheamus likes me and believes I would be a suitable son-in-law. I believe Laureen is smart and wise. She's probably at best lukewarm on the idea. She's very right to doubt."

"You're a good guy. Why should she doubt?"

"Because she's already lost a sailor husband on a ship everyone thought was unsinkable. Why would she want to open herself to that kind of pain again?"

"You don't think we'll sink, do you?"

"Leroy, our boat is light years ahead of all the rest. It's designed and manufactured better. But all it would take is a lucky hit, or a mechanic fucking something up, and we'd go down. There is a non-zero probability of our demise. Why would she risk it?"

"Then, why are going there tomorrow?"

Because I like the old man. Because I want to be helpful and don't mind a day of work. Also, because I'm not the kind of person who spends their life hiding instead of living."

"Oh, then you like her?"

"Yeah, I do."

USS LIVERMORE

1441, 31 March, 1942

Captain Huber, "So, is there anything you can actually do to protect yourself on the surface?"

Morrison, "We can fire torpedoes from the surface, but that's only effective against large floating targets. We have a watch with a rifle, but that's about it."

"How much water do you need to dive?"

"We like a hundred fathoms. We need forty or fifty feet under our keel, so at least one hundred fifty feet. In truth, I would want to know for certain what the bottom conditions were at that shallow a depth."

LCDR Henry Morrison, "Can you use sonar to map it out?"

"Generally, we only use passive sonar. In 1990, using active sonar would be suicide. High frequency sonar would be detected by any other sub and act as a 'come kill me' beacon. Right now, it might work."

Huber, "Wouldn't people hear it?"

John, "We would transmit above audible frequencies. You get better picture resolution that way as well. It just has a shorter range and is bounced more easily."

Henry, "Bounced?"

"Changes in salinity and temperature can cause a sonar signal to bounce away like a ball hitting concrete."

STEWART FARM

0800, 1 April, 1942

Mike backs his car out of the way and parks. He gets out and grabs two bags out of the back. Sheamus comes out of the barn, "You'll need to change if ye wanna work."

Mike holds up his bags, "I brought work clothes. Any chance I might do my laundry, as well?"

Laureen, from the porch, "I'll do your laundry. Let me show you where you can change."

He follows her into the house and she leads him to a room, "If you like, I can wash what you're wearing, as well."

"Thank you very much. I wasn't expecting this."

"I think with your brawn, you'd be of more use to Sheamus."

He changes into jeans, a grey t-shirt, a flannel shirt, and a denim jacket. He takes his boots out to the rear porch and puts them on. The washing tub is on the back porch. Laureen looks up from her work, "Where did you get those clothes?"

Mike smiles, "Spokane, Washington, USA. I think I bought them in 1988 when I was at my sister's house on leave. I'm a time traveler."

"Oh. Um. Oh."

"My whole battle group came back in time."

"I heard of that, but I didn't know."

He stands up, "I'd be happy to tell you all about it, but I should probably get some work done."

"Over lunch?"

"Sure." He smiles and walks away. She watches him go, then turns back to her washing. She has two loads to run through the machine before she can get to his.

Mike joins Sheamus in the barn where he's repairing a milking stall. "One of my milkers has a wicked kick. She mostly takes it out on the stalls."

Mike holds boards and hands Sheamus nails. When that is done, they go and clean out the water troughs. Then, they prepare the garden for plowing. Sheamus fires up his Ferguson-Brown Model A tractor and plows the garden. Mike goes to the wood pile and chops wood for the house. Soon, he's so warm, he's pulled off his jacket and shirts.

Laureen finally gets to Mike's laundry. She's sees him swinging the axe, splitting each round with one hit, shirt off, his skin glistening with sweat. She picks up his dirty clothes and puts them to her nose, breathing in. Her eyes lower, and she smiles. Another breath, and she opens her eyes. She puts the clothes into the machine.

LONDON ROAD, GLASGOW, SCOTLAND

1510, 1 April, 1942

The cab drops Cumberland off in front of a nondescript and faintly Victorian house. He pays the cabby and walks to the door. He's wearing jeans and a black leather jacket. Thinking, "Okay, the car is only a couple of blocks away at the train station. I know I have enough money. Time for some fun." He knocks.

A large, stocky man answers the door, "Yes?"

"I'm looking for Betty's?"

"And you are?"

"Does it really matter?"

"I suppose not. You're dressed strange." He lets Cumberland in. There are several women sitting in the lounge, all dressed nicely. An older woman walks up and curtsies, "May I get you anything, m'lord?"

"Would you be Betty?"

"I am, and you are?"

"James Bond."

"Welcome, Mr. Bond. Would you like a drink or would you prefer to get straight to business?"

"I'm not in a chatty mood."

"The ladies are two pounds for a gobble, five pounds for the hole. Ten, if you won't use a Tadger wrap. You've got your pick of 'em."

He points at one who reminds him of his ex-wife and hands Betty a ten. He goes to the woman and takes her hand. They head upstairs and she leads him to a room. "Sir..."

"Stop. No words. You remind me of someone." The room is fairly clean and the sheets changed. He'd asked for a classy place, and he'd got one. He undresses her, then turns her back to him as he disrobes.

He turns her around and pushes her onto the bed. He climbs on and mounts her without preamble. Her eyes widen, but she doesn't make a sound. He grabs her hair and growls, "Fucking cunt. Fucking whore. Beg for it."

"W...What?

"Beg."

"Um, um, fuck."

He yanks her hair and grins with gritted teeth.

She looks into his eyes, "Please. Please don't. Please."

He releases her hair and she relaxes a bit. He puts his hands on her throat and smiles. He slowly squeezes. Her left hand scrambles for a cord below the head board. Just as her hand touches the cord, he's done, growling, his hands still wrapped around her neck.

He smiles, and lets go, pushing away and standing up. Her hand is still on the cord, but she hesitates. He dresses, pulls a twenty out of his pocket and tosses it on her. "Shut up about it, or I'll really kill you." Smiling, he walks out of Betty's. He whistles as he walks down the street to his Navy sedan.

STEWART FARM

1730, 1 April, 1942

It's been a hard day of work. The four of them sit down to another amazing dinner. Mike regals them with stories. When they're done, Mike helps clear the table and organizes the dishes. Laureen fills the sink with hot water. She washes and Mike dries.

Jean Luc comes up to his mother, shutting his eyes. She smiles and lifts him to the side board, washing his face and hands. She speaks in French to him, then puts him down, "Go read with Papa."

"Okay, Mummy."

Mike, "So he knows French."

"I don't want him to forget. Knowing more than one language is an advantage."

"I agree." They finish the dishes and walk into the parlor. Sheamus has Jean Luc on his lap, reading to him. Sheamus looks up, "When must you return?"

Mike, "I don't wish to impose, but I must be back tomorrow night."

Sheamus, "We've a guest room and wish your company." He grins, "We just might get that garden planted tomorrow." He gives Laureen a sly look, "Laureen, why don't you show the lad our sunset?"

Jean Luc, "Can I go, Papa?"

Sheamus squeezes the boy, "But I haven't finished the story, little one?"

Mike and Laureen walk outside into the cool night. Mike, "Is he making you uncomfortable?"

"What?"

"He's trying so hard to match make. In truth, it makes me a bit uncomfortable for you."

"I love him. He's good to us."

"He's a good man and he loves you, but it's for you to choose, not him. Anyway, I'm no slam dunk."

"What is a slam dunk?"

He offers his hand and she puts her hand in his. "As I see it, you were already married to a sailor. If Sheamus is any indication, he was a great person. I have the majority of the war in front of me and no guarantee I won't be killed, as well. I believe my odds to be fair to good, but there's always that chance."

"I understand. What is a slam dunk?"

"Do you know the sport of basketball?

"Not really."

"Okay, if a person is tall and athletic enough, they can jump up and stuff the ball into a net. If they can do it, it's very easy. A slam dunk is something easy."

"You're tall. Can you slam dunk?"

He chuckles, "I'm not very good at basketball, but yeah, I've done it."

"Then you are a slam dunk." She smiles. They turn and look at the sky to the west. The setting sun is lighting up the loch and making the clouds glow.

"Do you understand what I mean? Us together would be very hard, and probably unfair to you."

"Nothing in life is certain. Yes, you may die. Truth, I may die. In time, everyone does. The question, then, is do we live?"

"Can you explain why you would even consider me?"

She holds up a finger, "You're a good man. You have a good heart and you are kind to my child." She holds up a second finger, "You're a serious person. You do not scoff at work or duty or responsibility." She holds up three fingers, "You're a sailor. Someone important. It's something honored here. Those that have served are revered and respected." She holds up four fingers, "You are beautiful."

Startled, he shakes his head, "I don't get the last, Laureen. I don't think you quite understand what you're getting into. I want us to go slow. I want to know for certain this is right for you, your family, and me."

"I accept to go slow. It's wise. When the war is over, what will you do?"

"I've been in the Navy sixteen years. There's probably four

more years left of the war. When I reach twenty years, I qualify for retirement. The retirement as a first class isn't much, but it's an income for life. Had I not come back in time, my plan was to stay in until they threw me out, buy a piece of land in a quiet place, and build a life. I expected to be alone. Now, that I'm here. Now, that I'm in this moment, I don't know what I want. I'm afraid of hurting you and Jean Luc."

"We are strong and you are a good person. If you stayed here after the war, would your family miss you?"

"They don't even know me. My parents are kids right now. My grandparents are...difficult. I would need to see my folks grow up from time to time, but I wouldn't want to live in their pockets. Um, too close. We need to think about this."

"I agree." She turns to face him, her body inches from his. She looks up into eyes, "Perhaps, we should sleep on it."

"Yes. Perhaps." He smiles.

Still holding his hand, she walks him into the house, then drops his hand. "Your clean clothes are in the guest room. I'll see you in the morning." She smiles at him and walks up the stairs.

ELECTRIC BOAT DESIGN LOFT, GROTON, CT

0950, 2 April, 1942

Lt. Mallory pours over blueprints for a proposed submarine design. Rather than writing directly on the plans, he's taking careful notes on a pad. He looks up at the clock, puts the notebook away, and walks upstairs to the conference room. He waits at the front as engineers and project officers file in. CDR Kevin Holloway, the submarine design lead comes in and sits down. Holloway came back in time on the Long Beach and had twelve years on fast attacks.

Mallory, "Is this everyone, sir?"

"It is. You can start."

Mallory, "Okay. I've found the items that must be corrected to avoid catastrophic failure, improve function, or improve repairability. First, a swivel snorkel will leak. There is no practical way to seal the join from the pressure of a deep dive."

"But you won't be using it in a deep dive. It'll be stowed."

"True, but when we come shallow again and try to use it, it'll be full of water. Gentlemen, it is unacceptable to dump 200 gallons of water through the vents and onto the head of the crew every time you use the snorkel. I understand your attempt at a longer reach. If that is a priority, then make the hull, and/or the sail larger, so a sliding snorkel can be used. In fact, I'm recommending two more feet of diameter for the sub. It solves some other issues we'll get to."

An engineer, "Two more feet will increase the hull thickness and energy needs while slowing down the speed."

"Streamlining will make up for the cost to speed. The additional beam serves a handful of purposes. First, it allows for a larger battery bank. Next, it solves the access issues beneath the engine and port generator. It also allows the proposed sonar dome to be three inches further forward, increasing the arc of detection and providing room for more effective sound isolation."

They ask questions and argue over Mallory's recommendations for twenty minutes. An engineer, "While the area is squared, the volume is cubed. This will work."

CDR Holloway nods, "Redraw the lines. The Lieutenant is right on all counts. Clyde, I need you to work with him to get a wave pool model made. Have we come up with a testing rig that can properly test a submerged hull design?"

Mallory, "I have that." He shows Holloway the plans.

The commander looks at the plans and hands them off to Clyde, Make it." He gets up and leaves.

NAVY PIER, SANDBANK, SCOTLAND

1945, 4 April, 1942

Mike Brown pulls his car to a stop and get out. He helps little Jean Luc out of the passenger seat as Sheamus and Laureen get out of the rumble seat. He gets his bag out and looks toward the San Francisco. He's in his working blues and he's going to sea.

Jean Luc, "Uppy." Mike picks him up. "You gots to go?"

"I do, little one."

"Why?"

Sheamus, "It be his duty, wee one."

"Okay."

Mike hands Jean Luc over to Sheamus, "Thank you, Sheamus."

"Thank you, lad. Now, you take care, aye?"

Mike, "I will."

Laureen takes his hands in hers, "We'll be praying for you."

OPERATIONS ROOM, ADMIRALITY CITADEL, LONDON

0910, 13 April, 1942

The First Sea Lord, Admiral Sir Dudley Pound calmly walks into the operations center. The place is buzzing with quiet urgency. The duty officer approaches, "Sir, the Tirpitz is underway. Western Approaches is rerouting convoys. We are sortieing the King George and Duke of York, with the Eagle and Unicorn. May we direct Task Force Yankee to engage?"

"Do we know its course?"

"No, sir. There are three convoys in danger of attack."

"I will make the call to Alconbury. Please dial me through."

In a minute, "Sir, Captain Holtz on line 1, sir."

"Captain, the Tirpitz is underway. We have three convoys scrambling. Can you attack it?"

Holtz, "No, sir. I would like to, but it is beyond our mission. I will, however, send the San Francisco. It's about 800 miles away, but it's the best I can do"

"Can you locate the Tirpitz?"

"Perhaps. Is it alone?"

Pound, "No. I'm told it's with a cruiser and several destroyers. All have anti-aircraft missiles fitted."

"Understood, I'll keep you posted."

USS SAN FRANCISCO, BETWEEN ICELAND AND THE FAROE ISLANDS

2052, 13 April, 1942

Brown is on the mess deck reading a novel. The 'Hunt for Red October' is playing for the thousandth time on site TV. There's a faint vibration throughout the ship and the hiss of flow noise. The sub is sprinting in a high-speed run 800 feet down. It puts them well below any current sub, and well above the bottom, which is 1000 feet below.

He reads the same page for the third time. Right now, sea mounts terrify him. They have good charts from when they played here with the Russians. Still, you never know. Finally, he sets down the book and writes Laureen a letter

CHAPTER 31

BATTLESHIP TIRPITZ, 100 MILES NW OF VESTVAGOYA IS-LAND, NORWAY

2320, 13 April, 1942

Oberleutnant zur See Helmut Schmitt stands OOD on the bridge. The weather is snotty with a force 9 gale blowing out of the west and heavy seas forcing the large ship to work into the waves. He steps out onto the starboard bridge wing.

Somewhere out there is the cruiser Koln, but he cannot see it. Spray pounds his foul weather gear and the chill wind creeps into every seam. Looking forward, he spots a dark image a little higher than the waves. He studies it to assure his eyes are not playing tricks, then asks the lookout, "What can you make out two points off the starboard bow?"

"It's a ship. Sorry, sir."

"It's cold and miserable, but we must be attentive to our duties. Carry on."

Schmitt walks into the bridge. The warmth envelops him like as a fog. Steam rises from his foul weather gear. He dials a phone, "Sir, contact two points off the starboard bow."

"Do you have identification yet?"

"No, sir. Just the distant sighting."

"Call when identified," the captain hangs up.

The phone talker says, "Port lookout spots a second contact

dead ahead."

Schmitt, "Very well"

SS SHENANDOAH, OIL TANKER, 11 MILES NORTH OF TIRPITZ

Second Officer Torrance Breve studies the waters ahead. The seas just keep pounding the large ship. Green water on rolls over the bow and along the deck. The ship was well made and only three years old, but the seas were disquieting.

He is restless and puts on his foul weather coat and walks out on the starboard bridge wing. All is endless waves to the front. To the starboard he can see the Canadian destroyer, HMCS Ottawa, H-60, also laboring against the wind and waves.

He looks astern and sees a formless shape. He adjusts his binoculars and sees blooms of orange-yellow appear. He freezes, hearing the shriek of a million pieces of paper ripping at once. A column of water rises up behind them. He rushes back into the bridge and grabs the phone, pushing buttons with shaking hands. The ship's master, David Langtree, walks in, "Are we under fire, Breve?"

"Y...Yes, sir."

"Calm. It will be what it will be. Ring the engine room for ahead full."

"Yes, sir."

HMCS OTTAWA, H-60

Commander Colin Donald walks onto the bridge just as the battle stations alarm stops, "What is it, Peters?" He hears the shriek of the next salvo and looks astern. "Ahead flank. Left full rudder. Run the torpedo tubes out as soon as manned.

Open fire with all guns as manned."

Lt. Peters, "Sir, are we in gun range?"

"It doesn't matter. We need them to focus on us."

Mount X, a QF 4.7-inch cannon starts firing.

Donald puts binoculars to his eyes. The ship is coming about smartly, heeling heavily in the waves, and picking up speed. Their rounds fall short. The next salvo from the Tirpitz lands behind them, "Right full rudder."

The destroyer heels again, all four of Ottawa's QF turrets firing.

Donald, "Left full rudder." The bow swings back toward the big German battleship. Another salvo. This time the Tirpitz splits fire and a round hits the Shenandoah. The two rounds aimed at the Ottawa land to their port side and a wave of water crashes down on the deck.

Donald, "Right full rudder." Again, in the hard turn, all four turrets fire. X turret scores a hit, starting a fire forward on the port side of the Tirpitz. "Left full rudder." B turret scores another hit. An explosion on the Shenandoah hits them with a shock wave, heeling the destroyer even more.

Then, at five miles, Donald, "Fire all torpedoes." Four torpedoes shoot off their launchers into the sea.

TIRPITZ

Kapitan Topp sees the flames from the torpedo launch. He can barely trace the faint line of their bubbles in the heavy waves. "Right full rudder. Ahead flank power limiting. We must avoid the torpedoes."

Schmitt repeats and relays the captain's orders. The lee helm is sweating, his hands trembling. Schmitt, "Easy Brandt.

They will miss. The British have no eyeglasses because every new pair they order, our submarines pour out on the bottom of the Atlantic."

"Yes, sir."

"Admiral on the bridge." Admiral Ciliax walks in, "Captain, we bled them. Time to withdraw."

Topp nods, "Yes, sir. I agree."

The Ottawa's torpedoes slide harmlessly down their port side.

HMCS OTTAWA

Donald watches the Tirpitz make the turn, firing its stern guns as it withdraws. The plucky destroyer scores three more hits, dodging the huge shells. Donald, "Right full rudder. Come to new course 355. The Shenandoah will need us."

The last 14-inch round from the Tirpitz hits just aft of Y turret and passes completely through the destroyer before exploding. The hit mangles both shafts and floods the stern of the destroyer. Five miles away, the Shenandoah burns.

As the destroyer slows, wallowing in the heavy swells, Donald realizes he cannot get to the tanker that needs them. His engineer comes onto the bridge and salutes, "Fires out. The bulkhead forward of Mount Y is holding. 27 dead. 19 wounded. We need a doctor and a tow, sir, but we won't sink."

He returns the salute, "Thank you, Clyde." Donald turns and looks out the windscreen. He sees movement on the water. He realizes he is seeing the burning Shenandoah backing toward them. He smiles, "Good. Man the boats. When they're close enough, we need to take them aboard."

USS SAN FRANCISCO

1710, 14 April, 1942

Cumberland, "We should be hunting submarines, not rescuing a Canuck destroyer dumb enough to fight a battleship."

Morrison, "We have our orders, sir."

Cumberland shakes his head, "Blow ballast, Morrison. It's going to be fucking cold out there. You have the bridge. Sarvis, Novogradic, are you ready?"

The two men, in unison, "Yes, sir."

Morrison is the first one up the hatch. The sub wallows side to side in the deep swells. When he gets to the top, he sees the destroyer close aboard. Its stern is awash, but both funnels have smoke coming from them. He uses a flashlight for a blinker, "Interrogative: How many survivors?"

"136 from both ships. Interrogative: What vessel?"

"San Francisco. Interrogative: Engines repairable?"

"In ship yard only"

"Understood. Tirpitz in port. Interrogative: Medical assistance?"

"Affirmative."

On the phone, "Sir, they need our doc."

"Morrison, I'm following below. How are you going to transfer him?"

"Sir, if we maneuver down wind, they could float us a ship's boat."

"Very well. Do it."

Morrison blinkers his plan. He maneuvers the sub downwind, off the destroyer's starboard bow, so the destroyer can moderate the wind and waves. The Ottawa puts a wooden boat in the water, strung out on a line with six rowers.

Morrison, "Hold the bell and rudder position. They're coming along side."

The wood boat bounces off the port side of the sub and Sarvis grabs the line, holding it in while Novogradic tosses his supplies into the boat, then jumps in. Then, the destroyer pulls the boat back alongside and hoists it aboard.

Morrison on blinker, "We will submerge now. A tow is coming. No submarine or enemy surface craft will get close."

"Thank you, San Francisco."

Sarvis climbs back up the sail, "Sir, what hit them?"

"A 14-inch round from the Tirpitz. That destroyer held off the Tirpitz and then, rescued the crew of a doomed tanker."

"Shit. Amazing they're still afloat."

"Yeah, it's a ship worth saving."

TIRPITZ AT ANCHOR, KAAFJORD, NORWAY

1845, 14 April, 1942

Helmut Schmitt walks around the forward port missile launcher. One of the destroyer's shells hit it and killed his friend. The smell of burning flesh still hangs on the air as the crew begins removing the jagged metal. Kapitan Topp approaches and Schmitt salutes. "Oberleutnant, do not fret that this launcher is hit. Rounds rarely fall on the same place twice."

"Sir, I was thinking of the men who died here. It seems so random."

"It is We must each do our best to minimize the enemy's opportunities to hit us again."

"Yes, sir."

"You do well, Oberleutnant, do not over react to what you see."

"Yes, Kapitan."

HMCS OTTAWA NEARING ABERDEEN, SCOTLAND

11 April, 1942

HM1(SS) Vince Novogradic does his rounds He's managed to improvise an infirmary and all of his patients are undercover. He has seven burn patients, nine with broken bones, and several other critical injuries. He's protecting the burn patient's skin with sterile wraps. A real challenge in this environment.

The worst is Boatswains Mate Billy Atherton's stomach wound. A piece of steel tore through his intestines. Novogradic had no choice but to perform surgery. He cut out the severely damaged portions of the small intestines, reattached the clean ends, and sewed together the torn muscles and skin. He filled Billy with antibiotics and wrapped him in sterile bandages. Now they wait.

He looks down at Billy, "How are you feeling?"

"No fever, doc. I think. Not quite ready to go dancing, but getting there. When can I eat?"

Novogradic peels back the bandages. The wound has stopped weeping and the redness is going down. "You are looking good. Sorry about the liquid diet. I need to keep your guts clean. Besides, the yogurt will help restore the biome the antibiotics are destroying."

They hear the sound of a helicopter, then, "Deck division. Standby to receive personnel at Mount A."

He redresses Atherton's wound, and touches his shoulder. He then goes to this next patient, "Chief Potter, how are you?"

"Doing well, considering my career as a pianist is over." Potter looks at the stump of his right arm, smashed by a collapsing bulkhead.

Novogradic smiles, "So, you play the piano?"

"Nope."

"Pretty sure you could manage the harmonica."

"I suppose I could."

The see a small man in black BDU's and carrying an enormous back pack come in and go to immediately wash his hands. Novogradic, "Who are you, sir?"

"HM1 Shockley, Seal Team 1. What do you have?"

Novogradic goes over the status of each patient. They change bandages and speak with each man, then walk out of the canvas division separating the infirmary from the mess decks.

Shockley, "How many did you lose?"

"It was almost a day before I got onboard. Those unsavable, were already lost."

"Where are you from?"

"San Francisco."

"You saved a lot of lives here. Good job."

"Thanks."

"Once in port, we'll transfer your critical patients by helo to Guys in London. Your boat is, I think, still underway. I could use you at Alconbury."

"Cool."

USS SAN FRANCISCO, 300 MILES SOUTH OF GREENLAND

8 May, 1942

Cumberland paces back and forth waiting for the radioman to finish sending their report. "Where the fuck are they?"

Morrison, "The convoys are getting through. There've been a few attacks in the med, but they got that one. It didn't happen in our history. I can't believe they would give up."

ETC Barton hands Cumberland a message:

FROM: COMNAVFORGB

TO: 711

REG: MOVEMENT

711, RTB morning tide, 5/16/1942 for tasking.

Holtz

Cumberland hands it back, "Jesus Christ, if he has a new assignment, why do we have to go back in to receive it."

"Sir, he's the boss."

"Fucking wing wiper. He doesn't know the first thing about what we do."

Quietly, Morrison says, "But, he's the boss, sir. It's wrong to criticize the boss in front of our crew, sir."

Cumberland looks around, "Morrison, they all get it. We should have a submarine officer commanding our squadron."

445

"Sir, there are no 1990 submarine captains or admirals, that I know of. A 1941 wouldn't understand what we can do."

"Neither, does he. Set our course. Let's hunt our way to Scotland."

"Yes, sir."

DAVID TAYLOR MODEL BASIN, CARDEROCK, MARYLAND

1250, 10 May, 1942

Mallory watches the submarine he designed being carefully lowered into the test tank. It is at the end of a six-foot pole with an instrument box and counter weight. It has fins to keep the model balanced straight in the water. When the rig is pushed through the water, the resistance is measured on a calibrated weight scale.

Admiral Klindt, "It's a sensible design."

Mallory, "Thank you, sir. I just hope it stays straight."

"Your counter balance and fins should do that. I can't find a flaw in your design."

The first model they run is that of a Gato class submarine. They run it six times down the course, making small adjustments to the controls. The runs share an average resistance number. Then they install Mallory's design. Eight runs later, the numbers speak for themselves. Though, the sub is wider, the resistance is substantially lower.

Mallory, "Sir, it's a start. With this tool I can refine the shape further."

"Do so, but keep in mind, we have to build the shape you settle on."

"Yes, sir"

STEWART FARM, SANDBANK, SCOTLAND

1815, 11 Mary, 1942

Jean Luc plays with this toy truck, stopping and listening to the birdsong. He picks a daisy and runs to his mother who's standing where she can see down the hill toward the loch.

Sheamus walks up beside her, "He's coming back."

"How do you know, Da?"

"You ken the large ship a floating out there with the destroyer tied to it?"

"Yes."

"That ship, tis here for your lad's submarine. As long as it is here, he'll be back."

Laureen hugs Sheamus, "Thank you, Da."

"Ye know there's a good bit of war left. He might be gone time to time, for even years. Ken ye live with it?"

She sighs, "I did for William. If he's for me, I'll wait. It...just now we're not anything. No promise. Not even a maybe."

"Dinnae fash yerself. He'll be back. I've seen him looking at you. He'll be back. You'll see. I'm pure right."

"Thank you, Da."

THE FIRTH OF CLYDE

0730, 16 May, 1942

Cumberland, "Blow ballast."

As they surface, Morrison is on the periscope, "Livermore at 230. Our guide boat is at 050."

Cumberland, "Very well. It's raining out there. Morrison, you have the bridge team."

"Yes, sir." The men on the bridge are all in foul weather gear. The sub works its way into Holy Loch. The tug parks them. Because it's their second time in, the crew knows where everything is. At 0915 liberty call goes down for section two and three. The Livermore anchors in the loch and sends over a launch.

The launch pulls alongside the San Francisco and the officer calls out, "Sirs, Commander Huber invites your wardroom, not on watch, to the Livermore tonight for dinner."

Quietly to Morrison, Cumberland asks, "Must we?"

"Sir, we are socially obligated to say yes."

Cumberland turns back to the boat officer, "My wardroom, of course, will attend. I hope you're also offering transport. As you can see, we're somewhat short on ship's boats."

"Of course, sir. It begins at 1600." He directs the coxswain back to the Livermore.

Morrison, "I'll give the wardroom the news."

Cumberland, "Do you suppose he has any information regarding our orders?"

"I doubt it, sir."

NAVY PIER, SANDBANK, SCOTLAND

1015, 16 May, 1942

Mike Brown, in his dress whites, carries his laundry off the pier. He sees his car, Laureen standing beside it and waving. His grin is uncontrollable.

MMC Jim Giblin walks up next to him, "You got yourself a

Scottish girlfriend, Brown?"

"No, Chief. She's from Marseille in France."

"But, she's your girlfriend?"

"I'm not sure, yet. Ask me on our next duty day."

"What is she doing here?"

"She's a widow. Her husband was on the Hood."

"Kids?"

"One amazing little boy, Jean Luc Stewart."

Giblin laughs, "He needs to make up his mind. Is he Patrick Stewart or Jean Luc Picard?"

Brown chuckles, "I forgot about that. Do you want to meet her?" They walk up to the car, "Laureen, this is one of my watch chiefs, Jim Giblin. Chief, Laureen Stewart."

Smiling, she offers her hand, "How do you do?"

Giblin, "Well, but not as well as Brown. A pleasure to meet you."

Laureen, "May I invite you to dinner?"

Giblin smiles at her, then looks over to Brown, "I'm afraid I have an engagement in town. Thank you very much."

Mike, "Take care, Chief."

"Oh, I will. You as well."

Mike and Laureen get into the car and he fires it up.

"Did you get any U-boats."

"Have you ever gone fishing before?"

"I have."

"Some days, there are no fish to catch. When that happens,

nothing you can do will fix it. Still, the convoys are getting through and that's the point. How have you been? How's Jean Luc?"

"He's been missing you. He keeps asking where his sailor is. He's so cute."

"Well, his sailor is home for a few days."

"Home." She smiles.

CHAPTER 32

USS LIVERMORE

1621, 16 May, 1942

Cumberland and Huber are at the captain's table, talking. Nearby, Henry and John are eating and talking. "Well, grandson, did you know that the Commodore's chief of staff is a woman?"

"Commander Samantha Hunt. Yes, I met her in Australia."

"What do you think of women in uniform?

"Grandpa, this is an item you do not want to be a dinosaur about. It's coming. In time, destroyers like this one, will have female officers and crew. In fact, one of the destroyers with the carrier group, the Fife, is skippered by Commander Laura Wakefield. It's the way of the future.

"When I met Commander Hunt, I think she had 35 kills, though she hates to talk about her kills. If you meet her, don't ask her. She considers it a barbaric, if necessary, part of warfare. She won't talk about it."

Henry, "What's she like?"

"She's very athletic, thin, with short blonde hair. She has a grace about her, but she also has steel. Cumberland talked bad about her and she took him to task immediately, and effectively. She doesn't smile much, but when she does, her face transforms. She's warm and beautiful. But, Grandpa, she's very reserved."

"Do you like her?"

John smiles, "Not like that. I have an enormous amount of respect for her. I told you I was married before we went back in time, right?"

"No, you didn't."

"Her name is Lisa, and she was my one and only. There's no room in my heart for another." John stops, then tells Henry everything about Lisa and their history.

Finally, "John, may I be frank?"

"Of course."

"That's fucking ridiculous. Despairingly foolish. You denied yourself any measure of happiness because you could not have your perfect happiness. It's the conduct of a fool. Please tell me you are smarter; that you have a heart wiser than that?"

John lowers his head, then looks up into his grandfather's eyes, "I've been an idiot, haven't I?"

"You have. Romantic love belongs to poets and writers. It will hold a relationship together," Henry snaps his fingers, "that long. Relationships are built on respect and compatibility."

"You love Grandma."

"We do have love for each other, but it comes from a place of respect. We are building a family and a future together. I respect her hard work, patience, and desire to build a better future. She respects my service, hard work, and desire to build a better future. We are compatible. We're also temperamentally compatible. Perhaps Lisa checked off all of those boxes for you. Great. In this vast world with millions and millions of people, there is, no doubt about it, thousands of women equally compatible. Do not close the eyes of your heart."

"I've been a fool."

"We're all fools, from time to time. The important thing is to learn. I take it I did not teach you this lesson forty or fifty years from now?"

"You tried, but I could not hear you. I...I martyred myself to her love. Once on that cross, I got comfortable there."

"Well, step down, we need the wood."

ELECTRONICS MANUFACTURING FACILITY, RICHLAND, WASHINGTON

0932, 16 May, 1942

Lt. Andrew Brown parks his Dodge pickup in the front of a huge complex of buildings. There are at least 500 cars in the lot. He gets out and squares away his combination cover. Orders in hand, he walks through the front door. Up four flights of stairs he finds the executive offices. A pretty woman typing at a desk looks up, "May I help you?"

"Is Captain Richardson in, ma'am?"

"He is. May I have your name?"

"ET 1...um...Lieutenant Brown, ma'am. I'm reporting from the Los Angeles class boat, San Francisco. It's a 1990 anti-submarine platform."

"Did Admiral Klindt send you?"

"He did."

She picks up a phone. After a brief conversation, she gets up and ushers him through a door. Inside, Captain Richardson is at a desk and on a call.

While he waits, Brown looks around. The office is smaller than he expected, with a sitting area and a large desk. The desk is clean and very tidy, the work boxes are stacked high with paperwork. There are two book shelves holding scintillating reading like Computer Architecture: A Quantitative Approach, Principles of Compiler Design, Reactor Plant Principles, Design and Repair of Electronic Subassemblies, and Principles of Electronic Engineering. He sees two other doors into the office.

Finally, Richardson puts the phone down, "How can I help you, Lieutenant?"

Brown hands over his orders. "Admiral Klindt assigned me to you."

"Do you know anything about electronics?"

"I was commissioned in March. Before that I was a nuke ET1 on the San Francisco. It's a 688 class."

Richardson leans back, "I asked for a competent ET. If Craig sent me you, then you are up to the task. Do you have a place to live?"

"I can sort that out later, sir."

Richardson shakes his head, "Go sort it out now. Take the whole day and part of tomorrow, if you need it. You'll need a comfortable house or apartment. Make yourself a nest where you can recharge, because, Lieutenant, I'm going to work the crap out of you." His phone rings, "I'll see you tomorrow."

LONDON ROAD, GLASGOW, SCOTLAND

1820, 17 May, 1942

This time, Cumberland parks his car a few blocks away and walks. He's in jeans and a flannel shirt. He pays attention, and realizes there's another house just down the road from the last one. He walks up and knocks. A man answers. "Yessir?"

"Can I find a girl here?"

"Who are you?"

"Does it matter?"

"No to me. Ye a boaby?"

"A what? I'm American."

"Come in, then."

The room is dim and there are several women sitting in the lounge. One is Asian. He smiles at her. An old woman walks up and puts a hand on his shoulder, "Ye wanna beer, ferst?"

He shakes his head. A woman in the corner catches his eye. He hands the madame a ten-dollar bill and walks over to the woman. Her hair is the right brown. She's the right age. The face is wrong, but she'll do. She leads him upstairs.

MC AND MAC'S PUB, SANDBACK, SCOTLAND

The pub has expanded into its back yard by putting in a flag-stoned floor and putting a roof up. There are no walls, but the weather is warm enough to be comfortable. Guthrie and some of his watch team, including a couple of nukes, are enjoying a beer. There are a few British sailors off the other tender and its subs. There are also a few American sailors off the Beaver. The locals are clustered in groups, watching the sailors.

Their waitress, Ashley, stops by their table, "Anything more for you, fellas?"

MM1 Jackson asks, "Could we get another round of beer?"

"Of course."

Guthrie, "May I have a date?"

Ashley smiles, "You're sweet."

A local stands and steps toward Guthrie with a cocked fist, "Hey, Yankee Doodle! Ye be keepin yer dick skinners off our lasses, or I'll be bustin yeer bucket!"

The ten San Francisco sailors stand as one. Another man swings a bottle at Jackson, missing his head and hitting his shoulder. Guthrie ducks a punch from the guy who mouthed off, then punches him in the gut. Other locals wade in, and soon it's a melee.

MMC Jim Giblin shouts, "KNOCK IT OFFF!" He dodges a thrown bottle, then the man who threw it charges. Giblin brings back his fist and pops the man in the nose. The man drops. "Come to me, guys! Circle it up!"

Another local swings a chair and Giblin ducks. Then he delivers a right uppercut. That man falls, knocked out. The sailors fight their way to Giblin, finally getting to his back. Any man facing Giblin, falls. Most stay unconscious.

ANNIE'S BROTHEL, LONDON STREET, GLASGOW

Cumberland, "What's your name?"

"Lisa," she smiles at him, coyly.

"Strip. No talking."

She stops and looks him in the eyes. Realization hits her and she shakes her head, backing toward the door, "No. Not you."

He rushes her, grabbing and throwing her onto the bed. He smiles and jumps on the bed and pining her legs. He pushes her dress up. She wriggles up to the head of the bed, and he grabs her arms. He holds her arms over her head, and holds her wrists with on hand, using the other to get under her clothes. "Stop fighting, or I'll kill you."

She goes limp. He penetrates, rocking, his head back. He takes his hand from her wrists, and puts his hands around her throat and squeezes. "My XO married a Lisa. I'm fucking Lisa. Beg whore."

She whimpers, fighting to breath, but she gets her hand behind the head board and pulls a cord.

MC AND MAC'S PUB, SANDBANK

The Frisco, and the some British, sailors stay in the circle while they work their way out the door. The locals are avoiding Giblin, but he keeps moving, protecting his men. Finally, the police and shore patrol arrive.

ANNIE'S BROTHEL, LONDON STREET, GLASGOW

Cumberland sees Lisa's hand behind the headboard and punches her in the face. Suddenly, he feels himself being lifted off Lisa and thrown onto the floor. He scrambles to his feet and swings at a huge man. The man brushes him off, swinging a haymaker. Cumberland slips the punch and walks into the bouncer's left fist, getting his right eye split open. Stunned, he wavers, and the bouncer hits him with a combination of body and head punches. The last one to his head hits him in the temple and he goes down, unconscious.

OUTSIDE MC AND MAC'S

The police and shore patrol break up the fight, and get the men sorted into groups away from each other. Constable Ann Lochlin asks Giblin, "Can you identify the man who started it?"

"I was behind him and only saw his back, sorry. The guy who threw the first bottle? Him I saw."

"Did any of your guys throw anything but punches?"

"No. Basic assault is one thing, throwing a weapon elevates it to aggravated assault, or even attempted murder. We just fought by hand."

"Several witnesses said you were knocking guys out with a single punch. Where did you learn to fight?"

"My dad was in the Army. We moved all over. After I got beat up, he decided I needed to learn how to fight. I tried karate, judo, and aikido. I learned from all of them, but I like boxing. I was a trouble maker in high school, so I continued the training. It kept me out of mischief. I boxed in college, too. I was an amateur, but I won four fights and lost only one. Anyway, that's how I learned."

"Where are you from?"

"I was born in West Germany. Raised in Germany, Italy, Korea, Japan, Texas, Washington, and Massachusetts." He smiles, "Army brat."

"Where do you call home?"

"Springfield, Massachusetts. My mom lives...um...will live there."

"The time travel?"

"Yeah."

Lochlin walks over to her team to conference.

ANNIE'S BROTHEL, GLASGOW

Cumberland wakes to water pouring onto his face. Three big men with clubs are standing over him. Annie, "Well, Commander George Cumberland. You had one hundred and twenty-three dollars in your wallet. You still have twenty-three. If we ever see you in this town again, we'll kill you and dump your body in the river."

"You didn't call the police?"

"We've enough trouble with them. Leave and consider your-self fortunate. If you had killed her, your body might never be found." She smiles and steps back, "Okay, boys. Let him go."

The men step away from the door. He staggers to his feet and stumbles out.

OUTSIDE MC AND MAC'S

The sailors are sitting with Chief Giblin, waiting. A helicop-ter circles and comes in, setting down on the road. A woman in aviation greens with the gold leaves of a lieutenant com-mander, gets out and approaches the police. She talks with them for a moment, then turns and walks over to the men. They stand and salute. She asks, "Which one of you is se-nior?"

Chief Giblin, "I am, ma'am."

"Do any of you need medical attention?"

Giblin, "No, ma'am. May I ask who you are, ma'am."

"Commander Hunt. I'm Yankee's chief of staff. He's flying right now. Which command are you with, and, can you ex-plain exactly what happened?"

"The San Francisco, ma'am. Some of us are from the Liver-more and Beaver."

She asks the men what happened, and they each give an hon-est description of the fight.

Hunt, "Okay, the police are comfortable with letting you go, and I agree. However, I want all of you to return to your com-mands tonight and let the town cool down some. I'll inform the OOD and let your captain know."

Morrison walks up and salutes, "Hello, ma'am. My apologies for this."

"It isn't their fault. I want to be clear. We do not discipline sailors for defending themselves. Understood?"

"Yes, ma'am."

Hunt, "Can you share what I said with the other commands?"

"Yes, ma'am."

"One more thing, the drinking establishments are closed to American sailors tonight. The town needs to cool down. I don't need a total recall. Just keep them out of the pubs."

Morrison, "Yes, ma'am."

Constable Ann Lochlin comes over, "We've enough to settle this. We want you to know the blokes who started all this are from a construction crew out of Glasgow. They're not locals."

Hunt, "Will they be charged with any crimes?"

"Yes. We're taking care of that."

"Thank you, Constable." She turns to Morrison, "Carry on." She returns their salutes and goes back to the helo.

Morrison, "I'll inform the shore patrol and the other commands. Thank you, Constable."

"You're welcome."

Morrison turns to the men, "Chief, get them back on board."

"Yes, sir." He salutes and Morrison leaves.

Lochlin asks, "She's closing the town?"

Giblin, "For the rest of the night, ma'am."

"I'll let them know."

TOPAZ INTERNMENT CAMP, WEST OF DELTA, UTAH

1610, 17 May, 1942

Himari Nakamura brings the mail into her hut. Her husband is training with the Army and her daughter is in the camp school. She sits at their rickety table and lays the envelope down. It is addressed by hand from John Morrison, with a US Navy return address. "I do not know a John Morrison."

After a long time, she picks it up and carefully opens it. There is a hand-written letter and a photo. She looks at the photo first. "Oh, he is handsome." The man is wearing an officer's white uniform, and he is, unmistakably, Japanese. She turns it over. On the back the writing says, 'LCDR John Morrison, February 11, 1942, Sydney, Australia.'

She unfolds the letter:

Dear Grandmother,

My name is John Morrison, and I'm your grandson. I am the executive officer on the USS San Francisco. Please, let me explain. First, I, with my carrier group, traveled back in time from December, 1990, to December, 1941. Before I go into an explanation as to how we're related, I must first tell you that the history I'm sharing, my history, is not set in stone. Our time travel has changed everything. The tragedy I'm about to share may not repeat itself. In truth, in all likelihood, will not repeat itself.

You, I know, are currently in internment in Utah. Your husband, my grandfather, is being trained as part of the 100th Infantry Battalion. He served, and fell, in Europe. I remember you, but never met my grandfather.

Your daughter, Kinuko, my mother, marries an Irish-American, Joseph Fallon, my father. Joseph joined the Navy after college and rose to lieutenant. I lost both my parents in a car accident outside of Norfolk, Virginia in 1956. The Morrisons were my parent's best friends. They, Mitchell and Amanda, adopted me with your blessing. It's for that reason, I grew up a Morrison. Grandpa Henry Morrison is currently serving as XO on a destroyer. His father, Peter Morrison, retired as a captain, having commanded a battleship during WWI.

From what I remember of our family history, you and grandfather were born in California. I think it was your parents who immigrated.

I hope that the tragedies that followed our family do not repeat. I also hope, very much, to meet you and my mother someday soon. I, and some friends, are also hoping to end the internment camp system. It was, is, a blight on America's history. I hope you are well. Once I'm certain of connecting with you, I will send what I can to help. My address is below. I hope we can stay in contact.

Your Grandson,

John

She carefully folds the letter and puts in flat on the table and places her hands on it. She stares at the wall, startling when she hears a knock on her door.

A neighbor comes in, "Himari, what is it that? Is Riku well?"

"I believe so, yes. I have received a strange letter."

"May I?"

Himari hands the letter to her friend, who reads it. "Himari, this could be good news."

"Why. I lose all I love."

"Oh, Himari, think. Because of this grandson it may not be

so. He says so. He comes back so your family may live."

USS BEAVER

0710, 18 May, 1942

Morrison is already eating when Cumberland comes in sporting a huge shiner. Cumberland orders breakfast and gets a cup of coffee. He sits down at Morrison's table, "I understand there was a brawl?"

"Yes, sir. There was. Some construction workers from Glasgow attacked sailors from the Frisco, Livermore, Beaver, and the British ships. The pretext was a sailor flirting with a waitress. The police, and our command, ruled it self-defense. There were no serious injuries. Hunt closed the town down for last night. What happened to you?"

Cumberland's food is brought to the table and he tucks in. After a few bites, "I want the full report. Some of them, no doubt, need to be disciplined."

"The Chief of Staff was clear. There is to be no discipline. What happened to you, sir?"

Cumberland lowers his head, "I got in a bar fight." He sighs, "We'll drop it."

STEWART FARM

1810, 19 May, 1942

Mike and Laureen walk in the field, holding hands and talking. She asks, "What do you wish to do after the war?"

"I want to leave the Navy and settle down."

"Where?"

"I don't know. He faces her, "What are we, Laureen?"

"I should ask you."

"I'm asking you. I need you to decide for yourself. Am I messing up your life?"

"No, Michael. My life was messed up before. Now, it feels more whole, not less."

"Laureen, I'm no saint. I've a terrible sense of humor. I need time alone sometimes. And, I'm way older than you."

"What is your sense of humor?"

He grins, "Okay, you asked for it. An American, a Frenchman, and a Russian all die and are in line together to get into heaven. As there is no language barrier in heaven, they get to talking and realize it was automobiles that caused each of their deaths. The American was racing up a mountain road in his sports car and ran off the road, plummeting to his death. The Frenchman was having sex in the back seat of his car with a lovely woman next to the river Seine when the brakes failed and they rolled into the river and drowned. And the Russian, well, he always wanted a car, so he saved and saved and saved...and he starved to death."

She folds in half, laughing. When she can catch her breath, she looks up at him, her eyes twinkling, "So, a local woman goes to a monastery and complains to the Abbot that one of the brothers got her pregnant. The Abbot assures her that is quite impossible, after all, the monks swore a vow of chastity. However, he devises a test. He has each monk disrobe and puts a bell on their manhood. He has the woman also disrobe and dance provocatively in front of the row of monks. If any of the bells ring, he will give the woman the compensation she is seeking. So, she dances down the line and the newest monk at the end starts sweating. None of the other monks react to the woman's alluring dance, but when she gets to the last man, his manhood reacts so strongly the bell rings fiercely and falls off. When the poor man bends over to pick up the bell, all the other bells ring."

Brown looks at her, his mouth open, then he laughs, "Oh my God, that's funny. Where did you hear it?"

"My father owned a restaurant. The customers were always telling jokes. So, you see, we just might be compatible. I do not care that you are older. It means you are a responsible person. That, and we all need time alone."

He looks at her for a long moment, then nods, "Yes. Laureen, will you be my girlfriend?"

"Yes, I want that very much."

Mike looks into her eyes, "I want you, too. You understand, I will have to leave. I cannot bear to hurt you."

"Boyfriend is a possibility, not a certainty."

"You deserve a certainty."

"Perhaps. But I want you."

Putting his hands on her shoulders, he draws her close, "How is this going to work?"

"Shhh," she kisses him. "We'll figure it out, dear."

On the back porch, Sheamus is watching them, smiling. Jean Luc is on his lap, "Are they kissing, Papa?"

"They are."

"Is he my Da now?"

"Na. Not yet, Jean Luc. It does mean he cares."

"He's my sailor."

"That he is."

KRIEGSMARINE HQ, BERLIN, GERMANY

2000, 19 May, 1942

SS-Oberfuhrer Victor von Bergan is ushered into the office of Grand Admiral Erich Raeder. The admiral stands and greets him, "How can I help you, Oberfuhrer?"

"I believe we have discovered a resource that requires your aid to recover."

"I am listening."

"Eighteen minutes after the time event, an American fighter successfully took off from Brendenmeyer. That fighter was seen parked, engines idling, at a special weapons facility. Four to six people worked in that bunker. None of them have been captured. We believe it likely they were killed when the field was secured. Finally, one of the captured servicewomen, a captain, has told us what was in that bunker. It held atomic weapons. These weapons could, with one bomb, destroy a city. As yet, we do not know how many there were. All the records were completely destroyed."

"What does this have to do with the Kriegsmarine?"

"The fighter turned north and ditched somewhere near Smygehuk Lighthouse, on the southernmost tip of Sweden. Although, the controls for the warheads may be damaged, the bombs themselves should have survived the crash. This is worthy of a serious effort."

"Perhaps, but you place the wreck within Swedish waters. We cannot barrel into their waters with total disregard."

"Grand Admiral, what could they do?"

"They could choose to join the allies and invite their aircraft to fly from Swedish territory. We would have to defend on four fronts. It's impossible. Find a discreet way to do this, or do not do it at all." Raeder thinks, "I could give you access to some small resources. As you should know, we have much more pressing matters. Thank you, Oberfuhrer. Good day."

"Heil Hitler."

CHAPTER 33

STEWART FARM

2307, 19 May, 1942

Sheamus and Jean Luc have gone to bed. Laureen and Mike are on the sofa holding each other and quietly talking. He kisses her, holding her tightly. "You know, you're an incredible kisser."

She giggles, "I'm French. Is that not required?"

"Perhaps." He kisses her again. When they come up for air, he asks, "Should we go to bed?"

She looks into his eyes, "You know I want you, Michael. We cannot. Not under Da's roof. It would be disrespectful."

"It would. Darling, I want you, too. But I want to do this right. Respectfully. For that reason, I keep my hands, um... nice."

She takes his hand and puts it on her breast. "This we may do." He kisses her, caressing her, causing her back to arch. He comes up for air and smiles, then kisses her again. Then, "It's time. Bed. Okay?"

"Yes, you are right." They stand together and go up to their respective beds. She shuts her door and leans against it, lost in the moment. "I love him, and he loves me." She moves silently to not disturb Jean Luc as she changes into her nightgown. She slips into bed. She can still smell him. She can still taste him. She falls asleep, smiling, contented.

USS SAN FRANCISCO

0845, 22 May, 1942

Cumberland paces, watching the weapons crew unload torpedoes from his boat. Under his breath, "This is so stupid."

Morrison climbs out, "That's the last one, sir. We now have eight torpedoes remaining and no missiles."

Cumberland nods."

Morrison sees two launches coming, "They're here, sir."

"Okay."

The launches pull up to the barge and SEALs scramble off, unloading their gear. Captain Holtz gets off one launch and walks up. They salute and Holtz returns it, "Are you critical?"

Cumberland, "Yes, sir. Once they're loaded, we can get underway."

"Here are your orders."

Cumberland takes the paper:

FROM: NAVFORUK

TO: 711

REG: Operation Hand Off

Deliver Seal Team 1 to the mouth of the L'Elorn River estuary no later than 0630 GMT, 25 May, 1942. The SEAL team will disembark, perform their mission, and return to your submarine. It is absolutely essential that the SEALs are back on board no later than 1430. If insufficient time is available, the mission will be aborted.

Holtz

Cumberland looks up, "I see. Yes, sir. Morrison, go below and make sure the SEALs stow their gear properly."

"Yes, sir."

Brown is in sonar going over the equipment and doing pre-underway checks. Giblin comes in and sits in the other chair, "I didn't get a chance to ask. Is she your girlfriend now?"

"Yeah, Chief. She is."

"We've served together for quite a few years. You've been divorced for what, thirteen years?"

"Yeah, Chief."

"How is this one different?"

Brown, "She's loyal, strong, sweet, smart, and funny as shit. Am I fucking up, Chief?"

"Don't know her. It was nice that she invited me to dinner, when she obviously wanted to spend her time with you."

"What was your engagement, Chief?"

"It was with a beer. You two needed alone time."

"She has a kid and lives with her father-in-law. Time together can be a challenge."

Giblin smiles, "Do you like the star ship captain? Excuse me, I mean the kid."

"Yeah, he calls me his sailor. The little guy has already decided I'm the one."

"Is there a down side?"

"One. She's adamant that she will not leave here. She will not separate Jean Luc from his grandfather. Jean Luc is all Sheamus has of his son who was lost on the Hood. Like I said, she's loyal."

Giblin looks at him, smiling, "Could you live here?"

"I don't know. It's beautiful. The people are nice. Do you think I would have to give up my citizenship? For me, that's a hard no."

Giblin, "No. No way. Being an expat means returning to the states once in a while and renewing your visa, but it should be fine. I don't know how far an E-6 retirement will get you here."

"Hopefully, I can make chief."

"I thought you declined chief?"

Mike, "Yeah, but I was alone then, and I didn't want to give up my panel. Now, I can see I'll need a better retirement check."

Giblin, "Okay, you've fallen hard. What will you do when you retire?"

"I'll help run the farm. There's about thirty acres."

"Thirty acres isn't much."

Mike, "True, but I'll have my retirement, and if need be, I have some skills."

"Not a big call for sonar technicians in Scotland."

"You're forgetting the North Sea oil boom."

"Right. Fair point."

"I also know more than a little about electronics, and even mechanics. You know I take care of my own Jeep. I'd get by."

"It sounds like you've made up your mind."

"Maybe, but then, I keep second guessing myself."

"If she was not in the picture, would you consider living in

Scotland?"

"I don't know. I didn't know I wanted a family before I met her."

"Seems to me you have one"

Morrison puts his head in, "We'll be setting the watch in a bit."

"Yes, sir."

STEWART FARM

Sheamus, Jean Luc, and Laureen watches the San Francisco being pushed away from the barge by the tugs. The tugs back off, and the big grey submarine gathers speed and disappears behind the headland. Jean Luc starts crying, "Mama, my sailor is gone."

"He'll be back, my love."

"You promise?"

She looks up at Sheamus, then bends down to Jean Luc, "Yes. I promise."

U-BOAT BUNKER, BREST, FRANCE

1300, 24 May, 1942

Admiral Donitz walks down the line of submariners. Heinrich Bleichrodt stands in front of his crew. Behind them is their boat, U-109. Donitz, "Kapitanleutnant, are you confidant in the repairs and changes made to your vessel?"

"Yes, Herr Admiral. We inspected all the work the yard did. We will miss the guns, but we understand the change in tactics."

"You understand that the Americans will hunt you by aircraft, helicopter, and ship?"

"It is the game, Admiral. A game in which we know no peer."

Donitz, "Unfortunately, the guided torpedoes are not ready yet, but we must send you out. Let us inspect your crew."

USS SAN FRANCISCO, 100 MILES WEST OF BREST, FRANCE

2314, 24 May, 1942

Backes quietly watches and listens to his watch standers as they get back into the routine. On a sub, everything has a rhythm. "Conn, Sonar. New contact. Bearing 092. It's a submarine diving. Designate Sierra 1."

Backes pushes the button, "Captain, we have a submarine."

Cumberland arrives in bare feet wearing boxers and a bath robe. He walks to the table, then into sonar. "Brown, what do we got?"

"It's a submarine. I heard it flood tanks. Two screws. Bearing is slowly shifting south."

"Does it match a sound profile?"

"The machinery noise is close to other profiles, but the screws have changed. It sounds like twin five-bladed screws. Flow noise is down significantly."

Morrison, in uniform, comes into control as Cumberland walks out of sonar. Morrison, "Sir, what do we have?"

"It's either a new or heavily modified German U-boat. Make our course 110. I need to get dressed."

"Sir, the mission?"

"I'm not dropping off SEALs with an enemy sub breathing down our throat." Cumberland smiles and exits control.

Morrison stares at the forward bulkhead for a bit, then sighs, "Load and make ready tube 1."

The SEALs have taken over the torpedo room. Their beds are set up among the empty torpedo racks and they've organized their gear for the mission. The torpedo division turns to, loading a fish into tube 1.

Lieutenant Issa, "What the fuck is going on?"

Trindle, "We're killing another U-boat."

Issa, "That's not the mission." He storms to control, but Cumberland isn't back yet. Backes barks, "You request to enter control, Lieutenant."

Issa takes a deep breath, "Request to enter control to enquire."

Backes, "Enter."

Issa goes to Morrison, "Sir, why are we loading a torpedo?"

Cumberland walks in as Morrison is answering, "Because the captain ordered us to. He does not want an enemy sub interfering with the mission."

"Sir, we have a time line and require stealth."

Morrison, "We are aware of that, Lieutenant." He looks at Cumberland.

Cumberland glares at Issa, "Fucking SEALs. You belong to the Navy, Lieutenant, now clear out of control. We'll notify you when you can proceed."

Issa bounces on his toes, looks at Cumberland for a long moment, "Yes, sir."

Two hours later, they are south of the estuary and within three miles of their target. It has surfaced and dived several times. Morrison, "It's on a sea trial."

Cumberland, "Flood tube 1 and open the doors."

"Conn, Sonar. New contact. Bearing 030. It's leaving port. It's flooding ballast, sir."

"Very well. Load and make ready tube 2."

The SEALs are conducting their pre-mission brief when the torpedo crew interrupts them to load a second fish. Issa, "What the hell?"

Kennedy, "They found a second sub."

Issa, "We go in three hours."

Kennedy, "Sorry, sir. We have our orders."

GERMAN SUBMARINE U-109

"Control, Sonar. We have a submerged target at 340. I think it flooded torpedo tubes."

"It's likely Otto Gericke in 503."

"But I cannot hear him, sir."

Bleichrodt is quiet for a moment, "Perhaps the sound isolation is working. Still, load tubes 1 and 2."

"Conn, Sonar. A new contact at 010. It's flooding ballast."

"That must be Gericke submerging and we two are the only boats out here. We have hunter out here. Come to 340. Flood tubes when ready."

USS SAN FRANCISCO

"Conn, Sonar. Sierra 1 is flooding tubes."

Cumberland, "Match bearings with Sierra 1 and fire tube 1." Cumberland pushes the button. Thud, whoosh.

"Conn, Torpedo. Tube 1 fired electrically.

"Conn, Sonar. Fish is running hot, straight, and normal."

Backes starts the countdown.

GERMAN SUBMARINE U-109

"Captain, torpedo fired. Bearing 346. Bearing is constant."

Bleichrodt, "Blow ballast. Ahead flank. Set tube 1 and 2 to a 2-degree spread on the reciprocal course at maximum depth."

The order is repeated back.

"Tubes are flooded."

"Open doors."

"Doors are open."

"Fire tube 1 and 2." They feel the thud, whoosh as the torpedoes fire. Moments later, they surface, "Right full rudder. Get the diesels running. Up scope."

He spins the scope. He sees the Pointe de Raz light. "Ahead flank." He hears the high-pitched pings of the torpedo before the diesels start.

USS SAN FRANCISCO

"Conn, Sonar. Torpedoes inbound. Sierra 1 is hit. She's breaking up."

Cumberland dances around control, "Thank you, Brown. Make our course 010. Depth 200. Ahead 2/3rd. Dodge the torpedoes, then find Sierra 2. Morrison, your boat." He leaves the bridge.

He walks into his stateroom, locks the door, then pulls down his coveralls. He grabs a sock and a bottle of lotion, "It's been too long. Yes."

GERMAN SUBMARINE U-503

Kapitanleutnant Otto Gericke looks over his sonarman's shoulder, "What is it?"

"It must be a submarine, sir. But it is extremely quiet."

"Thank you." He looks at his crew, "Heinrich Bleichrodt, the submarine ace is gone. It is left to us. Load all tubes. Bring us to periscope depth. We need to call in and report."

USS SAN FRANCISCO

Morrison studies the chart table. "Conn, Sonar. Sierra 2 is shallowing out."

"Very well. Flood tube 2. Match bearings for Sierra 2." The U-boat is at the outside range of the torpedoes, but allowing the German to report in is a problem. "Captain, Sierra 2 is going shallow. They're trying to report in. Do I have permission to fire?"

"Just a minute." Cumberland walks in and looks at the table and torpedo status "Firing tube 2." He pushes the button with a huge satisfied smile, "Carry on." He walks back to his stateroom, "Fuck, yeah.

GERMAN SUBMARINE U-503

Kapitanleutnant Gericke, "Up scope. Raise the VHF antenna."

"Captain, torpedo fired. Bearing 203. Bearing constant."

"Understood. We go back down. Lower the scope and antenna. Let us get close to the bottom. The torpedo will pass over us."

GERMAN LOOKOUT, ILE DE SEIN, WEST OF BREST

"Headquarters, Watch Point 1. There was an explosion to the northwest of our position. I identified a periscope, then the explosion."

"Understood. Are there any survivors?"

"We can't see any from here, sir."

USS SAN FRANCISCO

0613, 25 May, 1942

Morrison is studying the chart. Lieutenant Issa and HTC Fronzak walk in, "Request to enter."

Miller, "Enter."

Issa walks up to Morrison, "Where are we?"

Morrison, "Twenty miles out of position."

"Conn, Sonar. New contact. Bearing 084. Designate Tango 9. It sounds like a surface ship exiting the harbor at hi revs."

Miller, "Very well." He looks at Morrison. Cumberland walks into control.

"Conn, Sonar. New contact. Bearing 087. Designate Tango 10. Another surface ship, sir."

Miller, "Very well." He looks at his CO and XO, "We kicked over a hornet's nest."

Issa, "Fucking hell. The operation is scrubbed." He turns on a heel to leave.

Cumberland, "You're out of line, Lieutenant."

Issa, "What are you going to do about it...sir." He walks to the aft hatch.

Cumberland, face red, "Lieutenant!"

"Fuck you, sir."

Fronczak smiles at Cumberland, "Sir, I thought you were the silent service." He goes out after Issa.

Morrison, "Left full rudder. Ahead standard. New course 295."

Cumberland looks at Morrison, confused. They can hear the unmistakable ping of active sonar. Cumberland's mouth tightens, "Evade the destroyers. Set a course for England. We'll dump the SEALs on a beach somewhere."

Morrison, "Yes, sir. That should make the captain happy."

Cumberland stares at his XO, "Carry on." He leaves and heads straight for torpedo. Fronczak waits outside the hatch, "You're call, sir, but I would suggest you not go in there."

"Why?"

"Sir, you've pissed off sixteen SEAL's. If you walk in, you'll be carried out. Do you understand me, sir?"

"You're being insubordinate."

"Perhaps, sir, but you're being an idiot. Now, most folks have a survival instinct. What sort of childhood disease deprived you of one?"

Cumberland looks Fronczak in the eyes. There's more compassion in the eyes of a shark. He turns on a heel and leaves.

STEWART FARM

1015, 27 May, 1942

Sheamus trowels mortar from a wheel barrow as Jean Luc plays nearby with his truck. He's on the last course of a square foundation he's putting in at a corner of their home. He took apart the corner of the porch for the eighteen square foot addition. The foundation goes three and a half feet into the ground and the walls are two feet thick. He uses a mallet to hammer the stone into place and a spirit level to check it.

Jean Luc runs out into the yard to look again. Because of trees and the roll of the land, the loch can't be seen very well from the house. Laureen walks out into the bright sunshine bringing Sheamus a glass of cold water. She smiles at her son craning his neck trying to see.

Jean Luc turns and runs back, "It's him! It's him! Mommy, Mommy! It's my sailor!"

Laureen scoops him up and walks to the edge of the yard. Jean Luc is right. The tugs are meeting the submarine in the ways.

"Is it him Mommy?"

"It is, darling son. Our sailor has returned." She looks heaven-ward and smiles. The warmth of the sun caresses her face.

USS SAN FRANCISCO

Morrison is on the sail as they warp into port. It is a glorious day. This is the third time in and it is getting straight forward. He shouts, "Heave the lines." In a short time, they are tied to the barge and hooking up services.

Lieutenant Commander Samantha Hunt walks down the brow to the barge as the SEALs un-ass the boat, "Seals to me. Commander, when will you and Commander Cumberland be available for debrief?"

Morrison, "Once we get services on and the plant shut down.

About an hour, ma'am."

"Meet us in the commander's conference room on the Beaver."

Issa comes up and salutes, "It was aborted, ma'am."

"I know. You've an hour before the debrief. Please get your gear out and onto the Beaver. You have another mission in a few days."

Issa smiles, "Yes, ma'am. By your leave." He salutes.

"See you upstairs," she smiles and returns the salute.

Morrison, Cumberland, and Issa are waiting in the conference room on the Beaver. Hunt walks in, "Commander Cumberland, you have the first go. What happened?"

Cumberland, "As we approached Brest, we encountered two U-boats. As they posed a real and significant threat to the SEALs, I engaged both boats and sank them. The Germans sortied two destroyers to look for us. The destroyers were no real threat to the San Francisco, but Lieutenant Issa chose to cancel the raid due to the destroyers."

"Were you surprised that sinking two German subs within sight of France would result in a response?"

He looks her in the eyes, "Frankly, yes."

"Why?"

"We're so superior to any technology Germany fields, at this point. In truth, I didn't think anyone would notice."

"You are aware that the Germans are developing defensive positions up and down France."

"Yes, ma'am."

"Issa, your go."

"As he said, as soon as he picked up the subs, our mission requirements were set aside. With sonar and possible depth charges in the water, we had to abort. The element of surprise was lost. One other thing, ma'am, he tried to overrule me and send my divers out in that environment."

"I see. Morrison, do you have anything to add?"

"One thing of note, the Germans are improving their U-boats. Both targets exhibited lower sound profiles then all the previous boats we catalogued."

"Understood. Anything to add regarding the topic at hand?"

Morrison looks at Cumberland, then back to Hunt, "No, ma'am."

Hunt, "Cumberland, do you recognize that your actions revealed the presence of your vessel in the vicinity of Brest?"

He stares at her, "Ma'am, do you know anything about submarine warfare? You can't kill a sub silently."

She meets his gaze, her face devoid of emotion, "Cumberland, answer the question."

"I'm a commander and you...you're a lieutenant commander."

"I'm Captain Holtz's chief of staff. I represent him. Answer the question."

"Jesus Christ, they send a fucking chick airdale to teach me my job. Of course, it revealed our position. Afterward, we cleared datum. Then we lifted our skirts and scurried back to drop off your golden boys."

Hunt continues staring at him, letting the silence hang. Then, "Issa, stow your gear here and grant your team liberty. They're to be in uniform. The Budweiser is a naval logistics corps pin, clear?"

"Yes, ma'am."

Her gaze never leaves Cumberland, "You may go."

Issa and his team leave. Only Hunt, Cumberland, and Morrison are left. Hunt, "Morrison, tend to your command."

"Ma'am?"

"Cumberland, your penchant for insubordination is not charming. You have disrespected me, but far worse, you disrespected an order from Captain Holtz. You disrupted and destroyed a timed military action. Your tactical success is now a strategic disaster. In short, you made an absolute mess of a strategic and tactical plan to take out the sub pens at Brest and fool the Germans into thinking it was done by air bombardment."

Cumberland, "You should have...."

Hunt, "No. You did not need to know the entire plan, you only needed to follow orders. You could not even do that. That said, the question that needs to be answered is whether you should remain in command. Stay here, I have a call to make. Morrison, you have a submarine that requires your attention. Good day." She stands and leaves.

Cumberland looks at Morrison, "She can't relieve me. I'm senior to her."

"Sir, the captain can. Who do you think she's calling?"

"Who would relieve me?"

"I would, sir."

Cumberland laughs and snorts, "You? You lack the temperament."

"I need to go, sir. Good luck."

Cumberland sits, stewing, for nearly an hour. He paces, cuss-ing under his breath. Hunt finally walks back in, "Sit."

He reddens, lowers his head, and takes a step toward her. He meets her gaze and stops, looks away, and sits down.

"I've discussed this matter with Captain Holtz and Admiral Klindt. They'll be inspecting your command on the first of June. They'll decide then."

"Yes, ma'am."

"Keep in mind, Commander, your job hangs by a thread."

He takes a deep breath, letting it out slowly, "I understand, ma'am."

"Do you, Commander? When you disrespect any part of the chain of command, you disrespect the entire chain of command. A wet behind the ears ensign knows that. For you it should be like breathing. You need to prepare your command for an inspection and to support the SEALs on their next mission. Now, will you give me a tour of your command, so I can meet your people?"

"Yes, ma'am."

CHAPTER 34

NAVY PIER, HOLY LOCH, SCOTLAND

0830, 28 May, 1942

Brown walks to the gate carrying his bags. Laureen waits for him next to the car. As he gets closer, his smile grows. Nearing the gate, he hears, "Petty Officer Brown, what are you doing?"

Brown turns and faces his captain, "Sir?"

"Who is she, Brown?"

"She's my girlfriend, sir."

"Jesus Christ, of all the men on my boat, I thought you were immune to feminine wiles. There is no place for a woman in the life of a serious warfighter."

"Sir, are you requiring the entire crew to remain single? Like Mallory?" He looks over at Laureen and smiles at her.

"You know I can't. But I can deny promotions to people who do not listen to me."

"Sir, I've already turned down chief. I would prefer to continue as your sonarman." He pauses, "Most submarine officers know better than to fuck with the eyes and ears of their ship."

Cumberland stiffens, "Don't cross me, Brown. Just dump the bitch and get back to work."

"By your leave, sir." He salutes and holds it.

"Get out of here."

Brown doesn't move, still saluting. Cumberland returns the salute and storms away. Brown picks up his bags and walks out to Laureen.

Laureen, "What an awful man."

He pulls her into his arms and kisses her. Releasing her, "I'm sorry you had to meet my commanding assifer."

She pulls down his face and kisses him again, "I love you, Michael Brown. Jean Luc is waiting. Let's go."

On the way to the farm, she asks, "Can he order us to part?"

"No, Laureen, he can't. An officer cannot interfere with a subordinate's private life. It's against the law."

She breathes a deep sigh, relieved, "Are you angry?"

He glances over to her, "I've been dealing with him for months. Commander Cumberland is living proof that there are more horse's ass's in the world than there are horses."

She giggles, "I want to improve your mood. Can you stop, please?"

He pulls over and sets the brake. She slides closer to him and pulls him into a deep kiss. She takes his hand and puts it inside her blouse. After several minutes, breathing heavily, they move apart. Brown grins, "You do know how to improve my mood."

"We should go. Jean Luc is waiting for his sailor."

As soon as the car stops, Jean Luc rushes out, "Michael! Michael!"

Mike scoops him up and hugs him tightly. The boy quietens and looks up at Mike, his face glowing. Mike kisses him on the forehead. Sheamus walks up, grinning. "Hi, Sheamus. What are you building?"

"A watchtower. Laureen and the wee one stand too much out in the rain watching for their sailor."

Carrying Jean Luc, Mike walks over to the new foundation. He goes over it slowly, then asks, "What is more affordable, wood or stone?"

"We have no end of stone, but it requires a mason. Wood requires a carpenter and that is more within my skills."

Mike, "Carpentry is more in keeping with my skills, too. Are you looking at three stories, then?"

"I climbed onto the roof to check, and it's enough."

Jean Luc touches Mike's cheek, "Can you play with me before you work?"

"Mike smiles down at him, "I can."

USS SAN FRANCISCO

1130, 28 May, 1942

Morrison finally has the time to go to his room with his mail. He has a huge box from Grandma Morrison, a letter from his dad, and a letter from Liz. He opens the box and finds hard candy, fudge, cookies, and beef jerky. A separate box inside has soap, toothpaste, toothbrushes, underwear, shoe strings, shoe polish, and a new wind up watch. There is also a letter:

Dear John,

I guessed at your sizes from what Henry told me. Please send me your measurements so I can keep you in uniform items. I'm glad the two of you have met. To me, that's very important. By the way, he spoke very highly of you. It warms my heart.

Mitch's grads have gone up an entire letter grade since he found out about you. I think he's growing up. I really hope all is well with you.

Another thing that crossed my mind. Are there any sailors on your vessel who have no family? If so, please share their names and addresses with us. I'm starting a letter writing campaign for those sailors adrift with no family. I have thirty-five mothers looking to adopt wayward sons and daughters.

One other thing I must share. You said that in your past there was only Mitch and Gretta. In another seven months, or so, they'll have a little sister or brother. I'm very much looking forward to changing your future.

Much Love,

G.M. (Granny Morrison)

He smiles and reads it again, "I don't recall a miscarriage. Well, Grandpa, congratulations are in order."

He reads his father's letter:

Hi John,

Thank you so much for writing me and sending the picture. Mom has you on the wall with the family. I decided to run track so I could stay in shape, and I'm getting my grades up. I haven't told anyone in school except Mrs. Peterson. She's my favorite. She teaches English and makes it interesting. I tried to get mom to pack a football and basketball and stuff. In 1990 did they still do sports? Was it like with rocket packs in outer space?

It's so great that dad got to meet you. He was really happy. Anyway, I have to finish my homework.

Sincerely,

Mitch

He writes back to both of them, then picks up the letter from Liz.

Dear John,

God, that is funny, now that I think of it. It's not at all what I wanted to say. Let me start over.

My dearest Johnny,

Better. I got your letter, and thank you. I'm putting my address in Bremerton at the end of this letter. Yep. I was transferred off the CV in Norfolk. They gave me a full stripe and put me in command of power school. Not a sexy combat job, but it's important. My direct supervisor is Klindt, which is interesting in a good way. We've three classes working their way through the curriculum: 42-01, 42-02, and 42-03. It's weird. The CO of the Long Beach was handling it before I got here. We're also building a mock prototype. It's kind of a fake S-1. It's going to take a while. We both know it can't be rushed.

On to the personal. On my way across the country, I got a chance to visit my grandparents. They were a bit aghast about my career choice. I stayed for a couple of days, and they came around. Mind, my Nana desperately wants to marry me off. I told her about Tim. I hope that will give me at least six months breathing space. I still love them.

I really hope you're doing well. My thoughts wander to our time together in Sydney. I count you my dearest friend. I admit to worrying about you and the tyrant. Please know my thoughts and prayers are with you.

Liz

He grins and reads it again, then he picks up his pen and starts writing

STEWART FARM

Mike and Laureen are on the sofa after dinner, talking. Jean Luc plays on the floor with blocks Mike made from off falls from the ground floor construction of the tower. Sheamus sits in his chair smiling at his family. "We made some good progress, lad. We got the floor in. I'll say this, ye know your way around a hammer. On the morrow, we'll pound up some walls."

Jean Luc looks up to Mike, "Look Daddy. It's our house."

They all look at Jean Luc's stack of blocks. Sheamus, "It is, wee one. It is."

Laureen, "Very good, Jean Luc. It is our house."

"Yeah, and granda, Mummy, and Daddy and me live in it, huh?"

Laureen looks at Mike. He smiles, "We do."

Sheamus, "My bones are telling me it's getting late. Come, little one, it's time for bed."

"Now?"

Sheamus smiles at Laureen and Mike, "Come on, Jean Luc. It's time, I think."

"Yes, Papa." He picks up his blocks and puts them in his toy box, then goes to the stairs, dragging his feet.

Mike grins and stands up, "I'll help, Sheamus." He picks Jean Luc up, and they go up the stairs.

Sheamus walks to his room. When Mike takes Jean Luc into the room he shares with his mother, Sheamus says, "In here, Michael."

Jean Luc, "But, Papa, this is my room."

"Not tonight, wee one. You can sleep with papa."

They go into Sheamus' room and Mike puts Jean Luc on the bed. He steps back, "Sheamus, Jean Luc, may I ask you a question?"

Jean Luc's eyes get big, "Uh huh."

Mike, "Sir, I would like to ask you for your daughter's hand in marriage."

"Aye, lad. Ye've got my blessing." Sheamus pulls Mike into a hug.

Mike kneels down to Jean Luc, "Jean Luc, would it be okay if I married your mommy?"

"Would you be my daddy?"

"I know you have a daddy I can never replace, Jean Luc, but yes, I would be your daddy."

Jean Luc's eyes fill with tears; his little body unable to contain his emotions. He jumps into Mike's arms, "Yes, Daddy." After a long hug, he leans back and looks at Mike, "Are you still gonna have to leave?"

"I will, Jean Luc. It's my duty, son. But I will come back."

Will it be long?"

"I don't know. It'll have to be as long as it is, but I will come back."

"Okay." He lays his head on Mike's chest, smiling.

Mike holds him and looks at Sheamus, his own eyes tearing up. "Okay, little one. Can you go to bed now?" He kisses Jean Luc on the forehead, then helps Sheamus collect his things and get him ready for bed. Tucking him in, Jean Luc smiles, "Ni, ni, Daddy"

"Good night, son." Mike turns to Sheamus, "Thank you, Dad."

Sheamus wipes his eyes, "Yer welcome, son. Move your stuff to her room. We'll sort the wee one in the morning."

"Yes, sir." Mike goes downstairs, smiling. He takes Laureen's hand and pulls her up from the sofa, "Come on. Outside."

They walk out to where they can see the loch. Laureen, "Did he upset you, Michael?"

"No. He misses his father. It's natural for him to think that way."

"He loves you, Michael. He loves Da, but Da is Pappa, not Daddy."

"Its fine, love. Are you okay?"

"It's been a year. I miss him, but he's a distant memory. I love you. I do." She takes his face between her hands and kisses him.

"I love you, too."

"Michael, do you think I'm made of porcelain? I'm not. I'm a woman, a woman who loves you."

"I love you, Laureen. When I went upstairs it was to ask a question of the two men in your life."

"What?"

Mike takes a knee, holding her hands in his, and looks up into her eyes, "Laureen Stewart, will you marry me?"

Her eyes fill with tears and her throat closes. She struggles for a breath, then everything clears, "Oh yes. Yes. Yes. Yes. Yes." She pulls him up and he wraps her in his arms, putting his head on her shoulder. He lifts his head, tilts her face up and kisses her.

They hear from an open window, "Well then, why don't you go to bed, so this old fart can get some sleep?"

They smile at each other and she takes his hand, leading him into the house and up the stairs. When they get to her room, she leads him in, "Too much clothes." She unbuttons his shirt and slides it off. Holding his gaze, she undresses him. He follows her lead, unbuttoning and removing her dress. When the rough skin of his hands touches her, she gasps.

Mike, "God, you're beautiful."

She grins, "You're lovely, mon amour." He picks her up and puts her on the bed.

USS BEAVER

0810, 1 June, 1942

Vice Admiral Craig Klindt, "Commander Cumberland, I've a dozen reports attesting to you being a grade A, number one, one hundred percent, pure asshole. You seem to have an issue with authority, an issue with women, an issue with following orders, and an issue with respecting your men. In short, you've made a right ass of yourself. Why the fuck did you deviate from your orders on your last mission?"

"The submarines were quieter than before. I had to assume they had improved their sonar as well. When we cycled the air lock to let out the SEALs, they might have heard it. An exchange of torpedoes while divers are in the water would be a dangerous thing for the swimmers. I elected to engage the subs first."

"Why did you tell Issa you were sending his men out after the destroyers were pinging?"

"That was a simple misunderstanding. I had no intention of sending them out. I only meant to remind him I was in command. I felt he was infringing on my authority."

Holtz, "Why did you disrespect my chief of staff?"

Cumberland swallows, "Did she say that? She...um...I was just, well, animated. In no way did I intend my comments as disrespectful."

"Hunt has an eidetic memory." Holtz pull out a piece of paper, "Your words were 'Jesus Christ. They send a fucking chick airdale to teach me my job.' Now, Commander, please explain to me how that was not disrespectful?"

"Um. Sir. It was merely animated conversation. It wasn't intended as disrespectful."

Klindt snorts, "Commander, put in context with your previous behavior toward Commander Hunt, and your behavior toward other female officers, it can be taken no other way but disrespectful. Hunt rightly pointed out that disrespecting her was disrespecting your entire chain of command. It's disrespecting the Commodore. It's disrespecting me. I have an entire dossier on you, Commander. I know every unprofessional or disrespectful thing you've done.

"The issue is our schedule. You're getting underway on a critical mission. You will re-embark the SEALs and deliver them to Kaafjord in Norway. They will plant explosives on the battleship Tirpitz and sink her. You are not to engage any enemy units whatsoever until the SEALs have completed their mission and are safely back aboard."

Cumberland, "But, sir, the U-boats are out there. The Tirpitz is just taking up space in a fjord."

"Every convoy to Russia has to pass by that fjord. It forces the Royal Navy to dedicate forces that would be better used elsewhere. That battleship sank a cruiser and badly damaged an aircraft carrier. It's hit convoys, or forced them to scatter and be picked off by subs. It's a real and immediate threat. This time, to make certain the mission goes down correctly, Commodore Holtz will accompany you."

"Sir, shouldn't he be focused on the air war?"

"Were it not for how little I trust you, yes. Commodore Holtz, you have my full trust in this matter." He stands and Holtz and Cumberland stand as well.

"Yes, sir."

Klindt walks out.

Holtz turns to Cumberland, "I'll be on board in about thirty minutes and I'll need quarters. My apologies for kicking you out of yours."

Cumberland takes a deep breath, letting it out slowly, "Yes, sir."

Cumberland invades his boat. He sees Morrison helping the SEALs mount a contraption over the forward escape trunk. "XO, my stateroom."

They climb down the engine room escape hatch. Cumberland puts his head around the hatch into maneuvering, "Miller, where are we on start up?"

"Heating the plant, sir."

"How long?"

"Two more hours, sir."

"Carry on."

Morrison silently follows him through the tunnel forward

to the captain's stateroom. When Morrison shuts the door behind him, Cumberland turns on him, "WHAT THE FUCK ARE YOU DOING GOING BEHIND MY BACK TO THE BRASS! I GOT MY ASS CHEWED OUT BY FUCKING ADMIRAL KLINDT! A FUCKING VICE ADMIRAL!"

"Sir?"

"SHUT THE FUCK UP! SHUT THE FUCK UP! I'M NOT DONE!" Cumberland takes another deep breath, "I expect loyalty from my officers."

Morrison holds up his right index finger and waits.

Cumberland, "I expect loyalty. Legacy, or no, you have ended your career in this Navy. What you've done was inexcusable. What do you have to say for yourself?"

"Sir, you lost my loyalty when you recommended I be sent to a Utah gulag. Loy..."

"THAT'S THE FUCKING LAW, MORRISON. WE ARE FUCKING FIGHT..."

"SIR, SHUT THE FUCK UP. IT'S MY TURN." Morrison holds Cumberland's gaze, "Loyalty is a two-way street, sir. You threw mine away. You've been a tyrant to our crew and reduced our combat effectiveness with your behavior. It's your career on the line, not mine. No doubt, they said as much."

"Yes, but they wouldn't dare relieve me."

"Sir, do you know why you haven't been relieved? I asked them to give you another chance. You know that Admiral Klindt is NAVSEA-08?"

"Yes."

"He's in charge of all things nuclear, which means he's in charge of you, and he's in charge of me. Now, sir, are we going to work together to fix the mess you created, or am I going to recommend a transfer to Adak so you can count trees?"

"You wouldn't dare."

"I'd do it in a heartbeat. Adak is still better than a gulag in Utah. That's what you wanted for me."

"So, this is personal."

"Sir, if this was peacetime 1990, you wouldn't last six months. That's the honest truth. Hell, SUBRON-1 sent you to me because you were, in his words, rough around the edges. The Captain wanted me to keep an eye on you. Are we going to work together, sir?"

Cumberland grits his teeth and looks away, clenching and unclenching his hands, "This is mutiny."

"No, sir. I'm not trying to replace you. I'm trying to help you. You know this is how the Navy works. Are we going to work together, sir?"

"I have no choice."

"You always have a choice, sir. Submarine duty is voluntary."

"Don't push me."

"Don't abuse the crew and we'll get along fine. Straighten up and all of this might go away."

"Klindt. Holtz. They'll never forget."

"True, but they might forgive. Are we going to work together, sir?"

"Jesus Christ. Yes, you sonofabitch."

"Are we going to work together, sir?"

Cumberland breathes in, exhaling slowly, "Yes, XO. We'll work together."

"Good. Rein in your temper around the crew. No more snide remarks about their ethnicity or family. Understood?"

Breathing heavily, Cumberland lowers his eyes, "Yes."

"Thank you, sir. May I go?"

"Yes. Go. Go clear out of your stateroom. Commodore Holtz is coming with us."

Morrison walks straight to his cabin, closes his door, and collapses in his chair. He takes a huge clearing breath and puts his head in his hands, "Dad, you told me a competent officer always does the right thing, no matter the personal cost." Another deep breath and the trembling in his hands slowly calms. "This is so fucking hard. I hope you would be proud of me today."

He grabs his bags and packs his stuff, remembering to retrieve his letters.

News of the shouting match between Cumberland and Morrison has already passed through the crew. Guthrie and Brown are doing their pre-underway checks with Gordon and the new guy, ST1(SW) Walter Johnson. Johnson transferred from the Jarrett to replace Thorsen.

Johnson, "I've never heard of a CO and XO fighting like that."

Brown, "You didn't. It's like when the guy in the rack above you is beating off. Socially. Officially. You don't hear a thing. Focus on your job. We got the SEALs again, so we're about to go out and do something hairy. We're the eyes and ears, and I need all of you at your best. We're also going to have a flag officer on board, so you know this mission is important. No matter what happens, stay calm and focus on your jobs."

Gordon, "Do you think he's going to be relieved?"

Brown, "Maybe. If, and when, it happens, it will happen right behind us in control. That is why I say you must stay focused on your job. If you start listening to the fight behind you, instead of the world outside, we could all die."

Gordon, "Okay, Mike. You're right."

Brown looks at each man, and they all nod.

FISHERMAN'S QUAY, WARNEMUNDE, GERMANY ON THE BALTIC SEA

1450, 1 June, 1942

Six SS sailors in civilian clothes wait in a large fishing boat. A Mercedes pulls up and SS-Oberfuhrer Von Bergan gets out. He walks up the boarding plank, returning their salutes. "This is the last time you salute. You are common fishermen looking for a catch. Is everything in order?"

Their leader, SS-Hauptsturmfuhrer Seidel, "Yes, Oberfuhrer. We understand what needs to be done. The magnetometer has been tested and functions correctly. It will be a challenge, but we will find the devices you seek."

"Good. It will take time, and perhaps, several trips. Meanwhile, I must look out for our American guests. They have been most helpful. Heil Hitler." He goes back to the Mercedes and leaves.

FOREST NORTH OF SWISS-LIECHTENSTEIN BORDER

1614, 2 June, 1942

Sophia Newberg, wearing a heavy winter dress stolen off a wash line, walks into a hen house with a basket. She hates stealing eggs, but they've kept her and Jerry fed. For six months they've worked their way across Germany trying to get to Switzerland, stealing what they needed to survive. Her husband, U.S. Airforce Sergeant Major Jerry Newberg is hiding in the trees nearby.

She walks into the hen house like she lives there and begins gathering eggs. When she's got a dozen, she goes to the door. She opens it to see a German officer standing there.

"Frau, why do you steal from me?"

She lowers her eyes and curtsies. In her best German, "I'm sorry, sir. I am hungry."

He draws his pistol, "Where are you from?"

"Ireland, sir."

"No. No, you are not. Come. You will share more. I promise you."

CHAPTER 35

USS SAN FRANCISCO, 600 FEET, 200 MILES EAST OF THE FAROE ISLANDS

0517, 3 June, 1942

ST1 Johnson, "Conn, Sonar. New contact. Bearing 344. Designate Sierra 1."

Miller, "Thank you." He pushes the CO's button, "Captain, submerged contact, north and east of us."

Cumberland, in the XO's stateroom, "Very well. Start a track."

Holtz wakes to the report. At first, he's disoriented. It takes a few seconds to remember he is in a submarine. There is no wave motion this deep. He rises and dresses.

Cumberland walks straight in to the chart table. "Is it lying in wait for the convoy?"

Miller, "Yes, sir." Morrison and Holtz come in to control.

Cumberland, Load tube 3."

Morrison, "Sir?"

Holtz, "Belay that, Captain. Do not forget your orders. No attacks. No contacts."

Cumberland, "People in that convoy will die."

"Maybe. We have a mission more important than a single sub or a single convoy. Carry on." Holtz leaves.

Cumberland, "What an ice-cold mother fucker. The right thing is to take the shot."

Morrison, quietly, "Sir, the right thing to do is to follow orders."

Cumberland, in a fierce whisper, "Shut the fuck up, XO, and get the fuck out of my face."

HILL NEAR ARGELES-SUR-MER, SOUTHWEST FRANCE

2020, 3 June, 1942

SFC Henry Holmes uses the telescopic sight of his rifle to study the terrain below them. Near the coast is a concentration camp. There are guards and patrols everywhere. He looks over his five remaining charges. The lieutenant was gutted by a boar and died of his wounds. One of the techs fell down the side of a ravine to his death. "Van Zandt, you know where Andorra is?"

Tech Sgt. Tiffany Van Zandt looks up, "Yes, Sergeant. It's about sixty miles through the mountains."

Holmes, "I like mountains. Cover and concealment."

Van Zandt, "I know."

"You've held up well."

"My dad was in the Navy. Well, will be. He was a pilot and a bit of a survival nut."

"He'd be proud of you."

"Probably. God, I miss him. If I'd followed him into the Navy, I'd have a comfy rack in 1990."

"What does he fly?"

"He doesn't anymore. He was banged up ejecting from an A-4. He's assigned as chief of staff for Admiral Ren on the Carl Vinson."

"The captain's daughter."

"Yep. Let's get moving."

USS SAN FRANCISCO, 500 FEET, NEARING THE STRAIGHT OF STJERNSUNDET, NORTHERN NORWAY

1720, 4 June, 1942

"Conn, Sonar. New contact. Bearing 075. Designate Sierra 2."

Cumberland straightens up in his chair, gets up, and goes to the table, "What is it, Brown?"

"It's almost identical to the last one we sank outside Brest. Definitely German."

Cumberland looks at Holtz, who's watching him. "Carry on. Morrison, get us inside."

"Yes, sir."

INTERROGATION ROOM, SWISS BORDER

1845, 4 June, 1942

The two sergeants button their flies and leave. In passable English, SS-Oberfuhrer Victor von Bergan says, "Now, wasn't that fun. If you tell me what I want to know, it will all stop."

Sophia Newberg's eyes sting with sweat. Every part of her body hurts. She lifts her head, pushing against the chains holding her to the table, "I'm a librarian. I know nothing of use to you."

"That, my dear, is not true. Your name is Sophia Newberg. You are forty-eight years old. You burned your library so we could not have your very valuable books. It is important, because your past is our future."

She lays back, silent.

"Enough for today. I want you to look forward to a visit from your new friends tomorrow."

She is unshackled and carried back to her cell. When the door opens, she sees another woman sitting against the wall. They shove Sophia in and lock the door. She tries to walk, but her legs give way, and she sinks to her knees. She manages a drink of water from a bucket. Then she turns her head, "Who are you?"

The other woman is wearing torn, filthy jeans and a sweater set. Through the filth it is obvious the clothes are from the 1980's. "I'm Lina. The...um...who are you?"

"Where did you get your clothes?"

"Los Angeles." Her accent sounds mid-west American.

"When did you buy them?"

The woman starts crying, "With my husband. His family. They live there."

Sophia goes to her and puts an arm around her, "What happened to your husband?"

"I don't know. He worked on the planes. The jets."

Sophia is quiet, "I don't know where my husband is either."

"What did he do?"

"He was the base command sergeant major. We had five months before we retired."

Lina, "Oh. Mine was junior. He was a sergeant."

"Where are you from?"

"Um, Cleveland, Ohio. Why are you asking me these questions? I think I want to die. They raped me."

"Yes. They raped me, too. What you need to do is protect your mind."

Lina, "What?"

"Something my husband taught me. He did two tours instructing SERE."

"What is SERE?"

"Lina, your husband must have put you in a hole. Do you know the rule of three?"

"No. Um, why do they keep asking me about a special bunker?"

Sophia, "Apparently, they assume the Air Force can't keep a secret. Just forget it. That's the last thing you want to help them with."

"But, why? What's in there that is so secret?"

"You don't want to know, and neither do I."

"Do you know?"

"No, Lina. There are some things you just don't get curious about."

USS SAN FRANCISCO, 250 FEET, STRAIT OF STJERNSUN-DET, NORWAY

2115, 4 June, 1942

Backes, "We have 200 feet under us."

"Conn, Sonar. New contact. Bearing 105. Designate Tango 21. Twin screws."

Backes, "Very well." Cumberland paces. Morrison stands stationary, calm and quiet. Commodore Holtz is in torpedo briefing the SEALs. Backes, "It's shelving. 150 feet under our keel."

Cumberland, "Bring us up 200 feet."

"Aye, sir."

Cumberland, under his breath, "I hate this shit."

"Conn, Sonar. Tango 21 is approaching our position."

Backes, "Very well."

In fifteen minutes, they hear the rhythmic beats of screws overhead. "200 feet, sir."

Backes, "Very well."

"Conn, Sonar. New contact. Bearing 110. Designate Tango 22. Two screws turning at minimum steerage. We're picking up reflected machinery noises from ahead."

Backes, "Very well."

Cumberland, "They're all leaving. We're going to drop the fish boys off into an empty harbor. If we just waited outside, we could kill them all."

"Sir, it's getting deeper. We have 600 feet under our keel."

TIRPITZ

Kapitan zur See Karl Topp is writing a letter home when there is a knock, "Enter."

A radioman enters, "Message from Berlin, Kapitan."

TO: TIRPITZ

FRM: KRIEGSMARINE

REG: Operations in support of Sea Lion.

Due to operation Sea Lion being reconsidered, it is important for you to stay in port and prepare your vessel for a major engagement with the British navy. As long as your current harbor remains viable, you are to remain in port. Supplies are being sent and should arrive early morning 4 June.

GAdm Raeder

"Thank you." He hands it back to be filed.

USS SAN FRANCISCO, 200 FEET, ALTAFJORDEN, 10 MILES FROM TIRPITZ

The San Francisco works its way into the fjord. Backes, "Sir, it's shallowing up again. We've 200 feet under us."

Cumberland, "Very well. Right standard rudder. Make our course 168."

Holtz and Issa walk into control. Holtz, "How much longer?"

Cumberland, "We're taking it slow, sir. Twenty minutes."

Morrison, "Commodore, local time is 0142. This far north the sun won't set."

"I'm counting on that, Commander. The low sun makes it difficult to see into the water and most people are tired. That, and a daylight raid is unthinkable." He looks at Issa, "Get your boys to the hatch."

"Yes, sir."

The top of the sail is twenty feet from the surface of the water. The SEALs exit the sub into the garage. They open it and push out two submersible craft. Issa, using touch and hand signals, direct the two teams, and they silently motor to the Tirpitz. They're spaced so they can see each other. It's an eight-mile trip.

When they're clear, the sub sinks deeper into the black void.

Lt. JG Russell 'Triage' Jeremy sits behind BM1 Paul 'Grunt' Bruce, who's operating the submersible. He scans the water and watches the lowering sun turn the water above them into flowing diamonds. Navigation is easy in the dim waters.

They reach the torpedo netting, which is hanging all the way to the bottom and made of ten-inch squares of steel mesh. Issa's boat turns left, and Triage's turns right. They work along the net listening to it creak and groan in the wake of small craft and the light chop.

They reach the end where the net is fastened to the rocks of the fjord. The net is a tumbled mess at the bottom. Where the net is fastened at the surface, two Germans are standing guard. The clear space is too close, and too shallow. Grunt tugs at Triage, pulling him along. One of the guys finds a place where two rocks hold the net out of the way. It's a big enough hole for them to get through.

TIRPITZ

Oberleutnant zur See Helmut Schmitt walks the deck. Just off watch, he can't sleep. It's a secret, but word of Sea Lion has spread through the crew. Invading Britain. He paces. Can it be done? He looks out over the fjord, thinking.

SEALS, AT TURN OF THE PORT BILGE, TIRPITZ

Triage and Grunt work quickly. Triage hands his partner shaped charges and det wire. They gently place the magnetic charges against the hull, install the detonation wires, then, string the wires to connect with the next charge. As they are setting the fourth charge, Triage feels something bump his shoulder. He turns his head and the large liquid brown eyes of a harbor seal are looking at him. The seal looks him over, than swims away. Triage forces himself to breath calmly.

They hear something hit the water above them.

TIRPITZ

Schmitt leans against the rail, thinking. A mechanic from the engineering spaces walks out of a door and dumps a bucket of old parts over the side. When the young man walks aft, past Schmitt, he clears his throat. The mechanic looks up, startled, "Begging you pardon, sir," and salutes.

SEALs

Greasy nuts and bolts fall past them. The two men look at each other and continue. The find the first charge of Issa's team. Grunt expertly splices his detonation wires to the charges. They swim to the end, inspect the timer, then swim back to the netting and their submersible.

They hear the screws of a large vessel start turning. Triage looks up. They are no more than twenty feet from the huge screws of the battleship. The screws are motionless. They can see the charges attached onto the fairwater bearing.

USS SAN FRANCISCO

"Conn, Sonar. New contact. Bearing 130. Designate Tango 23. Sir, it has three screws."

Cumberland, "Three screws?"

Morrison, "Some of the German heavy cruisers had three screws."

Cumberland looks at Holtz, "Excuse me, sir." He goes forward and down to torpedo. With the ship at battle stations all the torpedomen are there. "Kennedy, load and make ready torpedoes in tubes 1 through 4. Call me on the sound powered phone when you're done."

Kennedy, "Yes, sir."

Cumberland leaves.

As soon as he is gone, Kennedy calls control, "Control, Morrison."

Kennedy, "Sir, Commander Cumberland just ordered us to load tubes 1 through 4."

"Proceed, Chief. Do not flood until our swimmers are safely aboard."

"Yes, sir."

Cumberland enters control. Holtz, "What are you doing, Commander?"

"Preparing for after the SEALs are aboard."

Holtz, "Be patient, Commander."

Cumberland stares at Holtz, then looks down at the chart table. He begins pacing, then walks into sonar, "What is 22 doing?"

Brown, "Sounds like they're getting underway, sir."

"Fuck. The SEALs are getting all the fun, and I have to sit on my hands."

Brown and Guthrie look at each other, and remain silent.

Cumberland, "Did you dump that girl, Brown?"

"We're getting married, sir."

"Fucking hell. No one listens to me. Do you think I'm a joke, Brown?"

"No, sir."

SOPHIA NEWBERG'S CELL

0010, 5 June, 1942

The two women hear a key in the door. A man enters holding a weapon. Sophia breathes out, it's her husband, Air Force Sergeant Major, Jerry Newberg. He motions for her to get up and follow him. She goes to Lina, "Come on, Lina."

"What?" Lina realizes what she's seeing and her eyes light up.

Sophia turns to Jerry, "We're taking her."

He whispers, "Is she American?"

"Yes."

He looks the woman over, "What was Watergate?"

"I don't know, a famous door?"

"Okay, what position did Calvin Klein play in baseball?"

Lina, "Pitcher, I think. I don't watch baseball."

"What was 'Top Gun'?"

"I don't shoot guns, they scare me."

"What color is the M&M's?"

"They are an African group, right?"

He butt strokes her, putting her out. He grabs Sophia and they run out down the hall and out into the predawn darkness. "I got the gun. Farm girl, I need you to drive."

"Okay." Outside the door is a Sd.Kfz. 231, six-wheeled armored car. He opens the hip hatch and she gets in after him. Reaching past her, he closes the hatch.

Sophia, "Gas. Clutch. Brake. Gear shift. One of these is low range and the other is six-wheel drive."

"Good. Drive. Turn left onto the road. The border is less than a mile."

Just as they lurch into motion, they hear a loud rattle on the side of the vehicle. Sophia, "Are they shooting at us?"

Jerry fires a burst through the top hatch, "Go! Go!"

She shifts gears, getting them moving, "Turning!"

Jerry, "Got it."

They are in high range, rear-wheel drive. Thankfully, the lights work. She runs up the gears and comes to a curve. She takes it at speed, and they sway around the corner, but stay on the road. A straight stretch appears in front of them and she floors it.

SEALs

Triage counts heads as his team swims through the gap in the netting one by one. When they are all outside, Grunt starts the submersible and neutralizes the buoyancy. They all grab on, and they start back. Triage checks his watch. They are running late. Worse still, a cruiser is crossing their path. They don't dare pass under it. A running pump could suck them up against the hull, or the screw could chop them into mincemeat.

USS SAN FRANCISCO

Cumberland, "Ahead 1/3rd. Bring us to periscope depth."

Holtz, "What are you doing, Commander?"

"We're fetching your fish boys, sir."

"Conn, Torpedo. Tube 3 and 4 are loaded."

Cumberland, "Flood tube 3."

Holtz, "Commander."

Cumberland turns his back.

NEWBERGS, NORTH OF THE SWISS BORDER

The straight road ends and Sophia pushes down on the brakes, trying to slow the heave vehicle. It slows a little, but the curve is coming up fast. "The brakes suck, love."

Jerry continues firing at the vehicle chasing them, "Okay."

She shouts, "Hang on!"

SEALs

Issa checks his dive watch. "Where the hell is Triage?" Finally, Triage's submersible appears out of the murk. Grunt turns, and side by side, the teams head to the rendezvous point.

NEWBERGS, ALMOST TO THE SWISS BORDER

Rounding the curve, they see the border gate directly ahead. Sophia realizes that the gates solid posts and barriers will be impossible for her to get through. On each side are fields and a double row of fencing with light poles. Immediately, she understands what she has to do.

Sophia, "Hang on!" She slams the armored vehicle into six-wheel drive at speed, and floors it. Turning the heavy vehicle sharply, she surfs off the road, slipping and sliding toward the border fence. Missing the posts, they smash through the first fence dragging it behind them. They hit the second fence, making it halfway through. Then, they're stuck, caught in the wire, wheels spinning.

Swiss soldiers run to them, and the Germans cease firing.

Jerry drops down next to her, "Nice driving, love."

"Thank you, kind sir." She looks up at her husband. "Love you, honey. Thank God, Greg was safe out to sea on the Stoddert when all this happened."

"Love you, too. I'm going to miss him, but at least, we know he's okay. Let's go meet our hosts."

USS SAN FRANCISCO

"Conn, Torpedo. Tube 3 is flooded."

Cumberland, "Open doors."

Morrison, "Belay that!"

Holtz, "What the fuck are you doing, Commander?"

Cumberland, "It's a heavy cruiser. By the time the fucking SEALs are on board, it'll be too late."

Morrison, "You'll kill them, sir!"

Cumberland, "Shut up! Shut the fuck up! All of you. I'm in command here. Open the fucking doors!"

Morrison, "Do not open the doors!"

Cumberland grabs for Morrison's throat. Morrison brings his arms up inside of Cumberland's and breaks the hold. "Sir!"

Holtz, "Stand down, Commander!"

Cumberland, "No! I'm in command. It's my boat and I am not letting that cruiser get away. It's my kill! Don't you idiots understand? My kills! Fucking SEALS!"

Holtz, "You are relieved. Get the fuck out of control!"

Brown, "Conn, Sonar. We have a heavy cruiser closing our position. No bearing change."

Morrison remembers Cumberland's last order, it was to come to periscope depth. The cruiser is on a collision course. "Five degrees down on the planes. Ahead full. Bring us to 200 feet."

Cumberland, "Belay that order! Open the doors!" He hits out at Holtz, who side-steps, grabs Cumberland's shoulders and spins him around. Holtz wraps Cumberland up from behind. Cumberland throws his head back and hits Holtz hard on the forehead. Holtz lets go, staggering back. Cumberland turns, and steps in, throwing a left hook at Holtz. Holtz falls against the chart table.

Morrison grabs Cumberland's shoulders and spins him around, pushing him away. Cumberland comes at him, swinging. Morrison steps to his left and hits him with an upper cut to the jaw. Cumberland drops to the deck, unconscious.

Morrison spins back to the watch, cradling his right hand, as the submarine accelerates. "Down full on the planes. Left full rudder. Make our depth 200 feet. Make our course 345. Ahead 1/3rd." They repeat back. "What do we have under our keel?"

The sound of the cruiser gets louder, "200 feet, sir."

Holtz rolls Cumberland over and puts a knee on his back. "Do you have a place to secure him?"

Morrison picks up the 1MC, "Medic, lay to control. SAR swimmer, lay to control." He goes to the chart table, "Left full rudder. New course 162."

HM1 Novogradic and BM1 Sarvis come into control.

Morrison, "Novogradic, the commander has had a mental break. For the safety of the ship, we need him non-violent. I'll leave that to you. Sarvis, protect Novogradic. Deadly force is authorized. Questions?"

Sarvis, "Where should we put him, sir?" The sound of the cruiser is loud overhead.

"Put him in the wardroom for now. Carry on. Helm, up 5 degrees on the dive planes. We have SEALs to pick up."

Novogradic, "I'll be back to take a look at hour hand, sir."

"Thank you. Later. I'll be fine." Then he turns to Holtz, "Are you okay, Commodore?"

Holtz, "I've been hit harder by a girl."

The crew chuckles.

CHAPTER 36

SEALs AT RECOVERY POINT

0210, 5 June, 1942

Grunt slows his submersible alongside Issa's. There is nothing but murky water. Triage checks his calculations again. He motions to Grunt to shallow them out so he can see the three points they are using for navigation. They are in the right spot.

The murk in front of them slowly turns solid and the submarine appears. Relieved, they go up behind the garage and Triage un-asses to open it. It takes an eternity for the door to open against the pressure of the water. They push the submersibles inside and secure them. Then, the SEALs all crowd in and they close the door. Issa taps on the hatch, then opens it. Issa and five men crowd into the air-lock and cycle it. Inside, a sopping wet Lt. Issa hands his gear to Broke Dick and heads forward to control. He stops at the entrance. "Permission to enter."

Morrison, "Enter."

Issa drips his way in and checks his watch. "Thirty-two minutes, sir."

Morrison, "Sorry, we were late. Something came up."

"The cruiser? It got in our way, too."

Holtz, "Is everyone on board?"

"They're in the garage and cycling through the air lock."

Holtz, "Tend to your men. We need to work our way out of here."

"Yes, sir"

SEAL GARAGE

Triage feels the sub turning and picking up speed. The air lock cycles open and he and the last of his team enter. He checks his air.

Grunt, "Little breaths."

Triage smiles and nods, twiddling his thumbs. The hatch closes. It's claustrophobic as they wait for the water to drain off. Most of them pull off their masks as soon as their heads are above water.

Steve 'Mac' Cook, "Who farted?"

The men chuckle. Triage, "He who smelt it, dealt it."

When the water is completely drained, the lower hatch opens. Two petty officers help them down. Dripping, they go down to the mess decks and forward to the torpedo room.

USS SAN FRANCISCO

The cruiser slows near the destroyer they passed earlier. They can hear the other destroyer that is between them and the sea. Giblin, "Conn, Hatch. All SEALs are aboard."

Morrison, "Thank you." He looks at Holtz, "We're running out of time. I would like to do something unorthodox."

Holtz, "It's your boat, Commander."

Morrison, "Flood tubes 3 and 4." Torpedo repeats back.

Morrison, "Gentlemen, can I get a fix on Tango 22 and Tango 23. Tube 3 for 22, and tube 4 for 23."

"Yes, sir."

Backes, "Are we going to fight our way out?"

Morrison, "I don't want to get caught in the shallows with the enemy behind us. Immediately after the Tirpitz blows, fire 3 and 4, cycle 1 and 2, and make a run out of here."

Backes smiles, "Roger that, sir."

Issa, in dry BDUs, "Request to enter and report."

Morrison, "Enter."

"Conn, Torpedo. Tubes 3 and 4 are flooded."

"Open doors. Match bearings."

TIRPITZ

Schmitt waits at the quarterdeck with his friend, Oberleutnant Hansel Zimmerman for the officer's boat to arrive. They have a pass to go ashore.

Kapitan Karl Topp, "Going for a beer, gentlemen?"

"Yes, sir."

The boat comes alongside.

USS SAN FRANCISCO

Lt. Issa counts down, "12. 10. 8. 7. 6. 5. 4. 3. 2. 1." The shockwave from the explosion shudders the boat and pushes it out of position. Twenty-four shaped charges detonated simultaneously at the turn of the bilge on the Tirpitz.

Morrison, "Fire 3 and 4."

"Conn, Torpedo. 3 and 4 fired electrically."

"Conn, Sonar. 3 and 4 are hot, straight and normal."

Morrison, "Very well. Cut the cables and shut the doors. What's the status of tubes 1 and 2?"

"Flooded. Refilling the slug tank, sir."

TIRPITZ, ENGINE ROOM 2

Obermaschinenmaat Vogt is cleaning an oil strainer on the starboard side when the detonation crushes the opposite bulkhead. He grabs two seamen and gets them up the ladder. The highest seaman is struggling with the hatch. Vogt looks down and sees the top half of his warrant officer in the surging water. The ship slowly rolls to port. "Schnell!!"

BOILER ROOM 1

Feuerwerkermaat Kuhn is caught in the churning water. As the ship rolls, he grabs a hand rail and pulls himself topside.

QUARTERDECK

Schmitt struggles to his feet. He grabs for Zimmerman as a secondary explosion shakes the ship. Zimmerman's neck is broken. He sets his friend down and looks for the captain. He watches the quarterdeck watch jump over the side into the water.

Schmitt sees Topp struggling to get out from under a fallen J-davit. He shouts, "Sir, we need to counterflood!" All he hears is a muffled mumble. He lifts the J-davit as the ship rolls onto its side. "Help me!" Men run past him, jumping into the water.

Topp, still tangled, pushes at Schmitt, "Go!"

Schmitt forces open a clamp and suddenly the davit comes free. He pulls his captain out and climbs the rail. He manages to get Topp over the rail and onto the, now, level side of the ship.

The Tirpitz continues its roll, picking up speed. Schmitt drags Topp until they are on the bottom. The great battleship settles until only a few feet of keel is out of the water.

USS SAN FRANCISCO

Holtz, "Thank you, Lieutenant Issa. Well done."

Backes, "5. 4. 3. 2. 1." The two torpedoes find their marks. Again, shock waves rock the Frisco.

Morrison, "Good job, Issa. Give our congratulations to your team." He turns away, "New course 285. Bring us up to periscope depth. Ahead full."

"Conn, Sonar. Tango 22 and 23 are breaking up."

Morrison, "Understood."

"Conn, Torpedo. We're ready to open doors."

"Good. Open doors."

Backes, "Sir, are we going to run the gauntlet at periscope depth?"

"It's the safest way. At the speed we'll be traveling, I'll need visual navigation to avoid the rocks."

"Yes, sir."

TIRPITZ

Schmitt shouts for help, but can barely hear his own voice. Blood pours out of Topp's chest, soaking his jacket. Topp pulls Schmitt down to him, "You have done your duty. I'm done."

"Sir?"

Kapitan zur See Karl Topp looks at Schmitt and smiles. His eyes go blank, open and staring at nothing. Schmitt's lowers his head, a tear falls on his captain's face.

SAN FRANCISCO

Morrison, "Up scope." He spins a quick 360. "Confirmed. The destroyer and cruiser are sinking. Right 5 degrees rudder." The Frisco turns in the slight correction. "Steady as she goes. Mark."

"308."

"Snap fire. Match for 1."

"Doors open. Bearings are set."

"Fire 1. Down scope." Thud, whoosh.

"Conn, Torpedo. Tube 1 fired electrically."

"Conn, Sonar. Fish is hot, straight, and normal."

Morrison, "Left full rudder." He quietly counts to ten, "Back to base course. The hear and feel a shell landing to their starboard and astern.

Backes counts down, "4. 3. 2. 1." The explosion shakes the sub.

Morrison, "Up scope." Again, a 360 spin, "Mark."

"306."

"That's the destroyer. Good kill. Right rudder." He counts as the ship turns, "Back to base course. What do we have under our keel?"

Backes, "800 feet and increasing."

"Good. Down scope. Take us down. Make our depth 400 feet. Ahead 1/3rd." The sub slows.

"Conn, Sonar. Torpedoes in the water. Sierra 2 at 348. Bearing is constant."

Morrison, "Ahead flank. Do we have a range for Sierra 2?"

"About 12 miles, sir."

"Match bearings."

"Yes, sir."

"Conn, Sonar. The torpedoes are passing astern."

Morrison, "Very well. Ahead standard."

"Bearings matched. Door is open."

"Firing tube 2."

"Conn, Torpedo. Tube 2 fired electrically."

Conn, Sonar. Fish 2 is hot, straight, and normal."

"Very well."

Backes counts down, "4. 3. 2. 1." Again, they feel and hear the explosion.

Morrison, "Backes, secure from General Quarters. Have your relief take us out to 100 miles from the coast at 2/3rd and 600 feet." The General Quarters watch team have been on watch since before entered the fjord.

"Yes, sir." Backes calls for their relief and turns over the watch.

Morrison, "Sir, could you excuse me?"

Holtz, "Of course."

Morrison walks into sonar, "Brown, thank you for calling out the position of the cruiser. I owe you a debt of gratitude. We all do."

"Just doing my job, sir."

"You saved the lives of everyone on board."

"Sir, I just wanted everyone to show up for my wedding."

"Right. We'll get it done. Brown, you've turned down chief in the past."

"Sir, I now have a family to care for."

"Would you take a commission?"

"Yes, sir."

"I'll sort out the paperwork. We'll do it in port so your girl can pin you."

"That would be great, sir."

Morrison walks back into control.

Holtz studies him, "Damn. I didn't know you could fight." He smiles, "You understand I'm giving you command?"

"Yes, sir."

"Who do you want for XO?"

"Backes. He's senior and we work well together. I'll move Miller to navigator and Cutting to Engineer. I also want to commission one of my sonarmen."

"The one who called the warning?"

"Yes, sir. He's ready."

"You have my approval."

"Conn, Torpedo, request permission to take the tubes down one at a time for maintenance."

Morrison, "Approved. Keep the conn informed."

Holtz, "You okay, Commander?"

"Yes, sir. Just another boring day at sea."

Miller, Backes' relief, laughs.

Morrison, "Miller, it's time to go home."

Miller, "Aye, captain."

THE END

GLOSSARY

16: VHF channel 16 is the international emergency channel. It is also, generally the channel used to communicate in the open, or non-encrypted communications.

1MC: General announcing system. Ship wide loud speaker system.

2nd Lt.: Second Lieutenant. Army and USMC rank. (O-1)

(Number)K: Fuel state. K for thousand pounds.

AA: Navy rank. Airman Apprentice (E-2).

AB: Navy enlisted rate. Aviation Boatswain's Mate. They do many duties on the flight and hanger decks and maintain other aviation equipment. ABAA through ABMC.

AD: Naval aviation rating. Aviation Machinist. ADAA through ADCM. AD's maintain aircraft structural components, flight surfaces, and engines.

ADM: Admiral. Naval Officer rank (O-10). Also used colloquially for Rear Admirals Lower and Upper, and Vice Admirals (O-7 through 9).

AE: Navy rate. Aviation Electrician. They maintain the electrical generation, conversion and distribution systems associated with jet aircraft. AEA through AECM.

AGL: Above Ground Level.

Ahead (Bell): The standard bells, or speeds of a ship are ahead 1/3, ahead 2/3, ahead Standard, Ahead full, and Ahead Flank. The number is the amount of revolutions per minute of the shaft.

Ahead Flank Emergency: Order to come to the fastest ahead speed as fast as possible. See Bell.

Air Boss: The ship's force air department head. The air boss commands all operations on the flight deck and hanger deck.

Air Chief Marshall: Royal Air Force Officer rank. Equivalent to Vice Admiral or Lieutenant General.

Air Commodore: Royal Air Force Officer rank. Equivalent to Captain or Colonel.

Air Marshall: Royal Air Force Officer rank. Equivalent to Rear Admiral or the current Rear Adm Upper Half or Major General.

Air Vice-Marshall: Royal Air Force Officer rank. Equivalent to Commodore or the current Rear Adm Lower Half or Brigadier General.

Amphenol: Multi-prong electronic or electrical connection.

AN: Naval Enlisted non-designated aviation rank. Airman (E-3).

AO: Enlisted rate. Aviation Ordinanceman. AOAA through AOCM. They inspect, care for and handle air delivered ordinance.

Arco: When an aircraft flies as a refueler they are given a special call sign. Usually the name of a gas station chain.

ASROC: Anti-submarine rocket. A torpedo delivered by a rocket.

ASW: Anti-submarine warfare.

AT: Navy rate. Aviation Electronics Technician. They maintain the complex electronic equipment associated with jet aircraft. ATA through ATCM

Auto-gyro: An emergency landing technique that uses the wind blowing through the helicopter rotors to keep them spinning, then uses the collective to slow the bird's descent at the last moment.

(AW): Naval specialist Badge. Air Warfare Specialist. Placed after rate such as AD1(AW).

Back (Bell): Astern bells for a marine engine. Back 1/3, Back 2/3, and Back Full.

Back Full Emergency: Astern bell to be answered as fast as possible.

Bandit: NATO code for enemy aircraft.

Battalion: Army/USMC tactical unit smaller than a brigade or regiment but larger than a company. Smallest unit designed to function independently. Generally commanded by a LT Colonel.

BDU: Battle Dress, Utility. The basic Army and Marine uniform.

Bell: The speed a ship is traveling at: Ahead they are Ahead 1/3, Ahead 2/3, Ahead Standard, Ahead Full, and Ahead Flank. Astern they are Back 1/3, Back 2/3, and Back full. In an emergency the order given is ahead flank emergency, or back full emergency which is a command to go as fast as possible.

Bearing: Compass or relative bearing in degrees from 0 to 360. Compass is true north, not magnetic north. Relative bearing puts 000 as straight in front of the bow of the ship and clocks degrees clockwise around the ship.

Bingo Fuel: Near the minimum to safely return to base.

Binnacle List: List of people sick or injured. Every unit and division maintains the Binnacle List and turns it in daily.

Blow: Submarines use ballast tanks to surface or submerge. By blowing high pressure air into the tanks water can be displaced and the vessel surfaces.

Blue Tails: Nick name for the VAW-122 Griffins. VAW-122 flies the E-2C Hawkeye radar plane.

Blue Water Ops: Carrier operations beyond reach of alternative air fields. You land on the carrier or swim.

Boatswain's Mate of the Watch (BMOW): In charge of all the lookouts, the helm and lee helm. The BMOW pipes (whistles) required ships announcements.

Bogey: An unidentified aircraft.

Boiler: Boilers generate the steam for propulsion, electrical generation, water distillation, and other uses.

Bolter: An aircraft missing the arresting wire.

Bridge: The ship's navigational control center. Where we drive the ship. The Officer of the Deck (OOD) is in charge except when the CO or XO are present. The Conning Officer directs the ship's coarse and speed. The Boatswains Mate of the Watch (BMOW), Quartermaster of the Watch (QMOW), Helm and Lee Helm are stationed here.

Brigade: Army/ Marine Tactical unit smaller than a Division and larger than a Battalion. Sometimes called a Regiment. Generally commanded by a Colonel or Brigadier General. They are usually armor, infantry, or airborne focused for the Army but still contain other units to permit independent operations.

BTOW: Boiler Technician of the watch. Senior watch in a boiler room.

BT: Navy Enlisted rate. Boiler Technician. BTFA through BTCM. Currently the BT rate is merged with the MM rate. Boiler Technicians operate and maintain marine boilers.

CAG: Commander Air Group. The CAG is in charge of all the air squadrons attached to the ship. The CAG is the counterpart to the ship's commanding officer. The carrier CO is always the senior.

Call the Ball: The Landing Signal Officer asks the pilot if they can see the Fresnel lens that shows the correct glide slope for landing.

Control: In a submarine Control is a room and watch station equivalent to both the bridge and combat control center on a surface ship.

Calico: NATO brevity code for an intruder on the radio net.

CAP: Combat Air Patrol. A fighter mission to circle an area ready to defend the fleet.

CAPT: Captain: Army and USMC rank. (O-3)

CAPT: Captain: Naval Officer rank (O-6).

CATCC: Carrier Air Traffic Control Center. This center controls all aircraft within 50 miles of the ship and manages take offs and landings.

CAV or Cavalry: Specialized Army Unit: These are units historically used for reconnaissance for larger units. They can be Armor, Airmobile, or Airborne. By WW2 the CAV distinctions were somewhat less than in wars past. Today the distinction is more historical than practical.

CDR: Naval Officer rank. Commander (O-5).

CHENG: Chief Engineer. Engineering department head.

CMAA: Chief Master at arms. A senior cop on a Navy ship.

COL: Army and USMC rank. (O-6)

Combat: Sometimes Combat control center. Weapon's and communications control center on a naval ship. The CO generally goes to combat during battle stations (General Quarters).

Combat Engineer: Specialized Army or USMC person who is trained to support combat operations by destroying obstacles. Structural engineers build things. Combat engineers blow them up.

Commodore: USN Officer rank. Equivalent to current Rear Admiral Lower half or Brigadier General. This rank was reauthorized in 1942 and discontinued after the war. It has been brought back, changed, and discarded since for the rank Rear Admiral Lower Half. If a unit of ships does not have an Admiral in charge, the senior or assigned Captain can take the title of Commodore to designate they are in charge of the group. This does not involve any change of pay or rank.

Company: Army/Marine tactical unit. Generally Commanded by a Captain. They are made up of a number of platoons and are organized into Battalions. Generally, companies are too small to function independently.

CORPS: Army tactical unit. Normally commanded by a Lieutenant General or General. It is a group of divisions and/or other units. Corps are not permanently assigned their divisions but rather receive and lose units based on need.

COTAC: Copilot Tactical Coordinator. Antisubmarine duty on S-3 Viking Aircraft.

Decimal: On radio the word 'Decimal' is used to indicate tenths. Thus, fuel at 9 decimal 2 is 9,200 pounds. Fuel is always given as weight.

Diesel Dyke: Nickname for women in the engineering fields, regardless of their rating. Obviously, it is not a term of respect and isn't tolerated in the modern Navy.

Division (Army/ USMC): Army and Marine Corps organizational unit. Army/USMC Divisions are tactical units commanded by a Brigadier or Lieutenant General that command a number of Brigades and supporting units. They are sometimes armor, infantry, airborne specific but contain all those other units needed to be an independent military unit.

Division (Navy): Naval organizational unit. Naval units are divided into Departments and Divisions. Divisions are functionally oriented units with all the enlisted members typically of one rating.

Eject: Order to initiate the ejection sequence for abandoning a doomed aircraft. Once ordered everyone must eject.

Electric Boat: Submarine Manufacturing firm based in Groton and other New England towns. In 1952 it merged with General Dynamics. Most US submarines are made by Electric Boat.

ELT: Navy Enlisted trade. Some MM's are qualified Engineering Laboratory Technician (Nuclear). They are chemistry and radiation specialists, though they also stand normal mechanical watches.

EM: Navy Enlisted rate. Electrician's Mate. Electricians operate the electrical distribution system on the ship, and also maintain all the electrical equipment. EMFN through EMCM.

EMP: Electro-Magnetic Pulse. A powerful change in the magnetic field. An EMP could damage or destroy electronic and electric gear.

Engine Room: Space where the main engines, electrical generators, and water distilling unit are located. This equipment is operated and maintained by Machinist Mates.

ENS: Ensign: Naval Officer rank (O-1). Junior most officer. Sometimes called a butter bar for their rank insignia which is a single gold bar.

EOOW: Engineering Officer of the Watch. Watch stander in charge of the propulsion plant. Normally a Lt. on a nuclear ship. Sometimes a senior or master chief on conventional powered ships.

ETA: Estimated Time of Arrival.

F-14: The Tomcat. An all-weather interceptor and fleet defense fighter.

Faking hose: Laying out a hose or line in parallel lines so the hose can be safely charged or the line let go without jamming.

Far CAP: Combat Air Patrol. Far CAP is a defensive position away from the fleet.

Feuerwerkermaat: Kriegsmarine (German Navy) enlisted rat and rank. Boiler worker mate.

Fire room: Location of the boilers in a fossil fueled steam ship.

Fire Team: An Army and USMC tactical unit consisting of two to four people and generally commanded by a Corporal. A squad will typically have two to four fire teams.

Flight Lieutenant: Royal Air Force Officer rank. Equivalent to Lieutenant Junior Grade (Navy) or Lieutenant (Army, USMC).

Flight Sergeant: RAF senior enlisted rank. Equivalent to Master Sergeant. May or may not be air crew.

Flying Officer: Royal Air Force Officer rank. Equivalent to Ensign or Second Lieutenant.

FN: Navy Enlisted rank. Fireman (E-3). A non-designated engineering striker. If designated his rate would precede his rank.

FOD Walk Down: Walking the flight deck looking for FOD

(Foreign Object Damage) that could damage aircraft.

Fox (number): Part of NATO brevity code. It is a call announcing the firing of a missile. The number designates the type of missile. 1 is short to intermediate range radar guided missile. 2 is a short-range heat seeking missile. 3 is a long-range radar guided missile.

Fregattenkapitän: Kriegsmarine (German Navy) rank equivalent to Commander.

Fuel state: How much fuel you have on board in thousands of pounds. (10 decimal 1 = 10,100lbs.)

'G's: Gravities. One 'G' is equal to normal earth gravity. Two is twice earth gravity etc.

General Quarters: The call to man battle stations and prepare the vessel to fight.

Gertrude: Nick name for a short-range underwater phone.

GMG: Navy Enlisted rate. Gunners Mate Guns. Gunner's Mates operate and maintain the weapons on a ship. The rate is split between Gunner's Mate Guns (GMG) and Gunner's Mate Missiles (GMM). GMGSA through GMGMC.

GMM: Navy Enlisted rate. Gunners Mate Missiles. Gunner's Mates operate and maintain the weapons on a ship. The rate is split between Gunner's Mate Guns (GMG) and Gunner's Mate Missiles (GMM). GMMSA through GMMMC.

Gold Eagle: Official nickname of the Carl Vinson. Every Navy ship is given an official nickname. The crews often give an unofficial nickname. In our novel series we sometimes use these as radio call signs. That would not normally be true ship to ship, but often used in air operations.

Group Captain: Royal Air Force Officer rank. Commander or Lieutenant Colonel.

GySGT: Gunnery Sergeant. USMC enlisted rank. (E-7) Generally an assistant Company commander or assistant to a higher rank officer or enlisted. As an assistant company commander, they are responsible for training the company commander and all servicemen under them. It is a critical and important job.

Hauptsturmführer: Paramilitary and Waffen-SS rank in the Nazi party roughly equivalent to an army captain.

HT: Navy Enlisted rate. Hull Technician. HT's are Damage control and repair experts. They also operate the sewer system on the ship earning them the undesirable nickname "turd chaser". HTFA through HTMC.

HY-80: Hardened steel used for special applications by the Navy. 3/8" will stop most rifle bullets.

ILS: Instrument Landing system. An aircraft system that helps pilots line up with a runway they cannot see.

Kapitänleutnant: Kriegsmarine (German Navy) rank equivalent to Lieutenant Commander.

Khaki: Navy slang term for chiefs and officers because they wear khaki colored uniforms.

Knight (number): Call sign of fighters flying for VFW-154, the Black Knights.

Landing Signal Officer: A pilot positioned near the rear of the carrier to help guide pilots in. The LSO also grades landings.

Law of Continuity of Suckage: Submarine phrase. Once the hatch is shut suckage can neither be created or destroyed. Meaning when one person gets a good deal another gets screwed. This is what happens when you lock a bunch of nukes in a tube for months on end.

Laze: Use a laser to designate where ordinance is to drop.

LCDR: Naval Officer rank. Lieutenant Commander (O-4).

Leutnant zur See: WWII German Kriegsmarine (Navy) rank. Equivalent to Lt.JG.

LPO: Naval enlisted position. Leading Petty Officer is the "Foreman" for a division. Usually an E-6.

Lt: Army and USMC rank. (O-2) Lieutenants are generally platoon officers or assistants to the commander of a larger unit.

Lt.: Naval officer rank. Lieutenant (O-3). Generally, a Division Officer in smaller units a lieutenant might be the XO or even CO.

Lt. COL: Army and USMC rank. (O-5) Generally commands a Battalion sized unit or serves as an assistant to the commander of a larger unit.

Lt. JG: Naval officer rank is Lieutenant Junior Grade, (O-2), a division officer or assistant to a more senior officer.

MA: Navy Enlisted rate. Master at Arms. Similar to Military police MA's enforce uniform and behavior rules. As such they are generally disliked. MA3 through MACM.

Magic (number): Call sign for an EA-6B Prowler, radar jamming aircraft of VAQ-133 Wizards.

MAJ: Major: Army and USMC rank. (O-4) Majors are sometimes company commanders but more often serve as assistants to higher rank officers. In the Pentagon you can't throw a stick without hitting a Major.

Marshall of the RAF: Royal Air Force Officer rank. The senior officer of the service. Equivalent to Chief of Naval Operations or Army Chief of Staff.

Master Chief: Naval Enlisted Rank (E-9).

Mini Boss: The air boss's assistant. They divide the observation duties in PRIFLY.

MM: Navy Enlisted rate. Machinist's Mate. They operate and maintain the machinery associated with ship's propulsion, auxiliary gear, and nuclear power systems. MMFA through MMCM. All nukes leave A school as MM3.

MMOW: Machinist's Mate of the Watch. Senior watch stander in an engine room. Sometimes called the Engine Room Supervisor. It is a watch station and not a rank.

MOS: Military Occupational Specialty. It is what a soldier or marine is trained to do. Be that infantry, armor, special forces, supply, radio operator, combat engineer or a myriad of other jobs. Generally, it is not used in the way ones' rate is in the navy. You don't call a sergeant in the infantry an infantry sergeant. There are some positional title changes for those in special units such as cavalry.

NAM: Navy Achievement Medal. A medal for individual meritorious accomplishment. When a V device is added for valor it signifies the award was for combat actions.

NAVSEA 08: Designation for the leader of the U. S. Navy Nuclear Power Program.

Navy Expeditionary Medal: Medal issued for service in a combat zone designated by congress.

NOE: Nap of earth. Order to fly as low as safely possible.

NTDS: Naval Tactical Data System. A system that shares sensor data with other ships.

Nuke: Nickname for anyone in the nuclear power career field. It is sometime used derisively. It is even said "Fucking-nuke" is one word.

Nuclear waste: Nickname for anyone who fails to complete nuclear training or is otherwise removed from the program. It is generally used with respect by nukes.

MW: Megawatt. One million watts. 1,000,000 watts. Most

nuclear power plants are measured in MW.

O-2 Plant: The oxygen generation plant which removes atmospheric oxygen and compresses it into liquid oxygen used by medical and as pilot breathing air.

Oberführer: Paramilitary and Waffen SS rank of the Nazi Party roughly equivalent to a senior Colonel.

Obermaschinenmaat: Kriegsmarine (German Navy) enlisted rate and rank. Senior machinist mate.

Officer of the Deck (OOD): In charge of the operation and navigation of the ship underway. In port the OOD is in charge of the ship's duty section and all operations during their watch.

Op-tempo: Rate of operations over time.

OPPE: Operational Propulsion Plant Exam. Same as ORSE for conventionally powered vessels.

ORSE: Operational Reactor Safeguards Exam. Scheduled examination of propulsion plant material condition and operational compliance. A poor grade on ORSE causes career ventilation. It can be a negative mark on every nuke on board.

Passageway: Navy speak for a hallway.

Petty Officer: Colloquial phrase for an E-4 through E-6. Generally, it is only used by officers or master at arms who are about to correct the Petty Officer's behavior. Instead a sailor will address the Petty Officer with their rate. MM1 instead of PO1.

PFC: Private First Class. (E-3) Army and USMC rank.

Phoenix: AIM-54 Long range air to air missile. The F-14 was designed to carry and fire this missile. In reality the USN never actually fired one at an enemy aircraft.

Platoon: Army and USMC tactical unit consisting of two to four squads. With armor this is three to four tanks. Platoons are generally commanded by a Lieutenant or Second Lieutenant and have a Staff Sergeant, called a platoon sergeant, to train the officer and men.

Plimsoll mark: The Plimsoll mark is an internationally accepted mark to indicate the maximum load or draft of a ship. It is based on the freeboard or distance from the water to the lowest deck opening and also stability. Being below the Plimsoll means the ship isn't safe for operations.

PQS: Personal Qualification Standard. PQS is the system used by the Navy to qualify sailors to do their jobs.

Propulsion plant drills: Engineering operator training practicing possible casualties and problems. Continuous training is the reality of most sailors. This is to prepare operators for problems that only occur very rarely but have huge consequences if the watch team does not know what they are doing.

PRYFLY: Primary Flight Control. The highest deck in the island structure where all flight deck operations are managed.

QAO: Quality Assurance Officer. The QAO manages inspection paperwork from repairs and also personally inspects critical repairs. No system, or aircraft can be used as designed until the QAO has approved the work.

Quartermaster of the Watch (QMOW): In charge of providing navigational information to the OOD and Conning Officer. The QMOW is required to keep the ship's position updated on paper and electronic charts.

Rainbow side boys: The traditional side boys for a senior visitor, only wearing the various flight deck colored jerseys.

Reactor Auxiliary Room (RAR): The RAR is the space where the reactor support and monitoring equipment is located. It shares most of the same functions that a fire room in a conventional vessel would have. Generally, the Naval Reactor is in a separate room inside this room.

Rear Admiral Lower Half: Naval Officer rank. One Star Admiral (O-7). See Commodore for WW2 usage.

Rear Admiral Upper Half: Naval Officer rank. Two Star Admiral (O-8). Called Rear Admiral in WW2.

RIM-7: Rail launched intermediate range air to air missile. Sea Sparrow.

RIO: Radar Intercept Officer. The RIO operates the radar and weapons system in the back seat of the F-14. They are a critical half of the in-flight team for fighting the aircraft.

RM: Navy enlisted rate. Radioman. They operate the radio communications gear for the Navy. They are, generally the most secretive because they are forbidden to share anything of what they see and hear.

Roger Ball (Number): Roger ball means the pilot can see the Fresnel lens glide slope indicator. The number is the total weight of the aircraft in thousands of pounds.

RTB: Return to Base.

Rule of Three: This is from SERE. A person can last three weeks without food, three days without water, three hours without shelter, three minutes without air, and three seconds without hope.

SAM: Surface to Air Missile.

SAR: Search and Rescue.

SERE: Survival, Evasion, Resistance and Escape training. It is survival and code of conduct training every pilot, air crew, and special forces soldier must go through. Every service has similar training and will take students from other services as well as DoD civilians who need the training.

SFC: Sergeant First Class. Army rank. (E-7) Generally an assistant company commander or assistant to a higher rank officer or enlisted. As an assistant company commander, they are responsible for training the company commander and all servicemen under them. It is a critical and important job.

SGT: Sergeant. (E-5). Army and USMC Rank. A sergeant generally is in charge of a tank, squad, or fire team. That or they serve as the assistant to more senior enlisted or officers. They are the back bone of any service.

SGT MAJ: Army and USMC enlisted rank. (E-9) Sergeant Major is the senior enlisted rank. They generally serve as senior instructors and advisors to major commands. They may have a staff under them.

SIS: British Secret Intelligence Service. Now called MI6.

SLQ-32: Called the "slick 32" it is a multi-function radar jammer carried on USN ships.

Snap 2: Early supply computer.

SOB: Son of a Bitch. Even cuss words have acronyms.

SSGT: Staff sergeant. (E-6) Army and USMC Rank. A staff sergeant is generally an assistant platoon leader or assistant to a higher ranked person. In the role of platoon sergeant, they are responsible for training the platoon officer in how to be an effective leader while also training all their subordinate servicemen. It is a vital position.

SSN: Submarine, nuclear powered. An attack, or hunter killer submarine.

Start the Music: NATO Code phrase for commencing jamming.

Squad: Army and USMC tactical unit. Generally made up of two to four fire teams and commanded by a Sergeant. In Armor this is typically one track or vehicle.

Squadron Leader: Royal Air Force Officer rank. Equivalent to Lieutenant or Captain.

Squawked: Identification, friend or foe (IFF) Code signal.

ST: Navy Enlisted rate. Sonar Technician. Responsible for operating sonar systems on ships and submarines. STSA through STMC.

Switch Gear Room: Space where the electrical distribution system is operated. EM's stand watch in Switch Gear.

TACAN: Radio beacon aircraft use to find the carrier.

TARPS: Tactical Airborne Reconnaissance Pod System. A camera system mounted on a hard point and controlled by the RIO.

TG: Turbine Generator. An electrical Generator powered by steam.

TG/DU: Turbine Generator and Distilling Unit watch. An Engine room watch stood by an MM.

Thwarts ship passageway: A hall way aligned from side to side rather than forward and aft.

TLD: Thermal Luminescent Dosimetry. A radiation measuring device to monitor crew exposure. The nukes sometimes call it "the little dicky."

VHF: Very High Frequency. A line of sight radio.

Vice Admiral: Naval Officer rank. VADM (O-9).

Wave off: Order to abort a landing and go around.

Wing Commander: Royal Air Force Officer rank. Equivalent to Lieutenant Commander or Major.

Yankee Search: Active sonar search.

YN: Naval Enlisted rate. Yeoman. Yeomen are the administrative grease that lubricates the functioning of the Navy machine. When an officer has a good yeoman, they guard him or her jealously. It is an unofficial sport to poach one's yeoman. YNSA through YNMC.

XO: Executive officer. Second in charge of a vessel or unit. Actual rank varies based on the size of the unit. A patrol craft or air squadron XO could be a Lieutenant. On a super carrier the XO is generally a Captain.

X-Ray: Material condition X-Ray. Lowest level of water tight integrity. Only set during a work day in port.

Yoke: Material condition Yoke. Middle level of water tight integrity between X-ray (in port on work day) and Zebra (Battle Stations). At sea yoke is checked at least daily.

Zebra: Material condition Zebra. Highest level of water tight integrity.

ABOUT THE AUTHOR

M L Maki

MM1 Maki is a retired US Navy nuclear field machinist mate with twenty-years of active service, who served on the USS Carl Vinson, CVN-70, and two cruisers. During twelve years of duty at sea, MM1 Maki circumnavigated the earth once, transited the Panama Canal three times, served on the USS Carl Vinson during Enduring Freedom, and earned multiple campaign awards.

Sofia R. Maki has a background in criminal justice and accounting.

BOOKS IN THIS SERIES

THE FIGHTING TOMCATS

Fighting Her Father's War

Divided We Stand

We So Few

Should England Fall

BOOKS IN THIS SERIES

*THE FIGHTING TOMCATS
HUNTER/KILLER SERIES*

Shark Among The Minnows

Made in the USA
Middletown, DE
23 December 2020